THE SEARCH FOR GRAM

BOOK ONE OF THE CODEX REGIUS

Chris Kennedy

Chris Kennedy Publishing
Virginia Beach, VA

Chris Kennedy/Chris Kennedy Publishing
2052 Bierce Dr.
Virginia Beach, VA 23454
http://chriskennedypublishing.com/

Publisher's Note: This is a work of fiction. Names, characters, places, and incidents are a product of the author's imagination. Locales and public names are sometimes used for atmospheric purposes. Any resemblance to actual people, living or dead, or to businesses, companies, events, institutions, or locales is completely coincidental.

Ordering Information:
Quantity sales. Special discounts are available on quantity purchases by corporations, associations, and others. For details, contact the "Special Sales Department" at the address above.

The Search for Gram/ Chris Kennedy. -- 1st ed.
ISBN 978-1942936053

As always, this book is for my wife and children. I would like to thank Linda, Jennie, Beth, Dan and Jimmy, who took the time to critically read the work and make it better. Any mistakes that remain are my own. I would like to thank my mother, without whose steadfast belief in me, I would not be where I am today. Thank you.

I would also like to thank Jim Beall and Dr. Robert G. Brown for their assistance with several aspects of the physics in "The Search for Gram." Any remaining errors are mine, in spite of their expert aid.

Author's Note

When more than one race refers to a planet or star, the same name is used by both races in order to prevent confusion. Also on the topic of planet naming, the normal convention for planets is to add a lower case letter to the name of the parent star (i.e., Tau Ceti 'b'). The first planet discovered in a system is usually given the designation 'b,' and later planets are given subsequent letters as they are found. In order to prevent confusion in this book, the closest planet to the star in a star system is given the letter 'a,' with the rest of the planets given subsequent letters in order of their proximity to the star.

"Any sufficiently advanced technology is indistinguishable from magic."

— *Arthur C. Clarke*

Chapter One

Bridge, Aesir Ship *Blue Forest*, Unknown System, March 15, 2021

"Continue firing all weapons," said the *Blue Forest's* commanding officer, Captain Elorhim Silvermoon.

"Lasers firing," replied the laser officer.

"Missiles launching," replied the missile officer. "For all the good it's doing," he added under his breath.

"Engineering, Captain," Silvermoon transmitted over his implant. *"We need more power. How's it coming back there?"*

"I'm sorry Captain, but this is the best you're going to get," said the assistant engineer. *"Engine Room One is open to space. Everyone who was in it, including the chief engineer, is* gone. *We're already 10 percent over redline, and I don't know how much longer the Number Two engine can take it! With the loss of the Number One engine, it's already pushing a bigger load than it was built for."*

"Do what you can," replied Silvermoon. *"They're gaining on us, and we're not going to make the stargate without more power."*

"I'll do what I can sir, but it won't be much. Maybe a percent or two. We're going to blow the motor if I try to do much beyond that."

"Do what you can," the commanding officer repeated. *"Silvermoon out."* He looked around the bridge. His crew was maintaining its composure, but he could tell the stress was getting to them. "How long until we reach the stargate?" he asked.

The navigator's pointed ears twitched. "It's going to be a little more than an hour at this speed," he replied. "Engineering just gave us another 10 Gs of acceleration, but it won't be enough to leave our pursuers behind."

Captain Silvermoon sighed internally, not letting his frustration show. He wished he had another courier drone, but they had launched both their drones earlier. Launched them and then watched as a second enemy ship destroyed them. They had no idea the second ship existed before then; it had just appeared between his ship and the stargate after the drones were launched. Unarmed and unarmored, the drones were easy prey for the enemy frigate. Whatever cloaking technology the enemy used was outstanding. All of a sudden, it was just *there*.

"The enemy's shields are down," said the laser officer. He didn't have to say he meant the smaller vessel's shields; none of the Aesir weapons had made a dent in the shields of the larger vessel that was slowly catching up with them.

"Destroy it," ordered Captain Silvermoon. Another volley of laser fire lashed the enemy frigate. The alien ship flashed on the screens as the missiles arrived, and something vital was hit.

"Target destroyed," the missile officer reported.

"One hour to the stargate," the navigator noted as the Aesir ship hurtled past the expanding ball of plasma.

The missile officer shook his head as he looked at his display. "I don't get it sir," he said finally. "The smaller vessel didn't defend itself after it destroyed the courier drones. It just sat there and let us destroy it. It's almost as if that's what the enemy wanted us to do."

"Yes," agreed Captain Silvermoon, already thinking along the same lines. "They were probably gathering information on our weapons systems...information we let them have. Too late to worry about it now; there's nothing we can do." He paused and then asked the question he'd been dreading, "Range to the other vessel?"

"One million miles," replied the laser officer. Last time, it had fired at 800,000 miles. They were getting too close, but there was nothing he could do.

"I've got the damage report from Engine Room One," said the damage control officer (DCO), "but I don't know if you're going to believe it. I don't."

"Go ahead," said Captain Silvermoon.

"The repair crew says the engine room is gone," said the DCO, "and they mean gone as in vanished. There is nothing left. No pieces, no bodies, and no equipment. Everything is just...gone. Where the structure of the ship ends, it ends with a clean cut. The repair crew says what's left is like nothing they have ever seen. They have no idea what could have caused it."

"Well, I don't know where it all went," said the sensor operator. "They asked me to mark the debris field so we could look for survivors later, but the missile didn't leave a debris field when it hit us. Everything just disappeared." In their three previous deployments, Silvermoon had never seen the sensor operator look shaken. He was an extremely competent naval officer, and he always had an answer in the past. The captain found he didn't like the new expression.

"Where did everything go then?" asked Captain Silvermoon. "Anyone have any guesses?"

The bridge was silent.

"Range to enemy vessel 800,000 miles," announced the laser officer. "Enemy vessel is firing. Six torpedoes inbound."

Damn it, thought the captain. The enemy ship had only shot one torpedo last time, and they hadn't been able to stop it. "Activate all defenses," ordered the captain. "Retarget main batteries on the torpedoes as well."

The Aesir ship's lasers and counter-missile lasers began firing at the incoming torpedoes, while missiles and counter-missile missiles leapt from their ports to join the energy weapons. Just like before, the torpedoes disappeared when the Aesir missiles would have hit them, only to reappear once the missiles were past. The lasers seemed to hit the torpedoes, but had no effect on them.

"No effect," said the ship's defensive officer. "Shields are as high as they can be with only one engine." He didn't say the shields hadn't stopped the earlier weapon, even with both motors running at 100 percent. He didn't have to.

"Any idea where the torpedoes are going?" asked Captain Silvermoon.

"I don't know," replied the sensor operator, the shaken look now a permanent part of his countenance. "They just vanish. It's not a shield because our missiles go through the space where the torpedoes were. It's like they're not there anymore. I don't know where they're going. *It doesn't make any sense.*" The sensor operator shook his head, barely able to contain the tears of frustration that Captain Silvermoon could see were perilously close to brimming over.

"That's okay," Captain Silvermoon replied. "Keep working; you'll figure it out."

"Five seconds to impact," said the laser officer a few seconds later. "Four... three... two... one..." Six torpedoes impacted along the length of the *Blue Forest*.

Chapter Two

Princess Merrorritor stared open-mouthed at the flame dancing on the Aesir's hand. "Why doesn't the flame burn you?" she finally asked.

The Aesir, who had introduced himself as Captain Salvan Nightsong, smiled. Generally humanoid in appearance, the Aesir was shorter and thinner than a normal Terran, and Captain Nightsong would probably have been able to pass as a Terran...if his skin hadn't been a light shade of green. He had also just called a flame into being, another giveaway he was definitely *not* a Terran. Although Calvin had been told Captain Nightsong was an Aesir, he couldn't help but think of him as an elf. It was probably the pointy ears poking out from under his long, blond hair.

"The flame doesn't burn me because it is my friend," the Aesir said. "Hold out your hand," he instructed, "and you can hold it, too."

"You don't have hair on your hands, but I do," said the Mrowry princess. A race of felinoid warriors that looked like Bengal tigers, the Mrowry were the Terrans' closest allies. The blacker the Mrowry, the higher up the individual was in the royalty. All of the Mrowry in the room were a solid ebony. "Won't the flame catch my hand on fire?" asked the princess.

"No," said the Aesir, "it won't burn you. It is a special flame." He put his hand next to the Mrowry's paw and blew gently. The flame hopped over to the princess' paw and began to dance rhythmically, but did not burn the young Mrowry.

"See?" the princess said, holding the flame out to Calvin, "I told you the Aesir were neat!"

"OK," said Captain Nightsong, scooping the little flame out of the princess' hand, "I need to talk to the adults, and the flame needs to go back to its world." He cupped his hands around the flame and blew gently into them; when he opened them again, the flame was gone. Despite the different cultures, everyone could tell the look on the princess' face was one of abject disappointment.

"Run along, Mimi," said the emperor. "You can talk with our guest later."

"If I have to..." she said as she walked to the door with her head down, dragging her feet.

"You can sit next to me at dinner," said the Aesir, "if your grandfather allows it."

"Can I, grandfather?" she asked, life coming back to her voice.

"Yes, you may," replied the emperor. "Now, *run along*."

Happy again, the princess bounded out of the room on all fours, stopping only to close the door.

Lieutenant Commander Shawn Hobbs, or "Calvin" to his aviator friends, had arrived at the home world of the Mrowry a few days before. The hero of the Terran war with the alien Drakuls, he had been given a few days of rest and relaxation, as well as some time to follow up on a quest an ancient civilization had given him. He returned from the quest to find the Aesir officer waiting for him although he had no idea why. He had never even seen one of the elves before.

"What can I do to help you?" Calvin asked.

"We have encountered a foe that is beyond us," replied the Aesir. "Our elders conducted a divination, and it was determined we needed to look outside our realm for aid. All of the signs point to you...we need your help."

"A divination?" asked Calvin.

"Yes. When we are faced with a decision that will have a major effect on our civilization, for good or ill, we conduct a divination. It is a means by which we attempt to foretell the best course of action. In this case, we were not shown the answer we were seeking, but our king had a vision of this planet, and someone walking around the large rock formation on the grounds of this estate. When I arrived here, I was told you and the princess were out walking around the rock. The vision showed a humanoid, not a Mrowry, so I believe you are the person we are looking for."

"I thought you were fighting the Teuflings," said the emperor. "They have never been more than you could handle before."

"That war ended," replied Captain Nightsong; "however, just after the Teuflings surrendered, our ships began disappearing in another quadrant."

"Well, I'm happy to do whatever I can for you," replied Calvin. "What do you need?"

"Steropes told me you have the qualities of a hero," the Aesir said. "We are in need of one, and we would like you to come to our star system. Our king would like to enlist your aid in determining what is going on."

"Just me?"

"No," replied the Aesir with a smile, "we would like to have your ship and crew come as well. It is likely the troops you lead will also be needed."

"Are you aware I am not the commanding officer of the ship?" asked Calvin.

The Aesir's eyes opened slightly in surprise. Calvin hadn't realized how green they were. "You aren't the commanding officer?" he asked. "I assumed the ship in orbit was your vessel."

"It *is* the ship I'm stationed on," replied Calvin; "however, I am not its commanding officer. I'm just the officer in charge of its fighters and space marines."

"You are in charge of both at the same time?" asked the Aesir. "How are you able to do both?" He shook his head in wonder. "It is obvious you are indeed the one we have been searching for."

"How that happened is a long story," replied Calvin, "but it was mostly a long progression of being in the wrong place at the wrong time."

"See?" asked Steropes. "Just as I told you, he *is* a hero spirit. They always find a way to be where they're needed, just like being here for you." A member of the Psiclopes race, Steropes appeared human, except for the fact that he was only three feet tall, and his head was much larger than normal. Steropes was one of three aliens who had made first contact with the Terrans almost three years previously and had helped guide their actions ever since.

Although the other two Psiclopes had their own agenda, which only roughly paralleled that of the Terrans, Steropes had proven his loyalty during the recently completed war against the Drakuls. Among their many differences, the Psiclopes also believed 'hero spirits' were born when needed to help pull civilizations back from the brink of anarchy. Although Calvin didn't believe in the concept of hero spirits, it appeared the Aesir was familiar with it.

Captain Nightsong nodded to Steropes. "I agree." He turned back to Calvin. "You are indeed the person we are looking for. You will need to have your commanding officer bring your ship to our home world."

"I'm his commanding officer," said the other Terran in the room. A large black man, he had proven as good at making decisions as the commanding officer of the Terran Space Ship (TSS) *Vella Gulf* as he had when he was the quarterback for the U.S. Naval Academy's football team. "I'm Captain James Sheppard. Lieutenant Commander Hobbs is going to need authorization from more than just me; he's going to need authorization from our chain of command on Terra. I'm sorry, but it's not my personal cruiser. We can't just go running around the galaxy, no matter how much you want his aid."

"While I understand why you want to get permission, our need is urgent and cannot wait. We have already lost several ships, and we do not know why."

"If you don't know why," said Captain Sheppard, "how do you know he can help? How do you know he's also not going to disappear or suffer the same fate as the rest of your ships?"

"Because we believe in him," replied the Aesir. "Hero spirits can do what no one else can."

"The fact remains that we can't go with you without authorization from our chain of command," said Captain Sheppard. "We will need to return to Terra to get that permission."

"Perhaps I did not make myself clear," replied the Aesir. "Our need is *most* urgent," he said, turning to Calvin. "We need you *now*. We do not have time to wait."

Emperor Yazhak the Third cleared his throat. "Excuse me," he said, "but I may have a solution. What if we were to send one of our ships to Terra while you take the *Vella Gulf* on to assist the Aesir? We need to send a delegation to Terra anyway, and I will tell your Admiralty that I sent you on. I will also give them the reasons for your journey, and we will take responsibility for any costs arising from this mission. If they have a problem with you assisting the Aesir, we will send our fastest courier ship to let you know. Would that be all right, Captain Sheppard?"

"It's going to hang my ass way out in the wind if they decide I shouldn't have done it," Captain Sheppard replied, "but I don't think we'll come up with a better compromise. I know the Aesir were part of the Alliance of Civilizations before it broke up, so I'm sure they are worthy of our aid." He took a deep breath and let it out slowly as he made his decision. "We will go."

"Excellent," said the Aesir. "Thank you very much."

"So, what is it you need from me?" asked Calvin.

"We need a new Gram," said the Aesir, as if that explained everything.

Calvin looked puzzled. "A new gram? What's that?"

"Have you heard of Wayland the Smith?"

"Wayland the Smith?" Calvin asked. "No, I can't say I have."

The Aesir looked disappointed. "Has your race forgotten its savior so soon? We remember him, even if you do not. How about Beowulf and Grendel? Can I at least start there?"

"I've heard of Beowulf," replied Calvin. Captain Sheppard also nodded his head. "I had to read that book in high school. I don't remember the story very well, but I think Beowulf was the hero of the story. Didn't he kill Grendel for some Norse king?"

"King Hrothgar of Denmark," agreed the Aesir. "Go on."

"Umm...I'm kind of hazy after that," Calvin said. "I think Grendel's kid then came after him, and Beowulf killed the kid too. After that, Beowulf lived happily ever after. Is that close?"

"Not really," said the Aesir. "Beowulf actually killed Grendel's *mother* in her underwater lair with a sword the legends say was 'forged for a giant.' After he killed the two monsters, the countryside was free again, and he retired to a life of luxury."

"OK," said Calvin. "You obviously know more about him than I do. I didn't even know he was a real person. I thought it was just a story. What does that have to do with Gram?"

"Wayland the Smith made the armor worn by Beowulf," said the Aesir, "and was responsible for re-forging the sword Beowulf used to kill Grendel's mother. I know this to be a fact because Wayland and Beowulf were the same person. Wayland was an Aesir who lived on your planet. When he saw the need, he became the hero, Beowulf, in order to kill Grendel for King Hrothgar."

"What was Wayland or Beowulf, or whatever his name was, doing on our planet?" asked Captain Sheppard. "Was he watching out for us?"

"No, nothing like that," replied the Aesir. "He was one of our warriors, who retired to your planet after a life of combat. He had always been fascinated with the art of sword-making, so he retired to a planet as far away from society as he could in order to pursue that art. It was nothing more than serendipity that he was nearby when Grendel began terrorizing the local populace."

"Did he change his name to Gram afterward?" asked Calvin, still not seeing where the whole conversation was going.

"No, he went back to being the sword-maker Wayland," replied the Aesir. "In addition to the sword used to kill Grendel, Wayland made a number of other swords, including many named swords with famous histories. One of these was 'Gram,' which was the sword of Sigmund."

"So you need a sword?" asked Calvin.

"Not exactly," said the Aesir. "Gram had a long history, including being used by Sigmund's son Sigurd to slay the dragon Fafnir. We are once again beset by dragons, although I use the term 'dragon' not as a living creature, but as a metaphor for something so big and monstrous that it will take someone of supernatural abilities to defeat it. We need a new Gram to help us defeat our dragon. You are the new Gram we have been searching for."

"I'm your sword?" asked Calvin.

"Metaphorically speaking, yes," said the Aesir, happy to finally be making some progress. "The divination we conducted indicated we needed the reborn Gram."

"How exactly is a sword reborn?" Calvin asked. "You want me to reforge this sword?"

"No," said the Aesir, shaking his head. "We want you. When Wayland first forged his swords, he incorporated the essence of a hero into each. Over time, when the swords were broken, the life essences escaped them. We believe your essence is the same essence he used when he forged Gram."

Calvin barked out a laugh. "That's not possible," he said, looking at Steropes. "According to Steropes, I was too busy being Zeus to be hanging out in a sword...unless the Psiclopes were wrong."

"Actually, that explains a lot," said Steropes. "There was a period when we were unable to find the hero spirit that we believe currently resides within you. If your spirit was captured and used to animate the sword Gram, it would explain why we weren't able to find you."

"Blah, blah, blah, hero spirit this and hero spirit that," said Calvin. "I still don't believe any of that stuff. Besides, there is another issue we haven't talked about that makes it difficult to help you right now."

"What is that?" asked the Aesir.

"I don't know how well you looked at our ship before you came down to the planet, but it is barely operational. It is in serious need of an overhaul to repair the battle damage that still remains from our last cruise. We stopped at Earth on the way here and replaced the personnel we lost in the war, but we're still missing several of our fighters. If we are going into harm's way again, I would rather do so with a full squadron. We have the pilots, but not the ships."

"I believe that is something we can assist you with as well," said the emperor. "We owe the Aesir several favors, and it would not take more than a few days to replicate the fighters you need for this endeavor. That would also give our shipyards time to fix the remaining damage to your ship if we gave it head-of-the-line status."

"I would appreciate that," replied Captain Sheppard. "One of our engines was a little twitchy on the way here. I would feel a lot better about going on this mission if we could get it looked at before we go. I don't know how we will be able to repay you for the fighters, though."

The emperor smiled, showing a mouthful of very sharp teeth. "It is not a problem to have your ship looked at," he said. "Nothing could be easier. As I said, we owe the Aesir. As to the fighters, just bring them back to us when you're done with them. Without scratches, of course."

Officer's Mess, TSS *Vella Gulf,* Grrrnow, 61 Virginis, May 17, 2021

"Moay I join you?" asked Calvin.

Steropes looked up. "Certainly," he said, seeing Calvin was carrying a golden rod and not a plate of food. "Not eating lunch?"

"I had something earlier," Calvin replied. "In all the excitement over the Aesir showing up, I never got to talk with you about this." He held the two-foot long rod, a product of an ancient civilization, where Steropes could see. Calvin had been given the rod with the guidance to seek out rock formations like Ayers Rock on Earth. The computer avatar that had given him the rod had told him he would 'know what he was supposed to do' when he was near the formations.

"What happened when you took the rod to Clowder Rock?" Steropes asked.

"When I went up on the rock, the entire rod started glowing a bright red, and one of the buttons glowed too. When I pushed the button, the glow faded from both the rod and the button."

"And that was it? That was all the rod did?"

"The only other thing that happened was this symbol appeared." Calvin pointed to two wavy lines, one on top of the other, next to another symbol. The other symbol looked like a balloon with a string lying on the floor, with a cursive 'n' standing over it. "Do those wavy lines mean anything to you?"

"No, not really," replied Steropes.

"Is that a 'no,' or a 'not really?'" asked Calvin, who had long ago grown tired of the Psiclopes' tendencies to avoid telling the Terrans everything they knew about a given subject. "Which is it?"

"Well, I don't know anything for sure," Steropes hedged. "Before I answer that, when did the other symbol appear?"

"Umm...I'm not sure. I don't *think* the symbol was on there when I first got the rod, but I put the rod in my closet and didn't pull it back out until we were headed to Terra for the final battle with the Drakuls. The symbol was there when I pulled the rod out, but I don't know when it appeared."

"Hmm," said Steropes. "My home world of Olympos had a formation like the ones you were supposed to find. I wonder if you got credit for the formation when Olympos went into the black hole." The Terrans had accidentally set off a black hole generator that had consumed the Psiclopes' home planet during the Drakul War. Steropes' tone of voice indicated it was still a sore subject with him.

"I don't know," repeated Calvin. "The symbol might have appeared then...but then again, it might have appeared any other time in the last six months too."

"The only things I have ever seen that looked like those symbols are two of the ancient Zodiac symbols. The reason I said 'not really' was that I don't see how the ancient Terran Zodiac would be relevant to something from the Progenitors."

"Progenitors?" asked Captain Nightsong, walking up with a tray of food. "Is that a rod from the Progenitors?"

"Yes," replied Calvin. He felt reluctant to hand the rod over to the Aesir, so he held the rod where the alien could see it, instead.

"Let me guess," said Captain Nightsong. "A gate appeared as you were transiting a known system, and you went through it. You found a system that had all the planets in a line, and you were met by some sort of computer avatar from the Progenitors, a civilization that disappeared long ago. The avatar gave you the rod and told you to look for a certain type of rock formation. Is that what happened?"

"Yes," said Calvin. "How did you know?"

"I have seen two of those rods previously. In both cases, that is how they were acquired."

"What happens when you complete the task or quest, or whatever the hell it is?" asked Calvin.

"I don't know. Both of the people who had them previously died before accomplishing the task. May I hold it?"

Calvin handed him the rod, feeling a little better about him.

"Only two symbols?" Nightsong asked. "You must have just received it."

"We've been kind of busy fighting the Drakuls since the avatar gave it to me. I was hoping to go around and get some more of the symbols, but I'm going to have to put it off to come help you."

The Aesir gave Calvin a wry smile. "In that case, you should try not to get killed. I have wondered about the reward for completing the quest for a very long time."

Calvin snorted. "As if I needed a better reason." He shook his head and then said, "Hey, I've been thinking about what you said on the planet, and there are a couple of things that puzzled me."

"I'd be happy to answer your questions if they help you accomplish your task," said Captain Nightsong. "What are they?"

"First, you mentioned something about putting a life essence into the swords Wayland made. How does that work? Were the people he took them from willing participants, or does your culture condone stealing peoples' souls?"

"Neither, actually," replied the Aesir, "although the full answer is much more complicated. Wayland didn't just retire to your planet; he fled there when our people found out he was experimenting with stealing peoples' life forces. What he was doing was against our laws and our beliefs, and it shocked all of us who knew him. When his experiments were discovered, he fled to your planet to hide. He would have been fine, but he spoke too freely about his sword. When he said it was 'forged for a giant,' it was. He had acquired it as booty in one of our wars against the frost giants."

"Frost giants?" asked Calvin.

"Yes, the Jotunn are a historical enemy of ours and the likely cause of our current troubles. When the first of our ships disappeared, we thought it was due to a giant attack. The frost giants live on a number of planets that are generally too cold for us and spend most of their time fighting amongst themselves. Every millennia or so, a leader will arise who is strong enough to unite them, and they will make war on one of their neighbors. Unfortunately, that neighbor is usually us. They haven't been heard from in about 1,400 years so we figured they were overdue."

"But it isn't the giants?"

"Not unless they have developed some new strategy that lets them sneak up on our ships and keep them from escaping," Nightsong said. "That has never been their style, though. Normally, they prefer a direct approach and try to overwhelm you with brute force. They also believe in single combat, which is where Wayland got the sword he killed Grendel with. He took it from a giant clan leader he killed."

"You seem well acquainted with Wayland's story," said Calvin.

"I should be," replied Nightsong. "We grew up together, and he was my best friend. The day I had to kill him was the worst day of my life."

"You grew up with him?" asked Calvin. "Didn't he live thousands of years ago?"

"Yes, he did," said Nightsong with a far-off look. "I am over 4,000 of your years old. We live longer lives than you, which tends to give us a slightly different view of the galaxy than most of the other sentient beings. We are less worried about short-term gains than long-term success, and rarely do anything quickly. The fact that this mission was put together so hastily is a sign of our unease at what is happening." He paused. "You said you had two questions; what was the other?"

"My other question is, if Wayland was an Aesir, how did he get away with it? I mean, how did he appear to be the human hero, Beowulf? Wouldn't he have looked like you?"

"You have to remember Wayland didn't want to be a hero. Quite the opposite, in fact. He fled to your world to *escape* prosecution. He didn't want the fame he thought would come from killing Grendel, but leaving Grendel unchecked had the potential to become even more of a problem. Wayland knew there was a Psiclopes' mission on the planet, and if Grendel killed enough people, they would probably come investigate."

"Why would they investigate a monster killing some of the local people?"

"Because Grendel wasn't indigenous to the planet, and Wayland knew the locals would never be able to kill it on their own. He knew the monster would eventually kill enough people that rumors of Grendel would make their way to the Psiclopes, and once they heard about the monster, they would come to determine if something needed to be done about it. He went looking for Grendel's lair, and when he found it, he killed Grendel. After the monster was dead, he found that it had some sort of projector that let its holder appear to be whatever he wanted. Grendel used it to appear human, so he could infiltrate human society when he wanted; Wayland also used the projector to appear human. Wayland went to the king and said that he would kill Grendel, then Wayland went back to the lair, cut off the monster's head and brought it back to Hrothgar. While he was in the lair, Grendel's mother showed up, so he killed her too."

"If Wayland didn't want the notoriety, why did he approach the king?" asked Steropes. "He had to know that might make us aware of his presence."

"He thought the projector would defeat anything you had, and you wouldn't be able to tell he was an Aesir," said Nightsong. "Obviously it worked because you never found out about him. Why did he do it? He wanted the reward and the fame. He needed funding to continue his experiments, and he wanted the fame to attract heroes to him so he could kill them and enhance his swords. He may have been crazy, but he was never stupid. He couldn't let an opportunity that good pass him by."

Squadron CO's Office, TSS *Vella Gulf,* Grrrnow, 61 Virginis, May 17, 2021

"Do you have a moment?" asked a voice. Calvin looked up to find an unknown lieutenant in the doorway. He swayed from side to side and generally looked uncomfortable; his eyes never left the surface of Calvin's desk.

"Yeah," said Calvin, "this paperwork isn't going anywhere fast. What can I do for you?"

"Hi sir, I'm Lieutenant Bill Bradford, the new Department X officer." He paused and then asked, "You've been briefed on us, right?"

"Yes, we had a representative from Department X with us on our last mission. You guys go through the alien databases looking for technology you can adapt to our uses."

"That is partially correct," the lieutenant replied, his eyes now at about Calvin's chest level. "You are right in that we go through the replicator databases looking for things we can use, but when our forces have needs Terran technology can't fill, we also look for alien technological solutions to fill them."

"Okay, I guess that makes sense. How can I help you?"

"Oh, you can't help me," replied the lieutenant, his eyes jumping up to Calvin's in his surprise. They quickly fled back down when eye contact was made. "Actually, I'm here to help you. I'm talking with all of the senior officers onboard to find out if there is anything you need. If there is a piece of gear or a capability you are lacking, I will get it produced for you."

"Like what?"

"I don't know; that's why I'm asking. This is my first time in space, and I only have a limited idea of what you *have*, much less what you might need. For example, the ship's commanding officer said that we don't have any way to communicate down the stargate chain once we proceed on our mission. I found out there are Aesir missiles that can fly back and report what we are doing so I got a few made. They're pretty expensive, so we won't have many, but if we get into trouble, it will give us the capability to transmit back to the nearest civilized planet so they know what happened to us."

"Hopefully we won't have to use them," noted Calvin, who had an aviator's fear of jinxing the mission by talking about something bad happening ahead of time.

"Uh, yeah…I mean…not that we'd *need* them," said Lieutenant Bradford, his face turning red. "But if we happened to want to…um…report what we were doing, they, um, might come in handy."

"I know what you mean," Calvin replied, taking pity on the lieutenant. "I saw a similar type of missile used by the Ssselipsssiss to call for help from the next star system over on our first mission. Gee, it seems like that was about 10 years ago."

"It will be two years ago next week," said Bradford, looking at his watch to confirm the date.

"How do you know that?"

"I reviewed the mission logs from all of your past missions, and I have always had a very good memory, even before I got implants." He paused and then asked, "Is there anything you need?"

"Not at the moment," said Calvin, "but if there is, I'll let you know."

Bradford looked up and met Calvin's eyes. This time, he didn't shy away. "If you need something, I *will* get it for you."

Combat Training Range, Grrrnow, 61 Virginis, May 18, 2021

Calvin surveyed the mountaintop from his observer position in an elevated stand 100 yards away. The two squads of his platoon were playing "Capture the Flag" to help integrate the new soldiers they had received. The squads were in combat with each other, but were without their officers and senior enlisted, who were in the observers' stand watching the evolution. The Ground Force, also known as "Bravo Squad," was defending the flag from the Space Force, or "Alpha Squad." Calvin frowned as he consulted his in-head display. "Where is your new cyborg?" he finally asked.

The cyborg conversion was one of the "benefits" of the new technology the Terrans received from the Psiclopes. The process saved a human brain by putting it into a robot body. Cyborg troopers were able to wield a huge variety of powerful weapons…if they weren't driven crazy by the conversion process first.

The Ground Force's new leader, Master Gunnery Sergeant Bob 'Mongo' Bryant, laughed. "Can't find him, sir? He's right there."

"I see where he is on the display," Calvin replied, "but I'll be damned if I see him. My display shows him next to the flag on top of the hill. He must be camouflaged, but his suit's camouflage is better than any of the other suits I've ever seen. I would have expected to see a shimmer or something, but it's as if he isn't there."

"He's not," said Mongo, scanning down the back of the hillside to check the rest of his squad's positioning.

"What do you mean?" asked Calvin.

"Our squad's new cyborg, Corporal Patrick Harris, is from Domus. He was a miner, until the day that the mine caved in on him. The cyborg conversion gave him a new lease on life. Still, he's lived most of his life in confined places, and he's comfortable in a hole. We dug a hole and stuck him in it. You can't see him because he isn't there."

"Wait, he's from Domus?" asked Calvin. The planet Domus had joined the Republic of Terra the year before. "I thought all of the new recruits were from Terra."

"No, sir. 'Tanker' Harris is from Domus. We had to take a cyborg from Domus since the Terran cyborg conversion program is on hold."

"What?" asked Calvin. "Why is it on hold? Lack of volunteers?"

"No, sir. Actually, it's just the opposite. All the warriors who got mangled in Iraq and Afghanistan are asking to come back in as cyborgs. It isn't so much a matter of finding people to turn into cyborgs as it is to find the right people to do it to. It's a mess."

Calvin raised an eyebrow.

"Why's it a mess?" asked Captain Paul "Night" Train, the unit's executive officer, or second in command.

"It's a mess because anyone with a psych degree is trying to get their noses into the selection process. The Navy's Bureau of Medicine is vying with the Army's Office of the Surgeon General and the Air Force's Medical Support Agency. They all think they can get a bigger stake in the new Combined Forces' Medical Bureau if they're seen as the experts. When you throw in the other countries' experts, the public sector folks who are looking to make a buck, and all of the people who want conversion for non-military uses…" He let the sentence trail off for a moment before finishing, "It's a mess."

"I see," said Calvin. "Now that the war's over, it's back to fighting amongst ourselves for a bigger piece of the pie?"

"Pretty much," Mongo agreed. "The two cyborgs we got from Earth, Sergeant Nelson and Sergeant Graham, will be the last two we get until they figure it out."

"If the process is so screwed up, how did they pick these two?" asked Night.

"George Nelson on Alpha Squad was easy. He was picked on his combat record in the Sandbox. He did three tours of duty in the

'Stans, picking up a Silver Star for valor, a Bronze Star for heroism and three Purple Hearts before finally stepping on the mine that got him."

"Sounds like he leads from the front," said Night. "My kind of guy." The leaders stopped to watch the troopers sneaking closer to the flag. It appeared undefended, which had all of them on edge.

"Sergeant Adeline Graham is a bit more…interesting," continued Mongo.

"Oh?" asked Calvin. "How so?" The squad had stopped at the tree line, and its members were looking at the last 50 yards up the hill to the flag. Only a layer of brush bearing some sort of orange berry separated them.

"Her background is a little more unconventional," said Mongo. "She was a history and classics major before going into the Canadian military. Sergeant Graham was taken by the indigenous forces during a peacekeeping mission in Africa. German Special Forces troopers got most of her back, but it wasn't pretty. Still, she survived and was a national hero; when she asked for the conversion, the Canadian government pushed hard and got it for her."

Calvin dialed up the comm frequency being used by the Space Force.

"*I gotta bad feeling about 'dis, mon,*" commed Sergeant Margaret 'Witch' Andrews. The Jamaican woman was a voodoo practitioner, among other things, and had an acute sense of impending danger. "*I not be getting any readings, mon, and I know I don't much wanna be walkin' up dat hill.*"

"*Me, neither,*" said Gunnery Sergeant Patrick Dantone. He knew from long experience to trust her feelings, but didn't see any other alternative. "*We'll go up in force,*" the cyborg finally said, "*and meet what-*

ever's waiting for us with overwhelming firepower. Fire Teams #2 and #3, keep your eyes out behind us; they're probably going to hit us here."

"*Roger that,*" chorused Sergeant Jones and Sergeant Burnie, the two fire team leaders.

"*Move out!*" ordered Gunnery Sergeant Dantone.

The squad started forward, nerves on edge, but only made it as far as the bushes before the comm net came alive.

"*Ouch!*" "*Damn it, Gunny, this shit hurts!*" "*Son of a bitch!*" "*FUCK!*"

"Why'd they stop?" asked Calvin.

Mongo gave a predator's smile. "I guess you haven't seen those bushes up close, have you, sir?" When Calvin shook his head, Mongo continued. "The Mrowry call them hell bushes. The thorns on them have a toxin that burns like hell. When the squad was setting up, they found out the thorns were so sharp they could even penetrate our combat suits. The Mrowry have eradicated them all across the planet, except for here on this range. The Mrowry who end up in the bushes are usually out of the battle for a good week afterward. Those bushes *suck.*"

As the leaders watched, the unity of Alpha Squad's advance was broken up as they each tried to find a way through the thorns, with only limited success.

"One of the benefits of having a history major in your squad," noted Mongo, "is that history majors know history. Sergeant Graham set up what's about to happen based on Hannibal's victory at the Battle of Trebia River."

All of Alpha Squad's troops were struggling with the hell bushes when Bravo Squad hit them from the left with a barrage of range grenades. Built to simulate the flight characteristics of the Terran antimatter grenades, they detonated with a flash although they did no real damage. Casualties were determined by the combat range's computer system, which had been fed the information on the Terran weapon systems' capabilities.

Alpha Squad instinctively reacted to the sudden onslaught by throwing themselves to the ground, which for about half of them meant throwing themselves into the hell bushes. Screams filled their comm network as the hell bush spines penetrated their suits. Calvin's suit showed five of Alpha Squad already rated as "killed" by the Mrowry computer system, including Sergeant Nelson, who was the target of three grenades. Judging by what Calvin heard on Alpha Squad's comm net, many more wished they actually *were* dead as the hell bush toxins ran through their systems. Calvin could see most of the squad pulling antitoxins and analgesics from their suits' pharmacopeia; judging by the traffic on the comms net, it didn't seem to be helping.

A Ranger long before his first trip off-planet, Gunnery Sergeant Dantone had trained his squad with tactics right out of the Ranger Handbook, and they responded to the ambush in the classic Ranger fashion. Without a word being spoken, his soldiers returned fire and threw smoke and concussion grenades. As they exploded, the remaining "live" members of Alpha Squad rose as one to assault through the ambush.

Expecting that reaction, Master Gunnery Sergeant Bill Hendrick had positioned several of his men on the back side of the hill behind Corporal Harris, and they rose with him to fire down the length of Alpha Squad as it faced left. The withering fire killed another four soldiers before the rest could throw themselves back down into the hell bushes. Another round of screams came across the comm net.

Alpha Squad grenadiers began firing into both ambush sites like there was no tomorrow. Calvin realized if they didn't do something fast, there probably wouldn't be. Although they had killed several of the ambushers so far, Alpha lost another two troops and was down to five.

"Follow me!" commed Gunnery Sergeant Dantone, the squad's only remaining cyborg. Before Bravo Squad could react, he rose to his feet and charged the second ambush. Lasers flashed off of his suit and several grenades burst nearby, but he made it to the ambush and began killing the members of Bravo, starting with the cyborg. The rest of Alpha made it to the ambush site as Dantone was put out of action, and he fell to the side. Seeing that the way was clear, the four remaining Alpha Squad members grabbed the flag and ran as fast as they could back down the hill.

Just before they reached the tree line, a simulated .50 caliber sniper round hit Corporal Pat Burke, and his suit locked, throwing him forward to hydroplane face-first into a tree. As he crashed to a stop, one of his compatriots brought up his rifle, aimed and fired at the sniper, before turning and continuing his flight. Calvin saw the sniper, located on the next hill, jerk as if hit.

"Who just shot the sniper?" asked Calvin.

"Corporal Nicholas Tomaselli," replied Master Chief Ryan O'Leary, the platoon's senior enlisted member. "He's one of the new guys. They call him 'The Kid.' He looks like he's about 12, but he's a natural shot. He'll be going to sniper school when we get back. The range was too far for him to get a kill with the laser, but he was credited with wounding the sniper. It was a heck of a shot."

"Well, it looks like a few of your guys are going to get away," said Night as the three remaining members of Alpha Squad made it to a gully that protected them from additional fire.

"Not necessarily," said Mongo. "The squad put together a plan in case anyone from Alpha made it to the gully. In fact, with two cyborgs on Alpha, my guys actually expected some of them *to* make it there." He pointed to a trooper hiding at the end of the gully with his back to them. The soldier watched the other squad work its way down the gully through a video monitor. "The gully's mined, and that trooper is watching via closed circuit TV. When they get in the kill zone, he'll trigger the mines."

"Who is that?" asked Calvin. "I don't recognize him."

Mongo consulted his suit's roster and rolled his eyes. "Aw shit," he said, "it's the Cat."

"You don't think he can do the job?" asked Master Chief.

"That's not it," said Mongo. "Sergeant Rowntree is one of the best soldiers I know."

"If he's so good," said Master Chief, "what's wrong with him being there?"

Mongo shrugged. "His call sign is 'Black Cat.' Although he's a great soldier, his abilities are countered by his bad luck. If anything can go wrong, it will go wrong...*to him*. He's as good as he is because he's always having to overcome some emergency or malfunction. I wouldn't stand next to him in combat if I were you. You don't want to be in the blast radius when his rifle blows up."

"Blast radius?" asked Master Chief. "These rifles won't blow up unless you set them to."

"His will. If he went on a fishing trip, a sea monster would probably pop up and eat him. *That's* how bad his luck is."

As Bravo Squad had planned, the remaining members of Alpha Squad were channeled into the gully Sergeant Rowntree was defending. Bravo Squad had laced the ravine with enough mines to knock out even the cyborgs if they were still operational. The platoon's leaders could see Sergeant Rowntree, and they watched as he armed the mines. Before he could detonate them, there was a loud "crack," and the plastic mount holding the video camera up in the tree broke. The monitor's picture started spinning, and Sergeant Rowntree played with its dials, trying to get the picture to stabilize. Finally realizing that the problem was with the camera and not the monitor, the soldier looked up just in time for the camera to hit him in the face, knocking him out.

The remains of Alpha Squad egressed the gully and made it to freedom.

"Black Cat, huh?" asked Calvin.

Mongo nodded. "They say cats have nine lives. I don't know how many he has left, but it can't be more than two or three."

Chapter Three

Bridge, TSS *Vella Gulf,* Grrrnow, 61 Virginis, May 20, 2021

"Five minutes to the Gliese 676 stargate," reported the helmsman.

"Good luck in your quest," said Emperor Yazhak from the front view screen. "Remember, you promised to bring my fighters back without a scratch."

"I'll do my best," said Captain Sheppard.

"I would also like it if you brought my grandson back in a similar condition," the emperor added, looking over Captain Sheppard's shoulder to where Lieutenant Rrower stood. As he had during the *Vella Gulf's* previous mission, the Mrowry would serve as the ambassador for his civilization. In addition to his diplomatic status, he had also proven his skills in a number of other tasks, including fighting alongside the *Gulf's* platoon of space marines when he was needed.

"I will do my best," Captain Sheppard repeated. "*Vella Gulf,* out." The screen went blank as he terminated the transmission. "Duty Engineer, sound General Quarters!" Captain Sheppard ordered.

"Aye aye, sir!" said the engineer, who was seated next to the helmsman at the front console. Responsible for all of the damage control systems, he was also in charge of the General Quarters alarm. "*Bong! Bong! Bong! Bong!*" sounded the bell. It was followed by the engineer's call of "General Quarters, General Quarters, all hands man your battle stations!" Setting General Quarters prior to transit was standard practice; the air crews also manned up all 12 of the ship's space fighters. You never knew what was waiting on the other side of a stargate.

"Helmsman, full speed to the stargate!" Captain Sheppard ordered. Under his breath he added, "Once more unto the breach."

Bridge, TSS *Vella Gulf,* HD 69830, May 30, 2021

"Entry into the HD 69830 system," said Steropes. The journey had taken 10 days, crossing through the systems of Gliese 676, Mu Arae and Epsilon Indi, but they had finally arrived at the Aesir's home system. "HD 69830 is a yellow-orange dwarf star that has a mass of 86 percent of Sol's, 89 percent of its diameter, and 45 percent of its luminosity. There are three large Neptune-like planets in the system that all lie fairly close to the star, with a large asteroid belt in between the orbits of the second and third planets."

"And this is the home system of the Aesir?" asked Captain Sheppard. "Which planet do they live on?"

"None of them, actually," replied Steropes. "The third planet, Asgard, has a mass of about 18 times that of Terra. Although the planet isn't Earth-like, it does have a moon that is."

"The moon's name is Golirion," said Captain Nightsong, "That is our birth world." He paused and then added, "It is good to be home."

"Didn't Steropes say there was an asteroid belt close to the planet?" Captain Sheppard asked. "Don't you have a problem with asteroid impacts?"

"Not anymore," replied Captain Nightsong. "The frequency of asteroid impacts throughout our history led us to have a very close relationship with nature, and it was the primary reason we became a space-faring race. Each asteroid impact set our culture back hundreds of years; we had to get off our moon so we could keep the asteroids from hitting us."

Bridge, TSS *Vella Gulf*, HD 69830, Approaching Golirion, May 31, 2021

"We are approaching the third planet," said Ensign Sara Sommers from the science station. She gave a puzzled look to the Aesir who had come onto the bridge to watch their arrival at his home world. "Captain Nightsong, I don't get it. Where is your civilization?"

"Are you looking at Asgard?" asked Captain Nightsong. "Our civilization is not there; it's on the moon."

"No," replied Ensign Sommers, "I know that. I'm looking at the moon, and I don't see any signs of habitation. There are some shipyards in orbit, but it looks like it's completely uninhabited." She put the long-range visual onto the front view screens. The bridge crew could see the planet Asgard as a backdrop, with its moon Golirion in the foreground. From space, the moon appeared very similar to Earth although a little smaller.

Captain Nightsong smiled. "You mean, where are all of our major cities? Where do our people live?" Sara nodded her head. "Most live below the surface of the moon," he said, answering his own question. "Our civilization developed there to protect itself from the asteroids which often hit our world. By the time we made it to space and could ensure the safety of our world, our civilization had adapted to living below the surface of the planet. Those of us who moved back to the surface live in harmony with nature; we enjoy its beauty and do not want to see it spoiled with the buildings and factories that pollute other races' planets." The Terrans could hear a large measure of pride in his voice.

"And what Captain Nightsong is leaving out," said Steropes, "is that very few outsiders have ever seen the surface of the moon. Usually, visitors are discouraged. When the Alliance of Civilizations moved off my planet, the Aesir were the only member nation that didn't want to host its headquarters."

"Look at our world," said Captain Nightsong. "If you were us, would you want that group of thieves and incompetents to come here and destroy its beauty? Many of the nations have no respect for nature or culture; they are only interested in what will make them the most money or gain them the most influence. We desire neither of those things. We desire peace and the opportunity to appreciate the finer things in life. Unfortunately, peace is often obtained only through strength of arms. We joined the Alliance of Civilizations, not because we wanted to, but because we wanted the peace we thought we would get by being part of a large defensive alliance. Other than that, we are content to stay out of the bickering and squabbling that goes on at Alliance meetings."

"You didn't want the prestige or monetary benefits from having the headquarters on your planet?" asked Sara.

"What is prestige when compared with the colors of a perfect sunset?" asked Captain Nightsong. "What is the value of artificial currency when compared with a still lake in the early morning before the fog burns off? We have no desire for anything the Alliance has to offer, aside from a galaxy-wide peace that would let us pursue our quest for knowledge and beauty."

"What is your society like?" asked Calvin. "What can we expect?"

"Unlike the other races I have met, we value our individual freedom more than anything else. We tend to be more solitary than the other races; even our cities are small. Most Aesir are very locally focused. We follow a local mayor, who follows a regional leader called a reeve, who owes allegiance to the king and queen who rule the planet. You would not be comfortable in our society; there are very few rules."

"How do you keep people in line then?" asked Captain Sheppard. "What if someone infringes on the personal freedom of someone else."

"Normally, most laws aren't needed," said Captain Nightsong; "most of our citizens don't do anything to harm anyone else. When someone goes rogue, which is extremely infrequent, the group will band together to modify his or her behavior."

"How do they do that?" asked Calvin.

"In whatever manner it takes," said the Aesir. "We try to be minimally invasive, but if the citizen refuses to change, stronger measures will be used."

"We're getting a communication from the planet," interrupted the communications officer, her voice full of confusion. "It's from someone called…the Thor?"

"That is our king," said Captain Nightsong.

"On screen, please," said Captain Sheppard.

The picture of Golirion on the front viewer was replaced with a male and a female Aesir; however, they were very different in appearance from Captain Nightsong. Where Nightsong's hair was blond and his skin green, the king and queen had dark hair and pale blue skin. A thin circlet was all that marked them as royalty; neither wore any other regalia. Nightsong bowed deeply.

"Greetings, people of Terra," said the king.

"Welcome to Aesir space," added the queen. "Thank you for coming so quickly."

Following Nightsong's lead, the Terrans who were standing on the bridge bowed as well. "Thank you for your words of welcome," said Captain Sheppard. "I am Captain James Sheppard. We are happy to come to your aid."

"Lieutenant Commander Hobbs is the hero we were looking for," said Captain Nightsong. "Although he is not the commander of this ship, he is the leader of their space marines and their space fighter squadron. Captain Sheppard is the commanding officer of the ship that supports them."

"That is…interesting," said the king. "Interesting and unexpected." He looked at Captain Sheppard. "Queen Farseer and I would be honored if you would join us for a strategy session in an hour. We will send you the coordinates of the closest transporter platform."

"I'm sorry, but I'm not sure what to call you," said Captain Sheppard.

"You may call me 'Thor,'" said the king.

"I'm sorry, Thor, but we are unable to transport down," said Captain Sheppard. "We haven't been scanned. The only way we can come down is via shuttle."

"I will have our technician send you the coordinates of a landing site. Please make it as soon as you can, but limit the number of people you bring to five, including your shuttle crew."

"Yes, Thor," said Captain Sheppard. "We will see you shortly."

The front view screen returned to the picture of Golirion as the transmission was terminated.

Captain Sheppard turned to Captain Nightsong. "The king and queen seem...dissimilar...to you."

"Indeed," said the Aesir. "They are of the Drow, or the underground Aesir; I am of the above ground clan, the Valir." He paused, gathering his thoughts. "When we emerged from our stay underground and took to the stars, there were those among us who chose to stay below. It was what they knew, and what they were comfortable with. Most, in fact, no longer desired the wide open spaces. Over time, those who stayed below ground lost the pigmentation from being in our star's light. Their hair grew dark while their skin became pale. Most of the Drow would look like I do if they chose to spend some time in the light; however, only a small percentage come up to tend our world's surface and take to the stars."

"What can we expect when we meet your king?" asked Captain Sheppard.

"I expect he will meet you in Reeve Hall," replied the Aesir. "As I mentioned, our regional leaders are called reeves. When the situation warrants, the king and queen will meet in Reeve Hall with the Council of Reeves to discuss important events. I expect the king and queen will meet you there, as you will be the first off-world visitors we've had in over three centuries. I imagine that qualifies your visit as an important event."

Shuttle 01, **Approaching Golirion, HD 69830, June 1, 2021**

"*Sir, this is amazing,*" commed Lieutenant Bryan 'Hooty' Hooten, the shuttle's pilot. The ship was descending vertically toward the landing pad, a tiny sliver of metal in the middle of a continent-wide forest.

"*The trees can't be more than 20 feet away on any side of the shuttle,*" said Lieutenant Larry 'Grocer' Albertson, the shuttle's weapon systems officer (WSO). "*It's incredible how they're able to keep them trimmed like this.*"

"*The trees aren't trimmed,*" said Nightsong. "*We just ask them nicely to keep this open. This pad is one of only two that exist on the continent.*"

"*What if you need to bring a larger ship down to the surface of the planet?*" asked Hooty.

"*We don't.*"

"*Wait,*" said Calvin, "*you ask them to keep it open?*"

"*Yes,*" replied Captain Nightsong. "*We have a very close relationship with nature…and some outstanding nanobots to assist us with the process.*"

The shuttle touched down gently on the pad, and its boarding ramp came down, allowing the shuttle's occupants to see two Aesir waiting for them. Calvin was the first person out of the shuttle, followed by Captain Sheppard and Night. Although the Aesir smiled as Calvin exited the shuttle, Calvin had also seen their faces before they masked them with smiles. He wasn't sure whether it was distrust or displeasure, but neither had looked pleased to see the Terran shuttle. "For a welcoming party, they didn't look very happy to see us," he said in an undertone to Nightsong, who was behind him on the ramp. "What's that all about?"

"It could be a number of things," replied Nightsong. "They might be unhappy about the shuttle. You are the first non-Aesir to land here in several centuries; some of my people are probably unhappy with this."

"I don't think that was it," said Calvin, who could tell the Aesir was being evasive. "What else could it have been?"

"Not everyone is happy we went off-planet in search of aid," said Nightsong. "Some of my people wanted to solve the problem ourselves and avoid becoming entangled with the Alliance again."

"But I thought the Alliance was no more," said Captain Sheppard, catching up with them.

"It's not," replied Nightsong, "but try telling that to my people. We have long memories, and there are a number of people who want to avoid any off-planet obligations ever again."

"Forever is a long time," Calvin noted.

"That is true," agreed Nightsong. "Let's hope they never come to power."

"Never is just as long," said Calvin.

"Indeed."

Calvin shook his head as Nightsong stepped forward to embrace the two Aesir waiting for them. Strange fragrances filled his nose. One smelled like pines, but not quite; a second had a scent of lemons and a third had an odor of oranges. None were quite like the corresponding Terran smells, but they had one thing in common; they all smelled clean. The forest pressed in on all sides, its foliage almost every shade of green in the spectrum. Lit by the warm sunlight filtering through, the leaves appeared to dance in a light breeze.

Captain Nightsong turned from his embrace to introduce his countrymen, both of whom were pale blue with dark hair. They were slender in build, like all of the Aesir Calvin could remember seeing, and remarkably similar in appearance.

"This is Senior Reeve Foron and his deputy Elhael," Nightsong said. "Foron is in charge of the Council of Reeves." Both of the Aesir bowed, and the Terrans returned the bows.

"Welcome to our world," said Senior Reeve Foron. "If you would follow me, the Thor and his queen are waiting with the rest of the council."

Captain Sheppard agreed, and the Aesir turned and began walking toward the forest. Without warning, the ground in front of them began moving, and an opening 30 feet long by 20 feet wide appeared as the ground was lifted up on four hydraulic rams. A ramp was revealed which led below ground, and the Aesir continued down without slowing.

The Terrans followed them below the surface of the moon into a well-lit passageway. As they stepped off the ramp and into the tunnel, the opening behind them began closing as the rams retracted. The opening shut with barely a whisper.

"I don't know about you," said Night, "but I sure liked it better when our way out was open."

"Yeah, me too," replied Calvin, repressing a shudder. "I'm sure they'll let us out again…"

His voice trailed off as they came to a doorway about 50 feet along the tunnel.

"Welcome to the real world of Golirion," said Foron as he opened the door.

The Terrans were amazed as they walked through the doorway. The walls of the tunnel were painted with murals of the surface so lifelike that it was almost like being above ground. The lighting was as bright as the daylight above, but there didn't seem to be a source; no light fixtures could be seen. Looking up, Calvin felt dizzy as he stared into the blue sky painted on the ceiling of the tunnel. He knew the roof was no more than 20 feet above him, but he was unable to tell exactly where it was.

"That's amazing," muttered Captain Sheppard in awe.

"Do you like it?" asked Foron. "Our craftsmen worked hundreds of years to craft a painting that makes you feel like you are on the surface."

"It's beautiful. Not only does it look like the surface, but it's almost like I can feel the warmth of your star and smell the scents of the forest as well," replied Captain Sheppard.

"Indeed," said Foron. "With scenes so lifelike down here, why would anyone ever want to leave?" He indicated a small tram sitting at the end of a railway. "This is our ride."

Calvin could see two sets of rails leading off into the simulated foliage from beneath the two little cars, but they were camouflaged to fit into the rest of the scene, and he lost sight of them within 20 feet. Each car could have held four Terrans comfortably, so there was plenty of room; Captain Nightsong got into one of the cars with the Terrans while the two Drow entered the other.

The cars started moving once everyone was seated, and they rapidly picked up speed. The pictures on the walls were just as remarkable as the cars sped past them; if anything, they were even more impressive.

"Was that a deer?" asked Calvin.

"I couldn't tell," said Night. "Whatever it was, it looked like it was moving."

After the first deer analog, the Terrans glimpsed a number of other life forms; all seemed to come alive as the Terrans sped past. Strange animals wandered through the underbrush; some stopped to look at the passing cars while others ignored them. Birds and other shapes flew overhead, but none close enough to identify.

All too soon, the tram coasted to a stop.

"We are here," said Foron as he exited his car.

Disappointed, the Terrans disembarked and followed him to a door, which was barely visible in the undergrowth.

"That was amazing," said Captain Sheppard.

"I am glad you liked the ride," said Foron. His smile seemed more genuine than it had on the surface, but then the smile faded as quickly as it had come. "I'm afraid what awaits in the Council of Reeves may be less to your liking." Before the Terrans could ask what he meant, he opened the door and walked inside, forcing the Terrans to follow along behind him.

Without warning, they found themselves in a giant horseshoe-shaped room with a packed dirt floor. The Terrans entered from the open end of the horseshoe to find two rows of elevated seating extending on both sides to meet at the opposite end of the chamber, at least 80 feet in front of them. The seating was terraced, with an eight-foot wall surrounding the floor of the horseshoe. Calvin looked up; the ceiling was at least 25 feet above him.

Aesir filled both rows on both sides; 15 to a row for a total of 60. Only a couple of seats were empty. Before Calvin could ask, Foron turned to the right and opened a door Calvin hadn't noticed. Stairs behind the door led up to the two open seats. Foron took the one in the lower tier; Elhael shut the door and mounted the stairs to a seat in the row behind and above Foron. The feeling was surreal; 120 eyes looked at them, but not a voice spoke.

A feeling of dread overwhelmed Calvin as he returned the stares of the Aesir.

"Welcome to Golirion," said a voice from behind them. The Terrans and Captain Nightsong turned to find the Thor and queen in an alcove above them, sitting on thrones.

"Thank you for your welcome," said Captain Sheppard, "but this feels less like a welcome and more like an inspection. We thought we were here at your invitation. Were we mistaken?"

"No, you are quite correct in that you are here at our request," said the Thor, "and the queen and I are very happy you have come. Our people have a pressing need which must be discussed, and an answer must be found to the troubles we are having. We need to determine what we are going to do about our missing forces; however, there has been a complication."

"What's the complication?" asked Captain Sheppard.

"One of our reeves has declared the right of trial by combat," replied the Thor.

"Trial by combat?" asked Captain Sheppard, not liking where this was going. "Trial by combat *with whom?*"

"With Lieutenant Commander Hobbs, actually," said the Thor. "The reeve disputes that Lieutenant Commander Hobbs is the hero we have been looking for. He wants to lead the mission and has challenged Lieutenant Commander Hobbs to single combat."

"*Swina bqllr!*" said Captain Nightsong under his breath. "I was afraid this would happen."

"With all due respect, Thor," said Captain Sheppard, "this is stupid. We come all this way to help you and find out we have to conduct some sort of challenge before we can? That is the dumbest thing I've ever heard. C'mon folks, we're leaving." He started walking toward the door through which they had entered, underneath the Thor's platform.

"It's okay, Captain Sheppard," said Calvin. "I've got this. This feels like something I need to do." He looked at the Thor. "What is the nature of this combat?"

"To the death," replied the Thor. "It is the only possible outcome of single combat. Do you accept?"

A momentary wave of panic darted through Calvin, and his eyes jumped from side to side as his body unconsciously tried to look for a way out. Shaking his head, he regained control. He took a breath, held it for a second and then released it. He'd been in worse positions; he'd get through this. He nodded his head. "I do," he said with more enthusiasm than he felt.

"Bring in the challenger!" called the Thor. A door on the other side of the room opened, and one of the blue Aesir came out, held by two of the green topsiders. "I'll kill him!" the Drow screamed. "I'll kill them all! No aliens should be allowed on our world! No more alien obligations!" Spittle flew from his mouth, and he jerked violently, trying to free himself from the two Aesir holding him.

"Thor, he doesn't…he doesn't appear totally sane," said Captain Sheppard.

"I'm afraid he's not," replied the Aesir. "He has his good moments and his bad. This, unfortunately, is not one of his good ones. He was exiled to a small county where he couldn't harm himself or anyone else; however, he somehow snuck back into the capital when he heard foreigners had come."

"You've got to call off the duel!"

"I cannot," replied the Thor. "Once accepted, it cannot be undone."

"It's okay, sir," said Calvin. "If he's crazy, he can't fight very well, can he? I need to do this."

Captain Sheppard raised an eyebrow.

"Really, sir," said Calvin with a nod. "I've faced worse odds."

"If you say so," said Captain Sheppard, not sounding convinced.

The challenger had stopped struggling and had fallen forward onto his knees although the two Aesir holding him maintained their grip. The Aesir no longer resisted, but he had lapsed into a litany of, "I'll kill him," which was even more frightening. A trail of drool from one side of his mouth reached the floor.

"Want me to take your place?" asked Night from Calvin's side. "Killing crazy aliens is my specialty."

"I have a feeling that, once accepted, there is no way for me to swap out," replied Calvin. He looked back at the Aesir and saw there were now drool streams from both sides of his mouth. "On the other hand, if I don't win, feel free to kill him afterward."

Night put his hand on Calvin's shoulder and met his gaze. "I will," Night replied. Calvin could see his eyes were like ice, and he stifled a shudder. If Calvin went down, Night *would* kill the Aesir; of that he had no doubt.

"Bring out the weapons," said the Thor. Two Drow came through the same door the challenger had used, each bearing a long box. One went to the challenger and the other crossed the open floor to stand in front of Calvin. The Aesir opened the box, and Calvin saw two silver rapiers inside. Although the metalwork on the guards and quillons surrounding the handles was exquisite, Calvin could tell the points were sharp and functional.

"Do I take one or two?" he asked.

"That is up to you," replied the Aesir.

Not having a shield or anything else to protect himself with, Calvin removed both of the rapiers from the box. Nearly a meter long and slender, the blades had cutting edges down both sides from their centers to their tips. He swung them back and forth to get the feel, and realized they weren't heavy enough for him to use the sides of the blades; like most rapiers, they were thrusting weapons. He tried to recall everything he had ever downloaded on fighting with a rapier. Unfortunately, it wasn't much. One of the points he did remember was that it took *years* to perfect rapier combat. He didn't have years; he didn't even have minutes.

"There is something you must know," said Captain Nightsong under his breath. "Reeve Farhome is an Eco Warrior."

Calvin stopped looking at the rapiers and spun in Nightsong's direction. "Really, this is a good time to tell me? An Eco Warrior? Just what the hell is that?"

"They are members of elite units who can manipulate matter using nanobots."

"Nanobots?"

"Miniature robots that act at the microscopic level. I believe Farhome's specialty is life."

"Okay, he has miniature robots, what can he do with them?"

"I'm sorry," said Nightsong; "in his case, I don't know."

Calvin could feel eyes on him, and he looked up to find Farhome staring at him. The Aesir was no longer talking or drooling; instead, the Aesir's gaze was now laser-focused on Calvin. Calvin found he liked the Aesir better when he was drooling. Two more Drow came and led Captain Sheppard, Night and Captain Nightsong from the dueling floor. The two Aesir holding Farhome also left.

"Is the challenger ready?" asked the Thor.

"Yes, Thor," Farhome replied. His voice was even, and his eyes never left Calvin.

"Is the challenged ready?"

"As ready as I will ever be." He assumed a defensive pose.

"Then let the contest begin."

Nothing happened.

Calvin stayed where he was, waiting for his opponent, but the Aesir remained motionless, continuing to glare at Calvin. Calvin remained ready, but didn't want to advance and put himself at a disadvantage. After about 10 seconds of tense waiting, the Aesir ran the blades of his swords together with a clash and said, "I hope you are ready, Terran; it's time for you to die." Holding both rapiers in front of him, he advanced toward Calvin, who waited at his end of the arena.

As the Aesir got closer on him, Calvin tried to remain calm, yet ready. He kept his upper body square to the Aesir, his right hand forward and high, and his left hand low.

As the Aesir reached him, Calvin feinted with his right hand and followed with a killing thrust from his left. Farhome blocked both thrusts with only a twitch of his weapons. "If that is the best you can do," said the Aesir, "this fight won't last very long." He let out a high-pitched giggle. "Neither will you."

Calvin unleashed a series of attacks, but all of them were blocked with ease. Farhome reached back and thrust one of his rapiers into the ground behind him so he could cover his mouth while he yawned. "This is really quite boring," he said when the yawn ended. "Time for some fun." He recovered his second sword without looking.

"Maior!" the Aesir said. In a blink, Farhome swelled in size, growing from just under six feet tall to almost eight feet tall. Worse, where before he had only been blocking Calvin's attacks, now the

Aesir began attacking him in earnest. With a shock, Calvin realized his opponent also now had a tremendous reach advantage. The additional height allowed his opponent to rain blows down on Calvin from an altitude he wasn't used to defending against, and after only a few blocks he could feel the muscles in his arms burning. Before he could adjust to the new fighting style, Calvin was hit in a number of places, and blood began streaming down his body.

"Maximus!" the Aesir said. Farhome grew in size again, now standing almost 10 feet tall. Along with the additional height came even more reach, and Calvin found himself blocking strikes from all directions. He was forced to backpedal as the Aesir reached over and tried to skewer him from behind.

The Aesir took two large steps and was back within reach of Calvin. The Terran took another cut at Farhome's midsection as the Aesir approached, hoping to land a blow that would even the fight.

It wasn't to be.

Calling out, "Minimus!" the Aesir shrank to just over three feet tall, and Calvin's sword passed over his opponent, doing no damage. Stepping forward, Farhome drove one of his rapiers through Calvin's right foot and into the ground, pinning him firmly in place. Before Calvin could adjust to his smaller height, he also stabbed Calvin several times with his remaining sword.

"Mediocris!" the Aesir said, returning to his normal height. He stepped back to survey the results of his attack, and he smiled as he watched Calvin try to remove the rapier from his foot.

The pain in Calvin's foot was intense, and his grip was too slick with blood to pull out his opponent's rapier while still holding onto his own swords.

Farhome turned to address the Thor. "This is the person that is going to solve our problems?" He giggled. "I don't see how. He seems to be having problems going anywhere at the moment." He giggled again.

Through the pain, Calvin had a moment of clarity. He knew he was never going to beat the Aesir the way he had been fighting; Calvin needed a new plan or he'd be dead. Dropping both his rapiers, he grabbed the hilt of the sword piercing his foot with both hands and pulled with all his augmented strength.

The pain was blinding, and he almost passed out, but slowly…slowly, he could feel the sword give way. Finally, with a spurt of blood, the rapier pulled out of the floor and through his foot. The pain was enormous, but no longer blinding, and his vision cleared as the Aesir turned back toward him. Seeing Calvin free, he said "Maximus!" grew to his full height and charged. He held his rapier extended in front of him, intending to run Calvin through.

Calvin could see the rage in Farhome's eyes, and knew the Aesir was done toying with him. This time, Farhome intended to kill him. Realizing he was out of time, Calvin took the Aesir's blade and threw it at Farhome with all his might.

The sword glimmered in the artificial light as it flew end over end toward the challenger. The Aesir saw it coming and stopped in place. "Mediocris!" he said, shrinking to his normal height. He grinned as he followed the flight of the rapier as it spun past him overhead.

A complete miss.

What he hadn't noticed was Calvin had followed the throw and was charging right behind the sword, leaving a trail of bloody footprints in his wake. As the challenger's eyes came back down, he only saw a flash, and Calvin was on him.

Calvin dove at the Aesir, hoping to tackle him, but Farhome was just as fast. "Minimus!" he said, shrinking to three feet tall as he dove to the side.

Seeing he was going to overshoot his opponent, Calvin reached out and grabbed Farhome's collar as he shot past. Unprepared to be grappled, the Aesir was spun around as Calvin's momentum whipped him back in the other direction, and both crashed to the floor.

Although the Aesir was half his normal height, Calvin realized he still retained all his mass, and Calvin was pulled up short. The Terran tried to pull Farhome closer, but the challenger struggled and, with a shout, shifted back to his largest size, kicking and flailing in all directions. Slick with blood, Calvin could feel his grip slipping as the Aesir rolled away. Coming to one knee, he got his good foot underneath him and sprang onto the giant Aesir. Farhome had his back to Calvin as he rolled and didn't see the Terran coming. Before Farhome could get up, Calvin got his right arm around the Aesir's throat and locked it into place with his left.

The Aesir changed size, going back to his smallest form, but Calvin was locked in and moved along with Farhome's body as it changed. Although slippery with blood, Calvin held on as the Aesir went through several more changes, one quickly following the other as Farhome tried to dislodge the Terran. Calvin was spun from side to side like a rag doll, and he realized that he knew nothing about Aesir physiology; while the choking attack would have worked against a human, he had no idea if it would be effective on an Aesir. As Farhome struggled, Calvin realized he was out of choices; if he let go, the Aesir *would* kill him.

With that thought in mind, he summoned all his waning energy and squeezed as hard as he could. The Aesir continued to fight and flip around on the ground for another five seconds, then his struggles began to lose strength. Within another five seconds, the Aesir went limp.

"If the Thor would be so kind, I believe the contest is concluded," said one of the reeves from behind Calvin. "There is nothing to prove with the death of someone who clearly lacks all of his faculties."

"I agree," said the Thor. "Lieutenant Commander Hobbs, this contest is at an end, and you have won. I would be in your debt if you would release Reeve Farhome instead of killing him as is your right."

Completely spent, Calvin slowly unlocked his hold on the elf, afraid of what the Aesir might do, but the challenger remained limp and unconscious. The Terran laid his opponent on the floor. Struggling up to one knee, his vision went gray as he turned to look at the Thor.

"If that is all–," he said, and then fell over unconscious on top of the Aesir.

Sick Bay, Golirion, HD 69830, June 2, 2021

The first thing Calvin was aware of was an overwhelming urge to throw up. He leaned over the side of the bed, and his stomach emptied, vomit coating the pair of shoes alongside his bed.

"Thanks," said Captain Sheppard, who was wearing the shoes, "those *were* my dress shoes."

His stomach empty, Calvin regained some of his strength and rolled over. "Sorry, sir," he said, the aftertaste threatening to set him off again.

Seeing the look on Calvin's face, his commanding officer moved a little further away from the splash zone. "It's good to see you moving," said Captain Sheppard.

Calvin got control over his stomach and looked up. "How long have I been out?" he asked.

"About a day," replied Captain Sheppard. "You had us scared there for a while."

"Yeah, me too."

"Hey, the war hero's awake!" called Night, walking into the infirmary. He started to walk up to the side of the bed the CO was on, but saw the puddle and went around to the other side. "I brought you something to eat."

"Oh really?" asked Calvin. "What have you got? I'd eat almost anything right now, just to get this taste out of my mouth."

"You'll have to," replied Night. "All the shuttle had were a few MREs…and the crew had kind of picked through them."

Calvin winced. The Meal, Ready to Eat was considered to be three great lies in one; it wasn't a meal, it would never be ready, and above all else, you should never, *ever*, try to eat one. "What flavors were left?" he asked with a sigh.

Night held up two brown packages. He looked at the one in his right hand. "Meal Rejected by the Enemy #1 is the vegetarian meal."

"Gross," said Calvin.

Night looked at the one in his left hand. "Massive Rectal Explosion #2 is chicken fajitas."

"Grosser," said Calvin with a sigh. "Give me the vegetarian one."

Night shrugged. "It's your funeral." He dropped the chicken faji-tas on the floor and kicked it under the bed. "Good riddance." He tore the top off the MRE and handed it to Calvin. "You must be really hungry if you're going to eat that."

"I just want to get this foul taste out of my mouth," Calvin re-plied. He dumped out the packet on the bed. "The candy bar and the gum are the only things I want from it." He pushed the rest of the items away.

"I'll take the tabasco sauce if you don't want it," said Night. "That always comes in handy when eating Navy food."

"Be my guest," Calvin said, putting the entire chocolate bar in his mouth. He turned back to Captain Sheppard. "Wha' did I miff?" he asked around the mouthful of chocolate.

"After you beat the reeve, you passed out from blood loss when you tried to stand up," the CO replied. "The Aesir brought you to their infirmary to patch you up. They have had contact with humans before, so they were able to take care of you…although they did say you might have a reaction to the anesthesia." He looked down and rubbed his right shoe on the bed frame, trying to get something off it. "Unfortunately, they neglected to mention what that reaction might be."

He shook his head. "In any event, once you beat the reeve, the other members of the council had no recourse but to allow us to try to solve their problem. It was obvious there were still some divisions within the council, but the Thor overrode them. We were just wait-ing for you to be able to travel so we could get the hell out of here."

"I see the victor is awake," announced the Thor, coming into the room with Captain Nightsong in tow. "I am very happy you defeated

Reeve Farhome; he was the wrong person to lead the mission to find our missing starships."

"Thanks, I'm happy I won too," replied Calvin, with a heavy dose of irony.

"I am sorry you had to go through that," said the Thor; "so sorry, in fact, that I have decided to dispatch one of my Eco Warrior teams with you. They will be helpful in facilitating your movement through a variety of environments." He started to come around to the side of the bed, saw the puddle and stayed where he was.

"I'm sorry, Thor," replied Captain Sheppard, "but I'm not familiar with Eco Warrior teams. Captain Nightsong mentioned Reeve Farhome was a member of one of the teams before Calvin's combat, but we don't have any idea what those teams are."

"An Eco Warrior team is a group of four or five specialists. Each team member has significant experience manipulating one of the natural elements: earth, air, fire, water and life. They have all practiced with their chosen elements over the course of many centuries, millennia in some cases, and are extremely experienced. Should they be needed, the Eco Warriors will serve you well." He looked back at Calvin. "If you can walk, it would be easier to show you than tell you."

"I think I can make it," replied Calvin, and he slid to the opposite side of the bed from Captain Sheppard. He started to get up, then realized he had a problem. "Perhaps someone could get me some clothes first?"

Eco Warrior Training Facility, Golirion, HD 69830, June 2, 2021

The Terrans were met at the training facility by one of the Aesir Eco Warrior team leaders. "Welcome," he said as he opened the door and stood aside so the Terrans could enter ahead of him. "Our Eco Warriors are some of the best and brightest craftsmen and women in our society. If they can't make an element do what you want, it can't be done."

Calvin's eyes scanned the large open room as he walked through the door. If this was a room of warriors, they were unlike any he had ever seen. One male was creating a sculpture of a tree, which was perfect right down to the veins in the individual leaves. Another male juggled what looked like five balls of fire. Calvin couldn't tell how he was able to catch them without being burned. A female, with her eyes half-closed and a smile on her face, sat in a large fountain that sprayed water in at least 25 streams. A second female sat in a corner with her legs crossed while electrical arcs danced around her and sometimes on her. A third male held something which looked like a hawk. While Calvin watched, the Aesir launched it into the air, and the 'bird' flapped over to the opposite side of the room and caught a small animal running away. The bird returned to the Aesir and dropped the captured creature in his open hand before landing on his other arm. The Aesir released the animal, and the process repeated itself.

Through several large open doorways, Calvin could see similar events taking place in other rooms throughout the building. Although the activities were interesting, the place didn't look at all like a training facility for warriors. Calvin glanced at the team leader, who had introduced himself with his team name of "Landslide." He was, at least, armed with a sword and laser pistol. "These are the Eco *Warriors?*" he finally asked.

"Indeed," replied the Aesir, "and you will not find more experienced veterans anywhere in our realm."

"I hope you'll forgive me," Calvin said, "but they look more like artists than warriors."

"They *are* artists," said Landslide. "While they may not seem deadly to the untrained eye, they are well versed in the combat arts as well." He paused and then asked, "How many years of training do you have as a warrior?"

"Well, I started out as an aviator and have about nine years of experience flying various air and spacecraft, as well as a couple of years of ground combat training. Why?"

"All of these warriors have over *300 years* of combat experience. Three of us have over 500 years of training. When you live as long as we do, you can take time out to pursue a number of specialties and still have time to do the things you want."

"Hmm," said Calvin. "I hadn't thought of it that way."

"Will you be leading the team coming with us?" Captain Sheppard asked. "If so, can you point out the members of your team?"

"Normally, I would be leading the team," replied the Aesir; "however, as this is a military mission, it requires a military leader." He held out a hand to indicate Captain Nightsong. "You already know Captain Nightsong; he will be leading the team. His team name is "Inferno." As you might guess, he is our fire expert."

"So that is how you were able to create fire for Princess Merrorritor," said Calvin.

"Indeed," said Captain Nightsong. "I have some small experience with fire nanobots and can use them to accomplish a variety of fire-based tasks."

"Inferno is being modest," said Landslide; "he is one of our most experienced Eco Warriors." Captain Nightsong shrugged. "The only reason he isn't a full-time team leader is that he left to pursue a career in the military. He still shows up periodically to refresh his skills." Landslide led them over to the female Aesir in the fountain. She was also one of the "up above" Aesir, with green skin and blond hair.

Calvin realized with a start that all of the Aesir in the room were green-skinned; there wasn't a single Drow in the facility as far as he could see. "Landslide, I don't see any of the Drow here," Calvin said. "Aren't they able to become Eco Warriors too?"

"They are able to become Eco Warriors," said the female in the fountain, whose voice flowed fluidly like the water surrounding her; "however, most Eco Warriors spend large periods of time on the surface, which most of the Drow choose not to do. There have been some Drow who stayed below and worked with soil, but aside from them, there haven't been many others."

"Tsunami is correct," said Landslide. "Most Drow do not choose to become Eco Warriors, aside from the handful who work with dirt. I am also aware of one who dabbles in life, but that's about it."

Looking down at the female Aesir, Calvin realized even though Tsunami was sitting in the fountain, the water wasn't touching her; an invisible barrier stopped it about a quarter of an inch from her. It was going to be interesting working with the Aesir, Calvin realized.

Landslide continued on to the female with electricity arcing all around her. Even from a few feet away, the Terrans could feel the hair on their arms standing up. "Cyclone is our air worker. As you can see, she also dabbles in things which aren't strictly 'air,' but are air-based." He paused to move out of Cyclone's area of effect.

"As you can probably guess, with a name like 'Landslide,' my area of expertise is working with soil," he said when clear. "That completes my normal team."

"I thought the teams also included someone who worked with life," said Calvin.

"While there *are* practitioners who work with life," replied Landslide, nodding to the Aesir with the 'hawk,' "they normally work at hospitals and are not assigned to teams. Generally, using life-practitioners to take life instead of save it is frowned upon in our society. That being said, there are a few who have trained to use their life skills to take life, and one of these *has* been added to my team for this mission. He was supposed to join us here…ah, there he is." Landslide nodded to an Aesir entering the room.

Unlike the other Eco Warriors, Calvin saw, this Aesir was a Drow. Not only was he a Drow, he looked awfully familiar…and the bruises around his neck confirmed his identity.

"No!" said Calvin. "I refuse to take *him* with us."

"I think you will find I am not as bad as I am made out to be," replied Reeve Farhome, who seemed more lucid than the day before…until a little giggle slipped out. "I *am* fairly sane, in fact…most days. Really. I'm still working on it. Hee hee."

Calvin turned to Landslide. "I thought Drow didn't leave your world. Besides, isn't he a reeve?"

"He renounced his reeve-ship," said Landslide, "but—"

"I did, hee hee, I did!" interrupted Farhome.

"Not only that," said Landslide, talking over Farhome, "he says he owes you for sparing his life. The only way he can ever repay you is to come along and assist you. And, if needed, to give his life for yours."

The giggling from Farhome vanished and his eyes achieved a clarity and focus Calvin hadn't previously seen. "I would have killed you if I could," he said. "I do not know why you didn't kill me, but I cannot be in debt to an off-worlder. I must go with you to erase that debt."

"This isn't something I'm just going to be able to forgive or release you from, is it?" asked Calvin.

"No," replied Farhome. "I have already given up my position as reeve. There is nothing tying me here." Just as quickly as it had come, the clarity left his eyes, and the smile returned. "Our lives and destinies are intertwined, hee hee."

Chapter Four

Bridge, TSS *Vella Gulf*, Golirion Orbit, HD 69830, June 5, 2021

"I wish you good fortune on your journey," said the Thor from the front view screen. The Aesir queen stood alongside him.

"Thank you, Thor," replied Captain Sheppard. "It is my greatest hope we won't need it."

The queen, who had been very quiet during the Terrans' visit, finally spoke. "You need to tell them," she said.

"It won't make any difference," replied the Thor.

"It will *to me*," the queen said.

The Thor gave her a small nod in acknowledgement and turned back to the Terrans. "While the crews of all of the ships are important to us, we would especially like it if you could find and return the crew of the *Blue Forest*. The commanding officer of the vessel, Captain Silvermoon, is our son and the crown prince of our people. His return is of the utmost importance."

"We will do everything we can to ensure his return," said Captain Sheppard.

"Thank you," replied the Thor. He gave the nod again, but this time to the Terrans. The transmission ended, and the screen went blank.

"Proceed to the gate," ordered Captain Sheppard. "Set General Quarters."

"Proceed to the stargate, aye," said the helmsman.

"Setting General Quarters," added the duty engineer.

The commanding officer turned to Captain Nightsong, who had taken the extra chair on the bridge. "You never thought it worth mentioning that we were looking for the crown prince?"

"It was not my story to tell," Nightsong replied, "but yes, the commanding officer of the last ship to vanish was the crown prince, who was sent to find the other ships that had gone missing. He is also the only child of the Thor, so the succession will be…difficult…if we do not bring him back. Very difficult."

"Thanks," said Captain Sheppard. "There wasn't enough riding on this mission already." He rubbed his forehead. "Is there anything you're holding back that could actually *help* us in our quest?"

Nightsong shook his head. "Nothing. Everything is silent beyond our outpost in Gliese 221. We still haven't heard from any of the ships that went through the stargate there."

"And that is three stargates from here?"

"Yes."

"Then there's no time to waste."

Bridge, TSS *Vella Gulf*, Groombridge 1618 System, June 5, 2021

"This is the Groombridge 1618 system," said Steropes. "It has a K-type main sequence star that has 67 percent of the mass of your sun and 61 percent of the sun's radius, but only radiates about 5 percent of its energy. The system has a low temperature debris disk that orbits at over 50 astronomical units (AU) or about five billion miles from the star, but no planets."

"Any reason to stop here?" asked Captain Sheppard. "Like, say, *are there any signs of enemy activity or anything else out of the ordinary?*"

"Um, no, not that I can detect."

Captain Sheppard shook his head. "Helmsman, proceed to the next gate."

Bridge, TSS *Vella Gulf,* HD 60532 System, June 8, 2021

"We have entered the HD 60532 system. HD 60532 is a white main sequence star located approximately 84 light-years from Earth in the constellation of Puppis. The system has two planets orbiting the star. The inner planet has a mass three times larger than Jupiter's and orbits at 0.77 AU, inside the habitable zone. The outer planet has a mass seven times larger than Jupiter and orbits at 1.58 AU in an eccentric orbit. Most of its orbit is in the habitable zone, but it is a gas giant and not fit for habitation."

When there was no reply Steropes looked up from his monitor to find the CO, executive officer, Captain Nightsong, Calvin and most of the bridge crew staring at him. "What?" he asked. "Oh! There's no sign of enemy activity or anything out of the ordinary."

"Baby steps," thought Captain Sheppard. He turned to the helmsman with a sigh. "Proceed to the next gate."

Bridge, TSS *Vella Gulf,* Gliese 221, June 10, 2021

"This is the Gliese 221 system," said Steropes. "Gliese 221 is an orange-red dwarf star with about 70 percent the mass of your sun, but only 10 percent of its luminosity. The system has three planets, a hot Super-Earth planet at five million miles from the star, a gas giant planet in the habitable zone and a Super-Earth planet just outside the habitable zone." He looked up and saw the yellow sticky note Calvin had posted at his station. "And there is no sign of enemy activity or anything out of the ordinary. There are, however, allied defenses and ships present in the system."

"This is our last outpost in this chain of stargates," said Nightsong. "From here on, we might find the frost giants at any time. They have tried to establish colonies on the third planet of this system on two previous occasions, but we were successful in making them withdraw both times."

"Is that why your defenses are set up here?" asked Calvin.

"Yes," replied Nightsong. "There's a battle station and an extensive mine field which guard the stargate into the system, as well as a minimum of two battleships present at all times."

"That's a lot of Aesir to be on station here," said Calvin.

"Not as many as you might think," replied Captain Nightsong. "The bulk of our defenses are automated, as most Aesir don't like extended deployments on the battle station. It is hard enough to get personnel for the ships which guard the stargate, much less the battle station."

"Sir, we are getting a transmission from the battle station," said the communications officer.

"On screen," replied Captain Sheppard.

The view screen lit up with the image of a green Aesir. "Welcome to Gliese 221. I am Admiral Valendil," he said. Unlike other battle stations the Terrans had seen, there were very few crewman in the background. "State your planet of origin and your purpose in this system."

"Hello, Brother," said Captain Nightsong. "This ship is the *Vella Gulf* from the nation of Terra. Its crew and I intend to go through the stargate to find out what has happened to our ships."

The Aesir visibly relaxed. "Good hunting then," he said. "Be safe; we still do not know what lies on the other side of the gate."

"Have you ever known me to be anything other than safe?" asked Nightsong.

"Yes, I have," replied the admiral, "Many times."

Chapter Five

"System entry into the Nu2 Lupi system," said Steropes. "The star is a yellow-orange main-sequence star located approximately 48 light-years from Earth in the constellation of Lupus. Nu2 Lupi is very similar to your sun although Nu2 Lupi is significantly older. Its habitable zone is also similar to your sun, from about 0.7 AU to 1.4 AU from the star."

He paused and then added, "I do not see any indication of alien activity, nor do I have any unusual readings. There are three planets, all Super-Earths, but they all lie outside the habitable zone."

A collective sigh filled the bridge; everyone had been keyed up, expecting a fight.

"Let's keep the fighters manned a little longer, just in case," said Captain Sheppard. "Helmsman, proceed to the next stargate."

"Aye, sir, proceeding to the next stargate," replied the helmsman. "Uh, sir, the navigation records the Aesir provided show three other stargates in this system in addition to the one we came through. Which would you like me to go to?"

Captain Sheppard looked over at Captain Nightsong, sitting in the observer chair. "Do you have any recommendations?"

Captain Nightsong considered for a few seconds and then said, "If memory serves, one of the stargates goes to an uninhabited pocket system with no other stargates out. I can't imagine how anything would have popped up there that could have caused our ships to go missing."

"I see that one," said the helmsman.

"The other two stargates go to chains of star systems," said Nightsong. "One of them, the gate to 14 Herculis, leads to where the frost giants live. The other goes to a system owned by hostile insectoids. It is unlikely they are to blame. Although they have space flight capabilities, they have some sort of hive mind and tend to stay close to their home world. If they go too far away, they go insane."

"So you are recommending the gate to 14 Herculis?" asked the CO.

"That would be my guess," replied Nightsong. "The giants are our traditional enemies and have no reason to wish us well. If they somehow made a technological breakthrough which gave them the ability to destroy our ships, they certainly would. My only question is, if they have the capability to destroy our ships, why haven't they shown up at Golirion to take back Asgard? It doesn't make sense for the giants to be the ones responsible for the loss of our ships; however, it makes even less sense for it to be anyone else."

"Perhaps there is an unknown race or some other factor that has yet to make its appearance," suggested Steropes.

Nightsong shrugged, something he had learned from the Terrans. "I do not know. We have explored many systems further down both chains of stars and never found a hostile race. That is why we moved the giants where we did."

"Well, we're not going to find out anything sitting here," decided Captain Sheppard. "Helmsman, proceed to the stargate to 14 Herculis."

Bridge, TSS *Vella Gulf*, 14 Herculis, Jun 13, 2021

"System entry," said Steropes. "Launching probes."

"Contact!" said the Defensive Systems Officer (DSO) and Steropes at the same time.

"What have you got, DSO?" asked Captain Sheppard.

"I'm picking up a lot of power spikes, Skipper," replied the DSO. "I'm still locking it in."

"Can you provide any more information, Steropes?" asked Captain Sheppard.

"Yes, I believe I can," said Steropes. "Give me a second, and I'll have it on screen." He paused for a few moments, and the picture of a Super-Earth planet appeared on the screen…along with the fuzzy image of a ship in orbit. "Based on the Aesir star charts, we are in the 14 Herculis system. The star is an orange dwarf with about 90 percent of your sun's mass, 71 percent of its radius and 36 percent of its luminosity. The star has a lot more—"

"*What about the ship?*" demanded Captain Sheppard.

"Oh! Yes!" said Steropes. "The ship is a quite large one. Initial analysis indicates it is approximately a mile and a half long, with a mass of nearly six million tons."

Calvin shook his head. "Another damn giant-sized ship to fight. I am so looking forward to a battle where we have the larger ship."

"Battles do not always go to the largest ships," said Steropes. "In this case, however, you are more correct than you know. I believe it actually *is* a giant ship, as it is crewed by the Jotunn. Although the ship is equivalent in size to a Mrowry dreadnought, it is a Jotunn battlecruiser. It is orbiting a Super-Earth planet in the star's habitable zone. There is also a gas giant about twice the mass of Jupiter three

AU from the star and a planet about five times the mass of Jupiter seven AU from the star."

"Sir!" interrupted the communications officer, "we're being hailed by the ship."

"On screen," said the commanding officer.

"Damn," said the helmsman, in awe, as the screen lit up to show an enormous humanoid. Although hard to tell, as everything around him was oversized, the being seemed colossal. Dressed in red-spotted pelts, the Jotunn had a chain-metal shirt over his torso. Light blue hair flowed out from under an outsized helmet with immense horns. The Jotunn's red eyes glared as he slowly surveyed the bridge of the *Vella Gulf.*

"Whoa," said Calvin under his breath. "He's got to be 13 or 14 feet tall."

Steropes shook his head. "Probably more like 15 or 16. Most of them reach at least 15 feet and weigh well over a ton."

The Jotunn's scan stopped upon catching sight of Captain Nightsong, and it laughed a long, deep belly laugh which was echoed by several of the other giants who could be seen at stations behind him. "This is the best you could do, Aesir?" it asked. "You come into our territory with this toy ship and these puny creatures to aid you? We had expected more...even from you."

Captain Nightsong's eyes narrowed, and a small growl escaped his lips. "This is not your system," he replied. "By treaty, this is our system, and we are here to find several of our ships that have gone missing."

"You banished us to Jotunheimr," said the Jotunn, "but we stay there no more. We have ventured forth to reclaim the worlds which once were ours. No longer will we do as you say. We have new friends who will restore us to Asgard. As to your ships, we have your *Blue Forest*, or what is left of it. You are welcome to come and get what few survivors remain."

"You destroyed our ship?" asked Captain Nightsong. "There will be war!"

The Jotunn laughed again. "Destroyed it? No, we did not. Nor will we destroy your puny ship, or seek to harm you in any way if you want to come and get your people."

"I am Captain Sheppard of the Terran ship *Vella Gulf*," said the commanding officer. "May I ask who it is I am addressing?"

The Jotunn turned and glared at him. "I am Fenrir, son of Loki, and captain of the Jotunn ship *Soaring Eagle*," the giant replied. "I am also the military commander of this system. Who or what is a Terran, and why have you come?"

"We are from Terra, a planet many light years from here. The Aesir asked us to help them find out what happened to their missing ships."

"Ho, ho, ho," the Jotunn laughed, "since you have come so far, I will make it easy for you and simply tell you what happened. The elves came into our systems and were destroyed. Now that you know, you may carry this word back to their leaders. You may also take them a warning. Tell them we are coming for them." He smiled and then added, "Ragnarok has begun." The screen went blank as the transmission ended.

"Huh," said Captain Sheppard, turning to face Captain Nightsong, "that was kind of abrupt. What do you make of it?"

"Like I said," the Aesir replied, "there will be war. I don't know how they destroyed our ships, but now that we know it *was* the Jotunn, they won't be able to fool us again."

"How do you know it was the Jotunn who destroyed your ships?" asked Steropes.

"Because Fenrir said they did," replied Nightsong. "His own admission damns him! We will muster our fleet and come back here to teach them the consequences of their actions!"

"Steropes is right," said Calvin. "How do you know it was the Jotunn? Fenrir didn't say the Jotunn destroyed your ships; he just said they were destroyed. Isn't that right, Solomon?"

"That is correct," replied the ship's artificial intelligence. The front view screen lit up with a replay of the conversation. The image of the Jotunn leader filled the screen and said, "Destroyed it? No, we did not." The tape jumped forward a little, and he added, "They came into our systems and were destroyed."

"You said before that the Jotunn periodically attack you, correct?" asked Calvin.

"Yes," agreed Nightsong. "They were actually overdue to attack, based on historical patterns. It has to be them."

"Wouldn't your ships' commanding officers also have been aware of this, especially after the first ship or two went missing?" asked Calvin. "Wouldn't they know to be on the lookout for a Jotunn attack? How could something so big have snuck up on one of your ships?"

"I do not know how it is possible," admitted Nightsong. "They have never been able to surprise us in the past. They must have developed some new technology; either that or they were given something by the new 'friends' Fenrir alluded to."

"Or maybe it was the new friends who destroyed your ships," said Captain Sheppard. "Steropes, do you have any indications of other ships in the system?"

"No sir, I do not," replied Steropes. "That does not exclude the possibility they exist and are cloaked, however."

"Understood," said the commanding officer. "Keep looking. Let me know if you find anything out of the ordinary that might be a cloaked ship."

"Aye aye, sir," said Steropes, turning back to his console.

Captain Sheppard turned back to Captain Nightsong. "So," he said, "what do you want to do?"

"If they have any of the crew of the *Blue Forest*, like he said they do, I want to get them back. If nothing else, the crew would be able to tell us what happened."

"Umm...how much do you trust them?" asked Captain Sheppard. "I'm not in a hurry to get close to that ship and have whatever happened to the *Blue Forest* happen to us."

"They *do* have a sense of honor," said Captain Nightsong, "but that doesn't mean you can necessarily trust them. They are very literal. For example, if Fenrir says the *Soaring Eagle* won't attack, all it means is that one ship won't attack. It *doesn't* mean any other Jotunn ships in the system won't attack. You have to be careful how you word things."

"Steropes, are there any other ships in the system besides the two of us?" asked Captain Sheppard.

"No sir, there are not, although my earlier warning still stands," replied Steropes. "There does appear to be the wreckage of a ship near the *Soaring Eagle*, possibly the *Blue Forest*, but that is all I currently see."

"Okay," Captain Sheppard said with a nod to Captain Nightsong, "so if I can get them to agree to give us safe passage, it *should* be safe to approach them closely enough to launch a shuttle and retrieve the remaining crew of the *Blue Forest?* Remember, you are risking not only your life, but the lives of all of the members of my crew in this assessment." Several members of the bridge crew turned to watch Nightsong's response.

The Aesir scanned the Terrans watching him before returning his gaze to Captain Sheppard. "Yes, it should be safe," he said finally.

Captain Sheppard turned to Calvin and raised an eyebrow. "Well, hero, what do you think?"

"I think I'd really appreciate it if you didn't call me that, sir," answered Calvin. "It's bad enough when Steropes does it. Regardless, we need to know what happened to the Aesir ships if we are going to find an answer. The only way we're going to do that is to get the remaining crew members from the Jotunn. Of course, I'd still say we ought to man all of the fighters and weapons systems…just in case."

"I agree," replied Captain Sheppard. "Communications officer, raise the *Soaring Eagle*. On screen."

Within a few seconds, the face of Captain Fenrir appeared on the front screen. "Yes?" he asked. "Is there some reason you haven't left yet? You are trying my patience."

"Captain Fenrir," said Captain Sheppard, "when we spoke earlier, you said you had some of the members of the *Blue Forest,* and we were welcome to come and get them. We would like to do so before we leave."

The Jotunn looked off-screen. "Did I say that?" He turned back to the *Vella Gulf.* "It appears I did; however, I never gave you the terms." A giant smile crossed his face.

"Terms?" asked Captain Sheppard. "What terms?"

"Well, you can't expect us to just *give* them to you. We rescued them from their derelict spaceship and have given them food, drink and comfort ever since. There is the matter of payment for our time and services. I choose to take that payment in the form of entertainment. One of you Terrans will fight me in the arena. If you win, you may take the survivors of the *Blue Forest* and leave. If I win, you leave and return with payment for your people."

"How much is the payment?"

"One billion mega-credits."

Captain Sheppard heard a sharp intake of breath from Captain Nightsong. Before he could say anything, Captain Sheppard said simply, "We accept," and ended the transmission.

"I do not know how you will get us out of this," said Captain Nightsong into the silence that followed. "You cannot beat him in hand-to-hand combat, and one billion mega-credits is more than the cost of a super dreadnought. There is no way the Thor will pay that with war upon us. He *can't*."

"Well then, Calvin, I guess we'd better not lose," said Captain Sheppard.

"No, I guess we'd better not," Calvin replied. "Night is better-suited for this, even if I wasn't still recovering. I'll go get him."

Bridge, TSS *Vella Gulf,* Proceeding to Jotunn Ship, 14 Herculis System, June 14, 2021

"Four hours until the rendezvous with the *Soaring Eagle*," said the helmsman. "Recommend rotating ship."

"Roger," replied Captain Sheppard. "Rotate ship; commence braking."

"Rotate ship, aye," repeated the helmsman. "Commencing braking, aye." He input the instructions that flipped the ship so its thrust could be used to slow the ship's approach to the Jotunn vessel.

"I have a question," said Calvin. "When we spoke to Fenrir earlier, he said Ragnarok was coming. I looked at the information we have available, and it says Ragnarok is the end of the world. What did he mean?"

"The Jotunn used to inhabit the planet Asgard," Captain Nightsong replied. "They achieved space flight at about the same time we did and immediately attacked us. After a series of wars, the Aesir were triumphant, and we moved the Jotunn out of the system for the good of both of our races. The Jotunn have never forgotten their ancient home, and they have a number of stories about what will happen once they return to it. Ragnarok is one of these stories, and it is more than just one event that results in the end of Asgard. The story is a series of future events all the Jotunn believe will occur. It includes a great battle which results in the death of a number of major figures on both sides, various natural disasters and the subsequent submersion of the world in water. How that's supposed to happen, though, is beyond me. Afterward, Asgard will resurface new and fertile, and the Jotunn survivors will live happily ever after, free of Aesir rule. It's a very nice fairy tale....from their point of view."

"It didn't sound like Fenrir thought it was a fairy tale," replied Calvin.

"No, to him it is not. Still, there is no way the events could happen as they prophesy. For example, it is extremely unlikely the major figures the story mentions would ever be together in the same system, much less together in a battle where all of them would die."

"Who are the major figures?" asked Captain Sheppard.

"Our ruler Thor and their ruler Odin, to start with," Captain Nightsong answered. "Also, Tyr, the head of our military and Freyr, the head of their military. A few others beyond that." He smiled. "It takes a certain kind of bravery on the part of the Jotunn leader to declare Ragnarok has begun when he knows that he is supposed to die as part of it. That is very interesting. Perhaps they have redefined the story; it is unlikely the Odin intends to die if he thinks the Jotunn can take back Asgard."

"Sir!" said the DSO. "I've got a new contact. It just appeared about 10,000,000 miles from us!"

"What is it?" asked Captain Sheppard.

"Unknown," replied the DSO. "It's not in our database. Initial indications are it is destroyer-sized, but that's all I've got."

"Talk to me, Steropes," said Sheppard, turning to the science station, "What have you got? Where did it come from?"

"I do not know," replied Steropes. "It just appeared. I did not have any indications of its presence before. Although it appears destroyer-sized, its power readings are unlike any I've ever seen."

"I don't like this," said Captain Sheppard. "General Quarters!" he commanded in a loud voice. "Emergency power. Get us back to the stargate."

"Aye aye, sir," said the helmsman and the duty engineer. Red lights began flashing as the engineer called for General Quarters.

"Lieutenant Commander Hobbs, get your fighters manned," Captain Sheppard added.

"Yes, sir," replied Calvin. He bolted for the door, already comming orders to the squadron.

"Sir," said the DSO, "something strange is going on with the unknown ship. There's something onboard that is using a massive amount of power."

"Is it a weapon system?"

"I don't know. If they are charging something, it's going to be something *big!*"

"He's right," said Steropes. "Something onboard is using enough power to drive the ship, but it isn't moving."

The communications officer sat upright in her seat. "Sir, we're being hailed by the Jotunn ship."

"On screen," said Captain Sheppard.

Captain Fenrir's laughing face filled the front screen. "Ho, ho, ho," he chortled. "One little ship appears, and you immediately try to run? Do you Terrans have no bravery or honor? Perhaps the ship is friendly."

"Is it friendly?" asked the CO.

"Of course not," replied Captain Fenrir. "You are about to find out what destroyed the Aesir ship. You asked who destroyed it; you're about to get your answer. It is unfortunate word won't make it back to Golirion, but we will be there to show them ourselves, soon enough."

Captain Sheppard pushed the button that ended the transmission, and the Jotunn's face disappeared. "What is the new ship doing?" he asked.

"Nothing that I can tell," replied the DSO. "It's just sitting there. Something on board is still using a lot of power, though."

"Communications, try to hail the vessel," ordered the CO. He turned to the helmsman. "How close are we going to get?"

"It's going to be close. We're probably going to come within 750,000 miles before we begin accelerating back away."

"We're within missile range," noted the Offensive Systems Officer (OSO). "Do you want me to begin firing?"

"No," replied Captain Sheppard. "Despite what the Jotunn said, we don't know that the unknown ship actually destroyed the *Blue Forest* or that they are our enemies. If we can talk to them instead of fighting them, maybe we can bring them over to our side."

Chapter Six

"The ship is still not responding to our hails," replied the communications officer.

"Keep trying," ordered the CO.

"Progress toward the Jotunn ship has been halted, and we are now accelerating toward the stargate," said the helmsman.

"Sir!" said the DSO. "I think the unknown ship just fired at us! There was a power spike, and then something launched that is heading towards us!"

"What is it, Steropes?" asked the CO.

"Unknown," answered Steropes. "The object is unlike anything I have ever seen, and it is impossible to analyze. Even though we can visually see the entity on the screen when it blots out stars behind it, the object doesn't exist on the sensors. I have never seen anything like it in all my life."

"That was weird," said the DSO. "Steropes, did you see the ship blink when it fired?"

"Yes, the ship was definitely not there for at least 0.27 seconds," agreed Steropes.

"What does that mean?" asked Captain Sheppard.

"I do not know," replied Steropes.

"OK, you don't know what the object is. Can I assume that it's probably a weapon?"

"With the wreck of the *Blue Forest* nearby and the other Aesir vessels missing, I believe the object is likely a weapon," agreed Steropes. "I do not think you want to let it overtake us."

"I agree," replied Captain Sheppard. "DSO, weapons free; defend the ship. OSO, let's see if we can kill the bastard. Fire all weapons!"

"Missile doors opening," both weapons systems officers chorused.

"Graser mounts extending," said the OSO as the offensive gamma ray lasers moved into position.

"Laser mounts extending," said the DSO as the defensive laser clusters deployed.

"ASMs away!" announced the OSO. The crew could feel the ship jolt as the big anti-ship missiles launched.

"Engaging the inbound track with AMMs," reported the DSO as he launched the anti-missile missiles.

All eyes followed the missiles on the main screen as they raced to intercept the incoming object.

"What the fuck?" asked the DSO as the tracks merged.

"What is it?" asked the CO.

"Sir, whatever is following us avoided our missiles. When our weapons should have hit it, their missile, or torpedo or whatever the hell that thing is blinked out."

"What do you mean 'blinked out?'"

"The same thing just happened to me," said the OSO. "I fired at the ship, and it just disappeared when the missiles should have hit. Our missiles flew right through where the ship was without hitting anything. Then, once the missiles were clear, the ship reappeared again."

"What the hell is chasing us, Steropes?"

"I don't know, sir. I've never seen anything like it. The weapon chasing us is much slower than any anti-ship missile I have ever seen. It appears to be some sort of torpedo."

"Helm," the CO asked, "are we going to outrun it?"

"No, sir. That torpedo thing is slower than a normal missile, but it's still a lot faster than we are.

"Are the shields going to stop it, Steropes?"

"I don't know, sir. Probably not."

"Shit," said the DSO, who had been counting on the shields. "10 seconds to weapon impact on the *Gulf.*" He switched to the ship's internal communications network. "*Missile hit in five seconds. All hands brace for shock!*" He turned off the comms system and said under his breath, "Three…two…one…"

The ship rocked as the torpedo impacted. Despite the acceleration dampeners, the crew could feel the ship decelerate, and the lights dimmed before coming back on full strength. Warning lights began flashing on consoles all across the bridge.

"Sir!" called the duty engineer. "We just lost Engine Room Two, and all of the equipment linked to it. I don't have any communications with anyone back there. Damage crews are responding."

"The unknown ship is moving," said the DSO. "It's turning to follow us and is accelerating."

"Launch the fighters," said Captain Sheppard; "maybe they'll have better luck."

"Fighters launching," replied the OSO. "Ops reports nine fighters launched. Lieutenant Commander Hobbs' fighter is having mechanical problems and is being repaired."

"We have 12 fighters," said Captain Sheppard. "Where are the other two?"

"I don't know," replied the OSO. "They are no longer showing on my board."

"What do you mean?"

"When the torpedo hit, the other two fighters must have been in its area of effect. They just vanished from my screens as if they no longer existed."

"Roger," acknowledged the CO. He turned to the communications officer. "Download our mission logs to a message missile and launch it back to Golirion," he ordered. "That way, at least someone will know what happened."

"Yes, sir," replied the communications officer.

Captain Sheppard turned to Captain Nightsong. "Any ideas, Captain?" he asked.

"None," Nightsong replied. "Everything you've done seems to be by the book. I expect your actions are very similar to what our ships would have done."

"Yeah, and look what that got the *Blue Forest*."

"Indeed," replied the Aesir. "We must come up with something else."

Asp 02, Proceeding to Unknown Ship, 14 Herculis System, June 14, 2021

"What happened to *11* and *12*?" asked the squadron's executive officer, Lieutenant Commander Sarah 'Lights' Brighton.

"They're gone, XO," said her pilot, Lieutenant Carl 'Guns' Simpson. "'Primo' Miller was talking to me over implant, and he cut out at the same time as the flash."

"I just heard from the *Gulf*," said Lights; "that flash was some sort of unknown weapon. Detach and let's get a quick damage assessment while the rest of the squadron launches."

"Roger that, ma'am," replied Guns. He switched to the *Gulf's* Departure frequency and called the ship on the radio. "Asp 02 *is ready for launch.*"

"*Roger, 02, you are cleared for launch. Detaching in three…two…one…launch!*"

"*02 is clear of the ship; proceeding on mission,*" commed Guns.

"*Roger, 02, get some for us!*"

Guns flew down the length of the ship toward the stern. "Holy shit," he said as he glimpsed the back ring where half of the Asps had been mounted. "Vella Gulf, Asp 02, *it looks like something took a big bite out of the back of the ship,*" he commed. "*I don't know how the weapon did it, but the cut looks smooth; there's no jagged metal at all. It's just gone!*"

"What do you suppose did that?" asked Lights.

"I've seen a lot of battle damage in my short time as a space fighter pilot," replied Guns, "but I have *never* seen anything like this."

Bridge, TSS *Vella Gulf*, 14 Herculis System, June 14, 2021

"What is the status of the strike?" asked Captain Sheppard.

"Nine fighters are approaching the unknown ship and are preparing to attack," replied the OSO. "Lieutenant Commander Hobbs' fighter is still attached to the *Gulf*. One of its motors has a problem that the maintenance technicians are working on."

"Who's leading the strike?"

"The squadron's XO, Lieutenant Commander Brighton, in *Asp 02*," replied the OSO.

Captain Sheppard turned to the duty engineer. "Do we have a casualty list yet of who we lost in the torpedo strike?"

"Yes, sir. We lost Lieutenants Danny Walling and Larry Albertson in *Asp 11* and Lieutenants Kenneth Miller and Ira Hensley in *Asp 12*. We also lost the assistant engineer and five other personnel in Engine Room Two."

"Damn," said the CO. "We absolutely can *not* take another one of those hits." He turned to Steropes. "How are we doing, Steropes?"

"The unknown ship is gaining on us," Steropes replied. "With only one engine operational, the enemy ship will catch us well before we get to the stargate."

"Continue firing," said Captain Sheppard; "maybe we'll get lucky." He turned to the duty engineer. "We need more power. When will they have the other engine back online?"

The duty engineer shook his head. "I've been listening over the damage control circuit. I'm sorry, sir, but I think this is the best you're going to get. The damage control party said the engine bay is open to space, and everyone that was in it, including the assistant engineer, is missing. They appear to have been sucked overboard. We're already running Number One harder than we're supposed to, and the chief engineer doesn't know how much longer it will last."

"Tell them to do what they can," replied Captain Sheppard.

"I will, sir, but from what they're saying, most of the motor has disappeared. It's just gone, sir, as in no longer there."

"Solomon, can you confirm the actual motor is gone?" asked Captain Sheppard.

"I have one camera in the engine room," replied the artificial intelligence, "and it appears a large portion of the motor has been physically removed from the ship."

"Can you play back the video and see how that happened?"

"I have played it back 237 times, and I have not been able to determine the cause. In one frame the motor is there; in the next it is missing. Its disappearance corresponds to the detonation of the weapon fired at us by the unknown ship."

"Sir, the mission logs have been downloaded to a message missile," said the communications officer. "It is ready to be launched to Golirion."

"Send it along with the video of the engine bay."

"Aye, sir," replied the communications officer. "Launching."

"New contact!" The OSO and DSO both called moments later.

"Sir!" the DSO added. "The new ship destroyed the message missile."

"What?" asked the CO. "Where is it?"

"It's only 100,000 miles off our starboard beam," said the OSO.

"Destroy the bastard!" ordered Captain Sheppard. "Fire all weapons!"

The OSO pushed a button. "Grasers firing," he said. The crew could also feel the jolts of more ASMs launching. "Grasers effective," added the OSO. "The new vessel is smaller than a frigate, and doesn't appear to have any shields. The grasers are going right through it! Missiles will hit in three...two...one..."

***Asp 02*, Proceeding to Unknown Ship, 14 Herculis System, June 14, 2021**

"Formation looks good, XO," said Guns. "All fighters are in a line abreast."

"Coming up on firing range," replied Lights. "It's odd they haven't tried to stop us yet..."

"Hey, I'm not complaining," said Guns.

"*All ships*, Asp 02," commed the XO. "*I just talked to the* Vella Gulf. *Whatever it was that hit the ship removed a large portion of one of the engine rooms. The* Gulf *cannot afford to be hit by another one of this ship's weapons. We have* got *to take it out. We will launch missiles and then close to laser range. Stand by to fire on my mark. Three...two...one...FIRE!*" 45 missiles detached from the fighters and leapt forward, racing ahead of the fighters as they continued toward the unknown ship.

Bridge, TSS *Vella Gulf*, 14 Herculis System, June 14, 2021

"Holy shit!" cried the OSO. "The new target didn't defend itself. All the missiles hit, and it has been completely destroyed!"

"Captain Sheppard," said Steropes, "I am getting increased power readings from the other ship, similar to the readings we saw just before it launched the weapon that hit us."

"What's the status of our fighters?" asked Captain Sheppard. "Will they be able to hit it before it launches again?"

"Torpedo launch!" called the DSO.

"No sir," said Steropes. "The ship has launched another weapon. The fighters' missiles will arrive in six seconds."

"Damn it!" said the OSO. "The ship disappeared before any of the fighters' missiles could hit. I was hoping we'd get lucky, and one would go for the torpedo, but that didn't happen. All the fighters' weapons missed, and the torpedo is still coming toward us."

"Fire everything you've got!" ordered the CO. "Kill that torpedo."

"I don't understand," said Steropes. "The smaller vessel didn't defend itself; it just sat there and let us destroy it. It was almost like the enemy wanted us to destroy it."

"Perhaps they were gathering information on our weapons systems," Captain Sheppard replied. He turned to the communications officer. "Launch another message missile. If nothing else, we'll at least get the word back to Golirion."

"Yes, sir, launching another missile back to Golirion," replied the communications officer.

"Defensive fire ineffective against the torpedo," said the DSO. "When a missile gets to where the torpedo should be, it disappears, and the missile flies through the spot. The lasers seem to hit it, but do not have any effect."

"Give me some options," said Captain Sheppard. "What else haven't we tried?"

"Lieutenant Commander Hobbs just launched, sir," said the OSO. "I'm having him fire his missiles at the torpedo, but that's all I can do."

Asp 01, 14 Herculis System, June 14, 2021

"**A**sp 01 *is clear, proceeding on mission*," commed Calvin.

"We just got retasked, sir," said his WSO, Lieutenant Sasaki 'Supidi' Akio. "We are supposed to try to stop a torpedo headed toward the ship. I have the target on your screen. We must turn quickly; there is little time."

Calvin pulled harder on the stick, yanking the fighter around in a tight turn.

"Stand by to fire," said Supidi as the nose of the fighter came into line with the target. "Fire!"

Calvin pulled the trigger on his stick, and the missiles launched. The torpedo was already close, and it only took a few seconds before Supidi said, "They missed."

"There's no way we're going to hit the torpedo with our laser," said Calvin. "One last thing to try…" He pulled the fighter back to the right and into the path of the missile.

"It's been nice flying with you, sir," said Supidi.

There was a flash, and the fighter was gone.

Asp 02, 14 Herculis System, June 14, 2021

"**S**hit," said Guns, "We just lost *07*." After the enemy ship launched the torpedo, a number of high energy lasers had opened up on the Asps as their crews raced to get within the range of their fighters' lasers. The Terrans had already lost *Asp 03* and *Asp 06* in the first attack; the loss of *07*, with its crew of Lieutenants John McCarter and Vernon Shepherd, made three.

No time to dwell on it.

The victor of fighter battles on Earth and in space, Guns continued to jink the fighter back and forth, seeming to instinctively know where the next laser bolt would go. The rest of the pilots followed him, dodging back and forth.

"Five seconds," said the XO, working the targeting solution. Sweat puddled in her suit as its environmental system strained to keep up. "Stand by…fire!"

Guns pulled the trigger, and laser fire splashed down the side of the alien destroyer. For the first time the vessel was hit. Although its armor withstood the majority of the laser fire, several jets of mist showed where holes had been opened in the hull, and atmosphere vented out.

Asp 05 followed, opening more small holes in the destroyer's side.

"*Pour it on,*" commed the XO. "*If we can open enough holes in it, maybe we can get them to disengage.*"

Asp 08 and *Asp 09* followed *Asp 05*, with *08* going down the port side and *09* down the starboard. Without warning, the alien vessel disappeared, and the two space fighters vanished with it. When the enemy ship reappeared two seconds later, *Asp 04* was in the same space as the enemy ship. The speeding metal slug that had been a space fighter, along with its crew of Lieutenant William Santiago and Lieutenant Keith Dodd, tore lengthwise through the alien destroyer until it ran into something explosive, and both vessels detonated catastrophically. There were several large pieces of the alien ship remaining; of the fighter and its crew, there was nothing.

Bridge, TSS *Vella Gulf,* 14 Herculis System, June 14, 2021

"Fuck," said the DSO under his breath. In a more normal tone he said, "The enemy vessel disappeared and then came back. When it reappeared, *Asp 04* was in the same space it occupied. Both *Asp 04* and the enemy vessel have been destroyed."

"Call back our fighters," said Captain Sheppard. His tone was muted; he could scarcely believe the devastation which had just overtaken his air wing. "How many do we have remaining?"

"Three, sir," replied the OSO. "The XO in *Asp 02, Asp 05* and *Asp 10.* The rest have all been destroyed or are missing."

"75 percent of the air wing gone in a single engagement," said Sheppard, shaking his head.

"Captain Sheppard, the Jotunn vessel has begun moving," said Steropes. "It appears to be heading in our direction."

"Helmsman, keep heading for the stargate. OSO, have the fighters join with us enroute."

"New contact!" called the DSO. "It's a little ways behind us…small ship…it's *Asp 01*, sir. *Asp 01* just reappeared!"

"Get them aboard ASAP," ordered the Captain, a little bit of hope seeping into his voice. "Have the other two fighters reappeared?"

"No, sir," replied the DSO.

"Keep an eye out for them," said the Captain. "If they show up, call them back." He turned to Steropes. "Is there any chance of the Jotunn vessel catching us or getting within weapons range?"

"No, sir," replied Steropes. "As long as we don't slow down, we have a large enough lead to easily beat the Jotunn ship to the stargate."

"Good," said Captain Sheppard. "While we're recovering the fighters, try to figure out what the hell just happened. There will be a staff meeting in my conference room once the fighters are back aboard."

Chapter Seven

CO's Conference Room, TSS *Vella Gulf*, 14 Herculis System, June 15, 2021

The aviators filed into the conference room, heads down and feet dragging. Most were covered in sweat; all looked like they had been crying.

Calvin and Lieutenant Commander Brighton took seats at the table, the remaining flyers sat down in chairs behind them. There were a lot of empty chairs.

Captain Sheppard could see Calvin and his XO looked particularly distraught. Charged with keeping the men and women under them safe, they felt the loss more than anyone else. Sheppard knew how they felt. He was ultimately responsible for the lives of everyone on the *Vella Gulf*. The entire fiasco was his fault. He had two choices: wrap himself in grief or learn from it and make sure they were ready the next time they met the aliens.

He intended to be ready.

Still…"Calvin…XO…I just want you to know how sorry I am for your losses."

Calvin nodded, not trusting his voice to say anything.

"I'm sorry…and I intend to make sure it doesn't happen again," continued Captain Sheppard in a firm tone. "The purpose of this meeting is to try to figure out what happened, so we'll be ready the next time we meet them."

"But—" said a voice from the back row.

The CO tried to identify who had spoken, but couldn't. "Yes," he said, "I know we destroyed their ship, but I doubt that was the only one they had. I don't know how many they have or how close they may be, but we need to get back to Golirion and report. We need to rearm ourselves, and we need to replace our losses. And *then*, we need to come back here and kick their asses! I intend to negotiate for peace with them…but only once I have knives to their throats and knees in their balls!"

Captain Sheppard saw the aviators were nodding their heads. They looked like they were back in the game. "All right," he said. "Before we can do that, we need to figure out what the hell happened. First, does anyone have any ideas on what it was that they hit us with? How was it able to destroy a large portion of our ship, yet still be survivable by Calvin's fighter?"

"Lieutenant Bradford and I have been discussing it," said Steropes. "We have come to a tentative conclusion, but it is one which will be hard to accept."

"Why is that?" asked Captain Sheppard.

"I'll get to that in a second, sir, but I need to give you a little background information first," replied the lieutenant from Department X. "When we started looking at the weapon, we realized this was the most important question, because we need to know what the weapon is in order to counter it. I searched the entire data banks of the TSS *Terra's* replicator and came up with precisely nothing. So, whatever that weapon is, I can confirm that it doesn't exist in alliance technology."

Steropes took up the story. "So, having ruled out what it *wasn't*, we tried to determine the nature of the weapon to figure out what it *was*. What could cause a clean cut like we saw in the engine room?

We ruled out explosives; they would have left the metal jagged, not smooth. Similarly, it couldn't have been some sort of laser weapon, or the damage would have penetrated further into the ship and not been localized to a single spot. The weapon appears to have affected a spherical area; if you were within that area, you disappeared. If you were outside the area, you weren't affected."

"So what the hell can do that?" asked Captain Sheppard.

"Nothing we know of," replied Steropes, "and if the engine room strike was all the evidence we had on the weapon's performance, we would probably never have figured it out. However, we also had the effects of the weapon that hit *Asp 01* to analyze, and that gave us the clues we needed."

"Well, how about telling us, then," said Calvin. "I have no idea what happened, and I was there. I thought I was dead."

"Had it been a conventional warhead, you most certainly would have been," agreed Steropes. "Even if it were just a solid piece of metal, you would have died from the impact. It was neither of those things, though; instead, it was a time bomb."

"A time bomb?" asked Captain Sheppard. "What the hell do you mean?"

"I mean that when the weapon detonated, its effect was to send everything within its vicinity back to where it had been about 10 seconds prior; however, everything was thrown 10 seconds into the future from when the torpedo activated."

"I see why you said we wouldn't believe it," replied Sheppard. "A bomb that sends things back to where they were 10 seconds prior, but then into the future? I don't see how that is possible."

"It's actually about 10.37 seconds in both directions," said Steropes. "The effect is impossible to measure more precisely than that."

Lieutenant Bradford took over. "We didn't believe it, either, and would never have figured it out if we didn't have the data from the weapon that struck Calv...I mean, Lieutenant Commander Hobb's fighter."

"It does not seem possible, but the data indicates that when Lieutenant Commander Hobbs' fighter detonated the weapon, the ship went back to where it was 10.37 seconds prior, although the fighter didn't appear there until 10.37 seconds *after* the weapon detonated. Once we came up with the idea that the weapon generated some sort of time distortion, I looked back at where we were when the first weapon hit us, and then extrapolated back 10.37 seconds along our route of travel. There was a debris field there of the same mass as is currently missing from the *Vella Gulf,* along with the mass of the two fighters that were caught in the weapon's area of effect. Despite the impossibility of its existence, I am all but certain the *Vella Gulf* and Lieutenant Commander Hobbs' fighter were both hit by some sort of time bomb."

"If I survived the weapon, maybe the crews of *Asps 11* and *12* did too," exclaimed Calvin. "We've got to go back and get them!"

"Even if the Jotunn allowed us to return," said Lieutenant Bradford, "which doesn't appear likely, I'm sorry, but there is no need. Both of the ships were cut in half by the weapon, right at the center of the cockpit; I'm positive both crews were also cut in half."

"So what you are saying," said Captain Nightsong, "is there is no explosive, at all, on the weapon? It just creates a bubble wherein everything goes back in time 10 seconds?"

"That is correct," agreed Steropes. "It would not be an efficient weapon to use on small targets, like fighters, that would be completely caught in its field. But for destroyer-sized or larger spaceships—"

"—its effect is fairly devastating," finished Lieutenant Bradford, "as it takes a bite out of the ship nearly 300 feet in diameter. If the ship or target is moving, like it would be if it was in combat, the resulting hole will be open to space."

"Okay, say for a minute that I buy the fact their weapon is some kind of time bomb," said Captain Sheppard. "How were they able to avoid our missiles? How were their ship and weapons able to disappear when our missiles should have hit them?"

"Unfortunately, that is something I don't have any information on," replied Steropes. "It wasn't a cloaking effect; that much we know. I analyzed the video from our fighters, and I can categorically state that their missiles went right through where the ship should have been. If it were only cloaked, the missiles would still have hit it."

"So what was it?"

"I don't know," said Steropes. "I have only seen one other being able to disappear in the middle of a fight. It was a couple of missions ago when we fought the—"

"Efreet," said Calvin and Captain Nightsong simultaneously.

Chapter Eight

CO's Conference Room, TSS *Vella Gulf,* 14 Herculis System, June 15, 2021

"Efreet?" asked Captain Sheppard. "You mean, like the ones you fought with Quetzalcoatl?"

"Exactly," replied Steropes. "The platoon fought them on Keppler 22 'b.' They also appeared to shift in and out of our reality, although we were never able to determine where they went when they disappeared."

"*You* have fought the Efreet?" asked Captain Nightsong, his voice full of disbelief. "And you survived?"

"Yes," replied Calvin. "We fought them once, and they were very hard to kill. They kept disappearing when we tried to hit them."

"That is to be expected," said Captain Nightsong; "they are not of our universe."

"Not of our universe?" asked Captain Sheppard. "What does that mean?"

"Remember when I told you about Wayland and Beowulf? I only told you part of the story; I have never told the rest, not even to the Aesir, because I knew they would think I was crazy. If you have fought them, though, you may believe my story. The Efreet are a race of beings who live in a different universe that is parallel to ours, called the Jinn Universe. Unfortunately for life forms in our universe, many of the races in the Jinn Universe draw energy from creatures here, so they tend to congregate where life exists. As they draw most

107

strongly from the psychic energy of sentient beings, most of the stronger types of Jinn live on planets that are the counterparts of inhabited planets in our universe. Some exist on the energy released at death, so cemeteries are also a common place to find them. As the energy released at death is random and chaotic, the cemetery Jinn also tend to be more chaotic in nature and are usually quite evil."

"I believe it," said Calvin. "Our experience seems to support that. My only question is, how do *you* know that?"

"I learned it from Wayland, who had more knowledge of them than anyone else I know. Remember Grendel and Grendel's mother? Both were Shaitans, members of the Jinn Universe's most powerful race. That is why they were so hard to kill. If you have fought them, then you can imagine how hard they would have been to fight at that time in your history. None of the warriors could hit them, and the monsters had free reign of the countryside."

Captain Nightsong paused, and then said, "In order to answer your question fully, I have to give you a little more information on Wayland, including some things you will not hear from any other Aesir. When he first came to your planet, he lived in the center of your largest land mass, and he was part of the court of a man named King Solomon. There was near-constant warfare in that area, which made it easy for him to find minor heroes for his experiments. While he was there, a number of Efreet came through from the universe in which they lived."

"How do you know the Efreet aren't from our universe?" Captain Sheppard interrupted; "maybe they are just from another part of our universe, a long way away."

"All the evidence points to a parallel universe," replied Captain Nightsong, "with planets in the same place as the ones in this universe; however, the conditions on those planets are sometimes very different. According to Wayland, their prisons use some sort of energy field that somehow brings the two universes closer together and makes it easier for the Jinn to cross over from their universe to ours. Even though the Jinn can cross over, they still have to return to their universe periodically, or they will die."

"So, the crews of *Asps 08* and *09* may still be alive...but trapped in the Jinn Universe, somewhere else, and unable to return?"

"It is certainly possible that they were inadvertently transported with the alien vessel when it shifted back to its universe," said Captain Nightsong. "If they then flew outside the range of the effect when the ship transported back into our universe, they would be trapped there, unable to cross back."

"We've got to get them back," said Calvin. "How is this transport between universes accomplished?"

"The Jinn have devices which allow them to move back and forth. It is usually in the shape of a small rod, but can sometimes be in the form of a ring. Both of these will transport two to three Jinn at a time. While Wayland was at the court of King Solomon, a high-ranking Efreeti named Asmodeus came over from the Jinn universe. Wayland was able to incapacitate Asmodeus and take his control ring. Knowing Solomon would grant him any number of favors for control of the Jinni, he gave the ring to Solomon."

"What did Solomon do with it?" asked Calvin.

"The ring gave Solomon power over the Jinn. He would transport with Wayland, capture Jinn and bring them back to your world. They had to do what he said, or he would keep them on your planet until they died. Asmodeus ended up helping King Solomon understand much of the Jinn society. He wrote all this information down in a grimoire called the Lemegeton, or Lesser Key of Solomon, which contained the instructions for evoking the 72 Jinn he was able to capture and interrogate with the ring. That ring became known as the 'Seal of Solomon.'"

"Does it still exist?" asked Calvin. "Who has the ring now?"

"No," replied Captain Nightsong. "The ring was later lost when Asmodeus tricked Solomon into giving it to him, and Asmodeus threw it into the sea…but only after going back to his universe to get one of the Efreeti control rods, which he used to escape."

Calvin had seen Steropes use a ring which appeared to have power over two Jinn. He looked at the Psiclopes and raised an eyebrow, but Steropes shook his head, indicating he didn't want to discuss it.

Captain Nightsong didn't see the glance and continued, "Wayland killed seven of the Jinn to infuse their spirits into swords he made especially for that purpose, hoping to create swords of great power."

"You've mentioned that before," said Calvin. "How exactly did he capture a life essence and infuse it into a sword? Is this some sort of magic?"

"There's no magic involved," replied Captain Nightsong; "it's science. You are aware, of course, that there is an animating force inside every living being, correct? If you look into someone's eyes as he or she dies, you can see the light go out of them. That is the spirit leaving the body. We have long known this happens; Wayland figured out a way to use magnetic containment to trap these spirits and then infuse them into a sword. He felt that by doing this, you could use the knowledge the spirits gained in life to help a sword-wielder fight better."

"Did it work?" asked Captain Sheppard.

"I don't know," replied Captain Nightsong. "He said it did, but the infused spirit had to be of the same moral outlook as the sword wielder. That is why he tried to capture a variety of Jinn. It was, of course, illegal and immoral to bind a soul against its wishes, so I never used any of the swords and wouldn't know whether it was true or not. For that matter, I do not know if he actually succeeded in doing so…although he claimed he did."

"Well, even if we had the ring or any of these swords," Calvin said, "I don't see how they would help us. We need something which will help us fight Jinn weapons and Jinn ships that can phase in and out of our universe. We need to figure out how to cross over and get my men back. And most importantly, we need to figure it out quickly, before we have to fight them again." He stopped suddenly as an idea came to him. "You know what? I think I may know a couple of individuals who can help us."

"Who are they?" asked Captain Sheppard.

"Some old friends of ours," said Calvin. "They're on Keppler-22 'b.'"

"I'm unfamiliar with that planet," said Captain Nightsong. "Who are these friends, and why do you think they'll be able to help us?"

Calvin smiled. "Their names are Sella and Trella," he said; "they're Jinn."

Asp 08, Unknown System, June 14, 2021

The stars seemed to flash and jump as Lieutenant Pete 'Rock' Ayre pulled out of his firing run on the alien ship. "What the hell?" he asked. "Are we hit? My implants just died."

"I don't know what happened," replied his WSO, Lieutenant Dan 'K-Mart' Knaus, "but it isn't your implants. It's the network; the entire implant network just went down. Mine are out too. I don't think we were hit, but the ship we were fighting must have exploded. It's gone."

"I don't know," said Rock. "It kept disappearing; maybe it just did that again. We'll set up a position here so we can pounce on it when it shows back up."

The radio came to life with a call. "Asp 08 *this is* Asp 09," said its WSO, Lieutenant Mark 'Chomper' Melanson. "*We've lost comms with the* Gulf. *Can you contact them?*"

"*Stand by,*" replied K-Mart. He tried several times with the faster-than-light communications system, but was unable to raise the ship. "*That's negative, 09, we don't have comms with Mom either.*" As the fighters were based on the *Vella Gulf*, it was their mother ship, or "Mom" for short.

"*They wouldn't have gated out without us, would they?*" asked Chomper, who was new to the squadron.

"*I don't think so,*" replied K-Mart. "*Besides, the* Gulf *was hours from the stargate. They wouldn't have made it to the gate yet. Stand by.*"

"This is strange," said K-Mart. "The *Vella Gulf* wouldn't have left without us. They wouldn't. And even if they *had* to gate out, they would have at least said something."

"Do you think they were destroyed?" asked Rock.

"No, I don't think they were destroyed. The alien ship fired another one of those torpedo things, but I doubt the torpedo would have completely destroyed it. I can't find the *Gulf* on any of my systems. Not radar, not radio, not even on the identification, friend or foe (IFF) system. Nothing. It's as if they don't exist anymore."

"What about the giants?" asked Rock. "Maybe they had a cloaked ship that appeared and destroyed the *Gulf* while we were fighting the alien ship."

"Maybe…" replied K-Mart, his voice betraying his skepticism. "Just a second; let me look and see what the Jotunn are doing." He looked down at his instrumentation and changed the settings on his systems. No matter what he tried, he couldn't find the giant ship…or anything else that had been in the system before the battle.

"Oh…fuck," he said as the realization hit him.

"I don't like the way you say that," said Rock, with a tinge of concern in his voice. K-Mart was one of the few sailors he knew who didn't curse like, well, like a sailor. To hear him swear was unusual; for him to drop an F-bomb meant something was really, *really* wrong. "What? Are the giants heading our way?"

"No, they're not. In fact, I can't find *them* either."

"Do you suppose they cloaked? I didn't know they could cloak a ship that big. Maybe they're behind a planet or something?"

"No, I don't think that's it."

"Well, where did they go then?"

K-Mart turned in his seat so he could meet Rock's eyes. "Remember how the alien ship kept disappearing, and we didn't know where it went?"

"Yeah."

"Remember how everything flashed while we were attacking the alien ship before it disappeared?"

"Yeah."

"I think we got caught up in whatever gadget or effect the ship used to disappear. Then, when it jumped back to our system, we were too far away to get caught in the effect again."

"What the hell does that mean?" asked Rock.

"It means that if you want to know where the alien ship went when it disappeared, look around. Go ahead and get used to it too. Not only are we in some new star system, or universe, or something, *we've got no way of going back home again!*"

Chapter Nine

"Okay, Steropes, give," said Calvin. "What do you know that you aren't telling?"

Steropes looked uncomfortable. "I misunderstood the nature and purpose of the ring. I had heard the stories of King Solomon and thought the ring gave you power over the Jinn; that if you had the ring, you could make them do what you wanted. I guess you can, but only under certain circumstances. Hmmm...that is why it didn't work on Keppler-22 'b.'"

"Yeah, I understand that," replied Calvin, "but that isn't what you were worried about. Why did you really not want me to tell Captain Nightsong you had the ring?"

"I don't know," replied Steropes. "I thought I had the Seal of Solomon, but now I wonder if it's something different. Until I figure out what I have, I thought it was probably better if we kept it quiet."

"So you don't know if you can go to the Jinn universe?" asked Calvin. "You never went there?"

Steropes shook his head. "All the information I had only said the ring was used to control Jinn. It didn't say how it worked or that there was another universe. I thought you only had to put it on your finger for it to work. When I fought Quetzalcoatl on Earth, he had one of the rings. He would command his two Efreet to do things, and they would go and do them."

"I wonder…"

"What?"

"I was wondering how they get their ship to cross over," said Calvin. "If they have some sort of giant ring or rod they use. Why haven't we seen them before? Why here? Why now?"

"All good questions," said Steropes; "unfortunately, I don't have any answers."

"So, I guess we push on to Keppler-22 and hope the answers are there."

"It would seem so."

Chapter Ten

Bridge, TSS *Vella Gulf,* HD 69830, June 26, 2021

"System entry into HD 69830–," said Steropes.

"Sir," interrupted the communications officer, "the *Terra* is here. They're calling us."

"On screen," replied Captain Sheppard. The face of Captain Lorena Griffin, the commanding officer of the TSS *Terra* filled the screen.

"Welcome back," she said. "The Thor has been anxiously awaiting your return. Were you successful in retrieving the prince?"

"No, we weren't," said Captain Sheppard. "We found the remains of his ship, but got chased off before we could find him. I don't want to say any more over an open channel; how about we send over a shuttle so we can meet in private?"

"We'll be waiting for you," said Captain Griffin.

CO's Conference Room, TSS *Terra,* HD 69830, June 26, 2021

"So that's the story," concluded Captain Sheppard. "We escaped, but we are missing one of our engines and the majority of our fighters. There is still at least one Jotunn ship in the system with the *Blue Forest* hulk, and that ship alone is more than we could have fought by ourselves. If another one of the suspected Jinn ships showed up, or even one of the Jotunn ships, we would have been in big trouble. I decided it was better to bring the word back, get our ship fixed and return with additional forces and better tactics."

"That makes good sense," replied Captain Griffin. "I can see why you would think the new enemy are from the Jinn Universe, but I don't understand why you think the Jinn in Keppler-22 will help us. If it is their spaceships that are attacking us, wouldn't they attack us there too, once they found out we were onto them?"

"It's possible, but I don't think so," said Calvin. "When we met the Sila in Keppler-22, they definitely did *not* seem warlike. They certainly weren't aggressive toward us; if anything, they helped us against the Efreet. If they were going to go to war with us, why didn't they attack us there while we were unsuspecting? Why wait and attack somewhere else? For that matter, we don't even know if the new enemy *is* the same Jinn; all we know is they seem to be able to go back and forth from some other place into our universe."

"You're sure it's not a cloaking system? Maybe one better than anything we have seen before?"

Captain Sheppard shook his head. "No, it can't be a cloaking system unless it's something that lets a ship become completely immaterial. I had my crew analyze all the battle video, and our missiles definitely go through the space where the ship was. Also, there is the matter of the two missing fighters. If the ship cloaked with them, why didn't they come back when it uncloaked?"

"Those are certainly all good questions," replied Captain Griffin.

"The bottom line is that we don't have enough information," said Calvin, "and we don't have a whole lot of places we're going to be able to get it. The Jotunn certainly aren't going to tell us any more than they already did. I have a feeling that Terra is at war with them now too, whether we want it or not. Whoever the enemy is, they didn't seem like they were in a talking mood. Our only hope is to go to Keppler-22 and talk with the Sila Jinn. They may be able to help us. Even if they can't, we're no worse off than we are right now."

"Speaking of worse off," said Captain Griffin, "the *Vella Gulf* is even worse off now than when you started on this mission. With only one engine, you won't be able to go as fast as you normally could, and I have a feeling speed is of the essence. We have to figure out who our new enemy is, and we need to come up with weapons and tactics to fight them effectively. Hoping one of our fighters is positioned where the enemy ship is going to materialize is a poor way to conduct combat; we can't expect to get lucky like that again."

"I wouldn't say it was lucky for the crew of the fighter," said Calvin.

Although the tone could have been taken as surly or disrespectful, Captain Griffin had lost plenty of her own crew members in combat, and she understood Calvin's sentiments. She also saw the bigger picture. "No," she said, "it wasn't lucky for them. It was, however, very lucky for us as it provided a means of escape for the *Vella Gulf*. The way the battle was going, I wouldn't be surprised if they did it on purpose. Much like someone I know who intercepted an inbound torpedo with *his* fighter."

"Sometimes you have to do what it takes for the good of the group," said Calvin, rubbing the back of his neck. He sighed. "Yeah, I imagine if I had been in their place, I would probably have done the same."

"Regardless, the only place the *Vella Gulf* needs to go is to the shipyards; it's in no condition to continue the mission."

"But—"said Calvin.

"Fleet Command sent the *Terra* to assist with your mission, and I intend to do that. Lieutenant Commander Hobbs, you are to transfer your platoon and the remainder of your fighter crews to the *Terra*. Although the *Terra* isn't made to carry fighters, we'll figure out a way to make it work. We will continue the mission to Keppler-22 while the *Vella Gulf* goes back for repairs." She smiled. "There's also the matter of briefing the Thor on what happened. I'm sure he is very anxious to find out. Perhaps the Aesir can put together a fleet to accompany us when we get back. If so, we can return to the system where you found the *Blue Forest*, destroy the Jotunn ship and find out what really happened to the rest of the Aesir ships that disappeared."

"So, you're just going to leave me here to talk to the Thor while you run off?" asked Captain Sheppard.

"I wouldn't say we're running off," said Captain Griffin, "just that we're going off to accomplish the mission since your ship is no longer capable."

"It still feels like you guys get a free meal while I'm left holding the check," said Captain Sheppard, shaking his head.

Captain Griffin smiled. "Well then, be a good boy and pay it for us, won't you?"

Asp 08, Unknown System, Unknown Date/Time

"*So, we're stuck here?*" asked Chomper. *Asp 09* had pulled alongside *Asp 08* to have a strategy session.

"*It would seem so,*" replied K-Mart. "*Unless you have some other way home.*"

"*So what do we do?*" asked Lieutenant Bryan 'Hooty' Hooten.

"Well, we've only got three choices I can see," said K-Mart. *"One, we can stay here and power down to next to nothing and hope they figure out where we've gone and how to get to us. If we do that, we would probably have enough power to last about 10 days. There won't be much to eat beyond the third day and only recycled fluids after the fifth day."*

"No thanks," said a chorus of voices.

"Considering the Vella Gulf *was running when we last saw her, that probably wasn't our best choice anyway,"* said K-Mart. *"The second option is to head out-system and look for a stargate. Maybe we could go somewhere…else…and find a way to catch up with the* Gulf."

"But I didn't think Asps could go through stargates by themselves," said Chomper.

"They can't," agreed Rock.

"Well, they can't do it where we're from," said K-Mart. *"Who knows what the rules are here?"*

"Pass," said Rock.

"Not my choice," said Hooty.

"What's behind Door Number Three?" asked Chomper.

"The third choice is to go to the Earth-like planet and see what's there. The only problem with this is, with all the fuel we burned fighting the alien ship, if we go to the planet, we won't have much fuel left when we get there. It will be a one-way trip."

"So, let me get this straight," said Hooty. *"We can either die alone and in the cold, or we can die alone and in the cold or we can go to the place where there's a slim chance we might not die alone and in the cold. I vote for your…what did you call it? Door Number Three?"*

"Me too," said Chomper.

"Works for me, mate," said Rock.

"I'm in too," said K-Mart. *"Let's go see what's on the planet."*

Chapter Eleven

"So, now that we're here, what exactly is your plan?" asked Captain Griffin.

"Yeah, you've been awfully close-mouthed about how we were going to contact them," said Master Chief O'Leary. "What *is* the plan?"

"I haven't wanted to talk about it with you, Master Chief," said Calvin, "because I am well aware of your misgivings when it comes to out-of-the-ordinary adventures."

"If you mean I don't like spooky shit," said Master Chief, "you got that right. And, I have to say, I don't like the direction of this conversation. Are we not planning on taking the entire platoon down with us to the surface?"

"No," replied Calvin, "we are not. I've given this a lot of thought, and I think it's best if just you and I go down. Sella and Trella seemed to have the closest connection to the two of us; if we take everyone down there, we run the risk of scaring them off."

"What if they show up with an army?" asked Master Chief. "A cyborg or two would be pretty handy to have if things go to shit...which they always seem to do with you around."

"I don't think it will come to that," replied Calvin. "They could have let us die the last time we were here, and no one would have ever known. Not only did they *not* let us die, they actively helped us defeat the Efreet. I don't think they will act against us now."

"You know they are aliens, right?" asked Master Chief. "They aren't pretty women we're trying to pick up in a bar on Friday night; they're no-shit *aliens*. You realize that, right?"

Calvin rolled his eyes. "I am well aware of that, Master Chief. Still, I don't think they, or their civilization, have anything against us."

"You're basing the intentions of an entire civilization on the actions of two individuals?" asked Captain Griffin. "Do you really think that's wise?"

"In most cases, no ma'am, I wouldn't," replied Calvin; "however, in this case, I just get the feeling they aren't the ones we have to watch out for. If they had hostile intentions toward us, I don't think they would have saved our lives or the lives of the native population of the planet the last time we were here."

"I learned to trust your 'feelings' a long time ago," said Captain Griffin. "I'm willing to let you and Master Chief go down to the planet by yourselves to try to get in touch with the Jinn, but I want the rest of your platoon on high alert and ready to transport down to the surface at a moment's notice. You *will* go armed, and you *will* take every precaution. If anything is even a little out of the ordinary, I want you to get back up here pronto. Even if the Sila aren't against us, it's still possible our new enemy is here, and I don't want to lose the two of you. Got it?"

"Yes, ma'am."

Mission Bay, *Shuttle 01*, Keppler-22 'b,' July 16, 2021

"Where do you want us to land?" asked the WSO of *Shuttle 01*, Lieutenant Neil 'Trouble' Watson.

"If you see the main complex of pyramids, there is an open area next to it big enough to land in."

"I see it," said Trouble, looking at his visual targeting screen. He pointed it out to his pilot, Lieutenant Jeff 'Canuck' Canada.

"We can do that, sir," Canuck added. "It'll be tight, but I can get it in there."

Shuttle 01 landed without fanfare on the local inhabitants' athletic field, and the boarding ramp came down. Once most of the dust had settled, Calvin took off his helmet and walked down the ramp.

The only problem with landing in the field, Calvin saw, was the ship was in plain view of the locals, who were at about the same technological level as the 11th century Mayan Indians of Central America on Earth. Of course, that is what they actually were, having been forcibly transported to the planet by an alien race called the Coatls. In fact, the Coatls had transferred so many of the Mayans to the Keppler-22 system that the Mayan civilization on Earth failed as a result.

The Coatls had continued to rule the Mayan civilization as gods on Keppler-22 'b' ever since, until they were dispatched by Calvin's platoon on an earlier mission. Although the locals had been in contact with the Terrans in the intervening months, it was still ingrained in their psyches that creatures from the sky were gods, a belief the Terran embassy on the planet hadn't been able to fully eradicate. Many of the small, brown men and women stopped and looked to see what the almost-gods were doing.

When nothing exciting happened after a couple of minutes, though, most went back to what they had been doing prior to the shuttle's landing.

"*All right, Master Chief, let's go,*" Calvin commed.

"*Are you sure you know what you're doing?*" Master Chief asked, getting up from the combat seating. He walked down the ramp, but much more slowly than the officer had. He also took his helmet off.

"No, I'm not," Calvin replied. He began walking toward the main pyramid. "Aren't you coming?" he asked as Master Chief stopped and leaned against the shuttle. "Trella might be nearby..."

"No sir," said Master Chief. "This is something you're better off doing yourself. The Jinn told *you* to call them, not me. Officers get to do all of the spooky, creepy shit. It says so in the manual."

"What manual is that?" asked Calvin.

"The manual for dealing with spooky, creepy shit, and what officers are supposed to do about it," replied Master Chief. "It says senior enlisted men and women are supposed to lead troops into battle, where they kill people and break things. Nowhere does it say we are supposed to deal with creatures that have supernatural powers, or turn invisible or immaterial or whatever the hell it is they do. Nowhere."

"So you're just going to sit there?"

"Yes I am," replied Master Chief. He paused. "On second thought," he added, "no, I'm not going to just sit here."

"You're not?" asked Calvin. "You're going to come with me?"

"No, sir, I'm going to go back inside and get a nap. Wake me up when you're ready to put this world behind us. Again."

Calvin shook his head and continued walking toward the central plaza in front of the main temple. He found he liked the plaza much better when there weren't a bunch of dinobears in it trying to eat him. "Sella!" he yelled. "Trella!"

He waited. Nothing happened. He looked around the plaza. The locals continued on about their business although a few of them looked at him curiously. Most of the parents with children tried to shepherd their youngsters away from the obviously crazy almost-god that was talking to invisible spirits. "Sella!" he yelled again. "Trella!"

He waited some more. Still, nothing happened. No magical genies. He didn't know what he had expected, or how he had envisioned them making their appearance, but he had expected *something*. They had told him that if he called, they would come.

"Sella!" he yelled one more time. "Trella!" Once again, nothing happened. He sighed, feeling extremely stupid. Most of the locals had stopped what they were doing to watch his strange display in the center of the plaza. Although Calvin didn't know much about the Mayan civilization, it was obvious to him that most of the locals questioned his sanity.

"Well, crap," he said. "I wonder what the heck they want me to do."

"Oooh, is the big strong soldier getting frustrated?" He jumped as a voice breathed in his left ear, causing goose bumps down his side.

"It certainly seems like it," another voice said in his right ear, causing a similar sensation down the right side.

He turned around, but there was no one standing there.

"Hi, ladies," Calvin said, not knowing a better way to address them. "Are you not going to make yourselves visible?" Looking around, he saw strange expressions on some of the locals' faces as they watched the foreigner talking to himself. Several mothers started dragging off their children to get them away from Calvin before his insanity infected them.

"In the center of the plaza?" the first voice asked.

"In front of all of these people?" the second asked.

"It would be nice," Calvin replied. "That way, they wouldn't think I'm crazy."

"Most of them don't think you're crazy," the second voice said.

"Well, not yet, anyway," the first voice agreed. "However, I think they *are* rapidly coming to that conclusion."

"Well, I guess that's to be expected," the second voice answered. "He *is* standing in the middle of the plaza talking to himself."

"And the longer he does it, the crazier he looks."

Calvin sighed again.

"He gets frustrated so easily," the first voice said.

"Yes, he does," the second voice agreed. "He sighs a lot. He really should learn some patience."

"You're both really funny," Calvin said watching one mother and her two young children hurrying past. They had taken a wide path around him, getting no closer than 30 feet. "I take it you're not going to show yourselves?"

"They don't know we exist," the first voice said.

"And we'd rather keep it that way," the second added.

"They need to learn to do things on their own," said the first voice.

"Won't the Terran presence keep them from learning how to do things on their own?" asked Calvin, directing his question to where he thought the first voice was.

When there was no answer, Calvin sighed again and began walking back toward the shuttle.

"There he goes with the sigh again," said the second voice. "Poor thing."

"I'm going back to the shuttle," Calvin replied, "and I'm not saying another word to you two until you're visible."

"Hey, Calvin," said the second voice.

"What?"

"You just said another word to us." Both of the voices giggled. The giggles quickly turned into laughter.

"Look, Trella," said the first voice, confirming his guess that she was Sella. "You made his face turn such a pretty shade of red. It's almost like the double sunset on Qualifret."

"Just like that," Trella agreed. "It's redder now, though."

Calvin put his helmet on to block out their laughter, but it still seemed to come to him anyway, so he walked faster to try to leave them behind. The giggles stayed with him the rest of the way back to the shuttle.

"Couldn't find them?" asked Master Chief as Calvin stomped up the ramp. Master Chief was lying across the webbed combat seating, using his suit as a pillow. "See, that's why the officer is supposed to go. That way you're the one who looks stupid yelling at the top of your lungs and I'm not. I could hear you all the way in here; I'll bet it was quite a scene."

Master Chief jumped up. "Hey! Something pinched me." He looked back at the seating for a second, and then he spun and reached out behind him. "Ha!" he said. "Got ya!" Trella came into view behind him. He had hold of her left wrist.

"How did you know where I was?" she asked.

"Because that was exactly what I'd have done," he replied. "Divide and conquer. I imagine Sella is sitting on the seating there."

"I am," she said, coming into view.

Master Chief looked at Calvin. "Sir, I'm afraid I'm going to have to do something I don't do very often. I'm going to have to tell you I was wrong."

"You were wrong?" Calvin asked with a smile. It wasn't often Master Chief admitted being wrong.

"Yes, sir," said Master Chief with an answering smile. "It turns out I'm a *lot* better at dealing with the spooky, creepy shit than you are after all." He started laughing, and the women quickly joined in. Calvin could see he'd been had. He resisted the temptation to sigh again and sat down along one of the bulkheads. The back of the shuttle had combat seating down both sides and a central double row that faced the two outside sections.

"Okay," Calvin said when the three began to wind down, "if you have all had your laughs, perhaps we could get on with our mission?"

"I guess," said Sella, sitting down across the aisle from Calvin so she could see him. "What brings you back here?"

"We need your help," said Calvin. "Well, I think you may be able to help, anyway. We are trying to figure out some things so we can help another race. I'm hoping you can help us...but I don't really know if you can."

"Well, that is certainly vague enough," said Trella. "I think I may need to sit down too." She sat down next to Calvin so she could look at Master Chief, who took a seat next to Sella. "Could you be a little more specific about the kind of help you're looking for?"

"Yes, I can," Calvin said. "I need to know how you are able to go invisible, or immaterial, or whatever it is you do. A race allied with us is fighting an enemy that can do the same thing. I'm trying to figure out how they do it, so we can help our allies."

"We can't tell you how we do it," said Sella.

"What?" asked Calvin. "You can't tell me? Or you won't tell me?"

"We can't tell you," Sella said. "We aren't allowed."

"So it is really a matter of you *won't* tell us," said Master Chief, joining the conversation. "Can you tell us why you can't tell us?"

"No," said Sella. She didn't say anything else, but looked instead at Trella. Calvin could tell they were communicating with each other somehow. As their conversation carried on, it appeared to get heated. Both began shaking their heads and gesturing at each other. Finally, Sella asked, "What is it worth to you to know?"

"Do you mean in money?" Calvin asked. "I don't know what you use for money, but I'm sure we have things you'd find valuable that we can give you for the knowledge."

"No, I meant exactly what I asked," said Sella. "What is it worth to *you*? Is it worth your life?"

"You want me to trade my life for the knowledge? Umm...will I be able to pass on the information to some of my friends so they can use it, or am I going to find out and then take the knowledge with me to the grave?"

"I don't *want* you to trade your life for that which you seek," Sella replied. "In fact, I kind of like you and don't want you to die. I would be quite happy if you *didn't* risk your life in the quest for this answer. But the fact remains, you would have to be prepared to risk your life if you want to gain the answer to your question. Are you prepared to do that?"

"The Aesir may be wiped out if we don't find an answer," said Calvin. "And then, once the Aesir are gone, it's likely the enemy will keep coming and fight us next. If I don't get the answer, I will still probably die, but it will be in combat with the enemy." He shrugged. "I'm going to die somehow, some time. We all are. If I have the chance to get the information needed to save the Aesir, then yes, I would give my life for it."

"What about you?" asked Trella, looking at Master Chief. "Are you willing to risk your life too?"

"This sounds a lot like the spooky, creepy shit I generally try to avoid," Master Chief said, "but if it involves Lieutenant Commander Hobbs risking his life, he's not going to do it by himself. I'm in."

"I knew you would say that," Trella said with a smile. She turned to Calvin. "You will need to take off your suit."

"Take off my suit?" asked Calvin. "Why?"

"Because it won't work where we are going, and it will only give away your presence."

"Oh," said Calvin. He took off his suit; Master Chief already had his off.

Trella reached across the aisle, and put her hand on Master Chief's arm. Sella reached across and did the same to Calvin. All four vanished.

Asp 08, Unknown System, Unknown Date/Time

"Asp 09, Asp 08, *are you seeing what I'm seeing?*" asked K-Mart.

"*If you're seeing some sort of big space station in orbit over the planet, then yes, I'm seeing what you're seeing,*" replied Chomper.

"*It's not that big. It can't be more than about 80 feet long.*"

"*No, it isn't. I don't see anything that looks like a weapon on it, either.*"

"Yeah, well we don't really know what their weapons look like, do we?" asked K-Mart.

"Should we call them on the radio, or should we just swoop in and blast them?"

"What do you think?" K-Mart asked his pilot.

"Well, we don't have enough fuel to go to the surface of the planet and then return to space," said Rock. "Once we're down, we're on the planet to stay, at least until we figure out a way to harvest some fuel. If we go down to the planet, I don't want to leave any of them up here where they can drop rocks on us."

"No, me neither."

"So, we either need to destroy the station or take it away from them," said Rock. "Personally, I don't think the station could have more than 15 or 20 people on it, even if they're really small. If one of us pulled up to the station while the other stayed back, the first crew could probably capture it. If things went badly, the second fighter could blast the station to pieces."

"Okay, so who goes in to clear the station?" asked K-Mart.

Rock turned toward his WSO and smiled. "We do, of course."

Asp 08, Unknown Space Station, Unknown Date/Time

"*Got it*," said K-Mart, finally catching hold of the edge of the station. This was his least favorite part of the whole plan, standing on the outside of the space fighter, trying to get it latched onto the space station. They had tried to contact the inhabitants of the station, but if the aliens' radios functioned the same way as their Terran counterparts, whoever was in the station didn't appear to have anything to say to them. Nothing was heard.

Communications having failed, *Asp 08* had approached the station while *Asp 09* waited half a mile back. The second fighter was close enough to be seen, but far enough away to not get caught in the same explosion if the aliens chose to attack.

The crew of *Asp 08* found the docking collar, but unlike its round Terran counterparts, the alien access tube was square. There was no way to join the fighter to the station, aside from tying it on, like an old-time rider roping his horse to the hitching post. "That's it," said K-Mart as he secured the metal line to the station. "We're tied up."

Rock turned off the motors and went to join his WSO, removing the ship's laser pistol and rifle from their mounting brackets. He had always wondered what they were there for, as he had never expected to actually land on a planet where he would need them. That's what the Marines were for. He also doubted the ship's designers had envisioned the weapons being used by the crew to assault a space station. It was ludicrous…yet here they were, doing it.

"*Which do you want?*" Rock asked K-Mart, giving him a choice of weapon.

"*I don't care,*" replied K-Mart.

"*Good, then I'll take the rifle. I used to do a lot of hunting back home when I was younger.*" He handed K-Mart the pistol and began walking toward the docking port.

"*How do you suppose we get in?*" asked Rock. The access port had a circular wheel, and there were a variety of dials and switches to the left of the access port. His suit wouldn't translate any of the writing that went with the dials and switches…if indeed it *was* writing. He could see a small room through the window that could be an air lock. *"I don't know,"* replied K-Mart. *"Maybe you should knock."*

Although the WSO had been kidding, Rock shifted the rifle to his left hand so he could bang on the door with his right hand.

After about 30 seconds of banging on the frame, a humanoid appeared. Its head was bald, and the being appeared nearly human, aside from the pale blue eyes that glowed so strongly they seemed to emit their own light. He was wearing a white full-body suit which covered most of his features, except for the 'hands,' which were two opposable talons on each side. The arms seemed longer and thinner than they would have been for a human, and the legs were also thin…and appeared to be backward-jointed like a bird. When the humanoid saw Rock, he jumped back in surprise, but then came closer, trying to determine what waited outside the window.

Rock pointed at himself and then the inside of the station.

The alien stood looking at him for a few moments, obviously trying to decide what to do with the stranger who had shown up, uninvited, at his door. His talons opened and closed repeatedly in distress. Finally, making a decision, he held up one claw and backed out of the room. He shut the other door, and the Terrans felt something mechanical operating through the soles of their boots. The vibration ceased, and a light on the panel next to Rock changed from yellow to blue.

"Suppose we should try the wheel now?" asked Rock.

"No, I think we should stand outside until we use up all of the oxygen in our suits," K-Mart replied.

"Eight billion people on our planet, and I get stuck with the king of sarcasm," grumbled Rock. *"Damn Yanks."* He magnetically locked his

boots to the station and turned the handle. It opened outward. Holding the door open with one hand, Rock motioned to the interior with the other. *"Be my guest,"* he said. *"Wouldn't want you to die out here, or anything. It would be so much better to do it inside."*

Leading with his pistol, K-Mart entered the station.

Chapter Twelve

Bridge, TSS *Terra*, Orbiting Keppler-22 'b,' July 16, 2021

"What the hell do you mean, 'they just vanished and haven't been heard from since?'" asked Captain Lorena Griffin. "Where the hell did they go?"

"I don't know," said Trouble, the WSO of *Shuttle 01*, from the main screen. "One minute they were talking to two pretty women and then all of a sudden, all four of them just vanished. I don't *know* where they went." He played with something off screen. "Here's the camera from the mission bay."

Trouble's face was replaced with a view of the shuttle's interior. Captain Griffin could see Calvin and Master Chief, as well as the two Sila Jinn she recognized from her last trip to the planet. She had seen them up close when they had materialized in front of her in the middle of a meeting. The two Jinn on the camera were Sella and Trella; she was sure of it. The two Jinn reached across the aisle to touch Calvin and Master Chief, and all four disappeared.

"What about infrared or any of the other sensors?" asked Captain Griffin. "Did you look at them?"

"Yes," replied Trouble, "when they disappeared, I tried all the sensors. Nothing. They just vanished without a trace."

"Trouble checked," added Canuck, the pilot of *01*. "I saw him. Not only did he check, but he ran diagnostics on all the equipment immediately afterward. They're gone."

"Roger that," replied Captain Griffin. "Wait there for now, and let us know if you hear anything. *Terra* out." The screen went blank. Captain Griffin turned to Steropes. "Well, Steropes, what do you think? Where did they go?"

"I do not know," he replied. "It can only be hypothesized they all went to wherever it is the Jinn live when they are not interacting with us. Whether that is another universe, another dimension or another reality entirely, I have no idea."

"Really?" asked Captain Griffin. The Psiclopes had lied to her enough times in the past she still didn't believe the first answer she received from any of them.

"Really," replied Steropes. "This is completely outside my experience. I have known Jinn existed for thousands of years, but I have never communicated with them. I didn't know the Jinn communicated with *anyone* who wasn't a Jinn. I didn't expect them to show up when the shuttle went to the planet, much less for them to converse with Lieutenant Commander Hobbs like we just saw them doing. No ma'am, I have no idea where they went."

Captain Griffin looked at Captain Nightsong. "What about you?"

"I don't know any more than Steropes," he answered. "They appear similar to the creatures Wayland said live in a universe parallel to ours, but it is beyond my ability to prove whether they *are* the same race, or where exactly they have gone."

"So, I guess we just wait."

"Yes, ma'am," replied Steropes. "It seems like that is the only thing we can do."

"Damn it," Captain Griffin said. She hated waiting.

Somewhere Else, Unknown Date/Time

Master Chief and Calvin fell to the ground as the shuttle disappeared from underneath them.

"What the hell?" asked Master Chief.

Calvin felt nauseous and lay back to settle his stomach. Looking up, he saw everything was different. The shuttle? Gone. The pyramids? Gone. Even the sandy desert-like planet's surface had changed. They were now lying in a forest with blue and red-leafed trees.

The girls' appearances had changed as well. Where before they had dressed like inhabitants of the planet Keppler-22 'b,' now they looked like something out of *1,001 Arabian Nights*. They wore brightly colored silks; Sella's were mostly light blue with a touch of purple while Trella's were mostly purple with a touch of light blue. Both had diamond-encrusted circlets on their heads, made from a reddish-colored metal. Silks flowed from the circlets to cover their faces. The only things he could see were their eyes, which glowed a solid light blue. Their hair cascaded in long pony tails behind them, reaching down to their waists.

Fighting the urge to be sick, Calvin stared at Sella, who stood in front of him. She was still pretty, but she was now very, very foreign. She held a short, golden rod in her right 'hand,' but it wasn't a hand like Calvin had ever seen; instead, it was a claw with four talons. Two wrapped around the rod on each side like a bird on a perch. He couldn't see her legs, but her arms appeared too long and thin to be human. He laughed to himself; he had intellectually known the Jinn weren't human, but it had taken seeing them like this to really understand that *they weren't human.*

Sella's hair matched her silks; it was mostly light blue with hints of purple. As he began to look around, the first thing he noticed was the sky was wrong. Where it had been blue on Keppler-22 'b,' the sky here was a medium shade of green. Looking at it made him want to throw up again. He focused on Sella's glowing eyes, instead. "Is this what you really look like?" he asked.

"Yes," said Sella, her voice a little deeper than what it had been on Keppler-22 'b.' "Welcome to our universe." She spun around once. "These are our natural forms. Do you like them?"

"I do," replied Calvin. "Umm...where are we?"

"You are now in our universe, which we call the Jinn Universe."

"That's interesting," said Calvin. "Did you know we call you 'Jinn?'"

"Of course," replied Sella. "You have it wrong though. We aren't Jinn; we are *from* Jinn. Our race is the Sila; there are other races which exist in this universe, like the Efreet. This is our planet, Ashur." Calvin didn't answer; he simply sat looking at her with his mouth open, so she continued, "You said you would give your life to find out our secrets. We brought you here, to our world, so you could have that chance."

"To find out the information or to give our lives?" asked Master Chief.

"That is up to you," Trella said. He couldn't see her face, but her voice sounded sad. "You may find the information you seek. You may not. You may die. Unfortunately, there is a very good chance of that happening. I kind of liked you, too, so that is a pity; however, it can't be helped. You asked to come, so we brought you. What you do with this opportunity is up to you. We will go see my father, the caliph."

"Caliph?" asked Master Chief. "Isn't that some sort of ruler?"

"Yes, our father rules here," said Sella. "His name is Harun al-Rashid."

"Can you put in a good word for us?" asked Calvin.

"We could..." said Sella, "but women aren't allowed to talk in court. You'll have to figure it out on your own. Come on, we need to go before we're discovered. The Efreet have random patrols which come by here."

"I don't know if you noticed," said Master Chief, "but wherever the hell 'here' is, it's a long way from anywhere with an implant network. 'On our own' is a good way to explain it. We're on our own, without any hope of support."

Bridge, TSS *Terra*, In Orbit Around Keppler-22 'b,' July 16, 2021

"Any word from Lieutenant Commander Hobbs or Master Chief O'Leary?" asked Captain Griffin.

"No ma'am," replied Lieutenant Watson from the main screen. "We haven't seen or heard from either of them. I've been in contact with the ambassador's staff and let them know to be on the lookout for them."

"Good thinking," said Captain Griffin.

"They also brought us dinner," Lieutenant Canada said, "but our crew day is getting to be pretty long. We're either going to need to come back to the ship or spend the night here."

"Give it another hour," Captain Griffin said. "If we still haven't heard from them, we'll send down another crew to relieve you."

"Yes ma'am," Lieutenant Canada replied. "We'll keep looking."

Ashur, Unknown Date/Time

"So that's what Efreet really look like?" Calvin whispered. He looked over the edge of a small hill as two creatures marched past. Although he had seen them previously, their appearance had been an illusion. In reality, Efreet looked like giant salamanders. Seven feet tall, each walked on its hind legs and carried some sort of tube-like weapon with a hose that ran to a container on its back. They were dressed in black armor with gold trim, which covered most of their torso and legs, and shiny golden boots. Their skin was dark brown with black patches; it was hard to tell where their skin ended and the armor began.

"Yes, that is their natural form," said Sella. "They conquered our planet a long time ago. Although they still let us govern our world, we do so only as long as we follow their rules. If we were to do something to irritate them, we would quickly find ourselves back under military rule."

"What are those weapons they are carrying?" asked Master Chief.

"They are flamecasters," replied Trella. "They can throw balls of fire or shoot a continuous stream of fire. They are devastating as we are allowed to wear nothing more protective than these silks." She nodded to the Efreet. "That is their patrol armor. Their combat armor covers their entire bodies and tails. Not only are they completely immune to fire when they are wearing it, they can also cover themselves in flames for a brief time."

"Our suits would probably have allowed us to withstand their fire," said Calvin, "at least for a little while."

"They might have," said Sella, "but there is an energy field here that would have shut down your suits' electronics. You would have had to carry them unpowered. The Efreet would also have known someone brought unauthorized electrical equipment into the restricted zone and would have come out in force to track it down."

"It's probably better we didn't bring them then," said Calvin.

"Much better," agreed Sella. She slid back, away from the hill's crest, and the rest of the group followed her as she began walking away from the Efreeti patrol. Both Sila seemed far more serious in their home world. Calvin could understand why; being conquered would tend to do that to you.

"Hey, sir," said Master Chief, after a couple of minutes walking, "I've got a question."

"Yeah, Master Chief, what is it?"

"So…we're going to see this grand poobah person, right?"

"That's right," Calvin replied, "I think Sella said he's called the caliph." Sella nodded her head in agreement.

Master Chief nodded. "Okay, the caliph. And we're going to have to talk with him because the women don't talk in court."

"Yeah. What's up?"

"So, we're going to have to talk with him in his own language."

Calvin nodded.

"Here in this other universe, we're going to talk to him *in his own language.*"

Calvin's brows knitted. "Not sure what you're getting at, Master Chief."

"Okay, sir, I'll be a little more blunt. How the hell are we going to translate some language we've never been exposed to? We won't have the processing power of the *Terra* to assist us through our implants. Our suits would be able to translate their language after they were exposed to it for a while, but we don't have them either. And, we're in another universe. Speech patterns may be way different here than at home. Their language may not be anything like our language. Maybe they talk with their feet. Maybe they make some sort of weird noises we can't pronounce or mimic. What the hell are we going to do then? How are we going to talk to him? *That's* what I'm getting at."

"Oh." Calvin ran his palm down his face. "I see." He took another couple of steps as he thought about it and added, "That could be a big problem."

"Officers," Master Chief said shaking his head. "Where would you be without us hard-working enlisted guys?"

"Okay, Mr. Hard-Working Enlisted Guy, do you have an idea?"

"No, but I'd rather find out here, rather than embarrassing ourselves in front of the caliph." He turned to Trella. "Say something in your language."

"Like what?" Trella asked.

"It doesn't much matter," Master Chief said; "I just want to see what our implants do to translate it."

Trella opened her mouth and emitted a burst of ear-piercing shrieks.

"That was your speech?" asked Calvin. "What did you say?"

"I asked what you wanted me to say, but asked it in our language."

"Did you get any of it, Master Chief?" Calvin asked.

"No, sir," Master Chief replied. "All it sounded like to me was two cats fuc…fighting. It sounded like two cats fighting."

"Yeah, me too."

"So what are we going to do?"

"I don't know," said Calvin. "I'll have to think of something. I don't think I can make that noise and besides, we don't have all day to try and figure it out. They're going to be missing us, back in our world, before too long."

"Sir, we disappeared without warning. They're probably already missing us."

"Yeah, they probably are…" His voice trailed off. The group walked for another two minutes, and then Sella said, "We're here."

"Where is 'here?'" asked Master Chief.

Sella pushed something inside what Calvin thought looked like a little bush, and the outline of a small trap door appeared in the ground with a 'click.' "This is our way to get to the castle without the Efreet seeing us." She lifted up the trap door and led them down a ladder into a small, but well-kept, tunnel.

Sella obviously knew the way; she passed several cross-passages without slowing. After about 10 minutes, the tunnel ended in another ladder.

"Where are we?" asked Calvin.

"We are underneath the castle," said Sella. "This leads into some secret passages which run through it. Only a few of us know they exist. The castle is on a hill, so it's a bit of a climb, and the ladder can get a little wet. Be careful going up." She climbed up the ladder, vanishing into the darkness. After a few minutes, a spot of light appeared far overhead as she opened the trap door at the top. Trella indicated the Terrans should go next, so Calvin went up the ladder after Sella, followed by Master Chief.

Trella checked the tunnel one more time and then climbed up the ladder. Having made the journey many times, she knew where the slick places were and avoided them, emerging into a small, 10-foot square room at the top of the ladder. She replaced the trap door and the carpet which covered it, and then turned to find the other members of the group had already left. Hurrying after them down the narrow passageway, she found the group as she rounded the first corner. They were 15 feet further down the passageway, surrounded by at least eight Efreet, who were aiming flamecasters at them. Sella and the Terrans had their hands up, and the Efreeti commander was holding Sella's control rod.

"Stop!" Trella heard the Efreeti commander order as he saw her come around the corner. "Give me your rod!"

"Okay," said Trella as she bowed her head in obedience. She walked forward, head down, and held the rod out to the Efreeti with both hands as custom dictated. As he reached forward to take it, she suddenly twisted the rod, exposing several buttons. The Efreeti screamed in outrage as Trella pushed one of the buttons and vanished.

Chapter Thirteen

Unknown System, Unknown Date/Time

"Well, that's fucked up," said Lieutenant Mark 'Chomper' Melanson. "They just left them here to die?"

"Yeah, they did," said Lieutenant Pete 'Rock' Ayre. It had taken over 14 hours for their suits to decode enough of the Sila's speech for them to be able to carry on a conversation. Normally, the suits were able to get the basics of a language in about four hours; 14 hours was a testament to how different their language was from anything in the Terrans' home universe. The translation still wasn't perfect, not by a long shot, but at least now they could get most of what they meant across. When Asp 08's crew heard the Sila's story, they called the crew of Asp 09 to join them in the station.

"The Efreet appeared in this system two months ago and destroyed all the space launch and recovery systems on the planet," confirmed Rock. "They also destroyed the spaceship that was supposed to take the Sila on the space station down to the planet. Yeah, they pretty much left them here to die."

"Why would they do that?" asked Lieutenant Bryan 'Hooty' Hooten.

"Because they are zzzzzt-breeding zzzzzt-zzzt mother fuckers!" said the station's commander, Major Zorr Zimba. "They enjoy inflicting cruelty on other races."

147

"Well, I see we've at least made some headway translating swear words," noted Chomper with a smile. "That will help with communications."

"Guess what else we found out?" asked K-Mart. "When the Efreet were here, they made the Sila go aboard their ship to clean out a clogged sewage line. Who do you suppose they saw while they were onboard?"

"A bunch of Efreet who will be dead the next time I get them in a fair fight?" asked Chomper.

"Even better," said K-Mart. "There were a bunch of prisoners on the Efreeti ship. That is why the sewage lines got stopped up; the ship wasn't built to hold that many people. Prisoners with green skin and pointed ears..."

"The Aesir!" said Chomper.

"Yeah, and they overheard the Efreet saying they were taking the prisoners to the giants' base on the planet," said K-Mart.

"We've got to go down and get them!" urged Chomper. "The prince may still be alive."

"Yeah, there's just one problem with that," said Rock. "The giants were in our universe, and we're not in our universe anymore."

"I'm sorry," said Major Zimba, "one of the words didn't translate. You are not where?"

"We aren't from here," said K-Mart. "We were fighting the Efreet ship, and it did something that brought us here from where we live. We aren't from here."

"Was there a flash?" asked Major Zimba.

"Yes," agreed Rock. "There was a flash, and all our friends disappeared."

"They must have made a zzzt which works for spaceships," said one of the civilians.

"A what?" asked K-Mart. "I'm sorry, my suit didn't translate that."

"Our government has a few devices that let us transfer between worlds. We used to go to the world of the giants to spy on them," said the same civilian. "We don't do it anymore now that the Efreet have come. It is too dangerous. The giants are not very smart, but the Efreet are excellent spies."

"So, if we get you down to the planet, you can get us to the world of the giants?" asked K-Mart.

"I can't, but the caliph can…if you can convince him."

"Bringing these people back to the planet might help convince him," K-Mart commed to the Terrans.

"Yeah, but we need to do it before the Efreet come back," commed Hooty. "We won't last long against their ship if they catch us here." Out loud he asked, "When do you expect the Efreet back?"

"When we heard you outside, we thought you were the Efreet coming back," said Major Zimba. "Our food ran out two days ago; we were hoping to lure them into the station and let the air out. We don't mind dying if we can take some of them with us."

"So, you don't have any way to get back to the planet?" asked Hooty.

"No, we do not," said Major Zimba.

"How many are there of you?"

"Eight."

Hooty looked at the rest of the Terrans. "How are we going to get them down?"

Chomper raised an eyebrow. "Very carefully?"

"Seriously," said Hooty. "In order to get them all down, we'd have to put four into each fighter. There isn't enough room for five people to fit on the WSO's side of the fighter, and I can't fly the damn thing with someone sitting on my lap. It wouldn't be a problem if we had enough fuel to make a few trips, but I don't think we have enough fuel to get my fighter back out of the gravity well once I take it down to the planet. Is yours any better off?"

"No, it's not," said Rock. "Still, we can't leave them here to die. We'll have to work something out."

"If it will get the civilians back to the planet," said Zimba, "Zzzzt Gorba and I will stay behind."

"Thanks for the offer," said K-Mart, "but we're going to get everyone down. I've got an idea. It will take a while to put everything we need together, but I think it will work."

Shuttle 02, Keppler-22 'b,' July 16, 2021

"Did you see that?" asked Lieutenant Tobias 'Toby' Eppler.

"Huh? See what?" asked his pilot, Lieutenant Phil 'Oscar' Meyer, from where he slouched in his seat. Like most people in the military, he could fall asleep at a moment's notice, regardless of his surroundings, and the waiting had been anything but exciting.

"The pyramid to the left," replied Toby. "A woman materialized about 10 feet above it and then fell down onto the side of it." He pointed. "Right there." Before Oscar could find her, she disappeared from Toby's sight. "Dammit, she's gone again."

"What did she look like?" asked Oscar.

"Hard to tell because I only got a quick look at her," said Toby, "but she kind of looked like something out of the movies...a belly dancer or harem girl...something like that."

"Well, I don't see her now."

"Yeah, me neither." Toby switched to his radio. "Vella Gulf, Shuttle 02. Interrogative, what did the Jinn who were with Lieutenant Commander Hobbs look like?"

"Stand by," replied the communications officer on the Vella Gulf. "The CO says they are short, pretty women. One is blond, the other has dark hair. Usually, they dress like the natives, but she has also seen them dressed in silks like Middle Eastern belly dancers."

"Roger that," replied Toby. "I think I just saw one of them materialize over one of the pyramids. She fell onto it but then disappeared."

"Copy all. The CO says to keep an eye out for her."

"Wilco. We'll keep an eye out."

"How do you look for someone who can go invisible?" asked Oscar.

"Beats me," Toby replied. "Look out the window and see if she reappears; I'll try searching on the infrared scanner."

"Maybe one of us should go outside," said Oscar after a couple minutes of fruitless searching. "We can't see very much out of the window, and she might have been hurt in the fall."

"If you are looking for me, that won't be necessary," said a feminine voice from behind the aviators. They turned to find a short woman at the back of the cockpit. Her long dark hair framed a delicate face with brilliant blue eyes. "I'm Trella, and I'm afraid your friends need help."

Ashur, Unknown Date/Time

The Efreeti commander motioned along the corridor. He barked out an order in a deep, raspy voice, but the translation software in the Terrans' implants couldn't translate it. "What did he say?" asked Calvin.

Without warning, the Efreeti standing behind Calvin slammed the tube of his flamecaster into Calvin's head, knocking him to the floor. The metal was much denser than it appeared; Calvin saw stars and nearly lost consciousness. The Efreeti commander said something else.

Sella helped Calvin to his feet. "He said to move," she said. "He also said, 'no talking.'"

The group headed down the passageway single file. It was so narrow in places the Terrans had to turn sideways to get through. As they walked, they heard voices on the other side of the wall and noticed peepholes which allowed them to see into the rooms on the other side. After a couple of minutes, they came to an open door and walked into the castle's throne room. Eight more Efreet were waiting there, pointing their weapons in the general direction of two male Sila. Though woozy from the blow to the head, Calvin guessed the larger of the two was the caliph. His robes were stunning, and he wore what looked like jewelry made from black metal all over his body. The second Jinn was taller and thinner, and he was dressed more plainly. Sella ran to hug the larger male, confirming Calvin's guess.

The Efreet soldiers prodded the Terrans into a group with the male Sila.

Calvin felt something running down his face. He reached up to see what it was, and his hand came away bloody.

"He whacked you good, didn't he?" asked Master Chief.

"Yeah," agreed Calvin. "My vision is kinda blurry, and it's pretty likely I've got a con, a conduct..., no, I mean a condominium..., no, a confab..."

"A concussion," said Master Chief. He looked into Calvin's eyes. One pupil was much larger than the other.

"Yeah, a concussion," said Calvin, smiling.

Damn, thought Master Chief; this day can't get much worse.

Chapter Fourteen

CO's Conference Room, TSS *Terra*, In Orbit Around Keppler-22 'b,' July 17, 2021

"The Efreet have captured your men," said Trella, who sat cross-legged on top of the table, with the *Terra's* officers seated around it. "They have the ones you call Calvin and Master Chief. I don't know how you will do it, but if you want them back, you will have to come and get them; the Efreet will never release them on their own."

"The Efreet captured them?" asked Captain Griffin. "What does that mean? How and why were they captured? What happened? What did they do?"

"I will tell you what I know," said Trella, "but I need to simplify things for time. The Efreet aren't known for being gentle jailors; the torture of your men will probably begin soon."

"By all means," replied Captain Griffin. "Go quickly then."

"Calvin and Master Chief wanted to know how we traveled between universes," explained Trella. "We were not able to tell them without permission, so we took them to our universe so they could ask our father, the caliph. Before we could ask him, the Efreet found us and captured my sister and your men. They will want to know where your men came from, and the Efreet can be very persuasive when they want to find something out."

"How do we know you're not leading us into a trap?" asked Night. "All we know is you and your sister appeared, took our men and now you say they were captured. For all we know, they were taken prisoners by *your* civilization, just like we will be if we go with you."

"You have to believe me!" cried Trella. "The Efreet—" she stopped suddenly. When she continued, she seemed more in control of herself. "I see what you are saying, and I can see why you might believe that. You don't know us. You don't know how the Efreet rule over our society, crushing all innovation and free spirit. Even though we saved those men's lives once before, it is possible my civilization captured them, and wants to capture more of you to study. It's not true, but I can see why you are worried it might be so. You leave me no choice."

Before any of the Terrans could move, she reached into the silks of her sleeve, leaned forward and placed a metal rod on the conference room table. Before the Terran's eyes, her appearance shifted, transforming into something very foreign. The hand the Terrans could see became a four-taloned claw with two opposing talons on each side. Her arms grew longer and thinner. The most striking feature, though, was her eyes. Although purple silks covered most of her face, her eyes were visible. They glowed a light shade of blue, almost as if they emitted light. Her purple hair matched her silks; both had hints of light blue which complemented her eyes.

She reached over and put two of her talons on the rod, which was round on both ends. Giving it a push, she sent it rolling along the table to Captain Griffin. "My life is now in your hands. Without that rod, I can never go home again."

Jail for Special Prisoners, Ashur, Unknown Date/Time

The prisoners were led down the hill from the castle. It was surprising how much form followed function, thought Master Chief as he looked around the castle grounds. The castle looked very much like a renaissance castle on Earth, with high walls and large towers in the corners. The towers were manned by Efreet, and Efreet patrolled the grounds. They all wore full armor and looked alert and ready for trouble.

As the group was led from the castle, Master Chief got his first look at the city, which spread out down the hill from the castle. He felt like he had been transported backward in time 250 years. The houses and buildings looked like something from out of the Revolutionary War paintings he had seen. They clashed on a technological level with the motorized vehicles that fought with the city's pedestrian traffic for control of the city's streets. It was a riot of colors...all of them wrong...under a putrid green sky.

Calvin threw up, the vomit making a splashing sound as it hit the stone road. Whether he threw up because of the concussion or because of the *wrongness* of the view, Master Chief couldn't tell. Certainly, the colors of the sky and the scenery below made him want to puke as well. The smell of Calvin's vomit didn't help.

They reached their destination. It was obviously a jail, as its walls were topped with the Efreeti version of barbed wire. It actually looked closer to razor wire, with blades sticking out at all angles. He looked at it with a professional eye and hoped he wouldn't have to go over the wall; the way the wire was coiled would make it difficult for anyone to get through in one piece.

Efreet manned the towers that encircled the jail. They were alert and faced outward. They didn't seem concerned about a breakout;

they were arrayed to stop the Sila from breaking in. Master Chief wondered who could be valuable enough to cause the locals to assault the walls wearing nothing but silk. Two foreigners and the caliph, he thought as they passed through the gates. He looked out as the gates shut behind him. None of the locals came within 30 feet of the jail, nor did they even look toward it.

Everything he saw reinforced the fact that he was in an occupied city.

All too quickly, they were pushed into a building and led down a set of nearly circular stairs. A long way down. Master Chief guessed somewhere between 80 and 90 feet, but he couldn't be certain.

He had hoped to rush the jailors before they were put in cells, but even more Efreet met them on the prison level to lead them to their cells. Each of the cells had bars set into the floor, which extended upward into a wooden roof six feet over his head. There were only about three inches of space between the bars; he wasn't slipping out between them. The prisoners were put into cells two by two, and then the Efreet withdrew. Calvin was in the same cell as the caliph, and Master Chief was locked up with the other Sila. Calvin immediately sat down in a corner and appeared to go to sleep.

As the cell doors were slammed shut, two Efreet led Sella away. She struggled, but each of them had hold of one of her arms, and they dragged her off. The caliph yelled something in a foreign language, but the soldiers ignored him and took her off into the gloom. The caliph continued to yell long after the last of the Efreet disappeared around a corner.

The single dim light further up the passageway gave off a minimal amount of illumination, but it was enough for Master Chief to see once his eyes adjusted. The light level was inconsistent, rising and falling, making shadows dance down the corridor. It looked to Master Chief like Calvin's head had stopped bleeding. That was something, at least.

The caliph stepped into his line of sight and said something.

"I'm sorry," said Master Chief, "but I don't understand you."

"How about this?" the caliph asked in Nahuatl, the language of the Mayans in the Terran Universe. Master Chief's implants were equipped to translate that language, due to his previous time on Keppler-22 'b.'

"That's better," replied Master Chief in the same language.

"I am Caliph Harun al-Rashid," said the caliph. "The man in the cell with you is my Grand Vizier, Jafar al-Barmaki. I believe you have already met my daughters Sella and Trella."

"I have," said Master Chief. "In fact, they were bringing us here to talk to you when we were captured by the Efreet."

"Sella said Trella went for help," said the caliph. "If your friends come quickly, they may make it back before you are tortured to death. That is the only hope you have. No one ever leaves this prison. Not alive, anyway."

"How do you know we have friends who will come?" asked Master Chief.

"You are not one of the people who live on the planet across the shroud of the universe," replied the caliph. "Unless my eyesight is failing me terribly, you are much taller and lighter-skinned than they are. I crossed the boundary many times in my youth; that is how I know the language I am speaking to you now. Although I may be growing older, I am not yet in my dotage. You must be from a planet on the other side of a stargate, am I correct?"

Master Chief twitched in surprise, but was too stunned to say anything.

"What, you didn't think we knew of other stars and civilizations?" asked the caliph. "We have been going to your universe for a long time and have known of the existence of stargates for several thousand of your years. What we didn't know was how to get our ships to your universe so we could *use* your stargates, or if your stargates would even work for us if we could get our ships there."

"It looks like you must have figured out how to get your ships to our universe," said Master Chief. "We fought a ship that went back and forth between universes just like I have seen your daughters do."

"Yes," said the caliph. "My daughters have always been fascinated with your universe and spend far too much of their time there. Unfortunately, this time it is going to be the undoing of all of us." He seemed lost in thought for a few moments and then shook his head. "My family problems are of little interest to you, I fear. I'm sure you are more interested in our ability to cross to your universe. Yes, 25 years ago, a scientist figured out how to make the jump system work for a ship. Before we could use it to flee, the Efreet captured the researcher who discovered the process."

"Based on our surroundings," said Master Chief, indicating the jail cells, "it doesn't appear you have very good relations with the Efreet. Your daughters said the Efreet conquered your world a long time ago. How long have they been here?"

"That is a long story," replied the caliph. He made a gesture with his talons which was probably the Sila equivalent of a shrug. "However, as we do not appear to be going anywhere, I will tell you."

"The Sila civilization has been a star-faring nation for thousands of years," the caliph said, sitting down. "It was necessary for us to go to the stars as our sun was in the process of going nova. Even though we knew we had many thousands of years remaining, the star was becoming more active, and bursts of radiation were making life difficult on our home planet. Our scientists explored a number of ways for us to escape our failing star. They developed devices to take us to other universes, ships to take us to new worlds within our own universe and machines that let us modify the new worlds for our use."

"The universe transfer technology never worked as well as we hoped," the caliph continued, "but our ship technology was solid, if nothing exciting. Unfortunately for us, soon after we figured out how to travel to the stars, the Efreet arrived. Neither of our races had achieved faster-than-light star drives, but while the majority of our research had focused on modifying other planets to fit our needs, the Efreet technology was focused solely on war. We filled all the ships we had built and launched them to the stars, hoping to find and colonize planets that were unknown to the Efreet."

"If there's one thing we've learned since leaving our planet," said Master Chief, "it's that there's always going to be a race which focuses on war, and they are going to have a distinct advantage when they meet other cultures. We have a saying on our planet that we usually forget when things are going well, 'If you want peace, prepare for war.'"

"Yes," replied the caliph, "that is a maxim we would have been well-served to learn *before* the Efreet showed up. Our home planet was conquered, and, as the Efreet were able to acquire additional ships, they sent them in pursuit of our colonization vessels. They have been chasing us around our universe ever since. They thought our colonies would be unarmed and easy conquests...and unfortunately, we were."

"They arrived here about 155 years after the establishment of this colony," the caliph continued. "We didn't have any space-based defenses, and we were quickly subdued. Since then, they have ruled us as our overlords, gathering the cream of our planet's production and sending it back to their home world. They have outlawed all research and technological advancement. Research can only be conducted in secret, as they kill everyone involved if they find out we've disobeyed their orders."

"How long has this been going on?" asked Calvin from the corner; his voice sounded steadier than before.

"I was coming to that," said the caliph. He looked back at Master Chief. "You asked how long they have ruled us. They have been here for 1,200 years."

"They've ruled you that long?" asked Master Chief. "Why haven't you done something to get rid of them? There can't be that many of them."

The caliph made the shrugging motion again. "As rulers, they are not overly harsh...if we do as we are told. However, harsh or not, they *are* rulers, and we continue to work on ways of throwing off their yoke. I'm sorry you arrived when you did. The Efreet had just caught me talking with one of our secret researchers when you showed up. They will not forgive this, nor will they ignore the fact you are from the other universe. They will want to know why you are here, and they will not take "no" for an answer. I'm afraid all you can look forward to is six days or so of torture, followed by being burned alive. Why don't we overthrow them? Because they are experts at spying, and they kill everyone who breaks any of their rules."

CO's Conference Room, TSS *Terra*, In Orbit Around Keppler-22 'b,' July 17, 2021

"Okay," said Captain Griffin. "Let's assume for a moment we believe you, and you mean us well. The Efreet have our men. What can we do about it?"

"You only have two choices," said Trella. "You can either go to my world and get them back, or you can consider them lost. Once the Efreet take someone to their jails, they are rarely seen again, unless it is for a public execution. I imagine that since your men are foreigners, they will be well-tortured. There may not be enough left for a public execution."

"We've got to go get them," said Night.

"I agree," said Captain Griffin, looking at Night; "however, I am reluctant to send more people into the other universe if it's just going to be a futile attempt that results in more deaths. We don't know anything about where they went or the creatures who are holding them." She turned to Trella. "What can you tell us about your world and where the Efreet are holding our men?"

"Our world is very much like the planet below us. The air is breathable by you and the seasons are generally similar. We have added certain trace elements to the atmosphere which will probably not affect you; however, they make the sky appear green. Our visual acuity is slightly less than normal on the planet below; although you probably won't notice, yours will be slightly less in my world."

She paused, considering, and then continued, "With regard to the Efreet, you have better weapons and technology than they do. The problem is they are very good at identifying and eliminating power sources. When your soldiers transfer to my world, the Efreet will get power readings on the suits your troops wear, and they will know you are there. Even worse, your men are being held at the jail. Trying to bring anything electrical close to that area will set off their detectors, and they will come with their devices which make electrical things stop working, like they did to your suits before."

"I remember," agreed Night. The first time he had been to Keppler-22 'b,' the squad that had gone to the surface had their suits short-circuited, and Night had to lead a rescue mission to get the suits off the planet before the antimatter in the suits detonated. "If the Efreet have more of those electromagnetic pulse generators, we're better off without our suits."

"Yes, that is correct," said Trella. "If you do not bring your suits, they will be less likely to know you are coming. There are tunnels that will get us close to the jail. We can sneak up on the Efreet through them."

"If they can sense anything electrical, they will see your cyborgs and weapons, won't they?" asked Captain Griffin. "Are you going to leave them behind?"

"I don't think there will be a problem with the cyborgs," replied Night. "The combat shell is built to minimize electronic emissions. If they were easy to track on a battlefield, they'd also be easy to destroy. Our weapons, though…they're another story. The Efreet might be able to get a reading on them, depending on how sensitive their equipment is."

"Do you have anything low tech in the armory?" asked Captain Griffin.

"Yes, ma'am," said Night with a nod. "We still have a full load out of legacy weapons. In fact, our sniper uses one now because it can shoot further with effect in atmosphere than our lasers can. The lack of weapons isn't the problem; the lack of intel is…"

Cells, Jail for Special Prisoners, Ashur, Unknown Date/Time

Conversation among the prisoners died as the sounds of marching feet were heard coming down the hallway, and hidden lights switched on suddenly as five Efreet came into view. Blinded by the sudden bright light, the prisoners covered their eyes and peeked out to see their captors. The first two Efreet were dressed in suits of combat armor similar to what the Terrans had seen earlier, solid black with gold trim and boots. Made from some sort of iridescent metal, the boots sparkled in the artificial light of the jail like a disco ball. They also carried flamecasters attached to tanks on their backs.

The two Efreet who followed wore golden armor on their legs, with some sort of brown robes covering their upper halves. Without the armor, Calvin was able to get a better look at the Efreet, and he was struck again at how much they looked like salamanders from Earth, albeit ones who stood seven feet tall. They each carried some sort of double-tube apparatus, but it was hard to see as the Efreet carried it beneath their robes.

The final Efreeti wore what looked like a black leather, form-fitting suit, with lots of blue and silver piping and braid. A band of blue and a band of purple encircled his left arm. This Efreeti stopped in front of the caliph's cell and began a conversation with him. The Efreeti quickly became upset with the caliph's answers although the caliph maintained a serene disposition.

"Are you getting any of that?" asked Master Chief. "My translation software isn't breaking it."

"No," replied Calvin. "It's not as painful to listen to as the Sila language, but I'm not getting any of it either."

The Terrans watched in frustration as the Efreeti got more and more agitated. Finally, it yelled something and pointed at the vizier. One of the robe-wearing Efreet pointed his tubes at the vizier and two little plugs fired out. They appeared to function like a taser, for when the plugs hit the vizier, he jumped and twitched as if he were being electrocuted. He tried to say something, but was unable to speak with the current running through him.

The vizier convulsed on the floor while the Efreet made some kind of noise. Master Chief realized they were laughing at the vizier's pain.

"Hey, you bastards, that's enough!" he yelled, but the electrocution continued, along with the laughter. He took two quick strides, grabbed one of the wires and gave it a hard tug. The thin wire snapped, and the vizier was released from his torture.

"Look out!" called Calvin.

Too late. The other robed Efreeti fired his weapon from behind Master Chief, and the Terran felt his body stiffen as the high-voltage current coursed through it. "F-, F-, F-, Fuck," he said as he hit the ground next to the vizier.

Master Chief felt like his muscles were being pulled out with a fork as he writhed in agony.

"Help him," Calvin said to the caliph.

The caliph said something to the Efreeti in charge, but the electrocution continued. For the first time, the caliph showed some emotion as he appeared to implore the Efreeti to stop.

The Efreeti holding the stun gun looked at the one in charge, who didn't say anything for at least five seconds and then uttered one syllable. The Efreeti turned a dial on the back of his arm, and Master Chief gave a final convulsion and went still. The trooper pulled the ends of the metal wires from the launching mechanism and tossed them through the bars onto Master Chief.

Loading another round into the weapon from a pouch on his upper arm, the Efreeti turned toward the caliph and aimed the launcher at him. Before he could fire, the Efreeti leader said something to him, and the soldier lowered his weapon. The leader then spoke to the caliph before turning and leaving with the four soldiers in trail.

When they had departed, the lights went out again, leaving the prisoners with the single dim source. "That is why we do not rebel," said the caliph. "Anyone who rebels ends up like that...or worse."

"Okay, that hurt," said Master Chief as he rolled onto his stomach.

"Are you all right?" asked Calvin.

"Yeah, mostly," said Master Chief. "All things considered, I'd rather not do it again, though."

"No doubt," said Calvin. He turned to the caliph and asked, "What did they want to know?"

"They think we are plotting to overthrow them, and that we are building weapons in private in order to do so. They wanted to know our plans. Their leader said they would be back in an hour, and then they would start on one of you." He paused and then asked, "Do you think your people will come and get you?"

Calvin glanced at the next cell over before giving the caliph a wry smile. "If Trella made it to our people, they will definitely come for us." His tone of voice seemed firmer; the slurring gone. "And woe be it to any of the Efreet who get in Captain Train's way!"

Chapter Fifteen

Unknown System, Unknown Date/Time

"That's the last one," said Hooty, fastening the chain. "You really think you can do this?"

Rock walked to the tip of Asp 08's wing and looked back toward the fuselage. He couldn't see it because the space station was now chained to where the wing root joined the fuselage. Although a "fighter" in terms of spacecraft, Asp 08 was 157 feet long, almost twice as long as the space station, and the station fit completely on top of the wing. "Yeah, I think I can. The computer thinks so, anyway. It's a shame we have to leave your fighter up here to get the station down, but mine will be just as useful to us once it's out of fuel."

"You know I'm not real comfortable riding down in the station, right? Are you sure you wouldn't rather have me fly the fighter, and you ride in the station?"

"Oh, stop whining. I'll get you down just fine," said Rock. Both of them heard the unspoken, "I hope."

"Fuel transfer is complete," commed K-Mart. He and Chomper disconnected the makeshift hose from Asp 09 and came back to rejoin the pilots.

"It's your idea," said Chomper. "Are you sure you wouldn't rather ride in the station and let me have your seat in the fighter?"

"No, Rock would get lost without me," said K-Mart. "Besides, the station is chained on. The only way anything bad can happen to you is if something bad happens to us. Now stop your whining and get in. We've got places to go, and hostages to rescue."

CO's Conference Room, TSS Terra, In Orbit Around Keppler-22 'b,' July 17, 2021

"How many Efreet are there?" asked Night.

"Our best guess is that there are about 1,500 of the Efreet on our planet," replied Trella. "Around 800 are in the capital area; the others are scattered around the rest of our planet in small groups."

"So we're going to be outnumbered about 20-1?" asked Master Gunnery Sergeant Bill Hendrick.

"Something like that," said Night with a smile. "Those are my kind of odds."

Hendrick raised an eyebrow, obviously debating the sanity of his platoon's XO. "Do you know something I don't, sir?"

"I know that we're Terran Space Marines," said Night, "and I know nothing has beaten us so far." Several shouts of "Gluck ab!" the platoon's motto, rang out from the long-time members of the platoon, and Night nodded to them in acknowledgement. "We haven't been beaten yet, and I don't plan on starting now. We'll find a way. Besides, that just means there are plenty of targets for everyone." He turned to Trella. "What can you tell us about this jail and its surroundings? Can you draw us a picture? How close will we be able to get without being seen?"

"Getting close to the jail won't be a problem," she said. "In fact, I can even get you into the jail, unnoticed."

All around the table, jaws dropped. "You can?" asked Night. "How are you going to do that?"

"We've been planning to overthrow the Efreet for a long time," replied Trella. "We weren't ready to do it yet, but with your help, maybe we can. Certainly, I want my father and sister back before the Efreet kill them. If we can capture the capital, the Efreet in other areas won't be able to hold out for long. The equipment they use to coordinate their efforts around the world and to talk to their ships in orbit is in the capital. If we can take that from them, we will have the advantage."

"I'm sorry, ma'am," said Night, "but I don't see how capturing the equipment gives you an advantage. If the Efreet have ships in orbit, they can just drop rocks on you until you surrender. How are you going to deal with them?"

"I don't know," replied Trella, "My father had a plan he thought would work, but I don't know what it was. You will have to talk to him. Before you can do that, though, we will have to get him back, and we will need to do it quickly before the Efreet kill him."

"That much is true," said Night. "Okay, tell us how you're going to get us in there."

.

Chapter Sixteen

"So that's the plan," said Night. "Are there any questions?"

No hands went up, but he didn't expect any. Their lack of intel on the target was obvious; the members of the platoon would have to make it up as they went along.

The troops went back to preparing their projectile weapons. Although some preferred more specialized weapons, most of the troops were armed with either an AK-74 or a FN FAL Paratrooper-version rifle, and they also carried either a Glock 17 or Heckler and Koch USP 45 pistol. Night already had his weapons ready, and he was checking the ones he had picked up from Calvin's office.

"Captain Train?" asked a voice from behind him. Night turned to find Captain Nightsong and the other four Aesir.

"Make it quick, sir," said Night. "We're in a hurry."

"I realize that," said the Aesir, "so I will be brief. We are concerned because it looks like you do not intend to take us."

"And you want to go?" asked Night. "I don't think so. We haven't trained together, I don't know any of your capabilities and you don't even look like you're armed. Why would I take you with us?"

"The short answer is we are experienced in manipulating the elements. No matter where you are going or what you are doing, we are force multipliers; we give you capabilities your unit doesn't have.

Please do not feel you need to worry about protecting us. As I believe Reeve Farhome has already demonstrated to your commanding officer, we can take care of ourselves."

Night scanned the Aesir, looking into each of their eyes. He saw one thing in all of them. Competence. They were supremely confident in their abilities. He didn't see any of the fear common to troops going into their first combat. They had obviously all done this before. He nodded once. "You're in. Just make sure you stay out of my way."

"What about me?" asked Lieutenant Rrower, the Mrowry liaison to the platoon, as he approached from the other direction. "If you're going to be outnumbered, I'd be happy to come along and help out."

"Thanks, but I've already got enough dogs and cats on this mission," replied Night. Realizing what he had just said, Night added, "No offense."

"None taken," replied Rrower. "If you need me, I'm available."

"Got it," said Night. He turned to Trella, who had been given back her rod and had reassumed her human form. "Did I miss anything? Is there anything else we should know?"

"No," she replied, "I think you covered everything."

"What about air power?" asked Master Gunnery Sergeant Hendrick from a nearby locker. "Do they have any fighter aircraft or anything similar?"

"No," she answered. "All they have are a few shuttles they use to fly people around."

"But they do have aircraft?" asked Night.

"Yes," said Trella.

"Have Nelson bring some anti-air missiles, just in case," said Night.

"Yes, sir," said Hendrick, who turned and walked off in search of the cyborg.

"Anything else?" asked Night.

"Yes," said Trella. "There is one thing I forgot. You should bring along all of the magic weapons you have."

"Magic weapons?" asked Night. "What the hell are they?"

"They are the ones made from the magic material. They would be especially effective in our world."

"What magic material?" asked Night. Annoyance crept into his voice; acutely aware of the passage of time, he could feel their window of opportunity for getting their people back closing quickly. "Does anyone know what the hell she's talking about?"

"She mentioned this once before," said Mr. Jones. "During the fight in the Mayan temple, most of our weapons weren't effective against the Efreet, and one of the Sila said, 'Use the magic ones.' Some of our weapons were glowing, and when one of them hit an Efreeti it *was* just like magic; the weapon killed it with only one hit."

"Which weapons glowed?"

"Well, Father Zuhlsdorf's, for one," said Mr. Jones. "He killed one of the Efreet, but he's no longer with us. Several other weapons were glowing, too, I think."

"One of 'dem be mine, mon," said Sergeant Margaret 'Witch' Andrews. She walked up to Night and drew her kris from its sheath. Night could see areas of dark and light running across the wavy blade. "The silvery areas started glowing when I had it out near the Efreet."

"Yes," said Trella, edging away from the weapon. "That is one of the magic ones. It has the same magic material in it."

"What are the light areas made of?" asked Night, taking the dagger from her to look at it more closely. The silver inlay was glowing softly.

"Dey be made of silver and nickel."

Night moved the weapon closer to Trella, and the glow became brighter. She edged away from the knife, and the glow faded.

"Doesn't that burn you?" she asked. "I can feel the heat from here."

"No," said Night, "it's not hot at all. What's wrong with it? The silver?"

"I don't know what you call it," said Trella, "but it is the same burn we get from most of the things the people on the planet use to adorn themselves. They wear jewelry made of the silver metal and the yellow metal. Whenever they are wearing it, we can't go near them. It reacts with us."

"So you're allergic to silver and gold?" asked Night. "Do you have the same problem in your world?"

"No," said Trella. "We don't have those metals in our world. Some of the elements you have in this world are not in ours. It is one of the reasons we like coming to this world. It is exciting, even though it is dangerous."

"Anyone got both silver and gold jewelry?" asked Night.

"I do," said Sergeant Adeline Graham. She hadn't lost her love of jewelry in the cyborg conversion, and she pulled a ring off each of her hands. One was silver, the other gold. Night took one in each hand and held them as far apart as he could as he walked toward Trella. Both started glowing.

"I don't know why they do it, but both of them seem to react," said Night, handing the rings back to Sergeant Graham. "Judging by your previous experience with the Efreet, I expect they have a similar weakness to both metals."

"Dude, that's like Superman and kryptonite," said Sergeant Jamal 'Bad Twin' Gordon.

"No, dude, it's more like a werewolf and silver," said his twin, Sergeant Austin 'Good Twin' Gordon. "Hey, dude, that's cool because it really *is* silver. She's prettier than a werewolf, though. Well, when she's not all alien-looking anyway."

"Whatever it is," said Night, "we need to find ourselves a whole bunch of silver bullets."

"I've got a question," said Sergeant Darrin Lancaster. "What's going to happen if we bring silver or gold into their universe? If the metal just glows here when it's around them, what are the silver and gold going to do when we're in their world? It might be better not to have them along if they're going to blow up or something like that."

"Good point," replied Night. "Now may not be the best time to experiment, and we don't have the time to waste getting them made anyway. All right, everyone, leave anything you have that is silver or gold here. Having a gold ring that blows your finger off isn't something we're going to want to deal with."

"You're not going to bring the magic metal?" asked Trella.

"Not this time," replied Night. "We need to test it first before we do. I will, however, start the process of having weapons made in case we need them."

"*Terra*," Night commed, speaking to the ship's artificial intelligence, "*could you please connect me with the logistics officer?*"

"*Certainly,*" replied the AI, "*stand by.*"

A window opened in his mind, and the picture of a dark-haired woman appeared. Under the picture, a line of text read, "Calling Commander Linda Pagant."

After three or four seconds, the text changed to "Connected," and a voice said, "*Commander Pagant.*"

"Hi, ma'am," commed Night. "*We are about to go down to the planet on a combat mission, and I need an emergency run on the replicator in case we need resupply. It appears silver and gold are highly reactive in the other universe, so we need some ammunition made with silver and gold.*"

"*Say that again?*" asked Commander Pagant. "*You need an emergency run on the replicators to make* silver *ammunition? I don't have any silver. Where am I supposed to get the input metal? What do you want me to do? Just toss my jewelry into it?*"

"*You know what?*" said Night. "*That's not a bad idea. Stand by.*" She waited while Night made a second call over his implant, and then the ship's intercom went active with several bells to get everyone's attention.

"*Bong! Bong! Bong!* All hands, this is the Captain!" the CO said. "We have troops going on a rescue mission, and they may need to use silver and gold ammunition in order to kill the enemy. Think of it as if they were going to kill werewolves, because it is not too different; our enemy is especially susceptible to these metals. I need all of you to bring your silver and gold to the replicator. If it's not an heirloom, we need it right now!" The message then repeated.

"Dude!" said Good Twin. "She used my analogy!"

Shuttle 02, Keppler-22 'b,' July 17, 2021

The shuttle touched down, its ramp already in motion. The platoon sprinted out, only to slow down and mill about as they realized there was no enemy to attack or defend against.

"Weirdest damn assault I've ever seen," Master Gunnery Sergeant Bill Hendrick said.

"Okay," said Night, "we're here. Now what?"

"Now I'll take you into my world, but I can only take two at a time. If I take any more, I run the risk of breaking the transporter."

"We wouldn't want that," Gunnery Sergeant Bob 'Mongo' Bryant said, "especially after I'm on the other side. Please don't break it."

"I'll go first," said Night, "along with Master Gunnery Sergeant Hendrick." He indicated Hendrick to Trella. Hendrick nodded his head and stepped forward. "Before we go, ma'am," he said, "I've got a question that's been on the minds of some of the troops. Ain't none of us ever been to another universe before, and we're all kind of wondering…umm…What happens if we die there?"

Trella looked confused. "You want to know what happens if you die in my universe?" she asked. He nodded his head. "If you die in my universe, you're dead."

"Yeah, let's try to avoid anyone getting dead, okay?" asked Night. "We stay together, we fight as a team and we support each other. We grab our folks, and we get the hell out of there. No one's dying today. Let's go."

He held out his hand to Trella, and she took it with one of her own. Her hand was cool to the touch and felt odd although he couldn't tell why…until he remembered what it really looked like.

"We all have to be in physical contact," Trella said, "or it won't work."

Night shouldered his rifle and reached over to take Hendrick's hand.

"Are you ready?" Trella asked.

Night started to nod, but disappeared before he could complete it.

Chapter Seventeen

Ashur, Unknown Date/Time

The sky flashed and turned green. A wave of nausea ran through Night, and he dropped to one knee. A splashing noise came from his right as Master Gunnery Sergeant Hendrick threw up.

"The disorientation will pass quickly," said Trella. "The more times you transfer, the easier it gets."

"I'll be fine," Night said. He looked at Hendrick, who gave him a thumbs-up, along with a wan smile. "Go get the next group." Trella nodded, touched a button on her rod and disappeared.

"That really sucked, sir," said Hendrick. "I hope we don't have to do this too often."

"She said it gets easier," replied Night with a wan smile of his own. Mentally forcing his stomach back into place, he stood up. His eyes scanned the surroundings, focused again, looking for danger. His vision didn't seem to work as well in this universe. They had materialized in an area of rolling hills, similar to the landscape in their universe. Short reddish shrubbery dotted the landscape, with a few larger blue tree analogues scattered widely throughout. Although as tall as trees, they didn't have leaves; instead, thin strands of something hung down from them.

Night pointed to the hill on his right. "Go take a look from that hilltop," he said. He nodded to the one on his left. "I'll check this one. Remember, don't transmit anything. We don't want them to know we're here."

Hendrick nodded and moved off toward the low hill 70 feet to his right. Night turned and jogged to the other hill, his eyes continuing to scan. His hill was closer, and he climbed up the 10-foot high berm, dropping to his hands and knees as he neared the crest. One of the "trees" was nearby. He still couldn't tell what the strands were, but he could see them moving, even though the air was still and heavy. Something seemed unhealthy about the way they twitched, and his skin crawled. The tree seemed to lean toward him, and he instinctively edged away from it.

"Don't let the creeval get any closer to you," said Trella. Night turned, and she pointed to the tree analog. He saw she was back to her normal, alien appearance; that didn't make the situation any less creepy. "I don't know if the spines of the creeval are poisonous to you, but they are certainly poisonous to us. Also, the vines hanging down will grab you and strangle you if you walk underneath them." She paused and then added, "There's nothing to see this way in any event."

She led him back to where Gunnery Sergeant Bob Bryant and Staff Sergeant Alka Zoromski waited. "There may be a problem," she said. "I did not know you had men made of metal. They may not transfer here. Also, when I try to bring them over, it may break my control rod. What do you want me to do?"

"Bring them last," said Night, "and one at a time. I don't want to break the rod, but if we're going to be outnumbered 20-1, we will need their firepower."

Unknown System, Unknown Date/Time

"I see it, damn it," said Rock; "you can stop pointing." He switched to his comm system. *"Hang on; we're going to land on a straight stretch of road. It isn't completely clear of traffic, so things may get a little…bumpy."*

Rock checked the fuel gauge and saw he was only going to get one chance; after that he was going to be flying a glider. One that wasn't meant to be a glider. With a big cylinder on top which increased its drag exponentially. He needed to do it right on the first pass because there wouldn't be a second.

A small column of smoke let him know the direction the wind was blowing, and he flew downwind a mile to the right of the road at 1,200 feet while he surveyed the landing area. Hopefully, not only would the pattern set him up to turn in and land, but also the people driving would get a chance to see him and would get off the road when they saw his intentions.

He extended 10 seconds past the end of the straight section and turned back in, letting his altitude drop slowly with the turn. The right engine coughed, but then settled out as his wings came back to level.

"Looks like there's a vehicle that's going to arrive at the touchdown point at the same time we are," noted K-Mart.

"I see it," Rock said. "I'm going to need every bit of that section to stop. He better see me coming and move."

The driver of the vehicle didn't see them and continued on toward their prospective collision point. At the last second, Rock gave the throttles a nudge, and the fighter jumped forward, just clearing the roof of the vehicle.

"Damn it, I didn't want to have to do that," he said. The burst of power changed their touchdown point from the end of the straight-away to about one quarter of the way down its length. As the wheels touched, Rock jumped on the brakes; even so, he could see the fighter wasn't going to stop before the road turned as it entered a forest.

All of the oncoming traffic saw the giant space fighter taking up both lanes of traffic and got off the road…except for one car, which continued straight at them.

"He's gotta see us," said K-Mart.

"You would think…" replied Rock

The vehicle continued toward them.

"He doesn't see us," said Rock.

"No, I don't think he does," agreed K-Mart, who was looking at the vehicle in his targeting scope. He had a great view of the Sila inside, who was looking down and tapping on something in his lap.

"*Crash positions!*" called Rock.

At the last possible second, the Sila looked up from whatever he was doing. Wide-eyed, he tried to swerve; however, all he succeeded in doing was to lose control of the vehicle as he jerked its control stick to one side. Out of control, it began rolling sideways down the road. Holding the fighter's control stick firmly, Rock averted his eyes so he wouldn't have to see the collision.

Still rolling, the car slammed into the right landing gear, tearing off the strut. The fighter's wingtip crashed to the ground, snapping off the outer 20 feet. The remaining wing dug into the ground and spun the fighter around. Snapping its chains, the space station broke free from *Asp 08*. Launching itself from the left wing, the station hurtled over 100 feet through the air before crashing to the ground and rolling in the direction the fighter had been headed. Not entirely round, imperfections in the space station's structure caused the station to hop and bounce as it headed toward the trees.

The station had enough momentum to make it to the trees, but not enough to break through the first big trees it came to, and it slammed to a halt.

"Is everyone okay?" commed Rock.

"Aside from some bruises and the fact I am hanging upside down from my seat at the moment, yes," replied Chomper. *"Now get us the fuck down!"*

"On our way," said K-Mart. He looked at Rock and asked, "Should we take our weapons or come back and get them?"

"Let's leave them here," Rock replied. "We don't want to look too aggressive on our first meeting with the locals here. Besides, we just saved their astronauts. We're going to be heroes!"

They exited the fighter and slid down the right wing to the ground. "Any landing you can walk away from is a good one, eh?" asked Rock as he stood up.

"I think Chomper is going to take some convincing if you want him to believe that," replied K-Mart as he came to his feet.

Rock and K-Mart raced over to the space station. As Chomper had said, it had come to a stop upside down next to a couple of the larger trees.

"Should we try to roll it back upright?" asked Rock.

"I don't think we can," replied K-Mart. He pointed to where the space station rested. "The station's already sunk several inches into the ground. It's not going anywhere fast. We need to find an entry port."

The two Terrans went in different directions around the station, looking for a way in.

"Got one," called K-Mart. He had almost missed the access door. It was partially under the station, and only the top two feet were accessible; fortunately, that included the handle, and the door opened inward. K-Mart opened the door, and both aviators slid into the station on their stomachs.

Rock pulled a light out of his suit and scanned the interior of the station. He got waves or thumbs-up from everyone but Chomper, who saluted him with a single middle finger. He had already removed a glove so Rock could see it better.

The aviators rescued everyone from their seats and let them wiggle out the access port. "After you," K-Mart said, waving Rock ahead of him. He followed his pilot through the doorway and stood up to find the other Terrans with their hands up, surrounded by Sila troops.

"I should have listened to you and brought my rifle," said Rock. "If those aren't guns they're holding, I don't know what they are."

Efreet Prison Headquarters, Ashur, Unknown Date/Time

"The queen hungers," said the colonel, touching both claws to his chest.

"The eggs hatch," replied the captain, mimicking the gesture.

"Report."

"The caliph and his vizier are in the containment cells, along with two foreigners."

"Foreigners?" asked the colonel. "Where are they from?"

"I believe they are from the other universe," replied the captain. "We caught the caliph's daughters sneaking them into the palace. It is obvious they are conspiring with the other universe. I suspect they are bringing in weapons to the Sila so they can try to overthrow us."

"They *have* seemed more restive recently," said the colonel. "If they were making weapons themselves, I think our spies would have informed us. If they were bringing them in from the other universe, though…we might not have heard about it yet."

"Those were my thoughts as well, sir."

"Obviously, you must torture the information out of them. Find out what they know. Just make sure you don't kill them too fast, like you did the last prisoners. They don't make good examples if you burn them after they are already dead."

"Yes, sir," replied the captain. "I will make sure I get *all* the information from them. It will be a challenge, as the foreigners do not seem to speak either our language or the language of the Sila."

"They may be feigning ignorance," replied the colonel. "After all, how would they do business with the Sila if they couldn't understand them? It makes no sense. They obviously speak the language. Perhaps they just need a little *persuasion*."

"I will do my best."

"I know you will," said the colonel with a smile. "Oh, yes…I know you will."

Chapter Eighteen

Ashur, Unknown Date/Time

"It no longer functions," said Trella, holding out the rod to Night. She had transported all of the Terran soldiers without a problem, but the third time she brought a cyborg, a loud 'pop' was heard from the rod on arrival. Now it appeared dead, leaving Gunnery Sergeant Dantone stranded back in their universe.

"How often does this happen?" asked Night. "Will it work again later?"

"This never happens," said Trella. "Once they cease functioning, they never work again."

"Not working?" asked Corporal Michael Higuchi. "Wait a minute. If it's not working, how are we getting home?"

"We're going to get home however the captain says," replied Master Gunnery Sergeant Bill Hendrick. "And he'll figure it out a lot faster if you shut the hell up and let him think. See that bush over there?" He pointed to a bush about 50 yards away. "Go set up a perimeter over there and watch for Efreet." The soldier jogged off.

Hendrick cocked his head and looked at the control rod. "So, sir, how *are* we getting home?"

"Damned if I know," said Night; "however, I *do* know the CO's in a jail, and we're not leaving without him, so it really doesn't fucking matter *how* the fuck we're getting home at the moment now, does it?"

"When you put it that way, sir, no it doesn't."

"Good. Get the troops rounded up and ready to travel. We're leaving *right now!*"

"Yes, sir!" Hendrick jogged off, already issuing orders. He didn't know much about the whole crossing universes thing, but moving out troops was something he understood *very* well.

"Since it doesn't work, can I have it?" asked Night, pointing at the control rod.

"Yes," said Trella, handing it to him. "I don't know if you are going to try to fix it, but I wouldn't open it if I were you. I hear they catch fire when opened."

"Like I told the master gunnery sergeant, we'll worry about it once we've rescued the prisoners. It looks like the troops are ready; take us where we need to go. And hurry!"

"This way," Trella said, waving to get Hendrick's attention. He nodded, and she ran off, her silks blowing in the wind.

"Move out," ordered Hendricks, and the point men started after Trella, with the rest of the platoon in close pursuit. He pulled Witch aside as she passed. "Keep an eye on the Aesir," he said. "Don't let them get lost."

"Wouldn't dat be a good thing for one of the newbies to do?" asked Sergeant Andrews.

"No, it would be a good thing for *you* to fucking do," replied Hendrick.

"Ya, mon," said the Jamaican sergeant with a mental sigh. "I'm on it."

The platoon didn't have far to go; after a five minute run, Trella stopped and reached into one of the little bushes that covered the landscape.

"We're here," she said. With a small 'click,' a small trap door appeared on the ground. "This tunnel will allow us to get to the prison without the Efreet seeing us."

"Is that the same tunnel you used earlier to go to the castle?" asked Night.

"Yes it is," replied Trella. "Why?"

"Because I thought you said the Efreet knew about the tunnel. It may not be safe any longer."

"There is no other way to get to the prison undetected," said Trella. "With the control rod broken, I can't even change your appearance. You would be spotted in an instant, and dead shortly thereafter. The Efreet have a saying, 'Kill first and ask questions later.'"

"We have a similar saying when it comes to fighting enemies," said Night, "but that one will work just as well." He looked into the tunnel and made up his mind. "We'll use the tunnel system, but my men will lead."

"I would be quite happy to have them lead," said Trella. "If the Efreet are in the tunnels, their flamecasters will be deadly."

"Zoromski, Yokaze, you two have point," said Night. "Watch for the Efreet. They may be down there with us. They have flame weapons. If you see them, don't wait for orders; kill them on contact."

Both men nodded in acknowledgement and started toward the tunnel.

"They should stop when we reach the second cross passage," said Trella. "We will need to turn there."

The two men nodded again and went into the tunnel. Yokaze was as silent as a ninja; Zoromski not much louder. They went down the ramp and slowed to let their eyes adjust to the gloom. Although there were no lights in the tunnel, something in the walls gave off enough light to see a short distance. They began moving down the passageway with Yokaze on the left and Zoromski on the right.

After they passed the first cross passage, Yokaze stopped suddenly. When Zoromski looked over, Yokaze gave him the hand signal to withdraw. Both men retreated about 50 feet down the tunnel.

"What's wrong?" whispered Zoromski.

"Didn't you smell them?" asked Yokaze. "They have a musty smell, almost fishy in nature."

"They?"

"Hai!" said Yokaze softly. "I heard something from both sides of the tunnel. I think there are at least two of them."

"I'll take the one on the right," said Zoromski. "You get the one on the left."

"When you are ready, kill him; I will kill mine at the same time."

Zoromski nodded and brought his FN FAL rifle to the ready. He gave Yokaze a couple of seconds and then advanced down the tunnel. As he passed the cross passage, he began to notice the musty odor Yokaze had mentioned. Just a little on the fishy side of smelly sweat socks. Zoromski knew he was close, and his eyes scanned back and forth as he crept down the tunnel. After a couple of steps, he could see the outline of an Efreeti. He couldn't see the creature, so much as he could see the lack of luminescence behind it.

The Efreeti moved a little as it readjusted its position, giving Zoromski the chance to see where its head was. The Terran took one more breath and slowly released it while stroking the trigger. As the suppressor on his rifle coughed, he heard a muffled 'twang.' Both Efreet fell backward.

He approached the pair and saw they were both dead. His had a bullet hole in the center of its forehead; Yokaze's had a crossbow bolt sticking out of its left eye.

Fifteen feet beyond the sentries was the second cross passage. "We're here," said Yokaze. "If you would like to get our guide, I will watch out for the enemy."

Zoromski left and reappeared a minute later with Trella and Night. "We go left here," said Trella.

"What lies down these other passageways?" asked Night.

"If you continue straight down the tunnel, you will come to the castle exit," Trella replied. "The tunnel to the right leads to another spot in the forest we use to go to a neighboring town."

Night pointed at the center passage. "So, this is where the Efreet are most likely to come from when they notice their sentries aren't reporting?"

Trella nodded. "Yes," she said. "The jail exit is disguised, so they probably won't have found it yet. We left the end of the tunnel unfinished in case any of the Efreet ever made it down here."

"Tanker, front and center," Night said in a forced whisper. Corporal Patrick 'Tanker' Harris eased his way to the front, the other troopers making room for the cyborg to pass.

"Tanker, I want you and Yokaze to guard this center passage," said Night. "If the Efreet come looking for their troops, they will be coming from this direction. I need you to hold this passage so we can get back out again."

"Will do, sir," said Corporal Harris. Yokaze gave a short nod of acknowledgement.

"Lead on," Night said to Trella. "I'm sure we're running out of time."

Cells, Jail for Special Prisoners, Ashur, Unknown Date/Time

"How are you doing over there, Master Chief?" asked Calvin.

"I'm having a hell of a day, sir," he replied. "I'm just loving my job. Where else can you go to new universes and get the shit tased out of you?" The sarcasm left his voice as he asked, "How about you, sir? How's the head?"

"Better," said Calvin, "but most of the trip here is a blur."

We're in some sort of underground prison," Master Chief related. "All the guards I've seen have looked alert. It's going to be tough to break out of here."

"Break out?" asked the caliph. "There is no breaking out of here. The only way to leave here is through death."

"We've been in worse dungeons," said Calvin, "and I guarantee our friends are on the way."

"They had best hurry," replied the caliph. "The Efreet are not known for their patience, especially when it comes to torture."

Chapter Nineteen

Tunnels, Ashur, Unknown Date/Time

Yokaze squeezed Corporal Harris' arm a full second before the Efreet appeared on any of Tanker's systems. Tanker didn't know how Yokaze was able to beat the best audio and visual technology the former Alliance had to offer, but he had. He nodded slowly, and Yokaze withdrew to the side of the passageway.

The only warning the Efreet had was a slight whirring sound as Tanker's M230 chain gun spun up to speed, and then 30 mm rounds tore the group apart. The weapon fired at a rate of over 600 rounds per minute, and Harris walked the shells back and forth across the passage like a fire hose. All the Efreet went down; most in more than one piece. Several were carrying flamecasters, and the tunnel was illuminated by the light of burning fuel as the holding canisters were ruptured.

Harris had only taken one step down the tunnel to confirm the Efreet were dead when the flames found the group's explosives, and the Terrans were blown backward as they detonated, the shockwave enormous in the confined space.

Even cyborgs aren't immune to brain trauma, and Harris was momentarily stunned. Lying on his back in the center of the tunnel, he realized his vision was beginning to cloud over. He forced himself to full awareness, realizing his systems *didn't* cloud over. He wiped his visual monitors, and they cleared, only to immediately start clouding over again. It took him a second, but then he realized what was happening.

Dirt was falling from the tunnel roof. The ceiling was collapsing.

He rolled over to find Yokaze a little way further back. Lighter, Yokaze had flown further in the explosion. Harris tried to stand up, only to find his right leg was inoperative. He ran a quick diagnostic; one of the drive motors was shot. He wasn't going anywhere quickly. He got his left leg under him and stood, just as a massive 'crack!' resounded through the tunnel as the beam above him split. Reacting without thinking, he put both hands up and braced the beam, pushing it back up into place.

"Yokaze!" he called. "Get up. Quickly!"

The Japanese man was already starting to move; when he heard Harris' voice, he shook his head and stumbled unsteadily to his feet. His eyes opened wide in shock as he turned to find Harris holding up the ceiling. "What can I do to help?" he asked.

"You can get the hell out of here," said Harris. "My right leg is shot, and the way the pressure on this is building, my other leg is going to fail in about 10 seconds. Once you're clear, I'll follow. *Go!*"

"We do not leave men behind," said Yokaze.

"You're not leaving me behind. There's nothing you can do. Just go, and I'll follow."

Yokaze turned and sprinted down to the cross passage. "I'm clear," he called. "Come on!"

Harris dropped his hands and began hopping down the passageway, leaning on the left side of the tunnel for support. As soon as his hands came down, the timber snapped, and the roof started caving in. The faster he hopped, the faster it seemed to him that the ceiling collapsed behind him. Within four hops, the falling roof had caught up with him; within six he was being buried. There was no seventh, as the roof completely let go, sealing the tunnel.

The tunnel continued to collapse, getting closer and closer to Yokaze. The Japanese man bowed in honor of his fallen comrade and ran to catch up with the platoon; they weren't getting Harris out from under that much dirt without an excavator.

Caliph's Retreat, Wendar, Day 2 of the Second Akhet, 15th Dynasty, Year 14

After their capture, the Terrans had been blindfolded and then subjected to two hours of extremely bumpy travel on some sort of electric vehicle. When the vehicle finally stopped, the Terrans were allowed to remove their blindfolds. They had arrived at a clearing in the middle of the forest. In the center was a house, or maybe a castle, surrounded by a 12-foot wall. It was probably a castle, as the wall was manned by a host of maroon-uniformed troops, all of whom were armed and alert. Before the gate closed, the Terrans could see the forest had been cleared at least 100 feet away from the wall to provide a clear field of fire.

The Terrans were ushered into the large sandstone mansion and brought to a small throne room. It had to be a throne room, K-Mart thought, as there was a large, ornate chair at the other end of the room on a small dais. A male Sila in flowing robes sat on the chair, with a well-dressed male standing on either side of him.

Based on the amount of orange braid on his uniform, the trooper that led the Terrans in appeared to be fairly senior. He led them to the dais and said simply, "Bow."

Seeing no reason not to, the Terrans all bowed as one.

"Thank you very much for coming here to meet me," said the male in the chair. "I am Khufu, Caliph of Abunar. To my right is Grand Vizier Nefermaat, and to my left is Vizier Kawab."

"You're welcome...I guess," said Rock. "It didn't appear we had much choice in the matter."

"Alas, that is true," agreed the caliph, "for which I am most sorry. Unfortunately, we are going through a period of...difficulties, and my military took you into custody for your own good."

"Our own good?" asked K-Mart. "What kind of problems are you having?"

"Some of our religious leaders want to return to the ways of old. They see the new technology we are working on as evil, and the arrival of the Efreet as a sign we have offended the gods. They want us to give up all technology and go back to living on farms."

"That's ludicrous," said Chomper. "How could you make that kind of transition?"

"We can't," said the caliph. "And yet, more and more of our youth follow those sect leaders every day. I expect they will begin calling for my head soon."

"We believe this effort is being financed by either the caliphate to the east or to the south of us," said Grand Vizier Nefermaat; "however, we have not been able to prove anything yet. Both have long desired parts of our caliphate for their own."

"Is there anything we can do to help?" asked Rock.

"I don't know if there is anything you *can* do to help," said the caliph. "A display of power would be nice, but I understand your ship is wrecked beyond our ability to repair."

"That's true," agreed Hooty, glaring at Rock. "Unfortunately, it was destroyed when we landed here."

"It was destroyed bringing back *your* space station," added Rock, "along with the astronauts the Efreet left there to die."

"For which we are in your debt," said the caliph. "However, since you are unable to impress my subjects with your power, it is best if we simply keep you out of sight. That way you remain mysterious. It will only work for a short while, but it is better than nothing."

Vizier Kawab coughed politely to get the caliph's attention. "In addition to Grand Vizier Nefermaat, who is responsible for the administration of the caliphate," the caliph said, "I have a few other viziers who handle certain areas of concern. Vizier Kawab is my Administrator for Other-Worldly Affairs."

"If my caliph will excuse me for interrupting," said Kawab, "I believe I have a solution that should work well for everyone involved."

"Please go ahead," the caliph urged; "tell me your solution."

Vizier Kawab bowed. "I believe the best thing for all concerned would be to send the newcomers on a mission across the boundary."

"What boundary is that?" asked Rock.

"The boundary between our world and yours," replied Kawab. "Our astronauts told me that you come from across the shroud of the universe; by sending you back to your universe, the caliph can say he has sent you on a mission. This increases his status by appearing to give orders to members of a star-faring race. It will make it harder for his enemies to call for his overthrow."

"It will also help me," continued Kawab after a moment. "I know the race on the other side of the boundary just received a large group of prisoners at their holding facility. I am curious as to whether the prisoners might assist us in the coming war."

"We do not know there will *be* war," Grand Vizier Nefermaat interrupted.

"There will be war," replied Kawab. "The only question is who will attack us first. Once one of them does, the other is sure to join. I would rather be prepared with allies than be destroyed."

"That makes sense," said Chomper. "You did, however, say there was something in it for everyone. What is in it for us?"

"For you?" asked Kawab. "You get to continue living."

Chapter Twenty

The lights snapped on, blinding the prisoners, and the sounds of marching boots echoed through the cell block.

"It sounds like the Efreet are back with reinforcements," noted the caliph. "I'm sorry, but it appears your friends are too late."

"Just hold on," said Calvin. "They will come."

"I implemented a plan for civil disobedience before we left the castle," said the caliph. "I do not know if it will help, or how much, but I had hoped it would slow the Efreet down and give your troops time to get here. Alas, it appears they will be too late."

Calvin saw the caliph was correct about the reinforcements. This time there were four of the brown-robed troopers and six of the armored ones with flamecasters accompanying the Efreeti in the black leather. All were armed and looked serious.

The Efreeti in black leather stopped in front of Master Chief's cell and said something to him.

"The captain wishes to know how long you have been coming here," translated the caliph, "and who your contacts are." The Efreeti spoke a little more. "He also believes you speak our language and should understand him on your own. He feels you are trying to hide your crimes by pretending to not understand him."

"Oh, I understand him, all right," said Master Chief. "I understand he is a worthless piece of shit that is too scared of me to come in and tell me that to my face."

"Are you sure you wish me to translate that?" asked the caliph. "Your punishment is sure to be swift and harsh."

"Yes, I want you to translate it," said Master Chief. "Word for word." He repeated what he had said so that the caliph could get it right.

If Master Chief had been hoping for a reaction from the captain, he was disappointed. The Efreeti continued to look at him and said a single word.

One of the brown-robed Efreet stepped forward and fired his taser weapon at Master Chief. Ready for the attack, Master Chief used a downward tae kwon do block, and he knocked one of the metal leads out of the air. The other lead penetrated his leg, but without the first wire, the circuit was incomplete and no current flowed.

With a look of disdain, Master Chief plucked the lead out of his leg and threw it on the floor. "Is that the best—"

Focused on the captain, he didn't see one of the other brown-robed Efreet move. The Efreeti fired on Master Chief without warning and both leads penetrated. Master Chief fell to the floor as the electricity coursed through his body.

"Sh–, sh–, sh–, shit," he was able to finally say as he convulsed on the floor of his cell. The electrocution continued for five seconds, then 10.

"Enough!" said Calvin.

The captain looked at Calvin, barking out a question. "He wants to know if you will talk," the caliph translated.

"Yes, I'll talk," said Calvin. The flow of electricity into Master Chief ceased.

"Don't do it, sir," gasped Master Chief, as the captain said something to Calvin.

"The captain wishes to know the same things," said the caliph. "How long you have been coming here and who your contacts are."

"Tell him I have been coming here for 10 years," said Calvin, "and those two Efreet are my contacts." He pointed at two of the Efreet in full armor. As the caliph translated, the two Efreet lost some of their intensity and began to shift their weight from foot to foot.

Both said something, obviously in denial.

"You lie," came the translated response from the captain. He made a motion with one of his claws, and the trooper restored the electricity flow into Master Chief. Sadistically twisting the dial on the back of his wrist, he increased the intensity, and Master Chief's struggles grew more violent.

After another 10 seconds, the captain made the claw motion again, and the current was turned off. Master Chief relaxed, breathing heavily.

The captain motioned, and one of the armored troopers opened the door to Master Chief's cell. Without hesitation, the captain walked over to where Master Chief lay and kicked him in the ribs. "Fuck!" Master Chief yelled.

The captain kicked him again, and Calvin heard one of Master Chief's ribs snap. This time, Master Chief saw it coming and only a muffled grunt escaped him. Several more kicks followed. Too weak to go on the offensive, Master Chief curled up in a ball, trying to protect himself the best he could. The captain kicked him several more times, but was interrupted by a distant 'boom,' that was felt more than heard.

The captain's head snapped up, and he looked around at his troops to see if any of them knew the cause of the noise. Seeing no recognition, he walked out of the cell and motioned for the armored Efreeti to lock it back up again.

He walked over and said something to Calvin. "I will be back shortly to discuss the issue with you further," the caliph translated. "It is unlikely both of you foreigners will survive our next conversation."

Tunnels, Ashur, Unknown Date/Time

"How much further?" Night asked.

"None; we're here," said Trella, walking alongside him.

The tunnel extended into the darkness past where she had stopped. On the wall was a small outcropping of rock, the same as hundreds of others they had passed along the way. This one was different; Trella pulled on it, and a six-inch cube slid out of the wall. Reaching in, she pushed a button on the left side of the hole, and, with a small 'click,' a doorway appeared in the wall next to it.

Trella pulled the door open and stepped aside. "We think this is the lowest level of the jail," she said. "We haven't explored any further, because we didn't want to get caught and let the Efreet know we had access."

A 'boom' reverberated through the tunnel from behind them.

"Shit," said Night. "There goes the element of surprise. Wraith, Zoromski, take point." Staff Sergeant Ji-Woo and Staff Sergeant

Zoromski moved to the door. "Trella thinks this is the lowest area of the jail, so we may need to go up to find our folks. Be on the lookout for stairs or doors that might lead to stairs."

The two soldiers entered the jail complex and found themselves in a 10-foot square cell. The sole occupant was a skeleton in the corner. The dank, musty smell of decay permeated the area.

Wraith crossed the cell to the door. Testing it, she found the door was locked.

"Really?" asked Zoromski. "Who locks a door they aren't using?"

Wraith nodded toward the skeleton. "Maybe they just locked the door and left the person over there to die."

"That would suck."

Wraith nodded as Night approached, rifle at the ready. "What's up?" he asked.

"It's locked," said Wraith. "Since they already know we're coming, want me to blow it?"

"Quickly," replied Night. "I expect we'll have company soon."

"I can take care of that," said a new voice. Night turned to find one of the Aesir. "Landslide?"

"Indeed," said the Aesir. He put his finger next to where the bolt extended from the locking mechanism. While the Terrans watched, the bolt dissolved to a fine powder, and the door eased open an inch.

"That's pretty handy," said Zoromski.

Night looked at Landslide, reassessing his earlier thoughts. He quickly came to a conclusion and nodded. "Thanks," he said in apology. He turned back to his troops. "What? Are you guys waiting on an engraved invitation? Let's go."

Caliph's Retreat, Wendar, Day 2 of the Second Akhet, 15th Dynasty, Year 14

"I'm not sure I like the tone of that, mate," said Rock. "What do you mean, 'We get to continue living?'"

"Ever since you crossed into our universe, you have been slowly dying," said Vizier Kawab. "I cannot confirm it for a fact, but I know that when we send people across the border for long periods of time, they eventually sicken and die. At first, we thought it was some new disease they had contracted, and we wouldn't let them return because of it. They all died. It wasn't until much later that we realized we are just not completely compatible with your universe."

"And you suspect we are similarly incompatible with your universe?" asked K-Mart.

"I do," replied Kawab. "If there is something that keeps us from staying in your universe long-term, our universe probably does the same to you. To avoid the effects, you will have to spend time across the border periodically or you will die. And while you're there…"

"We could accomplish your mission for you," finished Rock.

"Exactly," said the vizier with a Sila version of a smile.

"What do you know about the prisoners or the race holding them?" asked K-Mart.

"The race holding them looks more like you than us," said Kawab, "especially your hands. They also have fleshy appendages for grasping things, not bone like us." He clicked his talons together in emphasis.

"We call ours, 'fingers,'" said Chomper.

"Ah...fingers," said Kawab. "I will try to remember that. Yes, the race across the boundary is very much like you in form; however, they are enormous. They are almost three times your size."

"Giants!" said Rock.

"The Jotunn," agreed K-Mart, nodding his head. "We figured as much. Let me guess, the new race of prisoners also looks like we do, but they are a little smaller and either green or black in color."

"With pointed ears," added Hooty.

"Yes, the reports indicate they are green-skinned and have pointed ears," said Kawab. "How did you know?"

"The prisoners are our allies on the other side of the boundary," replied K-Mart. "In fact, the reason we came here is that we were searching for them." He looked at the other Terrans. "Looks like we found them."

"Yeah," said Chomper; "too bad there's no way to let anyone know."

"So you will go then?" asked Kawab.

"Yes," said K-Mart as the rest of the group nodded, "we'll go."

The vizier smiled again. "I rather thought you might."

Chapter Twenty-One

Jail for Special Prisoners, Ashur, Unknown Date/Time

The sound of gunfire reverberated through the cell block. *"We've found the stairs,"* commed Wraith, *"but we're taking fire. Literally, fire!"*

Night approached the staircase at the passageway's "T" intersection as a wall of flames came shooting down it. The fire cleared and Staff Sergeant Zoromski leaned in and fired a burst up the stairwell. He quickly ducked back as another sheet of flames roared down.

"They're hard to see up there," said Zoromski. "There are several wearing some sort of black armor. Looks like they are heavy on flamethrowers."

"No kidding," Night stuck his head in the stairwell, then dodged back out of the way. "They're going to be tough to kill up there." He switched to his comm. *"Nelson, we need you up front."*

"On my way."

Night checked the passageways which ran left and right. *"Wraith,"* Night commed. *"Take half of Alpha Squad and check the passage to the left. Gunnery Sergeant Bryant, take the other half and go down to the right. See if you can find us another way up."*

"I'm here, sir," said Sergeant George Nelson.

"Good," Night replied. "There are a bunch of Efreet up the stairwell, wearing some kind of armor. See what you can do about thinning them out some, would you? Beware, they have flamethrowers."

"I can take a little bit of heat," the cyborg replied. "As long as I don't have to stand in it too long, I shouldn't get all melty." He unclipped two boxes from his back and laid them aside. "I'll be even better without these," he added.

Nelson walked over to the stairwell. 10 stairs went up to a landing, and then the stairs looped back to the right as they continued up. "Be right back," Nelson said as he passed Zoromski.

Unlike the other soldiers who leaned into the stairwell to fire a burst and then withdrew, Nelson charged up the stairway to the landing and rounded the corner. He was met with a wall of flame and burning fluids. His sensors indicated the fluids were sticking to him and burning at a temperature that was much hotter than expected.

His proto-skin was already starting to gel as his Mrowry autocannon came into line with the fire he was taking. He swept the barrel of his weapon back and forth across the top of the stairwell, and the flames ceased. Realizing he was still on fire, he ran back down the stairs, dropping his weapon as he reached the landing. Throwing himself to the floor, he rolled back and forth, trying to smother the flames. Whatever liquid the Efreet were using was difficult to extinguish, causing him to have to lay flat on his stomach for several seconds to put it out, which allowed the fluid to burn his back until he could flip over.

Zoromski and Staff Sergeant Rainer Koppenhoefer charged up the stairs, with most of Bravo Squad in trail.

As Sergeant Nelson got to his feet, Night could see several places where the metal substructure of his back was visible.

"That was kind of hot," Nelson said. "I could feel my brain cooking." As he spoke, his nose drooped to below his mouth, and the right side of his face sagged noticeably.

"I'm amazed your rifle didn't blow up," said Night.

"The autocannon is tough," said Nelson. "The Mrowry know how to build them. The ammo in Tanker's weapon would probably have cooked off. You're lucky you had me." He attempted a smile as he re-clipped the two boxes to his back, but only succeeded in jiggling the proto-flesh a little.

"*We're clear up here on the next level*," commed Staff Sergeant Zoromski.

"*I copy*," commed Night. "*Wraith, Mongo, have you had any luck?*"

"*None here*," said Wraith. "*I'm at a dead end.*"

"*Me too*," added Gunnery Sergeant Bryant. "*Dead end.*"

"*All right, come join us on the next level*," replied Night. "*We're moving up.*"

Efreet Prison Headquarters, Ashur, Unknown Date/Time

"The queen hungers," said the colonel, touching both claws to his chest.

"The eggs hatch," replied the captain and lieutenant in tandem, mimicking the gesture.

"I need you to take a squad to the airfield," said the colonel to the lieutenant. "Something is jamming our transmission, and we need to get the alert shuttles launched immediately."

The captain looked out the window and could see smoke rising from several places. "What is happening?"

"The Sila are revolting," said the colonel. "We must put them down, and put them down hard. Lieutenant, take no chances along the way; kill any Sila you see. Let them experience the penalty for their insolence."

"As you command," said the lieutenant.

"What about the prisoners?" asked the captain.

"Kill them. Kill them all."

Jail for Special Prisoners, Ashur, Unknown Date/Time

"*This level is empty,*" commed Staff Sergeant 'Hoofer' Koppenhoefer. "*We have come to another set of stairs.*"

"*Hoofer, Wraith, up the stairs,*" said Night.

"*Gluck ab!*" they chorused. Reaching the top of the stairs Hoofer turned left, and Wraith turned right…and came face to face with a squad of Efreet. Although the reptilian Efreet were fast, Wraith was faster, and she emptied the entire 20-round magazine from her FAL rifle into the group. "*I'm out!*" she commed, diving for the floor to give Hoofer a clear line of fire.

The former German Kommando Spezialkrafte trooper had already turned, and he fired his Heckler & Koch G36 assault rifle into the two Efreet still standing. Hearing movement from further down the passage, he added a 40 mm grenade from the under-barrel launcher. The shock wave echoed down the passage as it exploded, and he could see dust coming down from the ceiling in a number of places.

Wraith saw movement from behind the German. "*Hoofer, look out!*" she yelled, frantically trying to reload.

A wall of flame engulfed Hoofer, and the smell of charred meat filled the passageway.

Gunnery Sergeant Bryant dove up the remaining steps and fired down the hallway as Hoofer collapsed; Wraith finished reloading and also fired. The smoke cleared to reveal two dead Efreet, hit in numerous places.

"*Medic!*" commed Wraith.

Within seconds, the Ground Force's medic, Sergeant Burt Yankiver, was at Hoofer's side.

"Can you save him, Yank?" asked Night.

"If he were in a suit, maybe," replied Sergeant Yankiver. "As it is, all I can do is make him comfortable."

"Do what you can," said Night.

Gunfire echoed from the floor below. "*We're getting hit from behind,*" commed Sergeant Rick 'Happy' Day. "*They've got some kind of – fuck! – flechette thrower. Corporal Holm is down. Holy shit! We need some help back here!*"

"*I'm on it, sir,*" commed Master Gunnery Sergeant Hendrick.

Fuck, thought Night. What else could go wrong?

"*Hey mon,*" commed Sergeant Andrews, "*has anyone seen the elves?*"

Chapter Twenty-Two

Caliph's Retreat, Wendar, Day 7 of the Second Akhet, 15th Dynasty, Year 14

"We normally cross the boundary here," said Vizier Kawab. "It is protected from prying eyes and comes out in a safe area." Another male approached the group. "This is Hori," Kawab added. "He will be your guide."

"How well does he know the area?" asked Hooty.

"He is our most experienced guide," said Kawab. "Hori has been across the boundary more times than anyone else."

"Hori, are you familiar with the plan?" asked K-Mart.

"I am," said Hori. "We will go through to the other side. It will take me two trips because I can only safely transport two at a time. Once we are all on the other side, I will lead you to a hill that overlooks the prison complex, so you can see if the prisoners are the ones you call 'Aesir.'"

Vizier Kawab walked a little way from the group and then turned and asked, "Lieutenant Knaus, could I have a word with you in private?"

"Sure," said K-Mart. "Be right back." He walked over to join the vizier.

"Right," said Rock to Hori, continuing in K-Mart's absence. "We'll see if there is any way to get close enough to talk to them. If so, we will attempt it. If not, we will come back and work out what to do next."

"Got it," replied Hori. "I am ready when you are."

"Just a second," said Rock, "we still have one more issue to decide."

"Whether to wear the suits or not, aye?" asked Hooty. "I still say we should wear them."

"They will give us *some* protection," said Rock, "but they really don't offer the same combat capability as the suits the platoon wears. They probably won't stop a bullet or laser."

"Yeah, but they give us some extra processing power if we have to learn a new language," argued Hooty. "They also have a limited pharmacopeia if we need that, too."

"I think we ought to conserve the batteries on them as much as possible," said K-Mart, rejoining the group. "We don't know how long we're going to be here."

"In the interest of time," said Rock, "why don't we vote. My vote is 'I don't care.'"

"I want to wear them," said Hooty.

"I'd rather not wear them," said K-Mart, "but then again, it really doesn't matter that much to me."

"I'd rather wear them," said Chomper, "but I'm like K-Mart; it doesn't really matter either way."

"Okay," said Rock, "the 'ayes' have it; we'll wear them."

The suits had been brought out earlier and checked; it was only a couple of minutes before everyone was dressed and ready. "We're ready, Hori," said Rock, "let's go."

Hori brought out a short golden rod with several buttons on it. "I need to be in contact with the first two people that are going."

"Good luck," said Vizier Kawab. "May the Protector watch out for you, in this world and the next."

"*Asp 08* leads the way," Rock said as he put his hand on Hori's arm. "Let's go, K-Mart."

K-Mart placed his hand on Hori's other arm and nodded once. "Let's go kick some giant butt."

Hori pushed a button on the rod, and the three vanished with a flash.

Cells, Jail for Special Prisoners, Ashur, Unknown Date/Time

The lights snapped on again and booted feet could be heard approaching quickly. Calvin looked through the gaps between his fingers while his eyes adjusted and saw the leader and six of the armored Efreet. No taser troops? That couldn't be good.

The Efreeti captain said something to Master Chief. "It appears the resistance has started, because he said the citizens are in revolt," the caliph translated. "He also said we shouldn't get excited because we will be dead long before any of them can get here."

"Wouldn't you like to come in here and kill me yourself?" asked Master Chief.

"He said that while it would be fun, he doesn't have time for you," said the caliph. "He is leaving to deal with your friends but wanted to see you burn, first."

The captain stepped out of the way and motioned his troopers forward. Three approached each of the cells. While two stood at the ready, the other unlocked the cell doors. As the doors opened, the

Efreet in front of the cells each took a step forward, arming their flamecasters as they stepped into the cells.

"*Maximus!*" yelled a voice from behind the Efreet. The air shimmered, and the Aesir team appeared, Farhome towering above the rest.

Over nine feet tall, Farhome stepped forward into Calvin's cell and took one of the armored Efreeti's heads in each of his oversized hands. Farhome slammed them together, then dropped their inert forms to the floor. With a giggle, he tossed a sheathed sword to Calvin.

Landslide appeared next to the two Efreet in Master Chief's cell. Before they could move, he touched the trigger mechanisms of their flamecasters, then dove to the side. Both tried to pull the triggers, but found them locked in place.

With a command in their own language, flames covered the armor of the remaining four Efreet, and they stepped forward to engage the Aesir.

The two facing Landslide reached forward to grab him in a burning embrace, but their flames suddenly extinguished.

"Oh, you like fire, do you?" asked Captain Nightsong from behind them as he stuck a finger into the joints of their armor. Both Efreet began screaming as flames appeared inside their armor, and their skin started to melt. Unable to escape the flames, they dropped and tried frantically to put them out by rolling on the floor.

Master Chief and the Aesir jumped out of the way of the slashing tails; the vizier remaining in the corner out of the way. Steam poured from the joints in the armor as the Efreet cooked.

The Efreeti trooper outside of Master Chief's cell saw the battle going against them and turned to run. As he passed Landslide, the

Aesir reached through the cell bars from his knees to slap the tanks on the Efreeti's back. The trooper made it four more steps before the tanks began falling apart. A hole appeared in the left tank, which was apparently the propellant for the flamecaster, as the escaping gas spun the Efreeti around to slam into the wall. With a splash, the bottom of the fuel tank fell off, and the trooper was doused in flammable fluid. Something sparked as the Efreeti slammed into the wall again, and he was transformed into a seven-foot tall tower of smoke and flames. The Efreeti screamed as he righted himself and ran down the hall, trailing smoke. Blinded by the smoke, flames and pain, he ran full-speed into the wall at the end of the passage. The Efreeti fell to the floor and lay still, flames crackling over his body as the rest of the fuel and flesh was consumed.

The final trooper charged into the cell, intending to kill the caliph, but was intercepted by Calvin who jumped in front of him. Calvin drew the sword, a rapier, from its sheath. As he brought the rapier to the ready position, the blade burst into flames and began glowing a bright blue down the length of its silver surface.

Faced with the rapier, the Efreeti stopped and grabbed the handle of his flamecaster. He brought it up to fire, but was hammered down from behind by Farhome with a double fist. "Oooh, hot!" cried Farhome. He began blowing on his hands, which had been singed by the flames on the Efreeti's armor.

Seeing no way out, the Efreeti captain grabbed the seemingly defenseless Cyclone from behind and put a knife to her throat. The Aesir smiled in his grasp and brought a finger up to the knife while her other hand reached back to touch the captain on his nose. As the circuit closed, 75,000 volts flowed through the captain, and all his muscles spasmed. Cyclone pushed backward to the wall so the captain wouldn't fall and continued to electrocute him. Turning her head, she watched until smoke began to trail from the corners of the captain's eyes before she released him. The Efreeti fell to the floor, dead.

In four seconds, it was over.

"You have interesting friends," said the caliph as a silence fell over the cell block. "I take it the dark one is the one you call 'Night?'" he asked, looking at Farhome.

"No," said Calvin, "these are some of our allies; Night is even more deadly."

"I am sure there is a story there," said the caliph, "and I would like to hear more about it later, but I need to go join my people and oversee the revolt. You will remember the Efreet accusing me of plotting to overthrow them? We were."

"I believe Night and the rest of my troops will be here in a few seconds," said Calvin as gunfire sounded close by. "If you wait a minute or two, we will have their support, too."

"I know where they are," said Captain Nightsong. He began walking down the passage. "This way."

"Thanks for the sword," said Calvin to Farhome as he stuck the rapier back into the sheath.

Farhome transformed back to his normal size. "Heehee, that was the sword I stuck through your foot," he said. "I thought you'd like it back."

"The flames were a nice touch."

"Flames?" asked Farhome, suddenly serious. "I thought you did that. The flames weren't mine."

Chapter Twenty-Three

"*O*strich has two flechettes in his leg," commed Corporal Michael 'Gooch' Higuchi, the Space Force's medic. "*I'll have him patched up in two minutes. Homey and Milly are both down.*"

With Hendrick directing, the firefight on the lower level was over within 30 seconds. Another six Efreet were dead, but the new flechette guns had not only claimed Corporal Steve Holm, but also Sergeant Milissa Story. Both were relative newcomers to the platoon; unfortunately, combat had a way of singling newcomers out. Corporal Pat 'Ostrich' Burke was another newcomer; at least he would live to fight another day.

"*I've got the next staircase up,*" said Wraith. "*Captain Train, you'll want to come see this. You're not going to believe it…*"

Damn it, what now, Night wondered as he sprinted toward the front of the group. "Well, I'll be damned," he said as he came upon Captain Nightsong leading Calvin, Master Chief and a number of civilians down the stairs.

"Probably," said Calvin, "but then again, so probably will the rest of us."

"What the hell happened, Skipper?" asked Night.

"It turns out there's a little more to an Eco Warrior team than meets the eye," replied Calvin. "They saved us just before the Efreet could roast us with their flamecasters."

221

"Flamecasters, huh?" asked Night. "Are those the things they're using as flamethrowers?"

"Yeah," said Calvin. "In addition to working like flamethrowers, they can also shoot fireballs with them, and the troops can cover themselves in flames. They're pretty nasty."

"I know," said Night, "We lost Koppenhoefer to one of them."

"Damn," said Calvin. "That's not a good way to go."

"No it's not," agreed Night. "One also melted most of the face off Sergeant Nelson. The Efreet have some sort of flechette thrower, too. We've lost a couple of troops to them."

"Shit," said Calvin. "Well, let's regroup and get the hell out of here. We need to get the caliph back to the castle, so he can direct the civil insurrection that's going on."

"Sorry, sir, but that will not be possible," said Yokaze as he ran up. "We were attacked by a group of Efreet coming from the castle, and when Tanker shot them, one blew up. The tunnel collapsed, and the roof caved in on him. We can't get out the way we came in."

"I'm pretty good with dirt," interrupted Landslide; "maybe there's something I can do."

"At least 50 feet of tunnel collapsed," said Yokaze. "How long will it take to get through that?"

"Hmm, that will take…a while," said the Aesir.

"There's got to be another way out of here, right?" asked Calvin. "The way they brought us in?"

"You were kind of out of it when they brought us down here," said Master Chief, "but I was paying attention. I think I can get us back out."

"Great," said Calvin, "let's go. I don't know about you, but I've got some payback to attend to."

14 Herculis 'a,' Unknown Date/Time

"That's awful," gagged Rock as they materialized. "I think I'm going to be sick. How are you doing?"

"My stomach's pretty good," said K-Mart. "I've had a lot of practice flying with you."

"What's that supposed to—" Rock stopped as he threw up.

"I'll be right back," said Hori. "It gets easier the more you do it."

"God, I hope so," said K-Mart, before he, too, threw up.

Hori reappeared several seconds later with Chomper and Hooty.

"Okay," said K-Mart, once Chomper and Hooty's stomachs had settled from the trip, "we're ready."

"Follow me," said Hori. "It's not far." He led them through a forest of something that looked like fir trees but were much larger; most were over 20 feet in diameter and soared several hundred feet into the sky. There was snow on the ground, and the temperature hovered around freezing.

"I'll bet you're glad you brought the suits now, aren't you?" asked Hooty.

"I don't know if I'm glad," said K-Mart, "but I'm certainly warmer for having brought them."

Hori pointed to a large hill in front of them. "The facility is on the other side of the hill. We will want to be quiet from this point on."

Talking ceased as the Terrans worked their way up the hill. Without the cover of the trees, the snow was almost a foot deep.

"Gah, I hate this stuff," said Chomper under his breath.

"What's wrong with…snow?" asked Rock, his breath coming out in puffs of steam as he climbed.

"Spent a lot of...time in the jungles...growing up," said Chomper. "I'm just...more used to the heat...I guess."

The group slowed as it neared the crest, and then everyone dropped onto their stomachs and crawled forward to look over the hill.

"Holy shit," said Chomper. "That place is huge!"

"No kidding," said K-Mart. "Although I knew they were giants, I guess I never really thought about what that meant. Crap! That building is over 50 feet tall...and it's only two stories. Words fail me. It's...it's enormous."

The jail was centered on a large stone building in the shape of an "X," with each leg nearly half a mile long. Almost 60 feet high, it only had two rows of windows. The building was surrounded by a 30-foot high fence that had rolls of some type of wire, probably barbed or razor, on top of it. There was an exercise yard big enough for four or five games of football to be played simultaneously. Guard towers with alert guards were in the corners of the fence, as well as several other places on each side. It would be a hard place to sneak up on.

"Movement, right side," noted Hooty. A door had opened, and 50 green-skinned people came out, followed by 10 of the Jotunn with giant two-headed axes on their shoulders. If they seemed worried about being outnumbered 5-1, it wasn't apparent in the way they carried themselves.

"They look like little bugs next to the Jotunn," said Chomper.

"They look miserable," said K-Mart. "They're all huddled in little groups. None of them have coats, and they don't look like they're used to the cold."

"Yeah," said Rock, "those are the Aesir. If they've got the prince, that's where he must be."

"Prince?" asked Hori. "Nobody mentioned we were looking for a prince."

K-Mart glared at his pilot before turning to Hori. "No, we're really not looking for him," K-Mart said. "I doubt he even survived, as badly as his ship was shot up. Besides, he's only some sort of minor prince of the Aesir; barely even worth worrying about."

"Oh," said Hori, sounding disappointed.

"All right," said Hooty, "I've seen enough. Let's get back so we can decide what we want to do." Catching a look from K-Mart, he added, "That place looks pretty impregnable; I think we should probably just write them off."

The group slid backward away from the crest of the hill, and Hori led them back the way they'd come.

"Why do we have to go back to where we came in?" asked Hooty. "Why can't we just jump back from here?"

"It's safest to exit where you came in or from one of the other surveyed points," explained Hori. "Although we believe the two planets started out the same, sometimes there are differences in elevation between the worlds. For example, if we dug a pit in our world and then transported from inside the pit, we would end up below ground when we got here."

"How would that work?" asked Chomper. "Would you displace the ground? Or would you become part of the ground?"

"I don't know," said Hori; "no one has volunteered to find out. Perhaps you'd like to try it?"

"No, I don't think I would," replied Chomper. "I'll stick to where we came in."

"If you remember, we also entered in a forest," added Hori. "I imagine transporting into the space occupied by a tree would be similarly fatal."

"I think I liked transporting in space a whole lot more," said Chomper. "There's a lot less shit to run into."

The group walked the rest of the way in silence.

"Well, I have some good news and some bad news," said Hori as they reached their destination.

"What's that?" asked Rock.

"Well, the good news is that we're where we need to be to transport back to our world. The bad news is you won't be coming back with me."

"And why exactly is that, mate?" asked Rock.

"Because you'll be staying with us," said a deep voice. Seven of the Jotunn came from behind the trunks of the large fir trees.

If the giants looked big from the crest of the hill, they were even more impressive up close, and the Terrans' jaws dropped. Fully 16 feet tall, they were enormous. Each weighed over 2,500 pounds and carried a double-headed axe, which was bigger than the Terrans were tall. The giants also smelled, badly, and the pungent aroma encircled the Terrans as the giants blocked off their avenues of escape.

The group was trapped; there was nowhere to run.

"What the hell?" asked Rock, nervously eyeing the giants as the ring around the Terrans closed.

"The fact of the matter is that we can't have you propping up the caliph," said Hori. "Your arrival has threatened to undermine all our plans."

"What plans?" asked Chomper. "Who do you work for?"

"Who do I work for?" asked Hori. He pulled out a length of cord and wrapped it around his upper arm. "I work for Grand Vizier Nefermaat. Who he works for is not my place to tell. Suffice it to say we were jumped by a group of giants, and I alone got away with my life."

"I'll kill you, you bastard," yelled Hooty. He took two steps toward Hori but was swept off his feet by the blade of one of the Jotunn. Not swept off his feet, saw K-Mart, but cut from his feet. The giant axe sliced completely through Hooty's torso, and the top half went spinning off while his legs and feet were left to collapse in the suddenly crimson snow.

Blood and guts sprayed everywhere.

K-Mart and Rock threw up; Chomper alone was left standing to glare at Hori. "I'll fucking kill you for that," said Chomper. "If it's the last thing I do."

"I'm sorry, but I really don't think you will," said Hori. He turned to a Jotunn wearing a chain mail shirt. "These people said that one of the Aesir you have is a prince. I don't know how important he is, but I figured you would like to know."

"You have done well, little one," said the Jotunn. "I look forward to many more profitable ventures with you."

"And I, as well," said Hori. He checked the tourniquet on his arm and then drew a knife from his belt. "This is the part I hate most," he said, slicing the knife across his arm. Blood poured from the wound, and he tugged the tourniquet tight, stanching the flow of blood. He walked over to Hooty's legs and wiped his knife off on Hooty's suit before sliding it back into its sheath.

"I *will* fucking kill you for that," repeated Chomper.

"Sure you will," said Hori. "Bye-bye." He pulled out his golden rod, pushed a button and was gone.

"Well, little ones," said the Jotunn with the chain shirt, "it appears you are going to be our guests. Would you like to walk, or do we have to carry you?"

Chapter Twenty-Four

Jail for Special Prisoners, Ashur, Unknown Date/Time

"I think this is it," said Master Chief, walking into the large room. "This is the first room we came to. I remember that drawing." He pointed to a black and white drawing of a large Efreet. "The door straight across is the way out of the building."

As they approached the door, the soldiers could hear explosions and screaming coming from outside. Calvin crossed to one of the windows. "Shit!" he said, looking out.

"What?" asked Night, coming over to the window.

"They've got fighters," said Calvin. Outside, Night could see the gate of the prison complex across a large open area. On the other side of the gate, civilians were running between strangely-shaped buildings as two red aircraft strafed them.

The aircraft didn't look particularly dangerous or deadly, as they were nothing more than flying boxes with wings. They were, however, more than enough to do the job of killing civilians, especially since the Sila didn't have any anti-aircraft weapons.

"I thought you said the Efreet didn't have armed aircraft," said Night, turning to Trella.

"They didn't," replied Trella. "I've seen those craft flying, but they never had weapons on them before."

"I have never seen them with weapons either," said Sella, who had been rescued from her cell on the platoon's way up to the surface.

"Well, they've got them now, and we can't take the civilians out there," said Calvin. "In addition to the aircraft, I can see at least two manned guard towers."

"*Nelson!*" called Night over his implant. "*Can you do something about the damn aircraft?*"

"*Right away, Captain Train!*" said Sergeant George Nelson. The cyborg moved past the rest of the squad, threw open the door and marched out into the courtyard. As he cleared the doorway, the two anti-aircraft missile launchers rotated up from his back where they had been stowed, with one pointing over each shoulder. He turned to the right, where one of the aircraft was attacking several civilians who were running toward the safety of a building.

The guards in the towers sensed the motion in the courtyard and began rotating their weapons toward the cyborg.

"*Snipers!*" commed Calvin. "*Take out those guards in the towers!*"

"*I've got the right tower,*" said the platoon's sniper, Sergeant Rick Day, as he smashed out the window on the right side of the room. "*I'm on the left,*" added Sergeant Nicholas Tomaselli, smashing out the window on the left. Although not officially 'sniper-qualified,' Tomaselli was the best natural shot the platoon had. Both men began firing.

"There's something you don't see every day," Sergeant Nelson said as he tried to lock the missile onto the aircraft. The ship wasn't a 'fighter' per se, but a modified transport onto which the Efreet had mounted rockets and a gun. The pilot used some sort of anti-gravity generator to hold the craft aloft, and a suck/blow system to propel it, but neither system generated enough heat for the infrared-seeking missile to lock onto.

Bang! Ping! Ping! Ping! Most of the flechettes bounced off Nelson although he could see a couple of them in his legs and one in his left arm. He pulled out the one in his arm and ran a status check. No issues. A thermal scan showed that although Tomaselli had killed one of the Efreet in the left tower, it looked like there were two, and the second one was reloading for another shot. The Efreet were starting to get annoying. *"Could someone keep the damn guards off me long enough for me to shoot down these damn planes? Left tower, reloading."*

Sergeant Tomaselli looked through his scope and found the second Efreeti. As Sergeant Nelson had commed, it was reloading its flechette thrower. Before the lizard could bring the weapon back up, Tomaselli took aim and fired. The bullet hit the lizard in the face, knocking him back and over the railing of the tower. *"Guard down,"* said The Kid as the Efreet fell.

"Thanks," said Sergeant Nelson. Looking up, he found the red aircraft again, silhouetted against the backdrop of the green sky. He switched the missile to contrast tracking, and it locked onto the aircraft. "Gotcha," he said as the missile roared out of the box launcher.

The weapon homed in on the unsuspecting fighter and detonated, tearing open nearly a third of its side. The explosion also damaged the system keeping the fighter airborne, and it flipped over sideways and fell from the sky, narrowly missing one of the buildings as it crashed to the ground.

"Now…where's that other one gotten to?" Nelson asked.

He turned to the left, searching, but the other aircraft had seen its companion go down and had turned toward the source of the threat.

Before Nelson could launch his second missile at the fighter, the Efreeti pilot fired his gun, and a line of explosions walked across the ground and into the soldier. The shells penetrated the cyborg, and Calvin saw his life signs immediately drop to zero across the board. Nelson fell to the ground in several large pieces.

"Dammit," said Master Chief, "he was the only one with anti-aircraft missiles."

"I've got this," said Sergeant Rowntree. He sprinted out the door to the remains of Sergeant Nelson. Reaching the body, he set his rifle down, unclipped the unused missile launcher from the mount on Nelson's shoulder and slid the missile canister from the box. Originally built as an infantryman's weapon, the missile still had all the hand-held launch controls built into it. Rowntree put the launcher up to his shoulder and sighted through the targeting reticle.

Nothing.

The sight was dead; the missile unpowered. He could still see through the lifeless sight, and he watched as the fighter turned back toward him. Taking the launcher from his shoulder, he scanned it, trying to find out what was wrong with the missile's power. The box launcher seemed undamaged, and he realized it had been powered by the cyborg's own electrical system. He found the power switch, turned it to "internal" and the missile began humming as it went through its power-up sequence.

Rowntree looked up and saw the aircraft closing in. He put the missile back to his shoulder and found the aircraft in the reticle. As the aircraft began firing, Sergeant Rowntree took aim, got a solid lock on the heat from the aircraft's gun and fired the anti-aircraft missile. "Eat that!" he shouted as the missile leapt from the canister.

His excitement was short-lived, as the plane broke hard to its right while launching a string of decoys. The missile followed one of the decoys, and spent itself on it. The aircraft immediately turned back toward Rowntree, continuing its attack.

The soldier dove to the side, and the aircraft's shells tracked through the space he had just vacated. The Efreeti aircraft roared past, pulling up and around for another attack. Sergeant Rowntree saw he had nowhere to run, and nothing to take cover behind, so he tossed aside the empty missile canister and picked up his rifle.

He sighted in on the aircraft as its pilot began firing, and it was a race to see who could put their rounds on target first. Sergeant Rowntree won, and a line of bullets stitched across the canopy of the aircraft, killing the Efreeti. Calvin watched in horror as the plane, already diving toward Rowntree, continued to accelerate as it arrowed straight at him.

"Move!" Calvin yelled.

Sergeant Rowntree turned and took two steps before the aircraft ploughed into him and detonated on impact with the ground. His implant transmitted one last update, and Calvin saw all the trooper's extremities had been ripped off...and what was left was shredded beyond repair. He hoped they'd find enough of him to bury, but didn't think it was going to be likely. Fuck.

Chapter Twenty-Five

Jotunn Jail, 14 Herculis 'a,' Unknown Date/Time

"Now what the hell are we going to do?" asked Rock, looking around the cell. There wasn't much to see. Four straw mats and a hole in the floor for refuse. The hole was far too small to try to go through, and even too small for one of the cell's previous inhabitants to use well. Feces covered the area around it, and the entire cell smelled like a sewer.

"We're going to try to find the Aesir prince and get out of here," said K-Mart.

"And just how the fuck are we going to do that?" asked Chomper. "Do you have some sort of magic wand you can wave and whisk us out of here?"

K-Mart motioned the other two men closer. "As a matter of fact, I do," he whispered. "Before we left, Vizier Kawab gave me one of the transportation rods. That's what he called me over for."

"Why did he do that?" asked Rock.

"Because Hori lost his partner on both of his previous missions. One time, his partner had the transportation rod when they left, yet Hori was the only one to return. He was also wounded both times but both looked self-inflicted to the vizier. Hori was the most experienced guide the Sila had…however, Vizier Kawab was starting to get the feeling something else was going on. He didn't tell anyone else he was doing it, but he gave me a rod because he was worried something might happen to us."

"Pretty justified in his thinking too," said Rock.

"So, if you had a transportation rod, Hooty's death wasn't necessary," said Chomper.

"No, it wasn't," said K-Mart, "but there was no way to tell you before now."

"Just get me back to the other world," said Chomper, "so I can kill that rat bastard."

"If you aren't worried about being in an official landing zone," said K-Mart, "we can go now."

"What are the odds they dug this facility out, and we're going to materialize in the ground?" asked Rock. "What about the forest in the vicinity of the caliph's retreat?"

"No way to tell," said K-Mart. "I guess I can transport back and, if I make it, come back to get you."

"If you don't make it, we're all dead anyway, so we might as well go together," said Rock.

"Okay," said K-Mart. He reached into his suit, pulled out the golden rod and showed it to them. "Kawab colored them for me. There are two main buttons, a green one and a blue one. Green means 'go back.'"

"Hey!" shouted a deep voice from the cell door. "What you got there?" K-Mart heard the sound of a key turning in the lock.

"Quick! Skin to skin!"

Both of the others touched him, and K-Mart pushed the blue button. Nothing happened.

The door grated as it was flung open. "Give me dat!"

K-Mart pushed the green button, and there was a flash of light.

Wendar, Day 7 of the Second Akhet, 15th Dynasty, Year 14

"Why'd you push the blue button, you dumbass?" asked Rock.

K-Mart flushed. "In the heat of the moment, I thought, 'blue for back.' I need a better mnemonic."

"At least we made it back safely," said Chomper looking at the trees surrounding them. "Sometimes it's better to be lucky than good. It would have sucked to come back inside a tree."

"Before you move," said K-Mart, "mark the spot where you came in. That way, when we go back, we know it's safe."

"Back?" asked Rock.

"Yeah, back," said K-Mart. "The prince is still there, and now the Jotunn know about him."

"One of us should go back to the caliph," said Chomper. "He's got to be warned about Grand Vizier Nefermaat's treachery."

"I guess that's you," said K-Mart. "Besides, don't you have a date with Hori?"

"Yeah," agreed Chomper with an evil smile, "I do."

"How is Chomper supposed to find his way back, though?" asked Rock.

"Let's see…" said Chomper. "I came back here facing that direction. In the other world, I was facing about 90 degrees to the left of where we came in. That means, if I turn right 90 degrees, it should be in that direction." He pointed.

"That's as close as I can figure," said K-Mart. "If anything, maybe a little more to the left. If you go more than two miles, try looping around to the left and coming back."

"Agreed," said Chomper. He began walking.

"That's weird," said Rock.

"What?"

"I just realized we didn't get sick coming back."

"Well, Hori said it got easier," said K-Mart.

"Yeah…" said Rock, not sounding convinced. "Maybe it's the direction we traveled."

"Maybe it's because we were too scared to notice this time."

"Yeah, maybe," said Rock. "So, what are we going to do about the Aesir?"

Courtyard, Jail for Special Prisoners, Ashur, Unknown Date/Time

"Before we go any further," Calvin said to the caliph. "I'd like some answers about what the hell is going on."

"Quickly," said the caliph, straining to look out the gate of the prison yard. "What do you need to know? My people are dying out there."

"*My people have been dying in here to get you out!*" Calvin yelled. "*They've been dying out there, too! Now, damn it, I want to know what the hell is going on.*"

"If I tell you everything I know, will you help my people?" asked the caliph.

"If you can help me figure out what's going on in my world, I will do my best to help you, as long as I can get the information back." He looked around and saw Sella and Trella. "Tell you what. You send Sella and Trella back to my world with one of my troops so I can get the information to my commanding officer, and I will do my best to help you."

"That is acceptable to me," replied the caliph.

"There's going to be a bit of a problem with that," said Night. "The control rod Trella had is busted. She tried to bring over the cyborgs, and while it brought three across, it died on the third attempt. Unless you have another transport rod, no one's going home."

"Do you have another rod?" Calvin asked.

"Yes, I do," said the caliph; "unfortunately, it is hidden in the castle. We only had three of them left. The Efreet took one from Sella when she was captured, and I have no idea where it might be. It could be here in the jail; they could have taken it to the ship they have in orbit. I don't know. The second was with Trella, but you say it is now broken. The only other rod is back at the castle."

"Well, at a minimum, I guess we'll be going back with you to the castle because that's our only way home."

"There are more of them in this universe," said the caliph, "but those are the only three that are on this planet."

Night reached into a pocket. "Here's the broken one," he said, handing it to Calvin.

"Do you know how to fix it?" Calvin asked.

The caliph looked at the vizier. "Can it be fixed?"

"The information I have says that they cannot be fixed once they break," said the vizier in a surprisingly deep baritone. Calvin realized it was the first time he had heard the vizier speak. "It is said they catch on fire when opened."

"But you don't know?" asked Calvin. "Why not?"

"The rods were not made here," said the vizier. "They were made back on our home planet, and it is said they were very difficult to make. When the diaspora began, each ship left our world with only eight of the rods; it was all they were able to make in time. Our ancestors brought them so that when they arrived at their target stars, they could potentially cross the boundary to interact with the civilization on the other side if they needed assistance. In our case, there was nobody on the other side until the flying snake people arrived, and when they did, they were more interested in sacrificing us than helping us."

The caliph sighed a very human sigh. "The bottom line is we do not know how to build them, nor do we know how to fix them. They were made on our home planet with a technology lost to us. When we started this colony, we had to do away with many of our advancements in order to sustain our people. We were building back to the level of technology we used to have when the Efreet arrived. They have limited our technology ever since."

"But you have still tried to advance?" asked Calvin.

"Yes, we have," agreed the caliph; "however, everything we do has to be done in secret, limiting our access to both supplies and manpower. Any time the Efreet find one of our scientific stations, they take all our research, kill the researchers and burn the facility to the ground."

"Realizing we were never going to achieve independence with what we had in this world," said the vizier, "one of our areas of research was in cross-boundary applications. Although we weren't able to produce the technology, we still had access to the files on how and why the cross-boundary control rods worked, and we were attempting to develop a way to get non-living material across the boundary."

"You were attempting it?" asked Calvin. "Or you succeeded?"

"We succeeded," said the vizier, with a voice full of pride. His face fell. "And then the Efreet found our facility and took both the research and the researcher who had made the breakthrough. They also destroyed all the files we had on the control rods and cross-boundary research, leaving us with nothing."

"Could what you invented be used to take a spaceship across the boundary?" asked Night.

"If given enough power, yes, we thought it was possible," said the vizier. "In fact, it was our intention to send equipment through to your universe, where we could build what we needed. The break-through was really quite amazing."

"Your breakthrough is responsible for the deaths of a lot of peo-ple on our side of the boundary," grated Night, "and will probably be responsible for the deaths of a lot more before it's all over. Many of them were my friends or people under my command. It would be much better for your long-term health if you weren't quite so excited about how 'amazing' a breakthrough it was."

"Well…umm…yes, there is that," agreed the vizier, "and I am very sorry for the loss of your friends. We had no idea the Efreet would get the technology nor that they would use it that way; we were only trying to get ourselves out from underneath them."

"*Lancaster! Front and center,*" commed Calvin. "I'm going to have someone take a look at the control rod. If we can fix it, we can cross back to our world, move closer to the castle and then cross back into this world."

"Yes, sir?" asked Sergeant Lancaster.

"Sergeant Lancaster is our tech guy," said Calvin. He handed the control rod to him. "See what you can do to get this going again."

"Yes, sir," said Lancaster. He took the device and turned it around several times. "Well, I see where the access panel is," he said. "It looks like there is either a screw or rivet holding it on..."

Lancaster pulled out a small tool kit and removed a mini-screwdriver. "This isn't really the right tool, but it may work to get it loose," he said, trying to loosen the fastener. The tip of the screwdriver snapped off at an angle. "Bitch," he said under his breath as he pulled another screwdriver out of the tool kit.

This time, the screwdriver won, and the access panel popped off. A blue glow suffused the inside of the control rod, moments before flames leaped out of it. "Shit!" said Lancaster, trying to blow out the fire. After a couple of seconds, he succeeded, and the flames went out, but the damage was done. Everything inside the compartment was destroyed.

"Damn it!" said Night, looking at the smoking remains of the control rod.

"I guess we'll have to do this the hard way, then," said Calvin. "You said there's another control rod at the castle?" The caliph nodded his head. "Then I guess that's where we're heading."

"You may not remember, sir, but there were a lot of Efreet guarding the castle when we last left it," said Master Chief.

"Then I guess it's a good thing I brought you along," Calvin replied. "It's time to kill people and break things, Master Chief. Move 'em out."

Chapter Twenty-Six

Outside the Castle, Ashur, Unknown Date/Time

Calvin leaned around the corner of the building and saw movement on the castle walls, only a block away. They had made good time but had been taking heavier fire the closer they got to the castle.

"How much longer?" asked the caliph.

"Just a couple of minutes more," replied Calvin. "I want to make sure we get you there in one piece. There were a lot of the Efreet at the castle, and I have some of my best men making sure all of them are dead."

"Ah, I see," said the caliph. "Thank you. In that case, I do not mind the delay."

A civilian ran up to the group and screeched something in the Si-la language. The caliph turned to Calvin. "We need to forget about this attack and flee the city," he said. "We are in great danger here."

"Great danger?" asked Calvin. "Why is that? I thought we needed to get you into the castle so you could coordinate the revolt of your people."

"Part of the revolt was predicated on keeping the Efreet from reaching the shuttles they use to get to their space ships. There are two of them at the airfield. A group of Efreet just recaptured one and took off."

"Okay, so why is that such a bad thing?"

"It appears they had the queen of the colony with them when they launched."

"And what does that mean?"

"There is only one female Efreet on this planet. She lays all the eggs that keep their colony here going. They would never bomb the planet from orbit while she was here. If she just made it off the planet, though…"

"They can bomb us at will," finished Calvin.

"Exactly," said the caliph. "We need to evacuate the city immediately."

"How long will that take?"

"To get the evacuation order to all the citizens in the middle of a revolt while the fighting is still going on?" asked the caliph. "Many hours, at least. And then to actually get everyone clear of the city once the roads get blocked with people trying to flee? Many hours more. That is why we must start now. Hopefully, we can at least get some of the people out of the city before the bombs start falling."

"Well ain't that some shit?" asked Master Chief.

"Yeah," said Calvin, "it certainly is. You know what's even worse?"

"Sir, you've got that look in your eye. I don't think I want to know."

"Probably not," agreed Calvin. He turned to the caliph. "You said there were two shuttles, right?"

"That is correct. My forces still hold the other."

Calvin turned back to Master Chief. "What's worse is we're going to have to take the second shuttle up and try to stop them."

"You've got to be fucking shitting me!" said Master Chief. "This isn't our war. We've already sacrificed a bunch of our people, and what do we have to show for it? *Nothing!* Not a fucking thing! We don't even have a way off this fucking rock!"

"That's why I want you to take the caliph and five troops and go seize the castle. Once the castle is secure, get the last control rod and send someone through the boundary to get the word back to the *Terra.* Someone's got to do that, and I know I can count on you."

"Oh, I see what you just did there, sir, and I'm not falling for it. If you're going off on some batshit-crazy rescue mission, you're not doing it without me. Who's going to keep you out of trouble if I don't go? No, sir; I'm going."

Calvin coughed to hide his smile. *"All Terrans, fall back and meet me two blocks straight out from the castle gate ASAP. There's been a change in plans!"*

Chapter Twenty-Seven

Wendar, Day 7 of the Second Akhet, 15th Dynasty, Year 14

"I'm going to transport back and forth until I find the Aesir, and then try to bring back as many as I can," said K-Mart. "Especially the prince, if I can find him."

"What am I supposed to do?" asked Rock.

"Mark my position and help me measure so I don't materialize in a tree," said K-Mart, "and help keep the Aesir out of the way…if I ever find them."

"Do you suppose the Jotunn are going to be waiting for you in our cell?"

"I don't know," said K-Mart. "I hope not."

"Wait a minute," said Rock, "doesn't that thing have some sort of invisibility or illusionary shape change function? I've read all of the mission reports I could get my hands on, and I seem to remember the first Sila that Lieutenant Commander Hobbs met could go invisible."

"Well, there are some additional buttons and knobs on the rod, but I'll be darned if I know what they do."

"Can I see the rod?" asked Rock. K-Mart passed it to him. "Yeah, I figured as much," Rock said. "It's kind of like a TV remote."

"What does that mean?" asked K-Mart.

"What does a TV remote look like after you've had it a while?" asked Rock in reply. "The buttons you use all the time have the symbols rubbed off, but you don't care because you know what each does. The buttons you never use still look brand new."

Rock pointed to the buttons as he explained further. "The two buttons to transport between worlds have their symbols rubbed off. They are used the most, so that makes sense. These other buttons on the end still have all their symbols, except for this one here, which is almost rubbed off."

He handed the rod back, and K-Mart looked at it more closely. "Huh," he said. "I never would have noticed that. I guess I don't have to worry about something bad happening if I push it. If that button did do something bad, it wouldn't have been used often enough to rub off its symbol, right?"

"Exactly," said Rock. "I don't know if there *is* a button to make you go invisible, but if there is, I'll bet it's that one right there."

"Groovy," said K-Mart, pressing the button. "Can you still see me?"

"No," replied Rock. "I can't see you at all. That's gotta be the right button."

"Well, in that case," said K-Mart, "here I go." He pushed the blue button and was back in the middle of his former cell. A Jotunn stood in the hallway, his eyes searching the cells. As his gaze swept over K-Mart, the aviator poised his finger over the green button, ready to transport out in an instant. The button wasn't needed; the giant's gaze kept moving as if K-Mart wasn't there.

So far, so good. His stomach was a little queasy, but controllable. On to the next step.

The cell door was shut, so he would need to get past it to get out of the cell. K-Mart measured from where he transported in; it was five steps to the bars marking the edge of the cell. There were at least five more to the wall on the other side of the passageway.

He went back to where he transported in, faced in the direction of the cell door and pushed the green button.

Back in the forest with Rock, K-Mart took seven and a half steps. No trees in the way. "Wish me luck," he said. He pushed the blue button and returned in the middle of the passageway, outside the cell. It worked; he was free to move around the complex. Now…where would he hide a bunch of Aesir if he were their jailor?

Outside the Castle, Ashur, Unknown Date/Time

"You're sure you know what you're doing, sir?" asked Master Gunnery Sergeant Bill Hendrick. "How do you know their spaceship won't blast you when you get up there?"

"I don't; that's why I'm going to need the caliph to send someone up to translate for us," said Calvin.

"It will have to be me," said Grand Vizier Jafar. "Only four people speak the language from the other side of the boundary, and two of them are women. The Efreet would know immediately something was wrong if there were a female voice on the radio. The caliph is much too valuable to risk on something as foolhardy as this mission. That leaves me." He looked at Night. "And perhaps, in some small way, it will help make up for my part in the deaths of your comrades."

"Okay," said Calvin, "here's the plan. Master Gunnery Sergeant Hendrick, you're going to take Sergeant Burnie, Sergeant Al-Sabani, Sergeant Hiley, Sergeant Jones and Corporal Rozhkov and secure the castle. If you can safely do it, you will then get the control rod and send people back to let the *Terra* know what we're doing and to bring back our suits if they can."

"Everyone else in the platoon," he continued, "is going to bust our asses getting to the airfield, where we're going to link up with the caliph's forces and board the remaining shuttle. Then we'll fly back here, get our combat suits and go up to the enemy destroyer in orbit, at which time we will commence to kicking ass and taking names. When there are no more Efreet alive on the ship, we'll figure out what we want to do next. Got it?"

All of the troopers' heads nodded up and down although more than a few had eyes that were about twice the size of normal. Can't blame 'em, thought Calvin. If I stopped to think about it, I'd probably be scared shitless too.

Calvin looked next at Captain Nightsong. "I don't think your Thor ever expected any of this when he sent you with us, but if you're crazy enough to join us, I'd really love to have you along. You are tremendous force multipliers, and we really need some multiplication right now."

"Your men have given their lives to help our people, even though there is no formal treaty between our nations. If we can play some small part in this endeavor, then play it we shall. We are with you."

"And I'm with you until the end," said Farhome, "no matter how many universes you try to sneak away into. Heeheehee."

"Everyone understand their parts?" asked Calvin. "Okay...ready, break!"

"*My group, with me to the castle!*" commed Master Gunnery Sergeant Hendrick.

"*Assault group, on me!*" commed Master Chief. "*We've got a destroyer to capture.*"

"How many Efreet do you reckon will be on the destroyer?" asked Night as the groups began jogging in different directions.

"Probably about 200," said Calvin; "give or take a few."

Night nodded his head slowly. "And we've got what? About 25 of us, so they only outnumber us by about 8-1?" A smile blossomed on his face. "Awesome; that's the best odds we've had all day."

Airfield, Ashur, Unknown Date/Time

"So, you think you can fly that thing, sir?" asked Master Chief as the force approached the Efreet shuttle. It looked nothing like the Terran *Reliable*-class space shuttle. In fact, it didn't look like anything aviation-related at all. It looked like a box with stubby wings and a window on the front.

"Master Chief, the only way we're getting to the destroyer is if I *can* fly that crate up to it, so yeah, I can fly that thing," said Calvin. "I hope."

"Maybe you'd like to take it around the block a couple of times to get the feel of it before we all get in?"

"I see it doesn't look aerodynamic," said Calvin, "and I admit I don't have any flight time in that model. Still, a shuttle isn't that complicated an aircraft. It's meant to haul things back and forth, and it doesn't need a lot of extraneous bullshit to do so."

"If you say so, sir."

Calvin climbed into the cockpit while the Grand Vizier spoke to the forces around the shuttle. As Calvin sat down, he realized something; there were more dials, buttons and switches than on his space fighter and shuttle combined. "Extraneous bullshit, my ass," he muttered.

The vizier slid into the seat next to him. "I figured you would need some help translating the controls," he offered.

"Yes please," replied Calvin. "This is the most complicated instrument panel I have ever seen. There are more damn buttons..." He shook his head. "Okay, where do we start?"

"How about with the lever that says, 'Engine Number One Start?'"

"That's as good a place as any, I guess," replied Calvin, grasping the indicated lever. He tried to advance it, but the level wouldn't move. "It seems to be stuck."

"The button under it says, "Push to Crank," said the vizier, pointing to the button beneath the lever. "Would that help?"

Calvin pushed the button and then tried to move the lever. Nothing.

"I heard something when you had the button pushed," said the vizier. "Maybe you have to move the lever *while* pushing the button."

"That's awkward," said Calvin. "With the controls in the center of the console, it's hard to push it with one hand and move the lever with the other."

"It is probably meant to be done with one hand," noted the vizier, "not two."

"But—"

"You forget our hands are different than yours," interrupted the vizier. "Watch." He pushed the button with one talon while using the backs of the two opposing talons to advance the lever. Calvin heard the motor begin to spin up and then, with a small 'boom,' the engine lit off.

"Progress!" said Calvin.

"Want to try the Number Two Engine?" asked the vizier.

"Sure," said Calvin. Having seen it done once, Calvin quickly had the second engine online. "Okay," he said. "Tell me what all the other buttons say."

"Aren't you going to start the third engine too?" asked the vizier.

"There's a third motor?" asked Calvin. "I didn't know that. Our shuttles only have two."

"We're all going to die, aren't we, sir?" asked Master Chief from the doorway.

"No, we're getting it," said Calvin; "we're just having some growing pains."

"Yeah, well, that's better than the dying pains us guys in the back are going to be having." He paused and then asked, "Would it help to have the shuttle's start-up checklists?"

"Yeah, it would," said Calvin. "Got a couple of those lying around, Mr. Smartass?"

"Sir, I try and I try to help you," said Master Chief, "and yet you're always wounding me." He pulled a booklet from the back pocket of each seat and handed them to the vizier. "Will these help?"

"What are they?" asked Calvin, craning his neck to see.

"This one is the 'Mark 17 Space Shuttle User's Manual,' and the other is labeled 'Mark 17 Space Shuttle Operational Checklists,'" translated the vizier.

"Yeah, those might be handy to have," said Calvin. "Thanks. Now, why don't you go back and strap in?"

"If you say so, sir," said Master Chief. "It's probably safer back there anyway. That way, I won't get sprayed by all this glass when we crash." Master Chief turned to leave but then faced back toward the cockpit. "Before I go, I should also probably give you the helmets that are sitting here. Those will probably be handy in a crash too..."

Castle Courtyard, Ashur, Unknown Date/Time

"Well, at least he got it airborne," said Sergeant 'Mr.' Jones.

"I'm not sure that's necessarily a good thing," said Master Gunnery Sergeant Hendrick as he watched the shuttle yaw as it approached, and then rotate extremely nose high. "Now he's got to set it back down again." Suddenly, the courtyard seemed a lot smaller. "Oh shit! He's going to try to land it *inside* the castle's walls. *CLEAR THE COURTYARD!*"

The shuttle continued to pitch, roll and yaw as it hovered, mostly, above the courtyard and began descending.

"I think he's going to make it," said Hendrick as he watched.

"No, he's not," said Lieutenant Rrower, bounding away from the impending catastrophe. "*Run!*"

The shuttle's wingtip screeched as it slid down one of the walls, spraying sparks and pieces of metal around the courtyard. After a couple of seconds that lasted an eternity, the shuttle yawed away from the wall, and the squealing ceased. Calvin slowly worked the shuttle down although it continued to awkwardly gyrate. He regained control of the ship, only to have it suddenly fall the last 10 feet, crashing hard to the ground.

Unlike the Terran shuttle, the boarding ramp on the Efreet shuttle was in the front, so Calvin and the vizier were the first ones out.

"Not too bad, eh?" said Calvin as he walked across the courtyard to where the other Terrans waited. "Any landing you can walk away from is a good one."

"Limp away from, you mean," said Master Chief as he hobbled up after Calvin. "Hey, does the right strut look bent to you?"

"Everyone's a critic," replied Calvin. He turned back to Hendrick. "Were you able to get the suits and the lasers?"

"Yes, sir, as well as Lieutenant Rrower, who was waiting with them."

"Master Gunnery Sergeant Hendrick thought you might need some help," said Lieutenant Rrower, "so I came along."

"Good to have you," replied Calvin. "Where are the suits?"

"They are inside the castle, guarded by Sergeant Hiley," said Hendrick. "I didn't think we wanted to advertise their presence, nor did I want any of them walking off with one of the locals. Paul said he'd keep an eye on them."

"Good thinking," said Calvin. "Let's get everyone into their suits and back on the shuttle. We need to get up to the destroyer before the bombing starts."

Chapter Twenty-Eight

Wendar, Day 7 of the Second Akhet, 15th Dynasty, Year 14

"The Aesir weren't on the first floor."

"Oh, no?" asked Rock.

"Well, if they were, they were hidden somewhere that wasn't immediately apparent to anyone walking through the facility," replied K-Mart. "I searched the jail for over an hour, and didn't find them."

"Do you suppose they are on the second floor or in some sort of dungeon?"

"I don't know," replied K-Mart, "and I didn't know how long the rod would keep me invisible, so I wanted to come back and let you know what I had found."

"I thought you didn't find anything," said Rock.

"I said I didn't find the Aesir," said K-Mart; "I *did*, however, find several interesting things."

Rock raised an eyebrow.

"First, I found a workshop that looks like it was built for the Sila, or some race fairly close in size to ours. I'm guessing Sila, because there were six Sila working in various sections of the area, with several Jotunn watching them closely."

"Any idea what they were working on?"

"No, unfortunately. It was something mechanical, but I couldn't tell what they were working on and didn't want to give myself away by trying to talk to them. We can always go back."

"Good plan," said Rock. "What else?"

"The second thing I found was a bunch of Sila in some jail cells. These were different; while the six in the workshop were all males, the 20 or so in cells were all females and children, and they didn't look like they had been fed very well. They were all thin and pretty sickly looking."

"Could they have been affected by whatever the "out of universe" disease was the vizier told us about?" asked Rock. "The Sila aren't native to our universe, so maybe they were wasting away from it. I wonder how long they've been there."

"I hadn't thought of that," said K-Mart, "but now that you mention it, the males were also thinner than any we've seen since we got here…even the starving astronauts."

"Okay, we'll add them to the list of people to be rescued once Calvin shows up with some ships and suits," said Rock. "You said 'several' things. Was there something else?"

"Yeah, I think I found the main admin offices," said K-Mart. "There was an almost continuous stream of giants coming and going through one of the doors, so I figured it had to be either the jail's administration or sleeping quarters. Since we saw a bunch of other buildings outside of the jail facility, I ruled out berthing and decided it had to be the facility's administration. If there's a head honcho, I suspect we'll find him or her there."

"So, mate, when are you going back to check the second floor?" asked Rock.

"*We're* going back right now," said K-Mart, holding out his hand. Rock took it, and they both vanished.

Mark 17 Shuttle, Ashur Orbit, Unknown Date/Time

"You know, sir, this thing doesn't seem to wobble as much in space as it does in the atmosphere," said Master Chief as he looked over Calvin's shoulder.

"Maybe I'm getting better at it," Calvin replied. "Did you ever consider that?"

"Yes, sir, I did," said Master Chief, "and I'm pretty sure it's just that it doesn't wobble as much in space as it does in atmosphere." He waited for the inevitable sigh and then added, "Sella and Trella are right; you do sigh a lot."

"I have a question," said the vizier. "What happens when the ship tries to contact us?"

"You'll have to answer them," said Calvin. "I don't speak their language."

"That much is obvious," replied the vizier; "however, I am wondering what your plan is if they want to see the pilot they're talking to." He tapped a little bubble on the instrument panel in front of Calvin. "The manual says that this is for video communications."

"Really?" asked Calvin. The vizier nodded. "Shit."

"I do not believe shitting will help the situation," the vizier replied. "Oh, I see, you intend to coat the lens so they can't see you?"

"No, that's not what I meant," said Calvin. "I was just…wait; I have an idea." He turned to Master Chief. "Go get Bob and Reeve Farhome, quickly."

Bridge, Efreet Ship *Incinerator*, Ashur Orbit, Unknown Date/Time

"Is it possible more will make it off-planet?" asked the *Incinerator's* commanding officer.

"I do not know the situation on the surface," replied the colonel. "The locals developed some sort of jammer that kept our outposts from communicating with us. Based on that, I thought it prudent to get the queen off the planet."

"As you should," said the commanding officer. "We will give our troops a little more time to see if any of them are able to make it to a shuttle and get off-world. Then we will make the Sila pay for thinking they could rebel against our rule."

"What are your intentions?" asked the colonel.

"I intend to make their planet burn," replied the commanding officer. "We will nuke them from orbit until there are not enough left to think about developing technology for *centuries*. We will turn them back into subsistence farmers. They will work...*and they will work for us!* They thought us harsh taskmasters before; they have not begun to see what harsh really looks like!"

"You will leave enough of the planet that we can restart the colony, of course?"

"Of course!" said the commanding officer. "She will never need to fear the air she breathes. We will start over on one of the smaller land masses. The capital, however, is going to be ash. Your men have another hour to get off-planet, then the bombs will start falling."

"Sir!" called the radar officer, "I have a target coming up from the planet."

The commanding officer nodded. "Very well," he said. "Verify they are indeed the colonel's men."

"You don't think the Sila could fly a shuttle do you?" asked the colonel.

"No, I don't," replied the commanding officer, "but when the queen is aboard my ship, I don't take any chances."

"The identification on the shuttle shows it is *Shuttle Five*," said the radar officer.

"Thank you," said the communicator. "I'm calling them now."

Mark 17 Shuttle, Ashur Orbit, Unknown Date/Time

The radio came to life. "Shuttle Five, *this is the* Incinerator, *over.*"

"There is a ship called the *Incinerator* trying to call a *Shuttle Five*," said the vizier.

"If no one answers," said Calvin, "then we must be *Shuttle Five.* The next time they call, answer them."

The radio crackled to life again, and the vizier answered. After a few back-and-forth comms, the vizier turned to Calvin and said, "They asked our cargo and intentions. I told them we were the last shuttle out, and that we had barely made it. I also told them we had six troops on board, and that we took fire that damaged our gear and some other systems."

"Think they bought it?" asked Bob.

Calvin shrugged. "We'll just have to wait and see..."

Bridge, Efreet Ship *Incinerator*, Ashur Orbit, Unknown Date/Time

"Sir, the shuttle confirms they are *Shuttle Five* and said they were the last ship out of the capital. They said they have six of the colonel's men onboard."

"It will be good to get some more of my men back," said the colonel.

"I can confirm the shuttle launched from the capital, sir," said the radar operator. "They are, however, flying a little funny, and their radar signature looks a little off."

"They were damaged by local fire," said the communicator. "One of their landing gear was broken, along with some other systems."

"That makes sense with what I'm seeing," said the radar operator.

"Did you have video of the pilot?" asked the commanding officer.

"No sir, audio only," said the communicator.

"Call them back and get video of the pilot."

"Yes, sir," said the communicator. "Shuttle Five, *please give me video of the pilot.*" His video screen lit up with the picture of a male Efreet.

"*Is there something I can do for you?*" asked the shuttle pilot.

"*No, we're good.*" The communicator turned to the commanding officer. "Video confirms the pilot is an Efreeti."

"Understood," said the commanding officer. "Pass docking instructions and welcome them aboard."

Shuttle Five, Ashur Orbit, Unknown Date/Time

"They believed us," said the vizier. "They just sent us docking instructions."

"Awesome," said Calvin. "Nice job everyone."

Bob got out of the pilot's seat and squeezed past Calvin. "I'm not going to get in trouble for impersonating an officer, am I?" asked the trooper.

"I won't tell if you don't," said Calvin. He turned to Farhome. "You can turn him back to normal, please."

"Aw, he looks better in black," replied Farhome. "Okay, never mind," he added, seeing the look on Calvin's face. He reached over and touched Bob's face, and Bob's features changed.

His color faded from black to gray, and his face transformed from Efreeti to tyrannosaurus rex. Corporal Bobellisssissolliss, or 'Bob' for short, was a member of the Kuji race from Domus. The planet had joined the Republic of Terra the year before, and their troops had been serving with the Terran armed forces ever since. In addition to Bob, Corporal 'Doug' Dugelllisssollisssesss was also a member of Calvin's platoon; several others had joined the space fighter squadron.

"Any problems?" Calvin asked the vizier.

"Not really…they just wanted to know why we were flying so badly."

Calvin sighed. "Everyone's a critic."

Chapter Twenty-Nine

Jotunn Jail, 14 Herculis 'a,' Unknown Date/Time

"That's not what I think it is, is it?" whispered K-Mart. The sole occupant of one of the prison wings, the silver creature uncurled from the ball it had been sleeping in. Its wings stretched, and its head soared to over 20 feet high. Golden eyes turned to look in their direction.

"If you think it's a dragon, then yes, it is," replied Rock. "Holy–"

"It's a dragon who could hear you coming half a cell block away," said the dragon. "And I could smell you from further. It's a good thing the Jotunn are neither particularly intelligent nor observant, or I'm sure they would have found you, too, invisible or not."

"But *you* can see us?" asked K-Mart.

"No," said the dragon, "but I have been following your activities for a while and hoped you would make it up here."

"Why is that?" asked Rock, as K-Mart pressed the button which made them visible again.

"Because I want you to let me out, of course," said the dragon. "Why else?"

The Terrans looked at each other, not sure what to do.

"*What do you think?*" commed Rock. "*He's obviously an enemy of the giants.*"

"*True,*" replied K-Mart. "*Just remember an enemy of our enemies isn't necessarily our friend.*"

265

"*But, he is also not your enemy yet either,*" replied a third voice. "*Freeing him from his prison would go a long way toward confirming your status as a friend.*"

K-Mart looked back at the dragon. "A telepathic dragon?"

"Most intelligent beings are," replied the dragon. "Are you not? How do you talk to each other without speech?"

"We have implants in our brains which allow us to," replied K-Mart. "It is not something we can do naturally."

"Well, of course not," replied the creature. "You have to be led to enlightenment; very few individuals ever find it on their own." He paused and then asked again, "So, are you going to let me out of here?"

"I'm reminded of a quote I saw on a t-shirt growing up," said K-Mart. "It said something about not meddling in the affairs of dragons because you are crunchy and taste good with ketchup."

"Do either of you have any ketchup?" asked the dragon.

"No, I don't," replied K-Mart.

"Then you are safe," said the dragon. "I don't have any either."

"I will let you out of there," said K-Mart, "but there are a few questions I'd like to ask you before I do."

"I don't appear to be going anywhere," said the dragon. "What are your questions?"

"Before I ask them, we haven't been formally introduced," said K-Mart. "I'm Lieutenant Dan Knaus, and this is Lieutenant Pete Ayre."

"Yes," said the dragon. "I know. K-Mart and Rock. I am Bordraab."

"Why are you locked up here?" asked K-Mart.

"The same things great minds have always been locked up for, throughout all of history," said Bordraab. "Subverting the masses, brainwashing children, et cetera, et cetera."

"Really?" asked Rock.

"Of course not," said the dragon. "I'm locked up because the Efreet came to our planet and took some of us off to give to the Jotunn, who wanted to use us in their arenas as victims of their sport. When they found out their best champion was not a match for even the weakest of us, they stopped putting us into the arena. When they found out we were telepathic and could coordinate a jailbreak without any indications, they split us up and sent us off-planet."

"If you were so dangerous to them, why didn't they just kill you?" asked Rock.

"Because they said they wouldn't and, believe it or not, they are true to their word," said Bordraab. "As telepaths, we knew their word was good when they said if 10 of us would return with them to their universe, they would spare our planet. They told us we would fight in their arenas, and if we survived, they wouldn't kill us. So here I sit, not being killed by them…and yet, every day I feel my strength and health fading away."

The dragon made a rumbling noise in his throat, and the Terrans realized he was laughing. "I, however, am under no such promise," Bordraab added. "If you let me out, I intend to kill as many of them as my strength allows. Better to die in battle, rending my enemies, than to slowly waste away. And *that* is why I want to get out." Bordraab's head spun around to look down the hall. "*Quiet!*" he said. "*They come.*"

The Terrans went invisible as two Jotunn approached, talking to each other while they conducted their rounds. One carried something that looked like a cow's leg the same way a human might carry a turkey drumstick at a county fair. The giant offered the animal leg through the bars to Bordraab. Recently severed, it still dripped blood. "Here dragon," the guard said. "Want a treat? It's nice and fresh."

When the dragon tried to seize it, the guard pulled it back out and took a bite. Both guards laughed. "Too slow," said the one with the animal leg as they walked off down the corridor.

"That's Plan B," said the dragon once they were out of sight.

"Oh?" asked K-Mart.

"Yes," said the dragon. "He does that every day, and every day my reaction has been slower and slower. They think it is because I am wasting away, which I am, but I have been feigning how slow I really am. Plan B is to take his arm off in the next day or two when he is the one holding the keys. I think I can get the door open before they can call for help; if so, I might be able to escape."

"It is my intention to engineer a much larger escape than just you," said K-Mart. "If you could be patient a little longer, I will return with aid and try to free everyone." He paused, thinking. "You said you weren't from this universe, correct?"

"That is correct," said the dragon. "The Efreet brought me here in one of their ships. They used it to cross over to this universe. Why?"

"Because freeing you is only half the task," replied K-Mart. "We also need to get you back to your universe, and I don't think the device I have will transport something, I mean, someone as big as you."

"Just a moment," said Bordraab. He closed his eyes and laid his head on the floor.

The Terrans waited.

And waited.

Finally, when K-Mart had come to the conclusion that the dragon had gone to sleep, the golden eyes opened. "There is a device which will take me back to my universe," he said. "It is on the level below us, not too far from here. There is also someone there who will use it to take me back to my universe."

"He knows how to use it?" asked Rock.

"He should," replied the dragon; "he built it."

Docking Port #2, Efreet Ship *Incinerator*, Ashur Orbit, Unknown Date/Time

"Looks like there are five or six armed soldiers waiting for us," said Doug as he looked through the airlock window. He waved. "I don't know what they were expecting, but they seemed to relax when they saw me."

"When they saw the 'new' you, anyway," giggled Farhome. He had worked his 'magic' on the two Kuji again, and both looked like Efreet.

"I like being this tall," said Bob as he looked out the window next to Doug. "Do you suppose we can stay like this when we're done?"

"Enough chatter, knuckleheads," said Night. "Focus." He looked around the cargo bay. Everyone else seemed focused. "Just like we planned," he said. "The Kuji go in, the Efreeti relax, and then we roll through and blast the shit out of them if they move. Any questions?"

There were none.

"It's time," said Bob as the airlock handle turned. The two Kuji filled the doorway as best they could, with the Terrans arrayed on both sides of the doorway out of sight.

The door opened into the larger ship, and Bob and Doug pressed forward, nearly knocking over the spacer who had opened the door. The Efreeti stumbled to the right and was knocked down by Night as he burst onto the destroyer. Wraith followed him to the right, with Staff Sergeant Zoromski and Gunnery Sergeant Bryant going to the left of the Kuji.

"Don't move!" yelled Bob, who had been coached by the vizier on how to say it in Efreet. Five of the Efreet froze, but one tried to bring his weapon around to fire. Night, Wraith and Mongo all fired at the same time, and the Efreeti fell, hit numerous times. The rest of the Efreet held their positions, but the damage was already done.

Bridge, Efreet Ship *Incinerator*, Ashur Orbit, Unknown Date/Time

"Sir, the computer reports laser fire in the shuttle docking port," said the communicator.

"Who fired?" asked the commanding officer. "What's going on?"

"Unknown," replied the communicator. "I have lost communications with the team you sent to meet the shuttle."

"Have you ever lost communications with a team while inside the ship?"

"Never, sir."

"Intruder alert!" ordered the commanding officer. He turned to the colonel. "Protect the queen at all costs."

"Yes, sir!"

Docking Port #2, Efreet Ship *Incinerator*, Ashur Orbit, Unknown Date/Time

Green lights began flashing, and an announcement crackled from a loudspeaker mounted in the upper corner of the docking port. Calvin stopped in the doorway of the shuttle to look over his shoulder. "What are they saying?" he asked.

"The voice said there are intruders in Docking Port Number Two. On-duty security forces are to converge on this area and kill them…er, us. It also said that all off-duty security people are to report to the queen's chambers to protect her. The message then repeats."

"They seem very protective of the queen," said Calvin. "If we could capture her, are they likely to do what we say?"

"Yes, very much so."

"Where would we find her?"

"She will be wherever the defense is heaviest."

"Which makes sense," said Calvin. "If there are guest quarters for visiting dignitaries, that is where I would look first, followed by the captain's cabin; they will be using the best rooms for her. Night, take the Space Force and the Kuji and go get the queen. We'll hold the docking port."

"I'd like to go with them," said Lieutenant Rrower.

"Go ahead," said Calvin.

"Are you sure you want to stay here, sir?" asked Night. "They know you're here, and you can't move. You're a sitting target, and you're going to bear the brunt of their attack."

"Someone's got to watch out for our ride home," said Calvin. "You go find the queen, and I'll keep the light on for you."

"If you say so, sir," replied Night. "Master Chief, move 'em out! Look for a schematic of the ship as you go and head for the bridge. The captain's cabin will be somewhere near there. I'll bet that's where she is."

"Wraith, Witch, you've got point," said Master Chief. "Let's go kill some 'Freets. Move out!"

Night proved prophetic; it wasn't long before the Efreet began arriving, and they arrived in force. Although the docking port only had one exit, the passageway outside extended to the left and right.

"Two on my side," said Sergeant 'Mouse' Patel, firing a burst to the left.

"Movers on my side too," called Gunnery Sergeant 'Mongo' Bryant, as he fired to the right. "Too many to count!"

"Back!" yelled Mouse. He grabbed Mongo and pulled him away from the doorway as a stream of fire burned past.

"This isn't going to work, sir," yelled Mongo. "They're moving up behind the cover of the flamethrowers. They'll be in the room with us real damn soon!"

A voice sounded over the ship's public address system. "They are directing the forces defending their ship," said the vizier. "They are sending more troops here."

"Damn it," said Calvin. "I see what Night meant. Not being mobile really limits our options." He turned to the Aesir. "Landslide, we need to get out of here. Can you cut us a hole in the bulkhead?"

Landslide put a hand on the bulkhead and the other on the deck. "I can," said the Aesir, "although it will take a while. The deck would be faster, but it's still going to take a little time."

"Go through the deck," said Calvin. "We'll hold them off as long as we can."

"We will buy you some time," said Cyclone. She led Captain Nightsong and Farhome to the doorway and spoke to the Terrans firing down the corridors. "We are going to the left; please do not shoot us," she said. Cyclone made a motion like she was throwing a double handful of something into the air. The three Aesir flickered and vanished.

"I hope they hurry," said Mouse. "The damn Efreet are getting awfully close."

"Me, too," agreed Mongo as he continued to fire his rifle to the right.

"Back!" yelled Mouse as another blast of flame rolled down the hallway. "Fuck. I hope they didn't just get fried." He peered around the corner as the flame receded. "Shit!" said Mouse. "One of them is on fire!"

The burning Aesir screamed.

Chapter Thirty

Jotunn Jail, 14 Herculis 'a,' Unknown Date/Time

"So, there is someone here who can build the devices which transfer people from one universe to the other?"

"Yes," said Bordraab. "He is being held on the level beneath us."

K-Mart's brows knitted. "If he can make transport devices," he said, "why doesn't he use one to escape?"

"Because the Jotunn have his wife and children," replied the dragon. "He says the Jotunn would kill them before he could get them out."

"But if I could get them out safely?" asked K-Mart, "Do you think he would help us?"

"I am sure he would," said Bordraab. "If you could save his family, that is. They are all wasting away too. The giants say they will free him when he makes enough transport devices for their ships. The giants are working on a plan for revenge against some other race, and they need them for their attack."

"And with that we come full circle," said Rock. "The reason we are here is that we are looking for some members of a race called the Aesir, which is the race the Jotunn are trying to get revenge on. Their allies, the Efreet, destroyed several Aesir ships and captured some of the Aesir, including an Aesir prince. We came here to get the Aesir back."

"Ah, I knew the Jotunn had brought in some new prisoners," said Bordraab, "but I didn't know where they were from. They are being held on the other side of the prison, which is, unfortunately, outside the range of my telepathy. I can smell them, but that is all."

"You can smell them?" asked K-Mart. "All the way on the other side of the prison, a mile away?"

"Not the way you understand smell," said the dragon. "My sense of smell is very...different. All my race have what you would call clairvoyant powers. Just like there are five senses, there are also five psychic senses. I am clairalient; I have the psychic ability associated with scent."

"I've never heard of anything like that," said K-Mart. "Umm...how does it work?"

"I have had it function a number of ways," said Bordraab, "and I can never be sure how it is going to work from one time to the next. Sometimes I will catch a scent associated with a feeling or idea. Other times I can smell the fragrances of locations far away or tell something which happened a long time ago by the psychic smell it leaves. Others of my kind say they can associate certain smells with non-physical beings, like the entities you call 'angels.' For me, the sense is very vivid and can sometimes be almost overwhelming. When I concentrated on the new prisoners the giants brought in, I got a smell unlike any odor I ever sampled. Whether that is your Aesir or something else, I cannot tell." He cocked his head and looked at the Terrans. "You wouldn't happen to have something from one of them, would you?"

"No," said K-Mart. "Sorry."

"In that case, I cannot be of any further assistance."

"Okay," said K-Mart, "so here's what I've got. The Aesir are probably in one of the wings on the other side of the prison. I know they aren't on the first floor because I checked there. We've got to get them out. There is someone in the level below us who can make a device to take a large number of people, or a dragon, to the other universe. He'll help us if we save his family. And finally, we have a dragon, who can smell things that aren't here, who wants to get out and kill giants. Is that about it?"

"Yes," said Bordraab.

"I think so," said Rock.

"If that's all there is, it shouldn't be any problem," said K-Mart with a smile. "Here's what we'll do…"

Task Force Night, Efreet Ship Incinerator, Ashur Orbit, Unknown Date/Time

"Hey Master Chief, you were looking for a diagram of the ship, right?" asked Sergeant Tomaselli. "I've got one."

Master Chief and Night moved forward to look where Tomaselli was pointing. There was a schematic of the ship on the bulkhead, with a number of places labeled for the crew's convenience. As it was labeled in Efreeti, the diagram was less helpful than it might otherwise have been. Still, they could see where the front and back of the ship were, and the diagram showed the ship sectioned into levels so they could see all the major spaces.

Master Chief looked at the diagram for a few seconds, then ran his finger from a purple dot to a space forward and two decks up.

"You speak Efreeti?" asked Night.

"No, but I've been on enough damn boats in my life that I can find my way around one," said Master Chief. He tapped the diagram. "I think this is the bridge," he said. "If we go there and then follow the trail of guards, I think we'll find the bitch."

"That's Queen Bitch to you," said Night with a grin; "where's your respect for royalty?" The smile faded as the ship's intercom came to life with another unintelligible message. "While we're near the bridge," he added, "we ought to put a stop to their command and control."

"Amen to that, sir," said Master Chief.

Task Force Calvin, Efreet Ship Incinerator, Ashur Orbit, Unknown Date/Time

"I'm on fire!" screamed Nightsong. "Ahhhhhhh!" Flames burst forth from him, coating his entire body. "And I love it!" He staggered, as if terminally wounded, toward a group of four Efreet firing from a cross passage. He could see their eyes get wider as he continued to draw closer without falling to the ground.

With a loud cracking noise, the head of the Efreeti on the left suddenly spun nearly all the way around. He started to drop, and Farhome appeared next to him. He scooped up the flechette thrower from the creature's lifeless hands and fired it at the Efreeti on the right, nailing him to the bulkhead.

The two Efreet in the middle began twitching as Cyclone appeared behind them and electrocuted them. She followed them to the deck, where they continued to twitch and spasm. Looking up, her eyes widened in surprise, and she dove out of the cross passage. "Look out!" she yelled.

Flechettes covered the Efreet on the ground like pin cushions. Cyclone rose from the deck and limped toward the docking port, with a flechette in her right leg. "Let's go!" she said to the other two Aesir.

The two male Aesir each grabbed one of Cyclone's arms and helped her along, Nightsong extinguishing his flames before he did so. "Cover us!" called Nightsong, pointing down the passageway in front of him.

Mongo looked in the other direction and saw several Efreet watching the drama of the burning Aesir. He fired several shots and was able to hit two before the third dove out of the way.

"Thanks," said Nightsong as the Aesir made it to safety. They laid Cyclone on the deck out of the way, and the Ground Force's medic, Sergeant Burt Yankiver, came to look at the flechette in her leg.

"I saw the group who shot Cyclone," said Farhome, "and you will want to hurry. There are at least 10 of them, and they look like they must be the Efreet equivalent of shipboard Marines. They are bigger and are carrying larger weapons."

Calvin looked down at Landslide, who was running his finger along the deck in a large circle. With each pass, his finger sank a little deeper into the groove he was making. He was through almost an inch of metal already, but Calvin had no idea how much further Landslide had to go. Firing from the doorway began again in earnest. "You're going to have to hurry," said Calvin, "We don't have much time."

"I know," said Landslide. "I'm almost through. Just hold them off another minute or two."

"Shit!" said Corporal Lopez, falling back from the doorway with a flechette through his shoulder. Staff Sergeant Zoromski jumped into his place and sprayed the hallway with a shower of laser bolts, driving the Efreet back.

"I don't know if we have another minute or two," said Calvin.

Chapter Thirty-One

Task Force Night, Efreet Ship *Incinerator*, Ashur Orbit, Unknown Date/Time

"*Right or left at the top of the stairs?*" asked Bob.

"*Go right when you get to the top,*" said Master Chief, consulting the diagram in his head. "*Look out, though,*" he added; "*the queen's room may be close by, and the passageway will probably have guards.*"

"*Got it,*" replied Bob. He reached the passageway at the top of the stairs and cautiously looked both ways. "*There's a door to the right about five feet down the hallway and six guards about 30 feet to the left,*" he commed. "Zlllpdrrrrzd blrrrgzd!" he added out loud to the Efreet looking suspiciously at him. "Don't shoot!" he said again.

Bob and Doug turned away from the guards and began walking to the door. "ZzzzLLprd Brrrlffffd!" shouted one of the Efreet from behind him.

"*The Efreet are saying something to us,*" commed Doug. "*They sound angry.*"

"ZzzzLLprd Brrrlffffd!" yelled the voice more insistently.

"*Keep going,*" repeated Master Chief. "*We're at the top of the stairs. We've got your back.*"

"*Okay,*" said Bob, not sounding the least bit convinced. He grabbed the door handle. It felt funny in his new talons. "*The door is locked,*" he reported.

281

"Really? They locked the door during General Quarters for an intruder alert?" asked Master Chief. *"Were you expecting a welcoming committee? Knock on the fucking door, you moron!"*

"Oh," said Bob. He knocked on the door but his claw barely made a sound. He knocked again with the butt of the flechette thrower he had liberated from an Efreeti at the docking port. Much louder.

The Efreet behind them yelled at them again. It was also much louder. *"We don't have much time,"* commed Doug. *"The guards are moving toward us and aiming their weapons at us."*

An Efreeti looked through a small window in the door. Bob waved at him. Bob hoped he didn't look as nervous as he felt.

The door started opening. *"We're in,"* Bob commed.

"Go! Go! Go!" ordered Master Chief, pounding up the last few stairs with Night at his side. They burst forth from the stairwell, nearly knocking over the approaching Efreet, laser rifles firing at close range as they cleared the stairwell. The rest of the Space Force poured into the passageway close behind.

The Efreeti opening the door jumped backward in surprise, pointing a talon down the passageway to warn Bob and Doug. It opened its mouth to yell a warning, but Bob shoved the laser pistol he had been hiding into the Efreeti's mouth and pulled the trigger. The creature fell backward, twitching in its death throes.

"ZzzbrrrllFFd; llrrrgzzd!" said Bob. "Don't move; claws up!" He realized as he said it the two orders were contradictory, but he had to go with it; that was what he had been taught to say.

There were seven Efreet on the bridge. A large chair sat in the center of the 20-foot by 35-foot space, with other positions around the periphery. All the Efreet were dressed in black leather uniforms, but two stood out because of the extra silver piping and braid they wore. The Efreeti in the central chair had large purple bands up both arms; the Efreeti standing next to him had a similar uniform, except his bands were blue.

Bob could see the Efreet were weighing their chances of success if they rushed the two Efreet who had just stormed onto the bridge; all of them seemed armed, and their claws strayed toward their weapons. The Efreet in the central chair barked out an order as Master Chief and four other troopers poured through the door, and all the Efreet at the peripheral stations dove for cover, reaching for their weapons as they went.

Bob shot the unmoving Efreeti in the central chair, striking him several times, while Doug shot the equally immobile Efreet with the blue bands on his uniform. Both collapsed.

"Shoot the armed ones, you morons!" yelled Master Chief, firing at one of the Efreet who had gone for cover behind a console. "Try to capture some of them alive if you can."

The Efreet returned fire, and the Terran Federation troops were forced to dive for cover. All except for Sergeant Adeline Graham, who strode across the bridge, firing a burst into the Efreet as they showed themselves. The smaller flechette pistols of the bridge crew weren't built to take on cyborgs and didn't have enough power to penetrate anything vital.

She reached the last console, which was being used as cover by the final two Efreet. She realized these Efreet had some training, due to the speed at which they reloaded, and how they covered each other. She wasn't worried, as they were still only armed with the little flechette pistols. She rounded the console and took five shots in rapid succession to her torso, then a sixth to her face, which put out her left eye.

"Dammit!" Okay, maybe she wasn't impervious to fire after all. She aimed her rifle and killed the Efreeti who had put out her eye, leaving only one alive. Chopping down, she knocked the pistol out of his hand and grabbed him by his tunic collar.

Weaponless and unable to escape, the Efreeti pulled a thin knife from one of his sleeves and stabbed himself in the stomach. Sergeant Graham grabbed his hand so he couldn't do it again, but it was too late. He had punctured something vital and died quickly, glaring all the while at her.

"Sorry, Master Chief," said Sergeant Graham, dropping the dead body to the deck. "I was trying not to kill this one."

"I saw," said Master Chief. "There's nothing you could have done about it." He switched to his comm. "*It was messy, but we've got the bridge,*" he reported.

"*And I've got the queen's quarters,*" replied Night, "*but we've got a problem.*"

Chapter Thirty-Two

Bridge, TSS *Terra*, In Orbit Around Keppler-22 'b,' July 17, 2021

"The Captain is on the bridge," said the quartermaster of the watch as Captain Lorena Griffin walked through the door.

"Have we heard anything from the other side yet?" she asked.

"No, ma'am," replied the operations officer. "Still no word."

"Damn it," said Captain Griffin. "We should have heard something by now. Next time, we're bringing more Marines. First a planetary assault and then combat in space? We need more troops!"

"Stargate emergence!" said Steropes and the defensive systems officer simultaneously.

"Get me an ID, ASAP," said Captain Griffin. "Communications officer, see if you can get them on the radio."

"The emergence was not from a gate we knew about," said Steropes; "there is a new gate much further out-system."

"How come we didn't know about this gate?" asked Captain Griffin.

"We must have missed it," said Steropes. "Things got exciting when we found life on the planet, and we might not have ever finished the survey. It is my fault."

"We can assign blame later," said Captain Griffin. "I'm still waiting on the identification of the ship."

"Long range scans indicate it is…" said Steropes.

"It's what?" asked Captain Griffin.

"I don't know what it is," Steropes admitted. "The ship that just came through the gate isn't in the database."

"Launch the fighters," said Captain Griffin. "Have them go take a look."

"Launch the fighters, aye," said the operations officer.

"Um…the ship is gone," said Steropes.

"What do you mean by 'gone'?" asked Captain Griffin.

"I mean, it just disappeared," said Steropes. "It appears to have jumped to the other universe."

Caliph's Retreat, Wendar, Day 10 of the Second Akhet, 15th Dynasty, Year 14

"You're just in time!" said Chomper, running out to meet K-Mart and Rock as they approached the retreat. "We're pulling out."

"What do you mean 'we're pulling out'?" asked Rock.

"When I exposed Grand Vizier Nefermaat's plot, the caliphate to the south, the Bargah Caliphate, attacked," replied Chomper. "Apparently, they had other spies besides Nefermaat and that slime Hori, and they passed the word to Bargah that their operatives' covers were blown. I never got a chance to 'talk' with Hori, either. Unfortunately, he heard I was back before I could find him, and he was shot while trying to escape. None of that matters any more. What does matter is we have to leave *right now* before we get overrun by the Bargah forces. They are already within 10 miles of here."

"If we leave, how are we going to go back and rescue the Aesir?" asked Rock.

"I don't know," replied Chomper. "I guess we're not…not now anyway. Maybe Calvin will get back with some air power so we can win the war and go get them. It doesn't matter; we can't stay here even if we wanted to. The reason Hori was going to the other side of the boundary was to put together some sort of treaty with the Jotunn to help the Bargah Caliphate; there have been reports of "enormously tall men" fighting for Bargah who keep breaking through the front lines. The caliph's troops are at about the same technology level as we had back in the late 1950s, so taking down one of the Jotunn is tough for them, especially since they don't have any air power. It's possible, but you have to hit them so many times they're already upon you before you can kill them. And, because it takes so long to bring the giants down, the rest of the normal troopers have reached your lines by the time you do."

"So, the caliph's forces are losing?" asked K-Mart.

"He calls it, 'trading land for time,'" replied Chomper. "I call it losing."

"At some point they're going to run out of land they can trade," said Rock. "Then what are they going to do?"

"I guess that's when they will start losing," replied Chomper. "Right now, the Jotunn are spread out enough that the caliph's forces can kill them almost as fast as they appear. When the lines get shorter, and the giants start coming closer together, there will be so many attacking at once that the caliph's forces will be overrun like that." He snapped his fingers. "I think it goes without saying," he added; "we *don't* want to be recaptured by the Jotunn."

"If we only had *one* of our fighters, this war would be over instantly," said Rock. "It wouldn't even be close."

"Yeah," agreed K-Mart; "unfortunately, the only fighter we have access to is wrecked beyond repair, and the functional one is out of gas and up in space. We can't get up to it, and even if we could, we couldn't do anything with it."

"So what are we going to do?" asked Rock.

"We're going to get our weapons and rescue everyone from the Jotunn jail," said K-Mart. "What else can we do? I'm not a combat trooper and, even though I like the caliph, this isn't my war. Our first goal is to rescue the Aesir. Then we need to stay alive long enough for Calvin to make it back here and pick us up."

"So you think he's coming back?" asked Rock.

"He'll be back," said K-Mart. "If he's able."

Task Force Calvin, Efreet Ship *Incinerator*, Ashur Orbit, Unknown Date/Time

"*L*ook out! Shit! Sergeant Day is down!*" commed Mongo from the doorway.

Calvin looked up to see the medic running over. He didn't need to see the fading life signs on his monitor to know the sergeant was done; he could see the three giant flechettes sticking through his face mask.

"*They just set up some sort of crew-served flechette thrower,*" commed Mongo, peering around the door frame. "*The projectiles are a hell of a lot bigger, and they are tipped with some sort of acid which eats a hole in whatever they hit. We need to get the hell out of here, sir; we're not going to be able to hold much longer.*" He dove back out of the way as another spray went by. "*The only good thing is that they can't come at us from both directions with that damn thing. It wipes out most of the passageway when they fire it, so the group coming from the other direction had to pull back."*

Calvin looked down at Landslide. The Aesir's finger now traced a groove nearly two inches deep. "How much longer?"

"This should about do it," Landslide said. His finger made one more circle, and a four-foot diameter section of metal detached, falling about six inches to rest on a number of pipes which ran below the deck. "Oops," he said. "I forgot there would be things below the floor. As long as these aren't electrical, it shouldn't be a problem." He reached in and grabbed one of the four-inch diameter pipes at the edge of the escape hole. His hand squeezed the pipe, and it crumpled in his grasp. Within seconds, he was through it, and water began spraying out.

"See?" he asked. "No problem." He grabbed the other end of the pipe and did the same thing. Once again, his hand went through the pipe, and the piece fell six inches to lie on what appeared to be the ceiling of the room below. Water began puddling as it poured from one end of the broken pipe.

Landslide grabbed the next pipe and squeezed, severing it. This one also had fluids running through it, but they were waste fluids; an unsavory smell wafted from the hole to assail the people standing above it.

"Oh my god!" Calvin said, fighting back the urge to vomit. "That is…the worst thing…I think I ever smelled." He looked into the hole and could see…things…floating in the pool of fluid.

"Better do something soon!" commed Mongo. *"We're almost at hand-to-claw."* He paused and then yelled, "Last frag out!" as he threw a grenade. They could all feel the concussion as it exploded; the Efreet were close.

"Almost done," said Landslide; "last one." He grabbed the third pipe and squeezed. He got about halfway through it, then went rigid as a "zzzzzzt" was heard. Sparks flew from his hand, and his body began spasming as electrical current flowed through it. "Aaaaaaaaaah," he cried, no longer in control of his actions.

Without thinking, Calvin dove into him, taking a jolt before the force of his contact separated the Aesir from the electrical line.

Calvin rolled to find the Aesir lying still on the deck. Sergeant Yankiver ran over to Calvin. "Are you okay, sir?" he asked.

"Yeah, I'm fine," Calvin answered. "Check on Landslide."

The Aesir wasn't moving, and a wisp of smoke curled up from his blackened hand. Yankiver took the Aesir's other hand and searched for a pulse. He couldn't find one.

"If you are looking for a pulse," said Farhome from above Yankiver, "you're looking in the wrong spot."

Sergeant Yankiver realized he had done it without thinking; he didn't know anything about the Aesir's physiology. The medic paused, unsure how to help Landslide.

"If you will move," Farhome said, "I will see what I can do."

Yankiver moved, and Farhome knelt next to Landslide. His eyes looked clear and focused. Farhome placed a hand on the fallen Aesir's stomach and closed his eyes.

"Not good," he muttered.

"Can you save him?" asked Calvin.

"Yes, but it will be a minute," replied Farhome without opening his eyes.

"Hurry," said Calvin. He stood and turned back to the hole. Tsunami had her hands in the hole, but wasn't being electrocuted. Cyclone had a laser pistol and was firing continuously into the hole. She stood awkwardly, favoring one leg, but no longer had the flechette through it.

Tsunami looked up as Calvin approached. "We'll be out of here momentarily," she said.

Calvin looked into the hole and saw the liquid in the pipes had stopped flowing; the ends of both fluid pipes were frozen solid. Not only that, but a hole had also been opened through the ceiling into the room below, and he could see where the pieces of the ceiling had fallen down onto the deck, along with the water…and things…that had been pooling. Cyclone had already cut through one side of the pipe with the electrical cable in it and was halfway through the other.

"Wha…" Calvin said. "How did you do that?"

"Water is stronger than you know," replied Tsunami. "It will carve rock given enough time." She smiled. "Or the right person to help it along."

"*Sir, it's now or never!*" commed Zoromski. "*30 seconds and they're in here!*"

The pipe dropped as Cyclone finished cutting through the second side.

"*Let's go!*" commed Calvin. "*Follow me. Careful not to touch both sides of the electrical pipe at the same time!*" He holstered his pistol and slid feet-first into the hole. Careful not to complete the electrical circuit, he dropped to the floor 11 feet below.

They were free.

Chapter Thirty-Three

Caliph's Retreat, Wendar, Day 10 of the Second Akhet, 15th Dynasty, Year 14

"I only need 10 of your troops," said K-Mart.

"That is impossible," said Vizier Bulah, who was in charge of the caliphate's armed forces. "Our men are already being overwhelmed. We don't have *any* men to spare, much less 10. And armed with heavy slug-throwers? We need these for your Jotunn! I don't know what you did to make them attack us, but the heavy slug-throwers are the only things which will bring them down."

"We did nothing to involve the Jotunn," replied K-Mart; "you have your own traitors to blame for that."

"Even if that is true," replied Vizier Bulah, "the fact remains; we don't have enough men to give you any."

"You're pulling out, right?" asked Chomper. "It seems to me that some of the men and weapons from the caliph's retreat ought to be extra. If you are abandoning it, its defenders are no longer needed to man it."

"But, but, but they are the caliph's own guards!" sputtered the vizier. "If you take them, who will guard the caliph?"

"How many of our men did these Terrans bring back from the space station?" asked the caliph.

"I believe it was eight, my caliph," replied Vizier Bulah.

"Then you shall find them eight soldiers for their mission," replied the caliph. "Those were eight men whose lives were returned to us, at great risk to the Terrans' own lives. I will risk my own life to give them those eight." He looked over to where his personal servants stood by the door, shifting from taloned foot to taloned foot. "No more discussion; it is done," he added. "It is time for all of us to go."

"Thank you, Caliph," said K-Mart as the caliph began to leave.

"You are welcome," replied the caliph. He stopped and turned back to meet K-Mart's eyes. "Those men have sworn their lives to me. Do not spend them lightly."

Task Force Calvin, Efreet Ship *Incinerator*, Ashur Orbit, Unknown Date/Time

"*W*e've got the bridge," commed Master Chief.

"*And I've got the queen's quarters,*" added Night, "*but we've got a bit of a problem.*"

"*I don't have a lot of time for problems,*" replied Calvin. "*We're on the run with a big group of Efreet chasing us. What's the problem?*"

"*I've secured the queen's quarters,*" repeated Night. "*The problem is, she's not here.*"

"*Are you sure?*" asked Calvin.

"*That she's not here? Absolutely. There's no place for her to hide. She's gone.*"

"*Where do you suppose she's gone?*" asked Master Chief.

"*The hell if I know,*" replied Calvin. "*Where would you go?*"

"Sir, you're looking at it wrong," said Mongo, who was alongside Calvin. "Take our leaders back home. They don't decide where they're going in the event of an emergency; the head of their security detachment does. You have to figure out where *you* would take your queen if you were in charge and under assault by a group you knew nothing about."

"On a spaceship?" asked Calvin. "I'd want to put all of my forces between her and the invading force. Failing that, I'd try to get her off the ship."

"Well, it sounds like the Space Force got through or around the security force. What does that leave?"

"The other shuttle we followed up here," said Calvin. "*They're going for the other shuttle,*" he commed. "*We've got to cut them off!*"

"Sir, we need to move," said Master Gunnery Sergeant Hendrick. "Any time we stop, they start shooting at our rear guard."

"We've got to get to the other docking port," said Calvin. "I think they're going to try to take the queen off the ship with the other shuttle."

"Well, why didn't you say so before?" asked Hendrick. He had committed the ship's layout to memory, and he traced out a path on his in-head tactical display to the other shuttle docking port. "Yokaze, you've got point. Head out and take the first right. Let's move, people! We've got a queen to catch."

Yokaze stayed to the right of the passageway as he hurried down the corridor with Staff Sergeant Zoromski close behind him. He reached the turn at the same time as a group of five Efreet, coming from the opposite direction.

Time seemed to slow as his senses went into overdrive. Firing from the hip, he shot the closest Efreet through the throat. Dropping the rifle, he whirled to his left, drawing his katana as he turned. Yokaze completed the spin, and the katana sliced through the neck of a second Efreeti. Yokaze saw his enemies bringing their flechette throwers up, and his katana flowed gracefully back in the opposite direction, removing a third Efreeti's left arm at the joint. He continued the spin to the left, disemboweling a fourth Efreeti, and turned back to find the fifth Efreeti already falling with a laser hole in its temple.

"Your mom never taught you how to share, did she?" asked Zoromski, finishing off the Efreeti with one arm.

"Hai!" replied Yokaze. "She did; I was just trying to be quiet."

"*We're in a hurry, gentlemen,*" commed Master Gunnery Sergeant Hendrick. "*Let's move! Take the second cross corridor to the left, then there should be a set of stairs to the right. We need to go up one level to get to the docking port.*"

"*On my way,*" replied Yokaze. Picking up his rifle, he led the group forward and found the passage and the stairs. He paused to listen for a few seconds before flowing quietly up the stairs.

"*I hear Efreet coming from the right!*" he commed after reaching the next deck. "*It doesn't sound like many. Which way is the docking port?*"

"*To the left,*" replied Hendrick. "*Take them if you can. Quietly!*"

Two Efreet hurried past from right to left. Unlike the Efreet they had seen earlier, these were dressed in some sort of spacesuit, and were carrying helmets. Yokaze and Mongo burst from the side passage. Yokaze slammed his tekkan down on the head of the closest Efreeti. Nearly the same size as his wakizashi, it had a blunt iron blade, which was used as a club. As the other Efreeti started to turn toward the sound, Mongo slammed the butt of his rifle down onto its head like a club.

Both Efreet went down.

"Nice job," said Calvin. "Put the bodies in the stairwell, and let's keep going. We're almost there. It's just around the corner."

Yokaze started down the passageway, but turned back when he got to the corner. "The queen's forces have already made it to the docking port and have set up a perimeter," he said. "They will be very difficult to get past."

"Did it look like the shuttle was leaving?" asked Master Gunnery Sergeant Hendrick.

"They did not appear to be loading it," the Japanese man replied. "They were stationary, as if they were waiting for something."

"Like what?" asked Hendrick.

"I do not know," replied Yokaze.

"I do," said Calvin. "The two Efreet we killed must be the shuttle's flight crew. The shuttle isn't going anywhere without pilots."

"So what's your plan, sir?" asked Hendrick.

"I intend to give them some."

Chapter Thirty-Four

Wendar, Day 13 of the Second Akhet, 15th Dynasty, Year 14

"Wait for us here," said K-Mart. "We will be back shortly."

"We will wait," said the sergeant, "but do not make us wait too long, or you will come back to find us overrun. The enemy is not far off; they will shortly be upon us."

"Understood," said K-Mart; "I just need to set up a couple of things first." He looked at the other Terrans and asked, "Ready to go?"

Both aviators nodded and reached out to make contact. K-Mart pressed the button and, with a flash, the Terrans appeared in their former cell.

"This is your plan?" asked Chomper. "Put us in jail?"

"No, this is just a defensible position to bring folks," said K-Mart. "Since we were the only ones on this wing, I'm hoping the guards won't come by here often. If they do, you can shoot them while they are unlocking the door."

The other two Terrans readied their laser rifles and K-Mart nodded. "Be right back," he said.

He vanished and returned with two of the soldiers. Both promptly threw up.

"Lovely," said Chomper. "That's going to make staying here even more sucky. Want to trade jobs?"

300 | CHRIS KENNEDY

"No thanks," said K-Mart. He brought the rest of the troopers in, and they began assembling their crew-serviced weapons…after they stopped throwing up. K-Mart disappeared again and reappeared a few minutes later with a woman and two children. He disappeared again and came back with a second woman and a child.

"That's all of them," said K-Mart.

"I thought you said there were about 20," said Rock.

"There were," said K-Mart. "They must have moved them." He shrugged. "I can't do anything about it now. On to Stage Two, where things get tough." He took a deep breath and let it out slowly. "Wish me luck." He vanished.

Jotunn Jail, 14 Herculis 'a,' Unknown Date/Time

"I don't know why K-Mart thinks he has it so tough," Rock said after a few minutes of waiting. "He's out running around while we're stuck here."

"No kidding," agreed Chomper. "He'd—"

"Fee, fie, foe, fum," rumbled a deep voice from down the cell block.

"I didn't really just hear that, did I?" asked Rock as two Jotunn came into view.

"Yeah, you did," said Chomper. "Don't let them say it again," he added as he sighted down his rifle. "*Fire!*" He fired his laser rifle, hitting the lead giant twice in the chest. He might as well have been shooting an avalanche; the giant kept coming.

That changed when both Sila slug-throwers opened up. The weapons fired rounds slightly larger than .50-caliber bullets, but that's where the comparison to a Terran machine gun ended. The bullets were fed into the weapon from the top by a loader in 40-round clips; the gunner then charged the weapon and fired off the entire clip. As the metal piece the bullets were attached to popped out of the bottom with a 'ping,' a second loader on the opposite side of the slug-thrower dropped in the next clip.

It wasn't the most efficient machine gun Chomper had ever seen, but with two loaders feeding it, the weapon put a respectable amount of ordnance downrange. It had a fairly rapid firing rate, and the over-size bullets were effective against the Jotunn. Mounted on a tripod, the gunners were able to direct most of their fire into their targets, blasting huge chunks out of the giants with accompanying geysers of green blood.

Combat veterans, the crew manning the slug-thrower on the right focused on the Jotunn on the right, while the other crew fired at the Jotunn on the left. Hit by over 50 rounds each, as well as a couple of laser bolts, both giants were quickly dispatched.

As the sounds of gunfire died away, a metallic voice could be heard coming from the vicinity of the felled giants. It kept saying, "Report," over and over in the Jotunn language.

"*K-Mart, you'd better hurry,*" commed Chomper. "*I think they know we're here!*"

Task Force Calvin, Efreet Ship *Incinerator*, Ashur Orbit, Unknown Date/Time

"Really? You can't tell?" asked Mongo. His voice was muffled coming through the faceplate of the helmet. Mongo and the squad's medic, Sergeant Burt Yankiver, were wearing the two Efreet spacesuits, as they were the two biggest men in the squad, and the two best able to simulate the size of an Efreeti.

"No," said Calvin. "I can't see your face. Not very well, anyway. The anti-glare coating on the facemask makes it difficult to see through unless you are up close and really looking." He turned to look at the medic. "You look good too, Doc. All you guys have to do is hold them for a couple of seconds. We'll be right behind you."

Mongo looked at the medic. He hadn't said anything since he put on the suit, but then he didn't say much at the best of times, either. He just got the job done. He slapped Sergeant Yankiver on the shoulder. "In that case," Mongo said, "we shouldn't have any problems. Let's go; the queen is waiting for her pilots."

Yankiver nodded once, signaling his agreement. It was more of a bend at the waist, as the Efreet suits didn't have flexible neck joints.

Mongo started walking. "Hey, you're going the wrong way," said Calvin. "The Efreet are this way." He pointed in the opposite direction.

"I know," said Mongo. "I wanted to get a running start. They will probably be expecting us to be hurrying, and it will cut down on the time they have to shoot at us. All we need is a moment's indecision, and we'll be on them."

"Good plan," said Calvin.

"*Ready?*" Mongo commed.

"*Yep,*" replied Sergeant Yankiver.

"*Here we go then,*" said Mongo. He started forward and then picked up his pace. He hoped a casual Terran jog was the same as an Efreet jog, but whether they even jogged at all was unknown. Yankiver caught up to him in a couple of steps, and they rounded the corner together, right into the line of sight of three Efreet standing shoulder to shoulder across the passageway with drawn weapons. Mongo could see more Efreet behind them, looking the other way.

One of the Efreet yelled something, and the two Terrans slowed, coming to a walk. They naturally put their hands up in the Terran display of surrender. Although it seemed to work at first, and the Efreet began to lower their weapons as they recognized the space-suits as being of Efreet origin, Mongo watched as their eyes went toward the rifles they were holding. Terran laser rifles, they were neither the same shape nor color as the ones the Efreet were hold-ing. He was close enough to see their eyes blink several times, and their weapons begin to come back up.

"*We're blown!*" Mongo commed as his rifle tracked back down.

The Terrans fired at the same time the Efreet did, while diving to the sides of the passageway. Mongo hit the wall on the left and con-tinued firing. Two of the Efreet were already down, and he shot the third twice in the chest.

A volley of laser bolts passed over his head to kill the other Efreet in the passageway as the rest of the Terran forces arrived, several with flechette wounds. Mongo rose and went to assist Ser-geant Yankiver to his feet, but the medic waved away the offer of help. Blood covered his chest and midsection. "*Didn't dive fast enough,*" Yankiver commed. "*I caught...most of a flechette blast...it's not...good.*" His hand dropped to the deck.

"*Medic!*" commed Mongo automatically. Realizing his error, Mongo knelt down next to him. "*Talk to me, Burt,*" he commed. "*What do I need to do?*"

"*Leave him,*" commed Calvin, looking at his monitor; "*he's gone.*" Firing could be heard from the interior of the shuttle as the remain-ing members of the squad assaulted into it. "*I need you and Zoromski, along with Corporals Dunn and Lopez, to set up a perimeter,"* continued Calvin when the firing had slowed. *"No one gets through."*

"Got it sir," said Mongo, standing up. *"No one through."*

"Sir, you better get in here," Master Gunnery Sergeant Hendrick commed. *"We've got the queen, I think, but...well, you're going to need to see this."*

Calvin nodded to Mongo and turned toward the shuttle. He immediately noticed the shuttle was different as he strode into the interior. It was the most opulent spacecraft he had ever been in. Come to think of it, there wasn't any ornamentation on *any* of the spacecraft he had ever flown on; they were warships. They barely could have been considered "comfortable," much less anything along the lines of "showy." Comparing the queen's shuttle to the shuttle they had flown up in was like comparing the Ritz Carlton to a fleabag motel somewhere on the wrong side of town.

There was no bare metal showing anywhere; the deck and the bulkheads (and the ceiling, too!) were covered in some kind of felt-like material in a variety of blues and oranges. It was beyond compare and almost beyond description; it was so garish that it was hard to look at.

He made his way to the passenger compartment to find...something... on the deck. Larger than the males he had seen, the eight-foot long creature looked vaguely like an obese Efreet, but out-massed the males by at least several hundred pounds. It was nearly round, with arms and legs only sticking out from the mass of flesh from the elbow joints down. While the males had some vestigial webbing between their claws, the creature's hands and feet were fully webbed, and it had a fin on the top and bottom of its over-sized tail. The queen's eyes were closed, and gallon after gallon of murky fluid spewed from underneath its tail, coating the felt of the floor and puddling behind the creature. A dead Efreeti lay nearby, and the creature on the floor pulled a strip of meat from the corpse's leg and popped the flesh into its mouth.

It was the most disgusting thing Calvin had ever seen in his life.

"I think it's laying eggs," said Master Gunnery Sergeant Hendrick, "…or something. I've seen a lot of sick shit in my 27 years in the Corps, but this is the most disturbing. It's even worse than when the company captured the sheep and…uh, never mind. This is just damn gross."

Calvin was at a loss for what to do with the creature. Before he could decide, an incoming call arrived.

"Hey sir," said Master Chief O'Leary, *"Have you guys captured the queen yet?"*

"Yeah, I think we just caught it…or her…or whatever it is," replied Calvin. *"Why?"*

"Because you need to get up to the bridge ASAP," commed Master Chief. *"It looks like we're going to have company."*

Chapter Thirty-Five

Bridge, Efreet Ship *Incinerator*, Ashur Orbit, Unknown Date/Time

"Did you have any problems getting up here?" asked Night.

"No," said Calvin. "Once you made the announcement we had captured the queen, all the Efreet stopped fighting. It's almost like there is some sort of cultural imperative to defend the queen at all costs, even if that means doing nothing that would endanger her."

"Well, that's good to hear," said Night. "We're already outnumbered, and it looks like it's about to get worse."

"Master Chief said we're going to have company; what's going on?"

"There's some sort of cargo ship inbound," said Night. "It jumped into this universe about five minutes ago. No idea if it came from our universe or somewhere else, but if it came from our universe, the *Terra* didn't do a very good job of stopping it. When the ship checked in, they didn't mention any problems or issues."

"Okay, I'll ask," said Calvin. "How were you able to find that out?"

"We had help," said Night. "Once you captured the queen, the Efreet became a lot more cooperative."

Night nodded toward a small alcove off the bridge that Calvin hadn't noticed before. Inside were two Efreet under the watchful eyes and ready weapons of two troopers while the vizier and Master Chief spoke to them. The alcove was unlit, and the dark-skinned Efreet blended into the shadows.

"None of the bridge crew survived the initial assault, but we bagged these two right after the attack. One knew how to operate the radio, and the vizier listened in to make sure he didn't warn the ship off. The vizier admits he doesn't know much about military communications, but the conversation seemed all right to him."

Calvin walked over to the alcove. "Have you been able to learn anything?" he asked Master Chief.

"Not a whole lot, sir," Master Chief replied. "They're both pretty junior. All they knew was that the freighter was bringing something for the ship, and their CO was looking forward to having it."

"Have we found out where the CO is yet?" asked Calvin.

"Unfortunately, yeah, we have," said Master Chief. He turned and pointed to the bodies by the chair in the middle of the room. "I think he is the one with purple stripes on his uniform. He took three laser bolts to the chest at the start of the fight; we're not going to be getting any answers from him or anyone else in the command group. They're all dead."

"Shit," said Calvin under his breath.

"So, what are we going to do with the freighter?" asked Master Chief.

"I don't know," said Calvin, "but give me a minute, and I'm sure I'll come up with something."

Jotunn Jail, 14 Herculis 'a,' Unknown Date/Time

K-Mart transferred back to the Jinn universe and hurried to where the workshop was in his own universe. He ran as fast as he could, knowing the Jotunn would soon notice the absence of the women and children. "If I...live through...this..." he puffed, "I'm going to...get in shape...when I get back."

He stopped at the transfer point he had marked out and waited to catch his breath. It wouldn't do to be panting so hard the giants could hear him.

"You there!" a voice called. "Don't move!"

K-Mart's head whirled around to see a squad of men dressed in black approaching. The enemy's color. One fired a weapon, and the slug slammed into the tree next to him. Without thinking, he pushed the button and disappeared.

He reappeared in the workshop, which was noticeably less crowded than on his earlier visit. Only one Jotunn was present, and it stood in the doorway watching two Sila. The giant was armed with an enormous rifle and had a small metallic box dangling from a strap that ran diagonally across his chest.

Still trying to control his breathing, K-Mart tip-toed to the Sila furthest from where the giant stood.

"Don't say anything," whispered K-Mart into his ear. "I am here to help you."

The Sila jumped and looked around wildly.

"Keep working," K-Mart added.

The Sila gave a small nod and went back to tinkering with the device he had been working on. His eyes shifted back and forth, looking for the source of the voice while trying to watch the guard and work on the metallic object all at the same time. It didn't work well, and the screwdriver-like tool slipped and scratched across the object.

"Easy," whispered K-Mart. "I'm going to get you out of here." The male's head snapped up, and he opened his mouth to speak. "Your family is safe," K-Mart added; "don't worry, I've already freed them from their cell, and we will join them shortly. Before we go, I have a request."

The Sila made a face; his annoyance obvious.

"I'm sorry," said K-Mart, "but there are more people here that need rescuing than just you and your family." The male appeared to understand, and his face relaxed. "Are you the person working on devices to transfer across to the other universe?"

The man nodded.

"I need a device which can transfer a large number of people at one time, and one that can transfer a really large creature. Do you have something that can do these things?"

"How many people?" asked the Sila under his breath.

"As many as I can," replied K-Mart. "There may be 100, and I would like to make the fewest number of trips possible."

"The large creature," said the male. "Is it the one on the level above us? Silver with scales and wings?"

K-Mart nodded, then added, "Yes," when he realized the male couldn't see him.

"I saw him once, and he speaks to me in my mind, sometimes," said the male. "I would like to free him, too, but there is a problem. The giants took all the transporters which can be used for large individuals yesterday. I don't have any more that are functional. I only have one, and it's broken."

"Damn," said K-Mart, "I really want to get him out."

"Me, too," said the Sila. "Let me think." He didn't say anything while he continued to work on the equipment. "I have an idea," he said finally.

"What is it?"

"I can use parts from the ship transporter to build a new transporter for large creatures, but the guard is never going to let me have it."

"How long would you need if you had access to the parts?"

"About 10 minutes," replied the male. "It isn't hard, but I can't rush it."

Gunfire sounded in the distance, and the giant turned toward the sounds, listening intently. A voice could be heard from the box on his harness. A radio. K-Mart set the transportation rod down on the table and became visible. The Sila said nothing as K-Mart calmly aimed his laser rifle and fired twice, hitting the giant in the side of the head with two long blasts. It crashed to the floor.

More gunfire sounded in the distance. As it died, Chomper called on the comm system. *"K-Mart, you'd better hurry. I think they know we're here!"* K-Mart looked at the Sila. "We need to hurry," he said. "Our time just ran out."

Chapter Thirty-Six

Bridge, Efreet Ship *Incinerator*, Ashur Orbit, Unknown Date/Time

"The freighter *Spark* is asking if the captain is available to come to the radio," said the vizier. "What do you want me to tell them?"

"Tell them his second-in-command is standing by and ask what they want," replied Calvin.

"The *Spark* said they are running behind schedule and will have to avoid an enemy warship on the way back. The *Spark* wants to know if we can send a shuttle to get our things, or if they should use their own shuttle. They would prefer that we send our shuttle so they can leave sooner."

"Tell them we'd be happy to send our shuttle," said Calvin, a smile brightening his face for the first time all day. "We will send it as soon as we are able."

"Sir, you're not thinking of doing what it sounds like you're thinking of doing, are you?" asked Master Chief. "We really don't–"

Calvin held up a hand, silencing him. "Ask the *Spark* what they have for us."

The vizier translated Calvin's request, then answered, "They have some supplies, payroll for the crew and the new modules for our engines which will allow us to jump to the other universe and back."

Calvin turned back to Master Chief with a gleam in his eye.

Master Chief sagged. "Yeah, I know," he said in a defeated tone of voice. "We have to go get them." He sighed and then straightened. "Okay, so how exactly do you propose we do this? I may not have been to all the math classes you have, but I can count. We've got 27 effectives, 33 if you count the Mrowry and the Aesir. If the Efreet decided to mutiny right now, we'd be hard pressed to stop them. The only thing we have in our favor is Sergeant Graham; the Efreet don't have a lot that can stop a cyborg."

"That's true," said Calvin, "but she's coming with us to the freighter. If things go badly, we'll need her fire support."

"If things go badly here," said Master Chief, "we might come back to find out we no longer control the ship. I don't like our chances if the Efreet bring this ship's weapons into play. They outgun everything else in this system put together. They could also wipe out all the Sila on the planet. We *can't* lose control of the ship."

"I know," agreed Calvin. The smile was back. "That's why I'm leaving you here as Lieutenant Rrower's second-in-command. I know I can count on you to make sure the ship stays in our hands while we're gone."

"Me? Stay here?" Master Chief asked. "What do you mean, I'm staying here? I'm the most qualified person you have to lead an attack on an enemy ship. Who has more training than I do?"

"No one," admitted Calvin.

"Damn right," huffed Master Chief.

"You also have more experience with guerilla warfare, booby traps and leading a small force against a much larger one. I'm leaving the lieutenant here to figure out the workings of the ship; you're staying here to lead its defense."

"Wouldn't it be better to destroy this ship and take everyone over to the freighter?" asked Master Chief, trying a new approach. "That way we bring all of our combat effectives to the fight and don't have to worry about losing control of the destroyer. Besides, who are you going to take with you in the shuttle to talk to the freighter? The vizier?"

"Hmm…I hadn't thought of that," said Calvin. "We need someone on the ship to talk to the freighter if they call, and we also need someone on the shuttle to talk to them. We definitely need someone on the shuttle, because we'll need guidance for getting to the docking port."

Captain Nightsong cleared his throat. "I am a little rusty, but I can speak a bit of Efreet. I haven't spoken it in a couple of millennia, but I've been listening to the vizier, and I think I can pull it off."

"Perfect," said Calvin. "Captain Nightsong will stay here to talk to the freighter if needed, and we'll take the vizier with us because we'll be doing more communicating. If we do it this way, we'll be able to keep the destroyer to help defend the Sila, and we will still have enough troops to go to the freighter."

Master Chief could see he was beaten. "Who are you leaving me with?"

"I'm going to leave what's left of the Ground Force, as well as the Mrowry and the Aesir. The Aesir are about out of nanobots, so they are less effective than when we started. Captain Nightsong will be in overall command; you'll have the nine members of the Ground Force, the other four Aesir, Lieutenant Rrower and yourself. That's 16 total to hold the ship. Hopefully, as long as you have the queen, the Efreet won't get uppity."

"And that leaves you what? All of 17 people to go capture the ship?" asked Master Chief.

"16 and a cyborg," said Calvin, "and we'll also have the element of surprise." He turned to Night. "Sound like enough to you?"

"What's our mission, sir? A quick smash and grab to get the engine components, or a full-blown assault to take over the ship?"

"Well, let me put it to you this way," said Calvin. "If we grab the engine parts, how are we going to get them to our universe? We already burned out one of the control rods, and that was just trying to bring a cyborg across. How well do you suppose it will work for engine parts? There's only one thing in this system that can get those components to our universe, and it's the ship which brought them here in the first place. It's also the best chance we have for getting our remaining cyborg back across. That freighter not only has the technology we need to be effective in our war with the Efreet, it's also our ride home. We're going to do a smash and grab all right…but we're grabbing the freighter."

"When you put it like that, sir," said Night, "how can I refuse?"

Cockpit, *Shuttle Five*, Ashur Orbit, Unknown Date/Time

"*S*huttle Five, *this is* Spark *control. The packages heading to the* Incinerator *will be waiting for you in Starboard Loading Bay Three. Are you familiar with where to go?*" translated the vizier.

"Beats the hell out of me," said Calvin, who was once again flying the shuttle. "Tell him our normal shuttle pilot is sick and ask for directions."

The vizier spoke on the radio again and then translated, "He said, 'Ah, that explains why your flying is so bad.' He also said the loading bay is on the starboard side of the ship, about halfway down. It will be the only compartment open."

"Do you suppose they have a force field to keep the air in?" asked Night from behind the co-pilot's seat. "Or do you think we'll be in vacuum in the loading bay?"

"I don't know," said Calvin. "Their tech level is all over the place. They have some stuff that isn't much better than what we had before the Psiclopes arrived, but then they have other things like the time bomb that are *way* beyond anything we've got." He thought for a second and then answered the original question, "Have everyone prepared for no atmosphere. Helmets on and buttoned up. We'll try to use the suits to their fullest. Full invisibility. Maybe we'll get lucky and make it to the bridge before anyone notices us."

"That would be nice," replied Night. "We don't have enough people for a running gun battle."

"No, we don't," agreed Calvin. "I'm hoping their freighters are like ours back home. Lots of open space for cargo, with a minimal amount of crew to run the ship."

Calvin paused as he scanned the freighter. "Got it," he said as he found the opening to the bay. "Some landing aids would have been helpful," he grumbled as he jockeyed the shuttle around for entry.

"Just take your time, sir," said Night, getting up to go to the back of the shuttle. "Even if you do it badly, they already know we don't have a professional pilot at the controls." He gave the vizier a grin before exiting the cockpit. Calvin was too busy fighting with the unfamiliar controls to notice.

It didn't help that Calvin was as inexperienced with the landing signals the freighter crewman was giving him as he was with the controls of the shuttle. He had to spin the shuttle slightly, then he overcorrected as he realized the position of the lineman's tail was just as important as the lighted wands he was holding. The shuttle started to oscillate, and Calvin allowed it to drop the final four feet to the deck of the ship, rather than fight the controls any longer.

Two orange lights illuminated on the control panel as the shuttle slammed to a stop. *"We're down."* He commed.

Cargo Bay, *Shuttle Five*, Ashur Orbit, Unknown Date/Time

"Yeah, we felt it," said Night as the ramp started down. *"Those of us who survived the 'landing' are proceeding on mission."*

Night looked into the shuttle bay and could see two of the freighter's crewmen waiting beside several large piles of boxes and equipment. He had already noted the crewmen had helmets on, but now he could also see they were walking normally. *"No air,"* he commed, *"but it looks like there's gravity at least."* The ramp grounded onto the deck. *"Let's go!"*

He led the troops down the ramp, and they spread out, looking for adversaries and defensible positions. The Efreet remained in place, waiting for the crew of the shuttle to disembark, unable to see the Terrans in their suits.

Night scanned the loading bay. The Terrans were in luck; although there were cameras mounted in a couple of places, there didn't appear to be a manned control room overseeing the bay's operations. Two other Efreet drove forklift-like conveyances toward the piles of equipment.

"*Cameras located* here *and* here," he commed, marking them on the tactical map which showed on all the troopers' heads-up displays.

"*I've got one more*," said Sergeant Jones. A number "3" illuminated on the map on the other side of the shuttle where Night couldn't see it.

Night trusted the former CIA agent to know what he was looking at. "*Okay*," Night said. "*You've got that one, Jones. Corporal Burke's got the first one and Sergeant Lancaster's got the second. We'll wait for the forklifts to stop, and then we'll go on my command.*"

"*How are we doing?*" asked Calvin. Night's suit showed his CO was on the shuttle ramp. Good; they wouldn't have to wait for him. A green light lit up on his display. Sergeant Graham was ready.

"*Good, sir*," replied Night as he sent out targeting instructions to his troops. Each soldier received a primary and a secondary target, based on their weapons and positioning. "*We're just about ready to go. Just waiting for the forklifts to stop.*"

"*Stand by*," he said as the forklifts neared the piles of gear. The waiting Efreet were starting to look a little antsy. The forklifts stopped. "*Fire!*" he commed.

A massive blast rocked the shuttle bay as the explosives Sergeant Graham had placed on the airlock door detonated. The door came off its hinges and fell toward the deck. The cameras exploded, and the four Efreet died before it hit.

"*Get the next set of charges ready!*" ordered Night. "*Now!*"

Chapter Thirty-Seven

Bridge, Efreet Ship *Spark*, Ashur Orbit, Unknown Date/Time

"What in the five hells was that?" asked the Efreeti CO as the ship shuddered.

"I do not know," said the intelligence officer, who monitored status both inside and outside the ship. "It appears there was an explosion in Landing Bay Three. It must have been a big one; all the cameras in the bay are out."

"Call the loading bay supervisor," said the CO. "Find out what happened."

"I have been trying to contact the loading bay supervisor," said the intelligence officer. "He isn't responding."

"As badly as the shuttle was flying, I'll bet it crashed," commented the shuttle control officer. "Its fuel must have exploded."

The ship shuddered again.

"Hull breach!" called the engineering officer. "Hull breach in the area of Landing Bay Three."

"Battle Stations," ordered the CO. "Get a damage control crew down there *now!*"

Task Force Calvin, Efreet Ship *Spark*, Ashur Orbit, Unknown Date/Time

In deciding their final battle plan, Calvin and Night had discussed whether to "go loud" or try to sneak their way into the ship. They had come to the conclusion there would likely be a control room or cameras which would give them away; "going loud" at least gave them the initiative. The plan would only work, though, if they could make it to the bridge before the Efreet realized there were intruders on the ship.

The race was on.

"*I've got a map*," said Sergeant Tomaselli for the second time that day. Calvin and Night raced to his side to look at the diagram.

"*Got it*," said Calvin, transmitting the intended route of travel to the group. "*Let's go!*"

A voice began talking on the ship's intercom, and Efreet surged into the passageways as they responded to the emergency.

"*Contact*," said Sergeant Lancaster, who had point. "*Two tangos down*," he added, indicating he had killed two of the enemy.

"Damn," said Calvin. Dead Efreet meant bodies that could be discovered. He had hoped to avoid that. "*Roger*," he commed. "*Pick it up; we've got to get to the bridge* now!"

Bridge, Efreet Ship *Spark*, Ashur Orbit, Unknown Date/Time

"Captain, I am getting strange power readings from the interior of the ship," said the intelligence officer. "I am also showing doors opening where no one can be seen on the cameras."

"What is happening in the loading bay where the shuttle landed?"

"There is nothing going on there," said the damage control officer. "My team just arrived, and there is no one there. The airlock doors have been destroyed, but there are no signs of life. Even our loading crew is gone."

"This is obviously a security test by the *Incinerator*," said the captain. "Initiate all security protocols. Alert the troops."

Task Force Calvin, Efreet Ship *Spark*, Ashur Orbit, Unknown Date/Time

"*Run!*" Calvin ordered as the green lights began flashing. By his estimation, they were about halfway to the bridge. They had been balancing the need for speed with the need to stay undetected. If the lights were flashing, only the need for speed remained.

"*Guards at the next stairwell,*" said Wraith, who was on point.

"*Kill them,*" Night ordered. "*Keep moving!*"

Calvin passed the guards moments later. Both had been shot through the head at close range.

The race to the bridge continued.

Bridge, Efreet Ship *Spark*, Ashur Orbit, Unknown Date/Time

"I've got them," said the intelligence officer. "The intruders appear to be heading for the bridge."

"Do you mean the security team from the *Incinerator?*" asked the captain.

"I do not believe the intruders are from the *Incinerator*," replied the intelligence officer. "They appear to be killing our guards, not incapacitating them. We are being invaded by an unknown force. The only group which matches the capabilities demonstrated by this group is an Alliance force wearing combat suits. We were warned about them by the Jotunn."

"But they are in the other universe, not ours," said the captain. "How did they get here?"

"That is unknown," said the intelligence officer. "All I can tell you, sir, is they are here, and they are rapidly approaching the bridge."

"Lock the doors," ordered the captain, "and get the marines up here *now!*"

Task Force Calvin, Efreet Ship *Spark*, Ashur Orbit, Unknown Date/Time

"*I am at the bridge door,*" reported Wraith.

"*Stack up and get ready to enter,*" said Night; "*we're right behind you.*"

The troops made two lines and prepared to enter the bridge. "*Go!*" Night ordered when he saw everyone was ready.

Wraith pushed the button to open the door, but it remained closed. She pushed it several more times in rapid succession. It stayed shut.

"*Jones, Lancaster, get up here and see if you can rewire the door panel,*" said Night. "*Graham, start cutting the door in case they can't. They obviously know we're here; there's no need for subtlety.*"

The squad made room for the cyborg to get to the door, and her laser snapped on in welding mode. Visors dimmed for the troops facing the door as their suits dealt with its actinic glare.

"Movement from the rear!" called Corporal Pat "Ostrich" Burke. He began firing down the corridor. *"Different troops,"* he added. *"These guys are dressed in green."*

"Holy shit!" added Sergeant Nicholas Tomaselli. *"They're better armed too. They've got lasers as good as ours. Look out Ostrich!"* He dove to the floor and returned fire. Burke crashed to the deck next to him and became visible, a laser hole through his visor. *"Ostrich is down! Medic!"*

"They can't see us," growled Night, *"it was just a lucky shot. Everyone get down and return fire."*

The Terrans dove to the deck, unable to find any cover in the empty passageway.

They were trapped.

Chapter Thirty-Eight

Jotunn Jail, 14 Herculis 'a,' Unknown Date/Time

"Moore of them coming this time," said Rock from the door of the cell. "Fuck!" he yelled as he dove to the side. Several laser bolts hit the bars near where he had been standing.

Rock stood up and crossed the cell to where the group waited behind their makeshift barricade. "This group is armed," he added.

"I saw that," said Chomper. He squatted down behind the only cover they had, the bodies of the fallen giants. "How many are there?"

"Too many," replied Rock. "K-Mart better get back soon."

Bridge, Efreet Ship *Spark,* Ashur Orbit, Unknown Date/Time

"The marines are asking for permission to use the device," said the intelligence officer.

"Will that affect us in here?" asked the captain, looking at the cut in the door. It was growing at an alarming rate.

"The bridge is shielded; it shouldn't affect us," said the intelligence officer.

"Kill the power to the rest of the ship," said the captain. "Tell the marines to proceed."

Task Force Calvin, Efreet Ship *Spark*, Ashur Orbit, Unknown Date/Time

"*Shit*," said several voices simultaneously as the lights went out.

"*Switch to infrared and keep up the fire support*," said Night. "*Graham is over halfway through the door*."

Calvin switched his visor to infrared. The Efreet didn't show up as brightly as humans did, but they could be seen well enough. He fired a couple of shots then turned to see how far Graham still had to cut.

"*What the hell's that?*" asked Sergeant Tomaselli.

Calvin turned back just in time to see the dim outline of a barrel-shaped object come to a stop in the middle of the passageway. It was about three feet in diameter and four feet high, with something small sticking up several feet from its center. A light snapped on at the top that was too bright to look at, causing all of the Terrans' visors to darken. The device started humming with a low electronic vibration which raised the hair on the back of the Terrans' necks.

The barrel looked familiar, Calvin thought. It took him a second, but then he remembered. "*Down!*" he yelled.

The noise from the barrel grew both louder and higher in pitch.

"*Should we shoot it?*" asked Sergeant Tomaselli.

Before Calvin could answer, the barrel detonated.

Chapter Thirty-Nine

Jotunn Jail, 14 Herculis 'a,' Unknown Date/Time

K-Mart paced back and forth, pausing periodically to look out the door to see if any Jotunn were coming. The fight on the other wing must be drawing all the remaining guards; it didn't appear anyone had noticed the giant he killed was no longer replying on the radio.

The Sila working on the transport device looked up. "You know, it doesn't help me to think with you walking around like that," he said. "I'm almost done. Just a couple of seconds more."

K-Mart stopped pacing and listened to the sounds of gunfire in the distance. The volume had dropped by half; one of the Sila slug-throwers must have been put out of action.

"Your friends need your help," said Bordraab. *"You must come and free me, and you must hurry."*

"I know I need to hurry," said K-Mart, *"but I need to wait for the box to get you out."*

"We must join the fight soon," replied the dragon. *"If we go now, we may yet be able to save them, but the Jotunn are readying for a final assault on their position. You must come get me, and you must do it* now!*"*

"On my way," replied K-Mart. He turned back to the Sila.

"I am finished," said the male working on the transporter box. He held it up for K-Mart to see. "It functions the same way the rod does, but has more power for bigger targets."

"Will it work for a large number of people simultaneously?" asked K-Mart.

"Sadly, no," the Sila replied. "I don't know why, but it won't. It wouldn't with the Efreet, anyway. They needed a box that was tweaked a little differently."

"The Efreet have already been here and taken the boxes for mass transportation between the universes?"

"Yes, several days ago," replied the Sila. "They took the 10 boxes I had ready and left. I can make another, but it will take me at least 30 minutes. I have most of the parts I need, but will have to make several of the connectors."

"Yeah, we'll need one of those," K-Mart said. "Keep working on it, and I'll be right back. I'm going to get help."

He pushed the button on his rod, turned invisible and left at a jog. He didn't need the invisibility; he didn't see a Jotunn the entire way to the dragon's cell.

He arrived at Bordraab's wing, out of breath, to find a Jotunn face down on the floor 50 feet from the dragon's cell. The giant was missing half an arm, and a trail of green blood led the rest of the way to the cell.

"Plan B?" K-Mart asked, becoming visible.

"Yes," replied Bordraab. "Unfortunately, my reflexes were slower than I thought. While I was able to bite his arm, I wasn't able to grab him before he could pull away. Sadly, he made it further down the corridor than I could reach. If you could get the keys from him, we can go help your friends."

A quick search of the giant didn't turn up any keys, nor did K-Mart see any places where they might have been. "I don't see them," said K-Mart. "If they are in a front pocket, I don't think I'm going to be able to get them. I can't lift him; he's too heavy." K-Mart went over to the cell. The bars were too close together to allow either him or the box to squeeze through. He turned the box in several directions, but it still didn't fit. "Crap," he said, "I don't think this is going to work."

"Well, then you should go back and save whomever you can," said Bordraab. "Without my help, your friends will be dead within minutes."

"Give me a second," said K-Mart. "There's got to be a way we can do this…I've got it. If you could move to one side of the cell, I will run toward the other side. When I get to the bars, I will push the button on the box and go to the other universe. Since we're on the second floor here, I'll be up in the air there. Once I materialize, I will push the button again and come back into this universe, but I will then be inside your cell. If I time it right, hopefully I can jump high enough that I won't be embedded in the floor when I come back."

"Can you do that?" asked the dragon. "Forgive me, but you do not appear very athletic, and there are many lives at stake."

"I think I can do it," replied K-Mart, "and the bottom line is we don't have much choice. Once I'm in with you, I can climb on your back and activate the box again. Hopefully, you can fly a little bit or something to break our fall. Once we're safely on the ground in your universe, we'll move to where my friends are, and transport back in, taking the Jotunn by surprise."

"I will be nearly as surprised as the Jotunn if all of that goes according to plan," replied Bordraab. "Still…it is better than anything I can come up with at the moment, so I am all for trying it. Hopefully, you'll at least get the box in here so I can escape, even if you kill yourself in the attempt."

"You're just a bundle of optimism, aren't you?"

"Getting free *is* a positive for me," said Bordraab. "I *am* being optimistic…from my point of view."

"Never mind," said K-Mart. "If you would give me a little bit of room, I'll give it a try."

"Now who is not being optimistic?" asked Bordraab. "There is no trying, there is only doing. You can either do it, or you can't."

"Yeah, right," muttered K-Mart, steeling himself for the attempt. "I think I've heard that before." He crossed to the other side of the passageway and took a breath. As he let it out, he started running. The bars of the cell came up fast, and he jumped and pushed the button. He vanished…

Wendar, Day 13 of the Second Akhet, 15th Dynasty, Year 14

*a*nd materialized in the other universe. As he had figured, he was in the air, and he began falling. He pulled his knees up to gain a little space and pressed the button again, rolling in the air…

Jotunn Jail, 14 Herculis 'a,' Unknown Date/Time

*t*o crash down onto the floor of the cell on his back, the box cushioned safely on his stomach.

"You made it," noted Bordraab. "Is the box okay?"

"I'm fine; thanks for asking," grumbled K-Mart, slowly getting to his feet. "No more than a broken rib or three. And yeah, I think the box is good too."

He turned to find one of Bordraab's eyes inches away from his face. The dragon seemed *much* bigger up close, especially the dragon's eye, which was bigger than K-Mart's entire head. K-Mart realized he wouldn't make much of a snack to the dragon; the creature was enormous!

"Hey, umm…we're still friends, right?" asked K-Mart.

"I have no intentions of eating you, if that is what you are worried about," replied the dragon, its breath smelling strongly of chlorine. "We are in a hurry, climb onto my back and let us get going."

"I never thought to ask," said K-Mart, sitting down in the space between its wings, "but you *can* fly, can't you?"

"I could fly quite well before my time in the prison cell," said Bordraab with a sniff; "however, I am sure my wings have atrophied somewhat since I have been caged. They should still work well enough to get us down."

"Ready?" asked K-Mart.

"I have been looking forward to this for some time," Bordraab replied.

"Here we go, then," said K-Mart. "On three. One, two, three!" He pressed the button, and they transferred to the Jinn Universe. The dragon's wings unfolded to their full 130 foot wingspan and flapped once before the pair crashed to the ground.

"*Guh!*" moaned K-Mart as Bordraab's bony spine was driven up between his legs.

"Sorry," said Bordraab, "it appears my wings have atrophied more than I realized. Hmm…it also appears I am not immune from some measure of hubris."

"Yeah…kind of…noticed that," gasped K-Mart, fighting back waves of nausea. "I—"

Pop! Pop! Pop! Bap-bap-bap-bap-BAP! The sounds of several guns firing interrupted K-Mart, followed by the sounds of high-speed projectiles hitting Bordraab in the chest, before whining off.

"If you would please dismount," said Bordraab, "I *am* capable of dealing with this."

K-Mart slid from the dragon's back, and Bordraab charged off in the direction of the shots. His bulk hindered K-Mart's view of what was happening, but to judge by the way several screams were cut off suddenly, he appeared to be winning.

It was over in less than five seconds, and Bordraab returned to where K-Mart waited, still hunched over. "Don't attack a dragon unless you're very sure you can kill it," said Bordraab.

"Important safety tip; thanks," said K-Mart. "I'll make sure I remember it. Umm…it looks like you have part of a…leg, I think, sticking to your upper lip."

Bordraab's forked tongue snaked out and removed the offending matter. He flapped his wings to circulate the blood, and hurricane force winds blew leaves and twigs in all directions. "I feel *better!*" the dragon roared. "Hurry! It is time to kill Jotunn!"

Task Force Calvin, Efreet Ship *Spark*, Ashur Orbit, Unknown Date/Time

"**D**ude," said Sergeant Jamal Gordon, his voice muffled by the confines of his dead suit. "Did anyone, like, get the license plate number of the bus that hit me?"

"Our suits are dead," said Calvin, removing his helmet. "So are our weapons and implants. I've seen this before. The barrel the Efreet just detonated was some sort of explosively-pumped flux generator." In counterpoint, all the suits beeped. "Those beeps are from the suits' emergency backups. We've got two hours until the containment fails, and our suits blow up."

"Blow up?" asked Sergeant Tomaselli.

"Yah, mon," said Sergeant Andrews. "In two hours, the antimatter in our suits is gonna meet the matter surrounding it and then ka-boom! We all go bye-bye."

"Back-up weapons everyone," said Night, shrugging out of his suit. Most of the squad was doing the same. "Pile up the suits; we'll use them for protection."

"Urr…" said a voice from behind Calvin. He turned to find Sergeant Graham leaning face-first on the doorway. She wasn't moving. "Graham, are you okay?" he asked. "Medic!"

"Not…okay," said Sergeant Graham as she slowly straightened. "Operating on…battery back-up. Primary life support…and systems…fried."

"What can we do?" asked the squad's medic, Corporal Higuchi, as he ran up.

"Nothing you…can do," said the cyborg. "Need specialists that…not here. Eight minutes…battery power…remaining."

The lights in the passageway came back on, illuminating the shapes approaching the Terrans.

"Efreet!" yelled Sergeant Lancaster, throwing himself to the floor. "Down!" Several flechette throwers fired, and a wall of metal hit the squad.

Corporal Higuchi fell forward onto the cyborg and slid to the deck, at least six large flechettes in his back. Calvin felt for a pulse.

There was none.

"Jones, Lancaster, get that door re-wired, *now!*" said Night. "We've got to get in there, ASAP!"

"Love to, sir," said Sergeant Lancaster, unconsciously ducking as a flechette ricocheted off the bulkhead next to him. "There's only one problem. It's fried too. There's no way we're getting in there with what we have available. We need something to power the board, and I don't have anything."

"Take...this," said Sergeant Graham. A panel swung open revealing an Alliance battery pack. She pulled it out and handed it to Sergeant Lancaster.

"What's that?"

"Emergency...life support...power," said the cyborg. "Won't last...long...anyway." The cyborg turned and slowly threaded her way through the troopers firing at the Efreet.

"Hey, where are you going?" asked Lancaster, who had appreciated having her bulk shield him from the flechettes as he worked.

"Going to...give you...time," said Sergeant Graham. Her Mrowry autocannon and her primary targeting systems were dead, but the shotgun in her right arm was still functional, as was the manual sight in her right eye. She fired several shells into the nearest Efreeti, whose head exploded under the double ought buckshot loads. She continued down the passageway, firing every few steps. Flechettes slammed into her proto-flesh and ricocheted off her exposed metal parts, but she continued down the hall.

Her life support system out, each step took more of her flagging willpower as her brain died from oxygen starvation. Operating on sheer determination, she reached the next intersection and fired a burst of shells into each of the Efreet hiding there. The last Efreeti dove into her, trying to bring her to the ground, but her bulk was more than he expected. Her combat knife extended from her left wrist and stabbed down into the top of the Efreeti's head. The enemy dropped to the floor.

She looked up just in time to see the laser beam that killed her.

Chapter Forty

Like the tide, the advance of the Jotunn this time was slow but unstoppable. Chomper knew it was a factor of the Terrans' weapons; they weren't big enough. They needed something bigger if they were going to stop the Jotunn…like maybe an M1A1 tank. Too bad there were never any tanks around when you needed them.

Demonstrating that even the Jotunn can learn if you kill enough of them, two giants had gone back to their armory and returned with oversized sheets of metal, which they used like police riot shields. Rectangular, and curved to shed thrown objects, they were strong enough to resist the Terrans' lasers and tall enough to go from the floor to above where the Terrans could see anything to shoot at.

The Jotunn with the shields advanced while the ones behind them provided covering fire. Both the Sila slug-thrower teams were down, proving that having to stand in the open to fire your weapon wasn't conducive to your long-term health in a combat environment.

Only the Terrans were left to defend the women and children, and Chomper saw that the only way they were going to stop the last six giants was to go around to the back of the shields. That meant exposing themselves to the Jotunn laser fire, which had already killed the slug-thrower teams. There was no good choice, Chomper knew; the Terrans could either wait and be overwhelmed, or they could attack and be shot once they came out of cover.

As he fired, Chomper could hear one of the Sila children crying. The child's mother tried to comfort him, but she was too scared to be very good at it. The giants were almost upon them.

Chomper looked over to Rock, who was trying unsuccessfully to bounce a laser bolt off the floor and under one of the Jotunn shields. "You go right, and I go left?" he asked.

"Might as well," grunted Rock. "I'm not having any luck doing it this way."

"Ready?" asked Chomper.

"Does it matter?"

"Not really," said Chomper. "Go!" He jumped up and ran to the left of the advancing Jotunn. The giants saw Rock move first, and they turned to defend themselves from his laser, leaving them unprotected on Chomper's side. Before they could turn back, Chomper shot the closest giant in the head, and it began its long fall to the ground.

As he turned toward the second giant with a shield, a glancing hit from a Jotunn laser burned through the left arm of his suit, searing his arm and causing him to miss his shot. The giant lifted his shield and slammed it down on Rock, smashing his head like an overripe watermelon.

Chomper fired again, hitting the Jotunn in the head with a long blast. He fell. Chomper started to turn toward the laser-armed Jotunn, but a battle axe struck his rifle, shattering it beyond repair and throwing him to the floor.

He tried to push himself up, every fiber of his being yelling, "Run! Escape!" but his left arm wouldn't function properly. Chomper looked down and saw the battle axe hadn't just destroyed his rifle, it had also removed the lower part of his arm. Blood spurted from what remained of his arm, which now ended just below the elbow. The pain hit, and everything went black for a moment. As his vision cleared, he looked up to see a giant standing above him, and Chomper watched in horror as the Jotunn raised his axe in preparation for the blow which would end Chomper's life.

Before the blade could fall, a mass of black fluid struck the giant from behind, and the Jotunn screamed. Some of the spray landed on Chomper, and he watched in rapt fascination as it began to eat through his suit. The burning sensation when it reached his skin caused him to forget about the pain of his missing arm, and his screams echoed the Jotunn's.

The giant threw himself to the ground, trying to put out whatever was burning his back. Chomper watched through graying vision as the Jotunn thrashed back and forth, until finally a massive claw appeared to pin him in place, and a silvery head leaned in to tear out his throat.

A smaller shape came into Chomper's view. He could hear a voice although he couldn't make any sense of it. The form shook him, and Chomper tried to focus. The voice became a little clearer, but still sounded like it came through a foot of water. "Hold on," said K-Mart. "We're here to help you."

"Took you…long enough," wheezed Chomper.

He closed his eyes and died.

342 | CHRIS KENNEDY

Bridge, Efreet Ship *Spark*, Ashur Orbit, Unknown Date/Time

"The marines confirm the device destroyed the enemy's suits," said the intelligence officer, looking up from the claw-held radio he was talking into. "The marine commander reports they have brought up one of their combat laser systems and are making great progress. He warned us to stay away from the door and says he will have the enemy destroyed within moments."

Task Force Calvin, Efreet Ship *Spark*, Ashur Orbit, Unknown Date/Time

"Ziiiiip-*PEW!*" The laser system that killed Sergeant Graham fired again, striking Sergeant Lancaster in the back. As he slid to the floor, Calvin could see a three centimeter hole all the way through him.

Calvin had seen the device as it turned the corner. It looked like a seven foot tall box on a tracked wheel system. It had to be a robot or something similar; Calvin didn't think there was enough room inside it for one of the Efreet. From the front, all the Terrans could see was a rounded shield which protected the machine behind it. A small firing slit was cut into the shield for the laser to fire through. Bullets from the Terrans' guns whined off ineffectively from its shield.

Gunnery Sergeant Bryant was down. Mongo had tried to charge the robot and had died with a laser shot to his chest.

"We're screwed sir," said Sergeant Jones from the door. "The laser bolt that killed Lancaster also struck the door control panel, and it's fused into a solid lump. We aren't getting in this way."

"Is there anything we can do?" asked Calvin.

"No, sir," replied Sergeant Jones. "Like I said, we're screwed. I can't do anything with the door."

"Ziiiiiip-*PEW!*" Sergeant Hiley's head exploded as the next laser bolt struck.

"We've got to get out of here, sir," said Night. "We can't stay here and take this."

"I know," said Calvin. "Let's try to break out and make it back to the shuttle."

"I've got this, sir," said Sergeant Tomaselli. He dodged as he ran down the passageway, arming a grenade. A flechette round struck him in the right shoulder, and he was spun around and knocked to the deck.

"Ziiiiiip-*PEW!*" The laser fired, the bolt going through the space where Tomaselli would have been, had the flechette not hit him.

Tomaselli scrambled forward, rising as he continued toward the robot.

"Ziiiiiip-*PEW!*"

Tomaselli fell as the next round hit him in the chest, the grenade rolling free from his lifeless hand to roll up against the bottom of the robot's shield. It detonated.

"Ziiiiiip-*PEW!*" The laser fired again, and the machine rolled forward, seemingly unaffected by the blast.

"Terrans! We are leaving," yelled Calvin as the ship shuddered noticeably. "Back to the shuttle on three. One…two…"

Before Calvin could say, "Three," the door to the bridge slid open. All the Efreet inside had their claws up. They were in.

Bridge, Efreet Ship *Incinerator*, Ashur Orbit, Unknown Date/Time

"Well, sir, you know I was a little disappointed when you left me behind," said Master Chief, "but then I realized you must have done it for a reason. I asked myself, 'Now Ryan, why would he have taken your squad and left you, his best assault tactician, behind?' The only thing I could come up with was that you were probably going to get yourself into trouble like you always do, and I would have to do something to save you, like I always do."

"I seem to remember you being in the jail cell next to mine when we were down on the planet," noted Calvin.

"True," said Master Chief; "very true. However, in my defense I'd like to point out the only reason we were in jail in the first place was because of you; I didn't want any part of coming to this universe." He paused. "I'd like to go get my ribs taped at some point today, sir. May I continue?"

"Be my guest," said Calvin.

"So, since I knew you would probably get in trouble, again, I knew I would probably have to come up with something to save you, again. Since we didn't have another shuttle pilot, I knew trying to fly over to the freighter was going to be difficult, so I had to think about a different means of saving your ass. Then it dawned on me. What has the biggest guns in this system? The Efreet ship we're currently on. I just needed to figure out how to use them, and everything would work out fine. Long story short, I told my plan to the Mrowry officer, and we grabbed a couple of them giant salamander things and convinced them it was in their queen's best interest to fire a few warning shots across the bow of the freighter you were in, just to get their attention. When we accidentally hit the ship with the second shot, their captain was more than willing to discuss his surrender."

Chapter Forty-One

Castle Courtyard, Ashur, Unknown Date/Time

"I am glad to see you again," said the caliph. "It is with great sorrow I note your numbers are much diminished. My vizier has already given me a quick report of your accomplishments, and I am astounded at the odds you have overcome. Although many of my own citizens were killed in the revolt, we are overjoyed to have thrown off the yoke of the Efreeti oppressors. I have arranged a ceremony tomorrow at which all of your men, both living and dead, will be honored for the sacrifices they made to help us in our struggle for freedom."

"I'm sorry, Caliph, but we will be unable to stay for that," said Calvin. "We have already been in your universe for far longer than we initially intended, and I am sure our people are extremely worried about us. We must get back."

"I was afraid you'd say that," said the caliph; "you must promise to come back as soon as you are able to formally receive your awards." He clapped his hands twice, and two stewards approached. The first steward carried a box, and the second brought a control rod on a crimson pillow.

The caliph handed Calvin the box. "This box contains your awards, naming each of you as a 'Hero of the Caliphate.' It is the highest military award we have."

"Thank you," said Calvin. "We were honored to help you free yourselves from the Efreet."

"And this is our last control rod," said the caliph, handing it over. "I would like to give it to you for your service to my people. It is my hope that someday you will return so my people can thank you properly for that service. If there is ever anything we can do for you, you only need to ask, and it will be done."

"Thank you for this gift," said Calvin. "We will use it to make more of them, so we *can* return to establish relations between our two cultures. I am sorry to leave you ill-prepared to defend yourselves if the Efreet return; however, we will leave the warship in orbit to help with your world's defense. You are going to have to begin training a space force of your own as you will need it if you intend to keep the freedom you have won."

"Your words are wise," said the caliph. "I have already appointed a vizier to oversee the creation of this 'space force' of which you speak. It will not happen overnight, but I hope to have a space force in place before the Efreet return."

"There is one other thing I would ask of you, Caliph," said Calvin.

"If it is within my ability to provide," said the caliph, "it shall be yours."

"It would be very helpful if we could have a couple of your people return with us to our universe," said Calvin. "We are going to take the freighter and some of their engineers with us, but we will need someone who can speak Efreeti to translate for us, at least at the start."

"There are only a few who are able to speak a common language with you," said the caliph. "I cannot leave during this time of upheaval, nor would it be proper for my daughters to return with you without appropriate chaperones."

"I will go in your place, my caliph," said Grand Vizier Jafar al-Barmaki. "I have already spent much time with them. Although they are strange, I am familiar with their ways."

"I will miss you, my friend," said the caliph. "Thank you for volunteering." The vizier bowed.

"Is there anything else you need?" asked the caliph.

"No," said Calvin. "The cost was great, but I think we achieved everything we came for."

Dendaran Valley, Wendar, Day 16 of the Second Akhet, 15ᵗʰ Dynasty, Year 14

"It's going to be tough to get through their lines," said K-Mart, looking over the crest of the hill at the battle playing out in the valley below. The longer he looked, the less it looked like a battle and more like a rout. The caliph's troops were fleeing toward a city on the horizon in disarray, pursued by a larger number of enemy forces. "They're all spread out…we're going to be seen, and when we are, we don't have the weapons necessary to fight our way through."

"I would fly you over them," said Bordraab, "but I am not strong enough to carry more than just a few at a time. I would have to make at least 20 round trips, and I do not think I have regained enough of my strength to do that yet."

"It won't be a problem," said the third person on the hilltop, Captain Elorhim Silvermoon. Although K-Mart and Bordraab had arrived too late to save Rock and Chomper, they had only met one Jotunn on the way to rescue the Aesir; it had been quickly dispatched by Bordraab, and the elves set free.

When they transported back to the Jinn Universe, though, they found the battle had passed them by, and they had spent most of the next several days trying to catch up with the caliph's troops while dodging enemy patrols.

"I'm not sure why you think it won't be a problem," said K-Mart. "Bordraab can't carry everyone over the lines, and I don't want to risk the women and children trying to sneak them through the Efreet."

"I have a couple of Eco Warrior teams in my group," stated Captain Silvermoon. His tone indicated he thought that explained everything.

"I don't know what those are," said K-Mart, "but without weapons, I don't see how even the best warriors are going to get us through that mess down there."

"The Eco Warrior teams *are* weapons," said Captain Silvermoon. "They have a number of types of nanobots they can use to accomplish more than you ever would have thought possible."

"If they are so powerful, why didn't you all escape before now?" asked K-Mart.

"Where would we have gone if we escaped?" asked Captain Silvermoon. "We haven't used them because we didn't have anywhere to go until now. Had an opportunity presented itself, we would have taken it; sadly, we never had the chance."

"So, what's your plan?" asked K-Mart.

"We wait until nightfall, then we slip through the lines," said Captain Silvermoon. He looked at the dragon. "We send the women and children back on Bordraab; hopefully, he can carry all of them."

"She," said Bordraab.

"She what?" asked K-Mart.

"Your language doesn't have a word which properly defines my gender," replied Bordraab. "Of the choices you have, I am closer to a 'she.'"

"My apologies," said Captain Silvermoon. "We wait until nightfall, then we slip through the lines. Hopefully *she* can carry all the women and children and fly them back to your ally's side of the lines."

"There are only two women and three children," replied Bordraab; "I can do that."

"Good," said Captain Silvermoon. "Okay, that just leaves us to sneak through the lines, and that's the easy part."

"That's the *easy* part?" asked K-Mart. "Sneaking through the enemy lines is going to be easy?"

"No, it will be quite challenging," replied the Aesir; "however, I have faith that my teams will get us through the Efreet. The problem is, what then? How do you plan to get us through the friendly lines without being shot? While I appreciate you setting us free, it really isn't much of a rescue if we get shot by the people we are risking our lives to help."

"Ah, I see," said K-Mart, finally understanding.

"Bordraab is going to have even more difficulty," added Captain Silvermoon, "as it does not appear there are any dragons on this planet. What would you do in the middle of a war if an enormous, unknown creature suddenly appeared?"

"I'd probably shoot first and ask questions later," said K-Mart with a sigh.

"I'd expect as much too," replied Captain Silvermoon. "I don't know how well her scales will stop bullets, but I'm sure no one wants to find out."

"Especially me," said Bordraab. "I think you will see, however, that just like your Eco Warrior teams, I am more than I appear."

"You are already quite formidable," said Captain Silvermoon. "What else can you do?"

"*I can also talk to them like this,*" said Bordraab telepathically. "*Hopefully, I can convince them not to shoot me before they are able to see me. Maybe I can even warn them about your arrival so you don't get shot by the caliph's troops when you approach.*"

"That would be nice," said Captain Silvermoon. "Is there a range to your telepathy?"

"Alas, it is rather short-ranged," said Bordraab. "You would already be within weapons range before I could hear you coming."

"Then we will give you a sign when we are close," said Captain Silvermoon.

"A sign?" asked Bordraab. "What kind of a sign?"

"I don't know yet," replied the Aesir, "but knowing my people, it *will* be obvious. You will know it when you see it."

Chapter Forty-Two

"So, we rounded up most of the Efreet and took them to the planet where the Sila could guard them," said Calvin. "We kept a few onboard the freighter to help us run it, and we left a few onboard the destroyer to help the Sila figure out how to operate it."

"Do you think that was wise?" asked Captain Griffin. "What if the Efreet are able to take back the ship from the Sila? They could wipe them all out."

"We moved the queen back to the planet," Calvin replied. "With her there, we didn't think the Efreet would randomly bomb the planet, even if they were able to take the ship."

"Based on what you already told us, I guess that makes sense," said Captain Griffin. "Bottom line; were you able to learn anything that can help us against the Jotunn?"

"I wasn't able to learn anything about the time bomb," said Calvin, "as they didn't have any onboard. I do, however, think it's safe to say the force allied with the Jotunn is the Efreet. Even though the destroyer we captured didn't have any bombs onboard, some of the Efreet said their ship had been in that system a long time. It is possible the weapon represents new technology or is only on certain types of ships."

"Anything else?"

"Yes, there is," said Calvin with a smile. "You'll remember the Efreeti freighter was bringing equipment for their destroyer? Guess what it was?"

"No idea," said Captain Griffin, "and I'm not really in a guessing mood. Why don't you just tell me."

"They were bringing jump modules for the destroyer."

"Jump modules? Are those what I think they are?"

"Yep, that's what lets them go back and forth between universes."

"Can we put them on the *Terra?*" asked Captain Griffin.

"Unfortunately, no," said Calvin. "We asked the Efreet, and they said two modules wouldn't jump a ship the size of the *Terra.*"

"Oh, damn," said Captain Griffin. "I was looking forward to giving them a taste of their own medicine."

"I figured you'd say something like that, ma'am," said Calvin, "which is why we brought back some more we found in the freighter's hold. They tell me eight will be enough to jump the *Terra*, so we brought back 10, just in case we were a little short." The smile faded from his face. "I hope it works," he added; "we lost a lot of good men and women getting them."

"I know," said Captain Griffin. "What do we have to do to get them linked into our system?"

"I brought back a couple of the Efreeti engineers and the vizier to help translate," said Calvin. "Our suits picked up a lot of the Efreeti language; it's too bad they were all destroyed in the attack."

"How does it feel to be without implants once you've had them?" asked Captain Griffin.

"It sucks about as much as it did the first time this happened," said Calvin. "As soon as we're done here, I'm headed to medical. I'm hoping they have a spare set they can give me. If not, I'll go to the replicator and make them myself."

"Well, that's all I had," said Captain Griffin. "We will return to the system where you found the *Blue Forest* and see if we can recover the Aesir. If we can get the jump modules to work, we will also jump through to the Jinn Universe and see if we can find the two fighters you lost. Are there any other questions?" She looked around the room, but no hands were raised. "In that case, you all know your jobs, and what we need to do. You're dismissed, although I'd like the chief engineer to stay a few minutes so we can discuss the jump modules."

As everyone rose to attend to their tasking, Calvin stopped Lieutenant Bradford, the Department X combat systems engineer and handed him the sword he had used in the Sila universe.

"Do me a favor," Calvin said. "Take a look at this sword, but...umm...be careful. When I drew it in the Efreeti jail, it burst into flame."

"Burst into flame?" asked Lieutenant Bradford. "Just like that, without any reason?"

"No reason I'm aware of," said Calvin. "I pulled it out of the scabbard, and it was instantly coated in flames."

Lieutenant Bradford held the sword a little further from his body, obviously worried the sword might spontaneously combust. He gingerly drew the rapier's blade out of the scabbard a couple of inches, but nothing happened. He pulled it out a little further. When it still didn't react, he drew it all the way and inspected the very normal-looking blade.

"Flames, sir?" asked Lieutenant Bradford. "Whatever caused them seems to have ceased functioning."

"I don't know what caused it," said Calvin. "All I know is when I drew it, the sword's blade glowed a bright blue, and then became completely engulfed in flames." He shrugged. "Looks normal enough now; I agree. Take a look anyway and see if you can tell what caused it. Maybe there was a coating or something on it we can use."

"I will look into it immediately," said Lieutenant Bradford.

"Good," said Calvin; "thanks. When you're done, take a look at this." He reached into his pocket and pulled out the golden control rod. "See if you can find out what makes these things function. When you're done, we need to get them scanned. I have a feeling we're going to need a bunch of them, and we'll probably need them soon. Very soon."

Bridge, TSS *Terra*, Epsilon Indi, July 28, 2021

"*E*ngineering, Bridge," commed the CO, "*are you ready for the test?*"

"*The Efreeti is giving us a thumb's up, or a claw's up, or something,*" said the chief engineer. "*We're as ready as we're going to be.*"

Captain Griffin hoped this test ended better than the previous three had. The first time, nothing happened because they had the power wrong. Instead of three-phase power, the Efreet used four-phase. Not only had the test failed, it had burned up one of the jump modules.

It was a good thing Calvin had brought extras, thought Captain Griffin. Having to completely disassemble a jump module to replicate it would have taken time...time they didn't have.

The second time, the tolerances were off. The modules were all powered correctly, but they had to fire within 0.01 seconds of each other in order for the fields to overlap correctly. That had taken over a day to figure out; most of it lost in trying to translate the Efreet troubleshooting instructions into English. It said something about the state of education in the Efreeti Empire, Captain Griffin thought. Technical instructions in the Terran Navy were generally written at the 10th grade level; in the Efreeti Empire, it seemed like they were written for 1st or 2nd graders. In order to explain things at that level, it often took several paragraphs of introduction just to explain the technical terms used in the procedure.

The troubleshooting instructions had finally been deciphered, and the cause of the jump failure determined. In order to get the required accuracy, the engineers had enlisted the aid of the *Terra's* artificial intelligence to run the module activation. Terra had assured Captain Griffin it was several orders of magnitude more accurate than what was needed, and it had sounded slightly miffed the question was even worth asking.

The third test, everything had appeared to work, but the *Terra* still hadn't jumped. Terra swore it had accurately activated the modules within the accepted tolerances, sounding even more miffed that its capabilities had been called into question a second time. One of the junior engineers found the solution several hours later, having decided to re-read the installation manual. As he noted, 'Dad always said, if all else fails, read the instruction manual.' At the back of the book in the "Things People Do Bad To Make The Stuff Not Work" section, the engineer found a note that said the modules at the front of the ship had to be initiated first.

Since all the modules were sitting next to each other in Engine Room One, he read a little further and found the modules had to be spread equally throughout the ship to work correctly. This necessitated moving seven of the boxes and reinstalling them, which took more time. The chief engineer swore it would work this time. Captain Griffin hoped it would, or she was going to maroon him on the next planet, habitable or not.

"Terra, are you ready for the test?" asked Captain Griffin.

"I am ready to do my part correctly, just like the last time," replied the AI. The snarky tone was still there, Captain Griffin noted.

"On my mark, then," said Captain Griffin. "Standby, *mark!*"

There was a flash on the front screen, but otherwise everything remained exactly as it had been.

"Did it work?" asked Captain Griffin.

"The Efreeti freighter *Spark* has vanished," said Terra. "Either we made the jump into the Jinn Universe or they did. I find it improbable that they jumped, much less that they picked exactly the same time as we fired our engines to do so. I find it greater than 99.9999 percent probable we have successfully jumped out of our universe although it will take my sensors some time to determine where we actually are."

"Thank you," said Captain Griffin. "That was well done, as expected." She changed to her comm. "*Engineering, CO, how's everything looking down there?*"

"*Good, ma'am, I think. Everything here appears normal...although I don't know what normal is supposed to be with these damn things. If nothing else, at least they didn't blow up...or meltdown...or something.*"

"*Outstanding. Any reason not to go back?*"

"*Not that I'm aware of, ma'am.*"

"Terra, please jump us back to our universe." As she said it, Captain Griffin realized her error. They shouldn't have jumped in a system without support. If they weren't able to jump back, and she was anything but certain about the jump system at the moment, no one would know what happened to them. They might have enough fuel to make it home, but home was 12 light years away. Even at 0.99 the speed of light, it would still take them over 12 years, objectively, to get home...and they would still be in the wrong universe once they got there. It was probably the dumbest thing she'd ever done. She didn't want to say anything and jinx it.

"Yes, ma'am," said the AI. "Jumping in three, two, one, now."

Once again the screen flashed, but nothing seemed to change.

"Is the freighter back where it is supposed to be?" Captain Griffin asked. Please be there, please be there, please be there...

"No," replied Terra, "it is not."

Captain Griffin's heart sank. "Any idea what went wrong?" she asked.

"Nothing went wrong," replied the AI. "We are back in our normal universe. The freighter isn't where it was expected to be, though. It has moved further than it should have in the time we were in the Jinn Universe. It is most puzzling."

"But we're definitely back in our universe?"

"Yes, without a doubt."

"Good," said Captain Griffin, uncrossing her fingers. "In that case, let's quit screwing around and get to where we're supposed to be."

Dendaran Valley, Wendar, Day 16 of the Second Akhet, 15th Dynasty, Year 14

Bordraab launched as darkness fell, her five passengers tied on with vines the Aesir had found. K-Mart watched them fly off until he couldn't see them anymore. Wishing it could have been that easy for all of them, he turned to Captain Silvermoon and said, "Ready when you are."

Captain Silvermoon nodded once and turned to seven Aesir standing in a small group. "Good hunting," he said with another nod. Two Aesir threw their hands up in the air, and the entire group vanished.

K-Mart looked for them, using all the sensors in his suit, but couldn't find them. "Where did they go?" he asked.

"Those are my Eco Warriors," replied the Aesir. "They will clear a path for us."

"But where did they go? I can't find them, even with my suit's sensors."

"Technology is only as good as the race which built it," replied Captain Silvermoon. He smiled. "It appears ours is better." He turned, and all the Aesir started forward at the same time as if connected by an invisible rope. The Sila males and K-Mart were drawn along after them.

One of the planet's moons was up, but it was only a small crescent that provided little light. The Aesir did not seem to have a problem seeing in the near total darkness, nor did K-Mart with the suit's enhancers, but both the Sila males were stumbling over small objects within seconds. Two Aesir came to their aid, with each of them taking one of the Sila by the arm.

They walked for 15 minutes after they reached the valley floor without seeing any of the Efreet although campfires and lighted areas were all around. K-Mart could smell food cooking several times and wanted to stop and ask Captain Silvermoon how they were able to avoid all the enemy, but then he came upon several Efreet bodies. Apparently the Eco Warriors weren't just avoiding the enemy, they were also silently neutralizing the Efreet when they needed to. Even with his suit's audio sensors turned all the way up, K-Mart hadn't heard a thing.

Without warning, Captain Silvermoon appeared in front of him, causing him to stop. "How are the local vehicles powered?" he whispered.

"They're electric," replied K-Mart. "They don't have fossil fuels on this planet."

"That will work," a disembodied voice said.

Captain Silvermoon turned back to the direction of travel. "What will it work for?" asked K-Mart.

The Aesir shook his head and indicated K-Mart should be quiet. The journey continued.

Their passage was incredibly surreal, K-Mart thought. To be close enough to see the Efreet all around, and even a few of the Jotunn around campfires, but never come into contact with them seemed incredible.

"Crap…" said K-Mart as they stopped at what had been an Efreeti camp site. At least eight of the enemy were spread out around a fire. All were dead, and most were bristling with flechettes…almost as if they had suddenly decided to shoot each other.

Several of their vehicles stood nearby with their access panels open; he watched as parts flew from the vehicles and stacked themselves near the fire, while the visible Aesir added Efreeti ammunition to the pile. The entire process happened silently, and K-Mart realized the Aesir must have some sort of implant network like the Terrans. If not, their ability to do things without saying anything was creepy. Damned creepy.

Only a minute or two was spent at the camp, then one of the Aesir waved for K-Mart to follow her, and the rest of the group started forward again. Two minutes later, the sky brightened behind them. K-Mart turned to look, and his facemask darkened to save his night vision. A massive fireball engulfed the Efreeti camp, with smaller streamers and pyrotechnics leaping out from the central mass as the ammunition cooked off.

Yeah, the Sila would know they were coming all right. It would take a blind man to miss that.

Combat veterans, the Aesir didn't stop to admire their handiwork. When K-Mart turned back to the Aesir, they were already moving toward the Sila lines, and he had to hurry to catch up. They raced forward into the darkness, and the commotion behind them faded quickly.

K-Mart had all his suit's sensors on high enhancement although it didn't help much. He wished he had one of the platoon's combat suits rather than his aviator suit; his was optimized for survival in space, not ground combat.

The Aesir continued into the night. After another five minutes of travel, K-Mart's suit began to pick up thermal images in front of him. He grabbed the closest Aesir and pointed in the direction of the heat sources, but the Aesir only nodded.

"You are almost to the friendly lines," said Bordraab mentally. *"I have alerted them to your presence."*

"Did you have any problems?" asked K-Mart.

"Not many...once they realized I wasn't going to eat them. Having the women and children along to vouch for me helped."

Within a minute, K-Mart was through the lines and welcomed by the Sila. He was safe.

Despite their enthusiasm for seeing his group, he could tell the defenders were tired, cold and dejected. K-Mart realized that even though he was safe, for now, he had put all of his effort into joining up with the forces who were losing the war.

He wasn't safe, after all.

Chapter Forty-Three

"Welcome back," said the Thor from the screen on the bridge. "Were you successful in finding the information you sought?"

"Yes, we were," said Captain Griffin. "Lieutenant Commander Hobbs made it to the other universe and brought back the technology we need to jump our ship into it."

"We never doubted his ability," said the Thor. "After all, he is the hero; we would expect no less."

"I appreciate your confidence," said Calvin; "however, I didn't do it by myself. I lost over half my platoon in the effort."

"If you brought back the technology," said the queen, moving into range of the camera's pickup, "then their sacrifice was not in vain. What you do with their sacrifice will give meaning to it. I have lived several thousand years, and I have lost many friends along the way. Each life is precious. To give one's life for a friend is a precious gift; one which must not be misspent. If their sacrifice prevents or shortens a war that would have cost millions, or even billions, of lives, their sacrifice was worthwhile. I know that doesn't make their loss any easier, and I am not trying to make light of it. My people will treasure the gift they have given us, and I will commission a tribute in their name."

"Thank you," said Calvin, the two words all he could manage through the lump in his throat.

"We are ready to go back to where we saw the wreck of the *Blue Forest*," said Captain Griffin. "Were you able to assemble any additional ships to aid us against the Jotunn ship in the system there?"

"You will find three battleships waiting for you in Gliese 221," said the Thor. "With the addition of your ship, you should have no problems with the Jotunn vessel."

"As long as they haven't brought in reinforcements, their ship shouldn't be a problem," agreed Captain Griffin. "However, as I understand it, that was one of their smallest types. I would hate to gate into that system and find one of their dreadnoughts waiting for us."

"Four battleships versus one of their dreadnoughts *would* be poor odds," agreed the Thor. "Let us hope you do not find one waiting for you."

"Let us also hope you find our sons and daughters," said the queen. "If so, please bring them home as soon as you can."

"We will," promised Captain Griffin. "If there is any way to do so, we will bring them home. *Terra* out." The screen went blank.

"Lieutenant Commander Hobbs?" asked a voice from behind Calvin.

Calvin turned to find Lieutenant Bradford, the combat systems engineer from Department X. It must be important, Calvin thought; he had never seen the engineer on the bridge before. "Yes?" Calvin asked.

"I just finished analyzing your sword, and it's all very strange, sir."

"Really?" asked Calvin. "You mean most swords don't spontaneously burst into flame?"

"No, they don't," said Lieutenant Bradford, missing the sarcasm. "I've been trying to reconstruct what happened, based on the residue, and it looks like there were some really interesting processes going on. I wish I could have been there to see it; it must have been really cool."

"I'm not sure fighting giant salamanders armed with flamethrowers is what I would call 'cool,'" said Calvin. "I'm afraid I was a little too busy at the time to appreciate the coolness of it all." He saw how excited the lieutenant was and relented. "Okay, what did you find that was so cool? Was there some sort of coating on it that caused the effect?"

"No, sir," replied Bradford; "it wasn't because of a coating. The answer is much more fascinating. It looks like there were at least two separate processes going on simultaneously. Either could have, and one of them probably should have, killed you. As it is, you probably did get irradiated, and you should get yourself checked out. The sword was still radioactive…although not *too* dangerously so. Still, you're lucky to be alive."

Calvin blinked; all kidding gone in an instant. "Killed me? What do you mean?" he asked, his attention focused on the engineer.

"The first process has to do with silver, which appears to be exceedingly unstable in the other universe. I found numerous traces of palladium on the blade where the silver was eaten away. All I can figure is that the silver was decaying into palladium. That actually makes sense now that I think about it." He paused for a second, deep in thought. "Yes, that would do it. If the silver decayed into palladium, it would have emitted a positron, which would have further decayed into some sort of gamma radiation when it annihilated an electron, and that would have made your sword glow blue." He nodded. "Hmm, that sort of fits the evidence. Positron decay. It seems like there's more to it, though…something I'm missing…." He focused on Calvin again. "Regardless, there was a nuclear fusion reaction going on at the same time, which was even more dangerous to you. It looks like a light gas, probably helium, was being adsorbed into the silver. That process would probably make it glow and maybe even break into flame?"

Calvin nodded.

"What do you know about cold fusion, sir?" asked Lieutenant Bradford.

"Ummm…not a whole lot," replied Calvin, thrown by the question. "Just what we got in the download when we got our implants." He paused to process what he had downloaded. "The Psiclopes figured out how to get around the Coulomb barrier and fuse helium-3 at low temperatures about 2,000 years ago. The only high-energy by-product of the fusion process is a proton, which is contained within an electromagnetic field. The proton interacts with the containment field and results in electricity generation."

"Correct," said Lieutenant Bradford. "A similar fusion process appears to have taken place on your sword with the adsorption of the helium. Not only did you have a flaming sword, but you also had one that wouldn't have run out of fuel any time soon, as only a tiny bit of nuclear conversion was necessary for the reaction. If you had let it keep going, the sword would have become brittle over time, but it would probably have taken centuries to use up even a fraction of the sword." He smiled as if that explained everything.

"Okay, I think I kind of get it," said Calvin. "There were two reactions going on, the fusion reaction and the...what did you call it? Positron decay?"

"Yes, for some reason, silver is unstable in the other universe, and it releases the positron as it decays into palladium. You should be glad it does."

"Why's that?" asked Calvin.

"Because the silver decay is competing with the fusion reaction. If the fusion reaction were allowed to run unchecked by the decay process, the nuclear conversion process would probably heat the sword beyond 800 degrees Celsius. That is the same as 1,472 degrees Fahrenheit, which is hot enough to melt lead. Your sword would have glowed red and started fires on touch; it also would have been very hard to hold onto or store."

"Yeah, I can see how that would have been difficult," said Calvin.

"It works the other way, too," said Lieutenant Bradford. "Having the fusion reaction kept the decay process from going out of control."

Calvin raised an eyebrow. "Now you've lost me. What?"

"If the reaction got out of control, the gamma rays from positron-electron annihilation would have been on the order of several mega-electron volts. They wouldn't have been able to scatter much in that small area, so the sword's holder would have received an enormous dose of dangerous, ionizing radiation, aside from the danger of what was actually happening in the sword. You need to keep both of these processes in mind, sir. Holding a nuclear reactor in your hand is rarely going to be a good idea, no matter which universe you're in."

"Um, yeah. I'll try to keep that in mind."

Bridge, TSS *Terra*, Nu2 Lupi System, August 16, 2021

"When last we were here, the Jotunn ship *Soaring Eagle* was in orbit around a planet about 51 million miles from the star," said Captain Griffin, "along with the remains of the *Blue Forest*. Our mission is to defeat the *Soaring Eagle*, recover the wreck of the *Blue Forest* and any remaining crew members, then the *Terra* will jump to the other universe to see if we can recover the fighters we lost. The *Terra* will lead the assault, as we are able to best deal with any Efreeti vessels we may find there." I hope, she added silently. "We will be followed by the *Shimmering Falls*, then the *Western Aurora* and the *Maroon Mountain*."

"It has been a couple of months since we were here, so it is possible the Jotunn or Efreet have brought in additional forces. The only way we'll find out for sure is to go through the stargate. Remember, you cannot see the Efreeti ships when they are in their own universe, and you *must* be ready for them to pop in without notice. Keep your weapons stations manned at all times. Any questions?"

There were none. "Good luck then," Captain Griffin said, "and good hunting." The screens went blank.

Captain Griffin turned to address the bridge crew of the *Terra*. "Although most of us haven't fought the Efreet, we have seen their freighter in action and know what to expect; we need to be ready at all times. The *Terra* wasn't designed to carry fighters; I want them launched as soon as we enter the system so they don't block our missile and laser ports. I know we only have four fighters, but the

Efreet could appear anywhere, and I don't want us handicapped. Any questions?"

There weren't any questions from her crew either. Combat veterans, they knew their jobs and were focused on doing them.

"All right then," she said. "Proceed to the stargate. Sound General Quarters."

Bridge, TSS *Terra*, 14 Herculis System, August 16, 2021

"System entry," said Steropes. "Launching probes."

"Fighters launching," said 'Lights' Brighton. She added under her breath, "What we have left, anyway."

"Contact," said Steropes. "I've got power spikes from the area of the first planet."

"Me too," said the DSO. "The harmonics match the data on the *Soaring Eagle* that the *Vella Gulf* passed to us."

"Concur," said Steropes; "it's the *Soaring Eagle*."

"The *Shimmering Falls* just gated in," said the OSO.

"We're receiving a call from the Jotunn ship," said the communications officer.

"Put it on screen," said Captain Griffin.

"The *Western Aurora's* here," said the OSO.

The front screen lit up with Captain Fenrir's face. "Ah, the Aesir's lackeys have returned with a bigger ship. And look, they brought friends this time. Isn't that sweet? Three battleships to take on our one, poor little battlecruiser. No wait, four battleships? You honor me."

"You will surrender your ship to us and return any Aesir crew-members you have," said Captain Griffin. "In return, you will be treated well and given a fair trial for war crimes against the Aesir nation. If you fail to do so, you will be destroyed. Do you surrender?"

Fenrir began laughing. "Ho, ho, ho. Us? Surrender to little people like you? Not today, midgets. Not tomorrow or any other time in the future either." He made a motion to someone off screen. "Our purpose wasn't to destroy you, or even to do battle with you. We were sent here to deliver a message, once the Aesir mustered an appropriate force. I say this to the Aesir and anyone else foolish enough to stand with them."

"The *Soaring Eagle* is underway," said the DSO. "It appears to be headed away from us."

"Beware, Aesir, for the Jotunn are coming for you," continued Fenrir. "We have begun Ragnarok, and it will surely end with your destruction. Run, puny ones, run, for we are coming to reclaim our homeland. Anyone who chooses to deny us our birthright will be destroyed. You have been warned." The screen went blank.

"The transmission ended at the source," said the communications officer.

"Try to reestablish communications," said Captain Griffin. She turned to Steropes. "If we went to flank speed, could we catch them?"

Steropes shook his head. "If they continue to accelerate at their current rate, we will not catch them before they reach the other stargate in this system."

"Understood," said Captain Griffin. "Proceed to the first planet and the wreck of the *Blue Forest*."

"Proceeding to the first planet, aye," said the helmsman.

"Sir, the Jotunn are not responding to our hails."

"I didn't think they would," said Captain Griffin. "It looks like they have given us their message, and now they are leaving. I expect they'll be back, but next time they'll be back in force."

"Do you want me to jump to the other universe to begin the search for our missing fighters?" asked the helmsman.

"Not right now," said Captain Griffin. "We said we would help recover any of the *Blue Forest's* crewmembers we could. If they are still onboard the *Blue Forest*, we will help get them. If they're onboard the *Soaring Eagle*, they are out of reach." She paused, looking at the tactical screen. "Besides," she added, "I don't want them to know we can jump to the other universe yet. We'll let that be a surprise for the next time."

"I'm getting power readings from the first planet, ma'am," said the DSO.

"Can you identify them?" asked Captain Griffin. "Could it be the missing Aesir crewmen?"

"No, I can't," said the DSO. "The readings are still very weak, but it looks like there's something on the planet."

"I can't tell what they are either," said Steropes. "We will have to get closer."

Dendara, Wendar, Day 4 of the Third Akhet, 15th Dynasty, Year 14

K-Mart shot the charging giant a fourth time, then a fifth, but the monster kept coming. It had crossed the open area between the battle lines faster than K-Mart would ever have thought possible, drawing the enemy forces along behind him. The caliph's forces were in trouble; K-Mart had seen a number of additional giants on both sides before his focus had narrowed to stopping the behemoth headed toward him. He doubted the lines would hold this time.

He fired again, but the bolt was far less intense and accompanied by the "beep" signifying the rifle's battery was dead. K-Mart knew that he was dead, too; the Jotunn was too close for K-Mart to change the battery in time. The giant was slowed by his shots, and a number of bullets from the caliph's troops, but it wasn't going to be enough.

The giant raised his enormous battle axe over his head, and K-Mart could see his opponent intended to split him in half. K-Mart held his rifle up in both hands to block the stroke. He didn't think he could stop the blow, but if he could just deflect it, maybe he would get another second or two of life.

As the axe fell, a wall of silver intercepted the stroke as Bordraab swooped in from the side. The earth shook as thousands of pounds of dragon and giant crashed to the ground. Bordraab tore out the throat of the stunned giant before it could move, then she looked up for new targets.

K-Mart could tell the dragon had been in the thick of the fighting as several bloody gashes ran down her side, and huge rents had been torn in her wings. Spying her next prey, she gathered herself and leapt into the air. She only made it 15 feet into the air before falling heavily back to the ground.

Her head snaked around to look at K-Mart. "I fear I am spent," said Bordraab, forked tongue hanging out of her mouth like a dog panting.

"Don't worry about it," said K-Mart as he changed out the battery in his laser. It was his last; he'd have to make his shots count. He motioned toward the dead giant with his rifle. "Thanks," he said; "you've certainly done your part today."

K-Mart scanned the battlefield for a target, but the bulk of the dragon blocked most of the enemy lines from his sight. The enemy had also learned it was death to approach Bordraab, and the enemies' common soldiers gave them a wide berth. Part of the battlefield was also covered in smoke from a number of burning Efreeti vehicles. The Eco Warrior teams had set several successful booby traps with the last of their nanobots the night before. It had slowed the enemy for a little while, but they were on the move once more.

"C'mon," said K-Mart as horns began blowing from behind them. "That's the order to fall back." He turned and trudged away from his position on rubbery legs. The Sila on either side of him weren't moving much faster. They all were spent.

"There is only one more set of lines to fall back to," noted Bordraab.

"Yeah," said K-Mart. "It's time to make our final stand."

Chapter Forty-Four

Bridge, TSS _Terra_, 14 Herculis System, August 17, 2021

"It looks like a Jotunn outpost," said Steropes, "but it appears to be abandoned."

"How do you know it's a Jotunn outpost?" asked Captain Griffin.

Steropes brought an image up on the front screen. "This building appears to be the main building in the complex. The imagery indicates each floor is well over 20 feet high. All the other buildings are constructed similarly although they are not as long."

"All right," said Captain Griffin, "I'll agree it is a Jotunn building as I don't know anyone else who needs 20-foot tall ceilings. Any guess as to what it is?"

"There is a fence around it, so I'd say it looks like a jail, or maybe a military compound. It doesn't appear to be inhabited now, though."

"So they probably kept the Aesir there but have now moved them. Are you getting any readings from the _Blue Forest?_"

"It's a hulk," replied Steropes. "It looks like it was hit by at least six of the Efreeti time bombs, as there are a number of holes down its side. Both engines are gone; it isn't going anywhere on its own."

"So it looks like the Jotunn took the Aesir crewmembers with them," said Captain Griffin. "The Thor will not be pleased."

"Is it time to go look for our ships, then?" asked Lieutenant Commander Brighton.

"It is," said Captain Griffin. "Recover our fighters and prepare to make the jump to the other universe."

Dendara, Wendar, Day 8 of the Third Akhet, 15th Dynasty, Year 14

They were doomed, thought K-Mart. It didn't take an army general to see it; the outcome was painfully obvious, even to an aviator. The capital city of Dendara occupied a peninsula which jutted from the northern end of the continent, although it was currently cut off from the rest of the land mass by the enemy troops who spanned the peninsula from east to west. Both the caliph's neighbors had thrown their most capable forces into the fight to end it; the caliph's troops were now outnumbered by more than 10-1, and their enemies had more armored vehicles than the caliph's troops had ammunition to kill them with.

The Jotunn had also equipped the caliph's enemies with lasers that completely outclassed anything the caliph's troops had in terms of range or damage.

The caliph's troops were doomed.

The final attack had begun at dawn. Bordraab had fought from the sky, spitting acid on concentrations of soldiers and their armored fighting vehicles until a group of Jotunn lasers brought her down. No longer able to fly, she scratched out a hole next to the trench in which K-Mart waited. It wasn't much protection for the dragon, but she wouldn't have to wait long; as quickly as the enemy forces were advancing, they would be in the trenches within the next hour.

K-Mart shot a scout who was sneaking up to their lines. With his suit and laser, he had a better tracking system and weapon than his counterparts in the caliph's army, and he was usually able to kill the enemies' scouts before his allies even knew they were present. Too bad his rifle's battery was down to five percent remaining.

He shot at another scout, but was distracted by a commotion from further down the trench.

He turned to see the caliph had arrived, along with the last 20 of his personal troops. The vizier in charge of the battle came running up, ducking to stay below the lip of the trench.

"What are you doing, my caliph?" asked Vizier Bulah. "This is far too dangerous a place for you. The enemy will be here soon, and it is likely this position will be overrun."

"I understand that," said the caliph, "but if this is to be the end, I intend to die in battle." He turned to one of his troops who was carrying a radio on his back. "On my command, give the order to charge."

"I guess this is the end," said K-Mart to Bordraab.

"I am afraid so," said the dragon, surveying the battlefield. "The time in jail has taken too much out of me. I will, however, die with one of the Jotunn in my mouth." She spotted a target and tensed her legs to join the charge.

"K-Mart, Calvin," his CO commed. "I don't know what it looks like down there, but from orbit it looks like you could use a little help. Tell everyone to close their eyes and keep their heads down; it's going to be a big one."

"Incoming!" K-Mart yelled. "Get under cover right now!" He dove into the trench.

Calvin's voice counted down, "Three…two…one…" He might have said "Impact," but it was drowned out by the supersonic shock waves of the incoming kinetic bombardment.

Accelerated to a speed of 36,000 feet per second, 12 of the telephone pole-sized tungsten rods slammed into the planet's surface, with each releasing the kinetic energy equivalent of 120 tons of TNT. Even though his eyes were closed, K-Mart could still see the flash. The blast effect was multiplied as the shock waves overlapped, reinforcing each other, and K-Mart felt himself hammered into the ground, which shook with the violence of a major earthquake. One of the trench walls collapsed, coating him with dirt. At least it helped protect him from some of the flying debris.

When the shaking ended, K-Mart risked a glance above the trench wall. A near-continuous mushroom cloud ran from one end of the enemy's line to the other. Underneath the cloud, there was a half-mile wide strip of...nothing. Everything that had been there, both men and machinery, was vaporized. Even the Jotunn were gone.

K-Mart turned to view his own lines, and what he saw was nearly as bad. Many of the caliph's troops hadn't heard his yell and were injured by the blast and flying debris. Many more had been looking in the direction of the enemy lines and were now flash-blind. At what price, victory, he wondered.

Bordraab had protected herself by throwing her wings over her head, and she didn't appear any more hurt than she had previously.

"*Did that help?*" Calvin asked.

"*Uh, yeah, that helped a lot...for those of us who survived it, anyway,*" said K-Mart. "*Did you have to do it so close to us?*"

"*Close?*" asked Calvin. "*That was 3/4 of a mile from your position. We wanted to make sure we got the enemy's attention.*"

"*Well, there's no doubt about that,*" K-Mart replied. "*Now I know why I'm an aviator. This ground-warfare stuff sucks!*"

"Tell everyone to keep their heads down. There's a second round coming."

When a second earthshattering series of explosions didn't immediately follow, K-Mart risked a look, hoping his suit's visor would protect his eyes from any further flashes. While the first round was anti-personnel, the second round was anti-materiel, and there were no flashes. The incoming rounds initially resembled the telephone poles of the first barrage, but this time the poles separated into a stack of Frisbee-like saucers as they passed through 15,000 feet. The saucers fanned out on both sides of the first strike's ground zero, with some close enough for K-Mart to get a better look as they initiated their attacks.

With the enhancements provided by his suit, he could see the saucers weren't symmetrical; a sensor stuck out from the underside. He couldn't tell whether the targeting system was based on infrared or optics, but the saucers unerringly found the remaining fighting vehicles of the caliph's enemies and homed in on them. Prior to impact, explosives on the upper part of the saucer detonated, firing an anti-armor dart down into the weaker armor on the top of the armored vehicles. Within 10 seconds, all the remaining vehicles were smoking hulks.

"This is our opportunity!" called the caliph. "Soldiers, to me! *Attack!*"

He climbed from the trench and started toward the enemy lines. Though the dust raised by the orbital bombardment was still thick, the devastation of the enemy's forces was visible to the troops, and they raced forward with a renewed enthusiasm to get in front of their leader as he charged toward his opponents.

"For the caliph!" they yelled as they assaulted the enemy lines, invigorated for the first time in weeks. Disoriented and demoralized, the remaining enemy troops were no match for the caliph's forces, and they turned and ran. Although only a few at first, platoon-sized units quickly joined the stampede, then entire companies fled en masse.

The battle was over in minutes; the rout continued for three days.

Dendara, Wendar, Day 8 of the Third Akhet, 15th Dynasty, Year 14

The shuttle landed, raising the dust which had just settled from the orbital bombardment. The ramp at the back was already in motion before the shuttle touched down, and suited Terran Space Marines poured out of the shuttle to set up a perimeter.

K-Mart watched the evolution with pride; the Terran soldiers were obviously professionals who knew their jobs and carried them out without any apparent oversight. The only thing that was odd was how few there were; K-Mart always thought the platoon had more men and women than the 20 or so he could see. He shrugged, deciding the rest of the group must have been employed on other missions.

Calvin walked down the ramp with the Aesir captain K-Mart had seen onboard the *Vella Gulf*. K-Mart climbed from the trench and went to meet them. Reaching the pair, he stopped and saluted.

Calvin and Captain Nightsong returned the salute, the Aesir in the hand-to-chest manner of his race. "We found one of the fighters in orbit," said Calvin. "Are you the only Terran who survived?" he asked, dreading the answer.

"Yeah," said K-Mart. "We had to ditch one fighter so the other would have enough fuel to carry their space station to the surface."

One of Calvin's eyebrows went up. "Space station?" he asked.

"Long story, sir," said K-Mart. "You can buy me a beer, and I'll tell you all about it. In any event, we crashed the other fighter bringing down the space station, which converted us from aviators to ground troops. With our weapons and suits, we were better armed and armored than the rest of the troops here, and we led a series of recon missions back into our universe to rescue the elves from a Jotunn jail."

"You led a recon mission to free the Aesir from a Jotunn prison?"

"Well, it wasn't me alone," said K-Mart. "All four of us did our parts, and it was a little more complicated than that."

"What do you mean?"

"Well, in order to free the Aesir, we had to free a Sila craftsman, so we could get a transportation device, so we could free the dragon, so we could get her help fighting the Jotunn. It's kind of complicated."

"I guess so," said Calvin. "But I see you're here, so I guess you were successful?"

"Yes, sir," said K-Mart. "We rescued the Aesir and their prince. There are about 40 of them left, I think. Assuming the prince wasn't killed in the fighting today, we should be able to return him to his people."

"Outstanding!" said Calvin.

"Yeah, it turned out pretty well," said K-Mart, "aside from losing Rock, Chomper and Hooty. The only thing we missed out on was rescuing some of the Sila scientists who were working on the time weapons. They were in the Jotunn jail we rescued the Aesir from, but we got there too late to save them. Apparently, the Efreet moved them to their home world for safekeeping."

"Did you get any information on where that might be?" asked Calvin. "As you can see, we were able to capture the technology to cross from one universe to the other. If we knew where they were, we could try to take them back from the Efreet."

"No, I didn't," replied K-Mart. "Apparently, every Sila who has been taken to the home world has never been seen again. It's some place named Efron."

"I was afraid of that," said Captain Nightsong.

"What do you mean?" asked Calvin. "What are you afraid of?"

"I know where the planet Efron is," Captain Nightsong said. "Efron is the planet across the boundary from Earth. The home world of the Efreet is the same as yours. Efron and Terra are the same planet; the Efreet could come through and attack your people at any moment."

"Oh, hell," said Calvin. "We've got to get back home right *now*."

Epilogue

Bridge, TSS *Terra,* Golirion Orbit, HD 69830, August 30, 2021

"We are forever in your debt for returning our missing crewmembers," said the Thor, "and I am personally in your debt for returning my son. Despite living long lives, our race does not have many children; to lose any we have is beyond tragedy."

"You're welcome," said Captain Griffin. "We're happy to have been able to rescue them. It is too bad we weren't able to get there sooner; we might have saved more of them."

"You did your best and honored your word," replied the Thor. "What more could we ask of you? If you ever need our assistance, you need but ask, and we will come."

"Thank you for your kind words," said Captain Griffin. "I'm sure my government will have someone here shortly to open up relations between our two civilizations. We, however, just found out the Efreeti home world in their universe is the same planet as Terra in this universe; we must get back to warn our leaders and help defend our world. We also believe the Efreet may have some Sila scientists there who could help us understand how their time-based weapons work. It would be extremely helpful if we could cross over to their universe and liberate them. We need to understand how those weapons work if we are to develop an answer for them."

"I understand," said the Thor. "I would do the same if our positions were reversed. I wish you a safe and speedy journey to your world. Once you are successful there, we would ask for your assistance here again in dealing with the Jotunn/Efreet alliance, if you have aid to spare. With their ability to pop up anywhere at any time, we might be overwhelmed with only a moment's notice."

"I understand…and that is why we must get back to Terra as soon as possible."

# # # # #

1st Platoon, Alpha Company, 1st Battalion of the
1st Regiment, Terran Space Force

Commanding Officer	LCDR Shawn 'Calvin' Hobbs
Executive Officer	Captain Paul 'Night' Train

<u>Space Force</u>

Space Force Leader	Sergeant Major 'Master Chief' Ryan O'Leary
Squad 'A' Leader	Gunnery Sergeant Patrick 'The Wall' Dantone
Fire Team '1' Leader	Staff Sergeant Park 'Wraith' Ji-woo
Laserman	Sergeant Nicholas 'The Kid' Tomaselli
Laserman	Sergeant Margaret 'Witch' Andrews
Laserman	Sergeant Adeline "Addie" Graham
Laserman	Corporal James 'Speedy' Swift
Fire Team '2' Leader	Sergeant John 'Mr.' Jones
Laserman	Sergeant Jamal 'Bad Twin' Gordon
Laserman	Sergeant Austin 'Good Twin' Gordon
Laserman	Corporal Irina 'Spook' Rozhkov
Laserman	Sergeant Darrin 'Homey' Lancaster
Fire Team '3' Leader	Sergeant Samuel 'Sun' Burnie
Laserman	Sergeant Ismail Al-Sabani
Laserman	Sergeant Paul 'Missionary' Hiley
Laserman	Corporal Pat 'Ostrich' Burke
Medic	Corporal Michael 'Gooch' Higuchi

<u>Ground Force</u>

Ground Force Leader	Master Gunnery Sergeant Bill Hendrick
Squad 'B' Leader	Gunnery Sergeant Bob 'Mongo' Bryant
Fire Team '1' Leader	Staff Sergeant Alka 'Z-Man' Zoromski
Laserman	Sergeant George 'Floppy' Nelson
Laserman	Corporal Steve 'Range' Holm
Laserman	Corporal Patrick 'Tanker' Harris
Laserman	Corporal Riley 'Scratch' Dunn
Fire Team '2' Leader	Sergeant John 'Black Cat' Rowntree
Laserman	Sergeant Rajesh 'Mouse' Patel
Laserman	Corporal 'Bob' Bobellisssissolliss
Laserman	Corporal 'Doug' Dugelllisssollisssesss
Laserman	Corporal Sergio 'Garcia' Lopez
Fire Team '3' Leader	Staff Sergeant Rainer 'Hoofer' Koppenhoefer
Sniper	Sergeant Rick 'Happy' Day
Spotter	Sergeant Milissa 'Milly' Story
Ninja	Sergeant Hattori 'Yokaze' Hanzo
Medic	Sergeant Burt 'Yank' Yankiver

Space Fighter Squadron-1

CO	Lieutenant Commander Shawn 'Calvin' Hobbs
XO	Lieutenant Commander Sarah 'Lights' Brighton

Pilot	Lieutenant Carl 'Guns' Simpson
Pilot	Lieutenant Bryan 'Hooty' Hooten
Pilot	Lieutenant Samuel 'Sammy' Jakande
Pilot	Lieutenant Hans 'Schnitzel' Hohenstaufen
Pilot	Lieutenant 'Tex' Teksssellisssiniss
Pilot	Lieutenant John 'Mack' McCarter
Pilot	Lieutenant Danny L. 'Brick' Walling
Pilot	Lieutenant Jiang 'Tooth' Fang
Pilot	Lieutenant Pete 'Rock' Ayre
Pilot	Lieutenant Pablo 'Bob' Acosta
Pilot	Lieutenant Jeff 'Canuck' Canada
Pilot	Lieutenant Tatyana 'Khan' Khanilov
Pilot	Lieutenant Kenneth 'Primo' Miller
Pilot	Lieutenant Denise 'Frenchie' Michel
Pilot	Lieutenant Miguel 'Ghost' Carvalho
Pilot	Lieutenant William "Vincenzo" Santiago
Pilot	Lieutenant Phil 'Oscar' Meyer

NFO	Lieutenant Tobias 'Toby' Eppler
NFO	Lieutenant Neil 'Trouble' Watson
NFO	Lieutenant Vernon 'Collie' Shepherd
NFO	Lieutenant Dan 'K-Mart' Knaus
NFO	Lieutenant 'Olly' Ollisssellissess
NFO	Lieutenant Faith 'Bore' Ibori

NFO	Lieutenant Erika 'Jones' Smith
NFO	Lieutenant Mark 'Chomper' Melanson
NFO	Lieutenant Sasaki 'Supidi' Akio
NFO	Lieutenant Gwon 'Happy' Min-jun
NFO	Lieutenant Larry 'Grocer' Albertson
NFO	Lieutenant Keith 'Pool' Dodd
NFO	Lieutenant Hakan 'Mays' Yilmaz
NFO	Lieutenant Ira 'Rocket' Hensley
NFO	Lieutenant Ali Ahmed 'Sandy' Al-Amri
NFO	Lieutenant Reyne 'Rafe' Rafaeli
NFO	Lieutenant Aharsi 'Swammi' Goswami

The following is an excerpt from Book 2 of the Codex Regius:

Beyond the Shroud of the Universe

Chris Kennedy

Available from Chris Kennedy Publishing

Fall, 2015

eBook, Paperback, and Audio Book

Excerpt from "Beyond the Shroud of the Universe:"

"The control rod only lets me take two other people," said Captain Nightsong. "We really don't want to take any more at one time, anyway, because the room where we're going is very small, and no one wants to transport into a wall. Since we can't go in with enough people to make a difference at the start, we should go in with just a small group, so there is less of a chance of them seeing us. They may have some kind of monitor or sensor which lets them know how many people are around; three is a lot less suspicious than 10. While three could be friends going for a walk, they're going to know 10 people are conspirators up to no good."

"I agree," said Calvin. "Okay, here's the plan. I'm going to jump in first with Captain Nightsong and K-Mart because he has the most experience with the Sila. We will take a quick look to make sure everything is still the way Captain Nightsong remembers, then we'll come back and get the rest of the platoon."

"Do you really think that's wise, sir?" asked Master Chief.

"What do you mean?"

"I mean every time you go somewhere without me, you always seem to get into some sort of trouble that I have to pull you out of. Wouldn't it be smarter and save us all a lot of time and trouble if I just went with you now?"

"I'll be fine, Master Chief," said Calvin. "Captain Nightsong has been here before and knows the lay of the land. We'll just take a quick look and be back to get everyone else. That way, we'll also know whether we can wear our suits or not."

"You know sir, I've been thinking," said Master Chief after a pause.

"Damn," said Calvin. "Master Chief's been thinking? Now I *am* scared."

"That's really funny, sir," Master Chief replied. "Seriously, though, what if the damn Psiclopes got it all wrong? What if I'm actually the hero, and you're just one of my sidekicks? Have you ever thought of that? I seem to have to save the day all the time; wouldn't that make me the hero? Perhaps you should let me lead this one. I've got a bad feeling about it."

"Now Master Chief, if you were the hero, you'd have to go to all the press conferences and do all the media interviews. Is that what you want? To be in front of the cameras all the time?"

"Screw that," said Master Chief. "Okay, you win. You can go, but please be careful for a change, won't you?"

"I will," said Calvin with a smile.

"Don't worry about it," said Captain Nightsong. "He'll be with me. What could go wrong?"

ABOUT THE AUTHOR

Chris Kennedy is a former aviator with over 3,000 hours flying attack and reconnaissance aircraft for the United States Navy, including many missions supporting U.S. Special Forces. He has also been an elementary school principal and has enjoyed 18 seasons as a softball coach. He is currently working as an Instructional Systems Designer for the Navy.

Titles by Chris Kennedy:

"Red Tide: The Chinese Invasion of Seattle" – Available Now

"Occupied Seattle" – Available Now

"Janissaries: Book One of the Theogony" – Available Now

"When the Gods Aren't Gods: Book Two of the Theogony" – Available Now

"Terra Stands Alone" – Available Now

"Self-Publishing for Profit" – Available Now

* * * * *

Connect with Chris Kennedy Online:

Facebook: https://www.facebook.com/chriskennedypublishing.biz

Blog: http://chriskennedypublishing.com/

Want to be immortalized in a future book?
Join the Red Shirt List on the blog!

The following is an excerpt from "First to Fight," Book 11 of the Empire's Corps:

First to Fight

_____

Christopher G. Nuttall

Available now in eBook from Christopher G. Nuttall

http://www.amazon.com/dp/B010E9QZJG

Excerpt from "First to Fight:"

The enemy, it seemed, recovered very quickly from the shock of our arrival and started to organise a proper welcome. I snapped awake hours later to the sound of mortar shells screaming towards the FOB, only to be picked off in mid-flight by the point defence. It might have seemed a pointless exercise, but the enemy knew that it wasn't impossible to overload the tracking radars and land a shell in the middle of the compound. The building itself had been strengthened, yet a lucky shot might kill a couple of us and convince our superiors to leave the factions to their mutual slaughter. And besides, it kept us awake. I might have grown used to only a few hours of sleep in Boot Camp, but it wasn't something I enjoyed. Tired marines made mistakes.

"Fuck it," Joker muttered. "This isn't funny, you know."

I shrugged. We'd trained for war endlessly, practicing in simulators and training grounds, but this was different. This time, real people could get hurt.

"Wake up, ladies," Sergeant Harris bellowed, crashing through the door. The rest of the platoon either sat up or jerked awake, depending on how well they'd managed to sleep through the welcoming barrage. "Stuff some crap down your throat, then grab your kit."

I nodded - salutes were forbidden in combat zones, with harsh punishment for anyone who dared - and reached for the MREs in my pack. The rations tasted better than anything I'd eaten in the Undercity, but I'd been told that complaining about them was an old marine tradition. I honestly hadn't understood why until I'd gone on leave for the first time. Joker crouched next to me and offered to swap one of his ration bars for one of mine. We made the trade, chewed rapidly, answered the call of nature and finally lined up in front of the sergeant, who eyed us all disapprovingly.

"1st Platoon is on QRF," he said, crossly. "2nd Platoon will take the first patrol, accompanying the old timers."

I felt a chill run down my spine. I was in 2nd Platoon.

The old hands met us as we assembled near the gates. There were four of them; Young, Benedict, Hobbes and Green. They looked less spruce than us, unsurprisingly; they'd been assigned to work with the army deployment here, instead of remaining with their regular companies. They had been intended to train the local soldiers, but apparently all attempts to set up a local militia to support the outsiders had floundered on political correctness and local realities, leaving them with little to do.

"Expect the wankers to test your determination as soon as they can," Young said. Wankers was an old term for enemy combatants, particularly those who didn't play by the rules. (As if there was any other kind, these days.) "Remember your training, watch your backs and don't let any of them come close to you. If you have to take prisoners, force them to strip. Better to walk someone through the streets naked than let them bring a bomb to you."

"Shit," Joker said.

The sickening feeling in my chest only got worse as we checked our weapons and body armour one final time, then advanced through the gates and out into bandit country. My hands felt sweaty as we slipped down the street, careful to give any piles of rubbish a wide berth. The enemy knew they couldn't face us - or even the soldiers - in open combat, so they resorted to all sorts of tricks to even the odds. Hiding an IED under a pile of debris and then detonating it when we passed was an old trick. I saw a couple of faces peeping at us from behind a curtain - were they reporting our progress to their superiors? - which vanished the moment I glanced at them. They had looked like kids, but that meant nothing. A kid could easily serve as a spy, his handlers banking on the fact we would be reluctant to shoot at them.

And if we did shoot a kid, I thought grimly, we would only create a new rallying cry for the enemy.

We turned the corner and strode towards a marketplace. I would have preferred to be somewhere - anywhere - else, but doctrine said it was important to convince the locals that we could go anywhere, at will, and there was nothing they could do to stop us. The locals scattered in front of us, the women hurrying out of sight while the menfolk looked ready to fight, if necessary. I didn't really blame them. They'd endured the attentions of a regiment more known for abusing the locals than fighting the enemy in the past, according to the briefing, and it would be a long time before any of them really trusted us. Stallkeepers eyed us warily as we passed, clearly expecting us to take what we wanted, but we had been warned not to take anything. If we wanted something, we'd been told, we had to pay for it.

The marketplace was a testament to human determination to survive, somehow. Everything was on sale, from meat (probably rat, but there was no way to know) to weapons and supplies smuggled in from outside the city. In a way, it was the only truly neutral ground in the city; I was mildly surprised the soldiers hadn't set up their base just inside the market. But then, there were weapons on display. We made a show of ignoring them as we reached the end of the market and headed down the next street. It looked cleaner than the others, which surprised me. In hindsight, it should also have worried me.

One of the wankers panicked and opened fire, a second before we walked right into the ambush. We snapped up our rifles and returned fire, putting several rounds through the windows to keep the snipers from continuing their attack, then ducked for cover and advanced, in fire teams, towards the house. It wasn't a big building, I noted absently as Joker prepared a charge to break down the door, but that wasn't reassuring. Our advantages were most pronounced in open battle, not close-quarter knife-fights. The enemy had worked hard to create a situation that maximised their advantages and minimised ours. Joker snapped the charge against the door, shouted a warning, then detonated the device. The doorway exploded inwards; I unhooked a grenade from my belt and threw it inside in one smooth motion, then followed up as soon as it detonated. Several wankers who had been lying in wait had been caught in the blast; I glanced at their bodies, then led the way through the house. Four other wankers made the mistake of running downstairs and straight into our waiting guns. We shot them down and advanced upstairs, checking the upper rooms one by one. The sniper who'd started the ambush was dead. There was no way to tell which of us had shot him.

The brief encounter expanded as the QRF arrived, then started setting up barricades to trap the insurgents. Determined to show that we would not be pushed around, we searched through a dozen houses, killing nine insurgents and capturing three more. I knew they'd go into our detention camps, rather than those run by the army or the local government, such as it was. Hopefully, we'd actually get some valuable intelligence out of them. Oddly, I no longer felt nervous. I was doing the job I'd trained to do.

It was nearly an hour before we heard the whimper.

MAKO

Did you like "The Search for Gram?" Take a look at "Mako" by author Ian J. Malone:

Mako (The Mako Saga, Book One) by Ian J. Malone

A down-and-out history professor leads a team of old friends to virtual glory as the first-ever group to beat Mako Assault, a revolutionary new game that has emerged from nowhere to take the online world by storm. As a reward for their achievement, and under the guise of publicity, the group is flown to meet the game's mysterious designer, only to learn that Mako's intent was never to entertain its players... but rather to train them.

"Mako" is an epic science fiction thrill ride of action, suspense, laughter, and romance; MAKO is the story of five ordinary people rising to the challenge of extraordinary events, driven only by their faith in each other.

Reader's Note: The Mako Saga continued in 2015 with the release of "Red Sky Dawning," Book Two of the series.

What readers are saying:

"Trust me, you'll enjoy this." — Arthur Harkness, The Brotherhood of the Evil Geeks blog.

"A marvelous adventure!" — John on Amazon.

"Fun story, great characters, hilarious dialogue... can't wait for the next one!" — Simon on B&N.

Sales links:

IJM website: http://www.ianjmalone.com/

"Mako" http://www.amazon.com/dp/B00BIWS3UI

"Red Sky Dawning" http://www.amazon.com/dp/0989032752/

Made in the USA
San Bernardino, CA
28 August 2016